Mohammad the Ninth

A Palestinian Saga

Book 3

Donn Hutchison

Text Copyright by Donn Hutchison c. 2016

Cover photograph by Lee Copeland

ISBN: 0-9970990-5-4

First Edition

As always, with love for Rana, Ramzi, and Kahlid, who showed me that, indeed, it *is possible* to have a foot in two very different worlds.

Acknowledgements

Words cannot express my heartfelt gratitude to Rana Hutchison Copeland, without whose prompting, encouragement, rereading, questioning, and determination the manuscripts would continue to rest in the bottom dresser drawer. It is through her perseverance and hard work that they live.

I will always be grateful to Carol Hutchison Vago, who read the chapters of all the novels as they were written and gave *instant* feedback: often critical, always insightful, and always supportive.

Credit must be given to Lee Copeland for the photo on the cover of a typical college campus, the kind of campus that Mohammad would have attended.

Index of Characters

Mohammad's Family:

Sitteh Hasna – the matriarch of the family; she had red hair and freckles and was a great teller of tales. Her story is told in the first novel of the series: "When I Was A Girl And Not Very Pretty.

Omar – Sitteh Hasna's son, the only one of her children to survive the 1948 massacre; he worked the land with his father before fleeing the village and becoming a camp refugee. He is a builder of stone walls; and though illiterate, is very wise.

Nijmeh – she is Omar's wife and the mother of ten. Like her name, she is the "star" in the lives of her husband and children; she is the most beautiful woman Omar has ever seen.

Mansur- he is the eldest of Omar and Nijmeh's ten children and the only one born in the village. He studied in Russia, became a doctor, and married a Circassian Russian beauty, **Zaleena**; they live In Amman with their three children.

Hasna- named after her Sitteh Hasna; she is the mother of seven boys and lives in the camp. Her husband is **Imad**. They live with his parents, **Abu Imad** and **Im Imad.**

Khalil- an unmarried lawyer living in Amman, he was imprisoned for seven years as a youth for throwing stones at the occupying forces. He sponsors his brother Mohammad when he goes to the States to study.

Mona- married to a Palestinian grocer from California.

Manal- also married to a Palestinian grocer from California; Mona and Manal are married to brothers.

Ahmed- killed at age ten while watching a confrontation between Palestinian stone throwers and Israeli soldiers.

Najla- married to a Palestinian engineer and lives in one of the Arab Emirates

Azeezeh- also married to a Palestinian engineer who lives and works in one of the Arab Emirates

Mohammad- the ninth of Omar and Nijmeh's children; he goes to the States to work on his Master's Degree; he is warned by his brothers NOT to get involved with an American Christian.

Issa- the tenth of Omar and Nijmeh's children; he is an artist and a political cartoonist; he lives in the camp.

Amr- a successful stockbroker; he was a cellmate of Khalil's for seven years; they are more than brothers and Omar and Nijmeh consider him one of their sons.

Saleem- Hasna and Imad's oldest son; he is married to **Aisha.**

Saji- The youngest of Hasna and Imad's seven sons; he is gentle and kind. He survives being attacked and brutalized by settlers. He and his grandfather Omar have a special link.

Im Najib- a neighbor woman. Though not a relative, she was Sitteh Hasna's best friend and is like an aunt to Omar and Nijmeh.

Yasmeen- Im Najib's granddaughter; she speaks English well, and becomes a dear friend to Sarah.

Sarah's family:

Dave Goldman is an Iowa farmer, a non-practicing Jew and Sarah's father.

Emily Goldman is a devoted Methodist; is married to Dave, and is Sarah's mother.

Sarah Goldman is a classmate of Mohammad's – the "American Christian" whom his brothers warned him against.

Ken Goldman is Dave's brother and lives on the neighboring farm.

Martha Goldman is Ken's wife and Emily Goldman's sister.

Mohammad the Ninth

Nijmeh despaired that Khalil would ever get married. He was almost thirty-seven and when Omar had been almost thirty-seven he was already a grandfather. She couldn't quite understand his reluctance; he was a lawyer; he was handsome; he was successful; he was good-natured; she thought he was the kind of a husband that mothers dreamed of for their daughters. If he hadn't been her son, and if she had been looking for a husband for one of her daughters, she would have snatched him up.

Tradition dictated that Khalil, as he was the older, should get married before Mohammad did, but she didn't think that was going to happen, and she didn't think she should stand in the way of Mohammad marrying. In a recent phone call with Khalil, *he* had broached the subject of finding a bride for Mohammad. He was concerned about Mohammad living in America without an Arab wife. He had implied to his mother that there were lots of *temptations* in the States and perhaps when Mohammad returned in the summer to renew his permit, he should get married and take his wife back with him.

As much as Nijmeh felt that Zaleena, even though she was Russian, was right for Mansur, she didn't want Mohammad to do what Mansur had done – *marry a foreigner*. She was going to actively look for the *perfect Palestinian* wife for Mohammad. When he came in the summer, he would be pleasantly surprised that the arrangements had all been made.

Chapter 1

Mohammad had to laugh when thinking about his brother Khalil's warning NOT to date. Mohammad had never been on a date. In the West Bank boys and girls didn't date – at least not those from the refugee camps. One didn't *choose* a spouse. A spouse *was chosen* for one. In some cases, at least in the camps, the only conversation a couple had before officially becoming engaged and married was a chaperoned hour before the engagement party. A couple was really never allowed to be alone together, at least in the camps, until *after* they married.

Before leaving for college, Mohammad had had *correspondence* with a woman journalist, Teri Bachman. He had reluctantly met with her alone *once*, for coffee at Birzeit University. The second time they had had coffee together he had taken his younger brother, Issa, along as chaperon. He had kissed her *once* on both cheeks – the kind of kiss one gave his brother or sister. He had never kissed a girl on her lips – *that came only after marriage.* At twenty-two, he knew he was inexperienced – naïve – when it came to girls. Khalil could have *put his hands in cold water* as his Sitteh Hasna used to say, meaning: *Khalil had nothing to worry about – there was no way Mohammad was going to get burned by a problematic situation.* There was no chance that Mohammad would be dating. He didn't know how one went about it.

He had almost completed his first year of graduate study. There were lots of things he liked about America but there was also some culture shock regarding social norms. From his year in the States, he had seen how college couples were: *they held hands; they kissed in public; some girls* (so he had been told) *slept with their boyfriends.* This all seemed very foreign to him. In the Old Country, *boys* who were buddies often walked arm in arm or held hands, sometimes with their little fingers hooked together, but a man did not hold hands with a woman unless they were engaged to be married. In the Old Country, men and boys kissed each other on both cheeks when they met, but one never saw *boys and girls* kissing in the street; and a girl in the Old Country (as far as he knew) *only* slept with her husband. If it was discovered that she *had* slept with a man who was not her husband, her father or brothers would *kill* her to preserve the family honor. That kind of put a damper on just sleeping with anyone.

Mohammad was conservative by nature and certainly conservative by up-bringing and culture, but he was in a new environment which was more casual. Perhaps he should make more of an effort to *adapt* to the culture and sample some of what the West had to offer.

He knew of two other Arab graduate students at Purdue who *dated* American girls; for them *dating* was translated into *sleeping with.* They had been quite candid with Mohammad. They had said that their American girlfriends had no problem doing their laundry, typing their papers, cleaning up after them and *sleeping* with them. In the Old Country, sex only happened *after* marriage; here it seemed marriage was *not necessary.*

When Mohammad had asked them if they intended to *marry* the girls, they had been vehement in their response: although one did say he may consider it *if it helps him get a green card;* they both intended to go back to the Old Country when they finished their studies and marry a nice Arab *virgin.*

They did suggest to Mohammad that he find himself a nice American coed, live with her while he was in school, and then when he was finished with school, go back home and get married to the girl his mother had picked out for him.

It was perplexing for Mohammad. He *wanted* to fit in, yet he *wanted* to hold on to the traditions in which he had been raised.

He had picked up some American profanities like *Holy Shit* and *fuck it* (but felt that they didn't quite compare to Arabic curses like: *May God destroy your house,* or *I'm going to break your legs and drink your blood)* and he had picked up some American clichés. He especially liked the one: *When in Rome do as the Romans do.* Why shouldn't he act as others were acting? No one would *really know* – no one who mattered like his parents and siblings. He had come a long way in his thinking from when he had been embarrassed by Teri Bachman hugging him and kissing him at the airport in front of his family. But no one from his family was around here to see what he did. Another cliché he had adopted was: *What they don't know won't hurt them.*

Mohammad had learned as a child that an angel sat on his right shoulder and whispered in his ear to *be good,* and yet he believed a *shetan* (devil) encouraged him to *be bad.* The *shetan* was talking him into believing that it would be all right to *date;* that it would be alright to get romantically involved with an American girl; that it would be alright to *sleep* with an American coed as she, apparently, didn't have the same attitude toward sex that Arab girls had. But he still had to get around the nagging doubts that he had. He still felt that sleeping with a girl who was not your wife was dishonorable. At least that is what the angel who was sitting on his shoulder was whispering in his ear.

Sometimes Mohammad *did wonder* if he really was just a little boy dressed in long trousers, as Teri Bachman had said. There were times that he did not feel like an adult at all, in spite of his height, his muscular build, his curly black hair, his five-o'clock shadow *and* his age. He looked like a man. He acted like a man – or how he thought an Arab man should act. But there were times when he felt he was still a boy on the inside, listening to that invisible angel perched on his shoulder.

This year in the States had caused subtle changes in Mohammad. He was finding himself getting comfortable with the freedom; comfortable with being independent, comfortable with being away from family. Oh, he still missed them; he still looked forward to their weekly letters, to the twice-a-month care packages from Mona and Manal; the phone calls from Khalil and Mansur and to his parents, but he found that the six thousand miles that separated them was really *not that far*. It surprised him to think this.

He wasn't used to thinking for himself. It was not always easy being *next-to-the-last,* when *next-to-the-last* meant that you were the *ninth child.* There were a lot of people who *think* they know how you should live your life, and *you* are not one of them.

Mohammad thought about his relationship with his brother Khalil. When he was only two years old, his Sitteh Hasna had *given* him to his sixteen-year-old brother Khalil. From the moment that his grandmother had placed him in his older brother's arms, Mohammad had become his. He slept on the same pallet with him; he sat in his lap to eat or to listen to the stories spun by his Sitteh Hasna; Khalil was the one who carried him around on his shoulders while the two-year-old Mohammad drooled into his curls and patted his head; Khalil had been Mohammad's teenage father until he had gone to prison for seven years for stone-throwing. Mohammad had slept in one of Khalil's shirts every night until he was released from prison when Mohammad was nine years old! It was Khalil who had taken over financial responsibility for Mohammad; he was the one Mohammad confided in about his attraction to Teri Bachman. He gave him advice – more in the form of *orders*. It had been Khalil who had said that he was NOT to date or become emotionally involved with an American. Khalil in essence pulled the puppet strings that made Mohammad dance.

Chapter 2

Mohammad had always just assumed he would eventually go back home and that his parents would arrange a suitable match for him. He *wanted* what his parents and married siblings had. He had been reared to believe that the only suitable wife for him was an Arab wife. The difficulty in the situation was that he couldn't just blindly accept what he had been taught. Like the fictional character, Pinocchio, whom he had read about when he first studied English in fifth grade; Mohammad may be a puppet, but he was a puppet with a *brain.*

There was a girl in the same program at Purdue he liked. She was vivacious; smart and hard-working; she worked in the lab, in the library, and was an assistant to one of the professors. Besides being beautiful, she seemed to like Mohammad, certainly a plus! The girl's name was Sarah Goldman. She was half-Jewish but didn't fit the stereotype that he had in his mind because of her fair skin, green eyes, warm, blonde hair with just a hint of red in it, and a spray of freckles across her nose. He thought that must be the Methodist side of her. (She had told him that her mother was a *Methodist,* of which he knew nothing, and that her father had no religion at all - though if asked would say he was a non-practicing Jew.) She had a bubbly personality, a lot like his sister Hasna's, and was easy to talk to. She knew nothing about Palestine or Israel for that matter and seemed really *interested* in learning more about Mohammad.

They had had the same classes for almost a year and had gone out for coffee together (he hadn't felt reluctant or that he needed a chaperone); they had studied together at the library; and had gone to a couple on-campus films. They had never held hands and certainly *never* kissed.

Mohammad found himself thinking more and more about her. He had never really had trouble sleeping, but the last few months he had lain awake long after he *should* have been asleep thinking about Sarah and all the *complications* that would arise if he really got serious about her. The situation was absurdly clear. She was *American* and a Methodist Christian with a Jewish father. He could just picture his Sitteh Hasna, if she were alive, dropping dead at the door if he tried to enter with an American-Christian wife named *Goldman*.

He was brought up to think that to take the *next step* in a relationship with a girl naturally meant *engagement* and *marriage*. A couple *didn't* go out together unless they were officially engaged and had already *signed the marriage contract*.

If he really got serious – he had to laugh at the thought; the very fact that he wasn't sleeping because of thoughts about Sarah Goldman was proof that in his mind it had *already* gotten serious. He didn't want to talk to the other two Arab guys about Sarah; their friendship was rather superficial. He didn't want to write or talk to Khalil or Mansur about Sarah as he already *knew* what they would advise. So he argued with himself; *a real man didn't discuss his feelings, a man made up his own mind.*

As he walked across campus for his morning class, he saw Sarah Goldman waiting for him. She was sitting on a bench, under an oak tree, in front of the ivy-covered brick classroom building. She had two cups of coffee with her.

"Hey, Mohammad, I was waiting for you. Here, I brought you some coffee," Sarah smiled as she handed him a paper cup of *McDonald's* coffee.

"Thanks," Mohammad said tossing his book bag on the ground under the bench and taking a sip of the hot coffee through the little slit in the plastic lid. "So, it's *McDonald's* and not *Starbuck's,* huh?" Mohammad joked.

"Some of us are not rich Arab *sheiks* with tents and camels and oil spilling out of the sand; some of us are just little Iowa farm girls. Besides, coffee is coffee." Sarah laughed.

"Ah, you have uncovered my secret. I thought I had successfully hidden the fact that I was *rich* and had a tent, twenty camels, and an oil well behind the tent," Mohammad kidded. "I see you are not buying the story that my parents live in a refugee camp, sans tent, sans camel, and sans oil well. That the only oil we have is what my mother uses in cooking!"

"What's with this *sans* tent, *sans* camels, *sans* sand and oil?" Sarah grinned.

"I remember we read the Oxford abridged version of *Hamlet* in high school and the word *sans* stuck in my mind." Mohammad laughed. "I thought I would just toss it into the conversation to show how *well-educated* we *camel jockeys* are in spite of our tents and camels and extreme wealth. We can even quote *Shake'a'spear.*"

"Shakespeare, my literary friend, Shakespeare, not *Shake'a'spear!*"

"I bow to your superior intelligence." And Mohammad made a mock bow as he smiled at Sarah. "I recognize that, *for a girl,* you are pretty smart."

"For a girl!? I only need to use a fraction of my brain cells to be smarter than you – oh, superior *male being,"* Sarah said poking him in the ribs and causing him to almost spill his coffee. "I suspect your mother and sisters are all smarter than your father and brothers but have learned the feminine skills of *making their husbands and sons and brothers* **think** *that they are smarter because they are men.* It is a skill we learn at our mother's knee. I can still hear my mother saying: *Now Sarah, you don't want to appear smarter than the boys in your class – even though you are. You must learn to make them feel smarter, even though they are not. You must make them feel that you really need them, when in reality they need you!"*

Mohammad thought about his mother, Nijmeh, his Sitteh Hasna, his sisters – they *were* all smart. Not necessarily *book smart.* His Sitteh Hasna had been illiterate, and so was his mother. Two of his sisters had been married off before they finished high school, but he realized that they *were* the real strength in their families.

Sarah noticed that Mohammad seemed deep in thought. "You men *do* have other qualities that make us women *willing* to make you *think* you are smarter. I imagine you are thinking about your own mother and sisters and how really *smart* they are. You are smart, my friend, just not *quite* as smart as me!" Sarah laughed and took Mohammad's arm. "It is time we were getting to class."

"You sure you want to be *seen* with someone so beneath you in intelligence?"

"I'll risk it; folks will just think *how kind I am being to a poor, male, foreign student.* Perhaps they will think I am after your *money,* you rich Arab *sheik."*

Mohammad had never felt so at ease with a girl who wasn't his sister, or mother, or grandmother. Sarah certainly *wasn't* his sister! He wondered if this was what *falling in love* was all about. He knew his father had *fallen in love* with his mother when he had first seen her at the well. He knew that his brother Mansur had *fallen in love* with Zaleena when she had tutored him. He wondered if he had *fallen in love* with Sarah.

Chapter 3

Nijmeh had gone with Hasna and Im Najib and Im Najib's granddaughter, Yasmeen, to pick wild *zatar* (thyme). It was wonderful to have a day away from the camp, to be out on the hillside, to be picking *zatar* and wild mint, and *ijer'ha'ma'me* (pigeon's feet) an herb that could be brewed into a tea when one had sand in one's kidneys. The sun was warm on their backs as they stooped to pick.

Yasmeen was just eighteen and had sat for the *tawjihi* (matriculation exam) and had done very well. She was interested in perhaps going to the local two-year women's college run by UNRWA and getting a teaching degree, but she knew her family thought it was *time she got married. After all,* her mother had said, *you **are** eighteen! And the more education you have, the less likely that someone will want to marry you.* Yasmeen was resigned to the fact that the next step for her was marriage.

Nijmeh had known Yasmeen since she was a little girl. She was kind and considerate; she was good natured and funny; she was smart – as her *tawjihi* scores had shown; she was modest and soft spoken; she was the oldest of six, and according to her grandmother, Im Najib, a wonderful help to her mother. Im Najib had told Nijmeh that Yasmeen was a *good cook, a good housekeeper, was obedient, and was great with her younger brothers and sisters – she was a born mother.* Yasmeen was also *beautiful* – she had dark eyes, raven hair and lashes, teeth like pearls, and deep dimples when she smiled. She was a dusky beauty. Nijmeh had seen a poster in a shop window once that depicted a Bedouin tent in a desert scene. There was a camel in the background and in the foreground was a beautiful Bedouin girl, her hand resting on the tent flap, staring at the mountains. The beautiful girl in the poster *could have been* Yasmeen.

Nijmeh looked at Yasmeen and thought to herself: *She would be perfect for Mohammad.*

Six thousand miles away, Mohammad tossed and turned in his bed. First he lay on one side and then on the other. He would adjust the pillow under his head and then adjust it again. Sleep seemed like it didn't want to come. He finally gave up and with eyes open stared into the darkness. His thoughts were full of Sarah. He stared into the darkness and the face of Sarah seemed to stare back at him. His mind kept playing over and over everything she had said to him, everything he had said to her. He wanted to ask her out, but he wasn't quite sure how one went about it.

The buzzer on his clock radio went off *just* as he fell asleep. He stumbled out of bed, went into the bathroom, brushed his teeth, showered, and shaved. He put the water on for coffee, and while it was heating, he prayed. As he faced east and went through the ritual, he added to his prayer the petition that Allah would show him *how to ask Sarah out.* And He did.

That morning he had decided to surprise Sarah with coffee from *Starbuck's* – after all *he did have that oil well in back of the tent,* he chuckled to himself. She was there on the same bench, under the same oak tree, in front of the ivy-covered brick classroom building.

"Good morning, Sarah. Here, coffee from *Starbuck's,*" Mohammad smiled handing her the large paper cup. "I got you a super size."

"*My* we *are* feeling extravagant this morning. To what do I owe this honor?" she laughed.

"I, my good and faithful friend, recognizing your vast *superior feminine* intelligence, would humbly like to ask you out to dinner." Mohammad said the words with some bravado he thought (though inside his stomach the butterflies were doing a traditional line dance).

"You are asking me out...on a *date?* Not to go with you to the library to study? Not to go together to see an on-campus film, but an actual *date* with dinner – in a restaurant – not at *McDonalds,* or *Pizza Hut,* or *Long John Silvers'?*"

"Sure, what is so strange about that? You have to eat dinner; I have to eat dinner. You *did* discover my secret about the oil well," Mohammad paused, trying to be casual, feeling anything *but* casual. "I would really *like* you to have dinner with me." He said seriously, hopefully.

Sarah seemed to wait, searching for the right words. "Mohammad," she paused, "we are *good* friends. I really like hanging out with you, studying with you, having morning coffee with you, but I have never really thought about us *dating.* I kind of don't want to spoil what we have. Once guys and girls start *dating* their relationship changes; their *friendship* changes; I like the way things are between us." She couldn't help but see the hurt look in Mohammad's eyes.

"It's okay. You are probably right. It was a dumb idea anyway." Mohammad didn't know what to say. He didn't know where to look. Having spoken, he *sensed* the relationship had already changed. "Hey, I gotta get going," he mumbled avoiding looking at her. He retrieved his book bag from under the bench and walked briskly away dropping his untouched *Starbuck's* coffee cup in the trash barrel.

"Mohammad! Mohammad, wait!"

Mohammad walked a little faster. He didn't want her to see the childish tears pooling in his eyes. He may have been wearing long pants, but he felt very much a little boy. The angel sitting on his right shoulder whispered sympathetic nonsense into his ear. The *shetan* said: *You sure bungled that.*

Mohammad was glad it was the weekend. He had two days where he wouldn't have to see Sarah. It was unfortunate, he thought, that *all* their classes were together. There was no way he could avoid seeing her. He would just have to make the best of it.

Mohammad didn't sleep that night at all. He did close his eyes, but he kept seeing the face of Sarah. He tried to sleep, but he couldn't seem to turn off his brain or silence the beating of his heart. He almost felt nauseated. Maybe the other two grad students were right; *he should pick up some coed who would be glad to move in with him – sleep with him. A girl who would do his laundry, type his papers, pick-up after him, have sex with him – a girl whom he cared nothing about; a girl as* **unlike** *Sarah as he could find.* The *shetan* whispered: *You're the man.*

After being awake all night, he slept all day Saturday. It was evening when he awoke. He had slept through breakfast, lunch and dinner. He showered, didn't bother shaving, put on jeans and a sweatshirt, ran a comb through his curls – *I really need a haircut*, he thought absently, put on sneakers without socks, and headed out to get a bite to eat at *McDonald's*.

He ordered two Big Mac's, a large order of French fries, and a giant Coke. He slipped into a booth; his back was to the door and the counter. He had automatically checked his mail box on his way through the lobby, and there had been a letter from Khalil. He had stuffed the unopened envelope in his back pocket. While eating his hamburger and French fries, he took the letter out, slit open the flap and was reading the letter when he felt a tap on his shoulder.

"So, trying to avoid me are you? I stopped by your flat and the receptionist told me you had gone out for a late dinner. I have already been to *Pizza Hut* and *Long John Silver's*. I knew I should have tried *McDonald's* first," Sarah said as she slipped into the booth. Mohammad looked at her and then dropped his eyes. "You ran off yesterday before we finished our conversation. I didn't want to leave things the way we left them."

"Hey, it's no big deal." Mohammad said finally raising his eyes and looking at Sarah. "I know that I have already spoiled what we had because I asked you out." He hesitated. "In the Old County men and women *don't date.* I didn't know *how* to go about it. I have never asked a girl on a date before. I *like* you. I *like* that we are friends. I *didn't* want to change that, and I did."

"Yes, you *did* change things a bit. I thought, because you had never *asked* me on a date before, that you were only interested in us being friends. And that was okay with me, because I *like* having you as a friend. At first, I have to admit, I thought it was a little *strange* that you never asked me out or tried to hold my hand or kiss me. Then I thought that this was just the way you were raised, and I kind of *liked* the idea that you weren't pushing an intimate relationship. It was *nice* having a *male* friend who didn't want to be my *boyfriend.*"

"And now I have changed all that, haven't I?" Mohammad questioned dejectedly. "I should have left well enough alone." *I am sorry I didn't*, he whispered to himself.

"Hey, Mohammad, speak to me. Yes, things, as I said, have changed a bit – but only *a bit*. We are *still* good friends, and I would really be *devastated* if I thought that that had ended. I *value* our friendship. You *are important to me* – and *not* just because you have that *oil well in back of your tent*," she joked, but there were tears in her eyes. "Let's just take things slowly. We *are* friends and let's just see where this friendship goes. We are still going to study together and go to on-campus movies together and have morning coffee together – *and* I'll even let you buy me a hamburger and French fries and a diet Coke; we will consider this *dinner* and our *first* unofficial/official *date.*"

When he went to place her order, Sarah thought to herself, *Be careful, Sarah, you could easily fall in love with him.* She wondered if she already had.

Their banter over hamburgers and French fries was casual, *almost* like it had been two days before. There *was* a bit of a strain, but only a bit. Mohammad walked her back to her dorm. They agreed to meet the next day in the library to go over the class notes for the class that Mohammad had missed. Unexpectedly, Sarah hugged him before she went in the door.

Back at his apartment, Mohammad took out the unread letter from Khalil. Propped up in bed he skimmed down through the Arabic. There were the usual *suggestions* that he study hard, make the most of his time, and NOT date, but he had added a postscript. "*Yum'ma* thinks she has found the perfect wife for you. We are concerned about you living alone in the States for two more years and think that you should get married when you come back this summer. I think you will be pleased with the girl that *Yum'ma* has chosen."

Mohammad slowly folded the letter and slipped it back into its envelope. He placed it on the nightstand and turned out the light. He lay awake all night, staring into space. His eyes were still open when the morning sun slid through the half-closed Venetian blinds.

Chapter 4

Nijmeh, in the back of her mind, always worried about Khalil. *It just isn't right that he is unmarried,* she thought. Over the years she had tried to arrange a marriage for him. She had suggested to him first the daughter of this person, then the daughter of that person. Each time he had joked, *Yum'ma, I am still looking for someone just like you. Until I find that woman I am not going to get married.* Nijmeh realized that the longer a man remained unmarried, the more choosey he became and the harder it was to find a girl who would meet all his expectations. *One should get married young, if one didn't, the chances of getting married faded until they disappeared,* she thought. She would sigh and wistfully wish that things had been different. She almost felt that she had somehow *failed* as a mother.

One night, as she lay in her familiar place with her head resting on Omar's chest, she broached the subject of Khalil with him. "I am worried about Khalil. He is almost thirty-eight and still unmarried. When you were thirty-eight, *habeebee*, you were already a grandfather."

Omar patted Nijmeh's shoulder and stroke her long, unbound hair. "Some men – a few men – choose not to marry. I don't understand why that is true, as I can't imagine my life without you in it, but I know that it is true. I think it tends to be especially true for *educated* men who postpone marriage while they are in school; then postpone marriage while they get established in a new job; then postpone marriage until they have enough money." He paused and kissed the top of her head. "We should have arranged a marriage for him before he went to Amman to university. But he seemed so anxious to leave and to study." He paused again as he tightened his arm around Nijmeh's shoulder. "He *is* only thirty-eight. That *is* not old for a man. Perhaps he will find the perfect wife for him, as I found when I was but a boy."

Nijmeh snuggled closer into Omar's embrace. "He does joke that he wants a wife just like me!" Nijmeh laughed.

"Ah, if *that* is the case, he will *never* marry. How could there possibly be someone who is *comparable to you?*" Omar whispered.

Khalil, less than a hundred miles away, also lay awake. He was worried about Mohammad. Mohammad was young, but *old* enough to be married. Khalil knew about the *temptations* of the States; his friend, who had met Mohammad at Purdue and seen him situated, had done his own graduate studies in the States. At that time he had had a live-in, American, girlfriend. He had even married her so he could get a green card and had stayed with her for three years until he had fulfilled the residency requirement for citizenship. Khalil thought he remembered that he had even fathered a daughter. Once he had his citizenship, he had divorced his American wife and come back to Jordan to marry a Jordanian girl whom his family had chosen for him. He now had dual-citizenship and lived in America with his Jordanian wife and their three children.

Khalil didn't want this for Mohammad. He felt there was something ethically wrong in marrying a girl *only* to get a green card and eventual American citizenship. He knew that others did it, but it didn't seem *right*. Marriage was sacred. He worried that Mohammad, so far from home, alone, would be tempted to get involved with an American girl. It would cause too many complications. He had been so thankful that the situation with Teri Bachman no longer existed.

His fears had prompted him to *suggest* to his mother that she find a suitable *Palestinian girl* for Mohammad. In his last conversation with his mother, she told him that she thought she had found the *perfect* bride for Mohammad. He *hoped* that Mohammad could be convinced to get married the coming summer when he was in the West Bank renewing his permit, but, there were times, Khalil worried, when it seemed that Mohammad was *not* listening to his suggestions as a *younger* brother should.

The butterflies in Mohammad's stomach all got in line to do their *debka* dance when he saw Sarah waiting for him at the library. Every time he saw her his heart seemed to flip and skip. He wondered, as he had a few days ago, whether this was what was meant when someone *fell in love*. This must have been how his father felt when he had first seen his mother. This must have been how Mansur felt after he had gotten to know Zaleena.

When he thought about the postscript in Khalil's letter, the butterflies dancing in his stomach seemed a little less energetic. *His mother had chosen a bride for him. His parents and Khalil wanted him to get married when he returned to the West Bank.* He *knew* this was the way it *should* be; he *should* marry someone *like* him; someone who was Palestinian and Moslem. He *knew* that his mother had probably chosen someone who was *perfect* in her eyes. But, like his father before him, *he had seen and his heart had chosen.* His *head* told him one thing; his *heart* told him another.

"Hey, I have been waiting for you," Sarah said pushing her books and papers aside and pulling out the chair next to her. "Sit here so you can see my notes and copy them." Mohammad sat next to her; she brushed against him as she leaned forward to show him where he should begin copying. He felt as though his arm had been burned. Her perfume was subtle and reminded him of the roses in the powdered-milk tins that lined the courtyard at home.

He faithfully copied as she explained the lecture he had missed. They worked quite steadily for two hours. "Let's take a break and go get a cup of coffee," Sarah stretched, easing the leg she had been sitting on out from under her.

"My treat," Mohammad smiled, "I'll even get you a *Starbuck's.*"

As they walked across the campus, Sarah slipped her hand into Mohammad's. His broad hand grasped hers, and their fingers intertwined; it was as though a hand had gripped his heart. He knew he was in love.

Chapter 5

Burning tires, tear gas, and rubber bullets seemed to punctuate the days. The children who were throwing stones at the soldiers were becoming younger and younger. In the paper, one day that week, there had been the picture of an eight-year-old child throwing stones. His hand was pulled back as though he were a pitcher taking aim to send the ball speeding over the plate. He was wearing a red coat that was a bit small for him; the fake fur on the collar framed the determination in his face. *He had a homemade sling shot made from the tongue of an old shoe and shoe laces,* so Hasna had read to Nijmeh. *Eight years old!* Nijmeh thought. *He was a baby!*

The walls of the houses and courtyards in the camp were covered with anti-Israeli slogans. The iron-shutters of shops were painted with graffiti. Periodically, soldiers would march through the camp, pound on metal doors, and order the residents to paint over the graffiti and slogans. Nijmeh had taken to having a pot of white paint and a brush already sitting by the door in preparation. (She had chosen white as it was easier for the boys who wrote the graffiti to write *over* the white. She didn't mind the painting she did – she saw it as part of the game. She knew by morning of the next day slogans and new graffiti would be written on the wall. She saw her job as *providing a clean slate.)*

She had also taken to setting, next to the can of paint and brush, a pan of *onions.* The women in the camp knew that peeled onions caused one's eyes to water. And if one had been exposed to tear gas, smelling the onion was a good cure for stinging eyes. Sometimes running children, who had been exposed to tear gas, would pound on her door and she would hand them a peeled onion as they ran off. All the women in the camp kept onions by their doors; the children knew that they could pound on any door for an onion.

Nijmeh also had friends among the women who would go out to the mountainside and *collect rocks*. She still had to chuckle over Palestinian women collecting *stones!* Palestine didn't have oil, but it had a *wealth of rocks*. The women would hide the stones – the perfect size for throwing – in the baskets they carried into the hills when they were looking for wild mint and *zatar*. They would place the rocks in the bottom of their baskets, and cover them with the wild plants they had picked. There weren't *enough* stones *just the right size* in the camp for the boys to throw, so the women were doing their part. Nijmeh and Hasna didn't go with them. They were in sympathy with what the other women were doing, but memories of Ahmad being killed, Khalil being imprisoned, and Saji being brutalized still haunted them.

Saji had gradually started to heal on the inside. He still, *only occasionally,* spoke a few words to Omar while they worked together. It was, Omar said, *as though he were testing his tongue.* He would say a few words; seem to *listen* to what he had said, and then smile at his grandfather. He had not yet spoken to Hasna or Imad or his brothers or Nijmeh.

Nijmeh was worried about Sami. Ever since the evening he had carried the brutalized Saji home, Sami had been different. Oh, he still went to work in the settlements with his brothers, Salah and Salam, but Nijmeh could tell he hated doing it; she felt that he *hated* himself for needing the money so badly that he continued to go to work *even* after *knowing* that settlers had almost beaten his little brother, Saji, to death. He had told her that he couldn't get out of his mind the tears on Saji's face after he had taken him to the bathroom, wiped him and pulled up his trousers; how he looked like a whipped animal. It had torn the heart out of Sami. There were days he felt like he would *explode*...days when he wanted to *explode!*

One of the bright spots in the daily game of *occupied and occupier* was that Issa had started to *sell* some of his drawings! There was an art shop, just inside New Gate of the Old City, in Jerusalem that had bought some of Issa's drawings. The shop catered to Western tourists and had found that framed prints of Issa's drawings were popular. When he had first approached them with his sketches, they hadn't been too interested. Just by chance, an American woman was in the shop and had seen Issa's portfolio. She had asked him how much he wanted for some of the drawings. Issa had tentatively named a price, and without any haggling at all, the woman had given him the money. She had said to the shopkeeper: *"If I were you, I would buy this young man's drawings, frame them and you will be astonished with how much money you make."* The shopkeeper had listened. The woman had been right. Issa was tickled that he was *making money* from his art and couldn't wait to tell Khalil when he next called. Issa thought that his Sitteh Hasna may have been right; *perhaps he would be the most famous of them all!*

Nijmeh thought that *even in the direst of circumstances, Allah gives wonderful surprises.* She had never thought that Issa would make money from his sketching. *If he really wanted to make money,* she thought, *he should sell political cartoons to the paper like that artist Ibn Omar.*

The petals of the buds of love were gently unfolding between Mohammad and Sarah. Mohammad felt himself relaxing; the tightness in his heart was lessening; he *could* envision himself married to Sarah; the hurdles that his mind put in the way were being leaped over by the hopes that were in his heart. The Quran allowed a man to marry a Christian – as she too was a believer – a woman of the *Book,* though not a Moslem. It, of course, *recommended* that a man marry a Moslem, but it was *permissible* to marry a Christian – even a Christian with a Jewish father. When he thought in terms of Sarah, he thought in terms of *marriage;* he never thought of *just living with her;* he thought of her in terms of a wife, *inshallah* (God willing), and the mother of his children. He *did* want to have what his parents and married siblings had, and he *knew* he could have it with Sarah. He was sure of his feelings; now he had to *convince* his family. In rasher moments, he even told himself that *if* they were not convinced, he would marry Sarah anyway and remain in the States. He couldn't imagine a life in which Sarah was not a part.

The school year was drawing to a close. He would soon be going back to the West Bank to renew his travel permit, to see his family, to tell them about Sarah. He couldn't imagine how he would endure the summer without seeing her every day. *She* would be going back to the farm in Iowa for the summer. They had promised to write each other, but it wouldn't be the same: morning coffee on the bench in front of the ivy-covered classroom building; holding hands as they walked across campus; studying in the library; *dinner dates* at *The Chinese Dragon* (It was ironic that they both had a passion for Chinese food; an Iowa farm girl and a Middle Eastern Arab); kissing her good-night when he walked her back to the dorm.

Yes, he had finally gotten up the courage to kiss her, or *rather, she had had the initiative to kiss him,* he thought ruefully. One evening after he had walked her back from *The Chinese Dragon,* they had stood in front of her dorm. He was holding both of her hands and looking down at her. She had reached up, standing on her toes, and gently kissed him on the lips. He had been startled and then had released her hands, and putting his arms around her he had drawn her close, and kissed her back. It felt *so right.* Any lingering doubts that he had had vanished with that kiss. No matter what happened, he was not going to let her go.

As he hugged her, she put her head on his shoulder and he had whispered into her hair – not so loud that she could hear – but loud enough that his heart heard : *I'm going to marry you one day, habeebtee, roh'el'be, ha'yati (my love, my spirit, my life).*

It seemed in the weeks before the term ended that they had talked about everything. He had told her about his family, about the camp, about the West Bank. He had even told her about Teri Bachman. She had listened, *really* listened. Her only comment about Teri had been: *I feel sorry for her. I can understand how she could have fallen in love with you. You are a person easy to love.*

Their relationship had definitely changed. They took moonlight walks holding hands, sometimes talking, sometimes *not* needing to talk. Everything seemed to take on an *enchanted* quality because they were together. They had gotten into the routine of taking all their meals together. Sometimes they ate out at the *Chinese Dragon;* sometimes they ordered take-out that was delivered to his studio flat.

At first, he had been somewhat reluctant to invite her back to his room; it didn't *seem quite right* to his conservative nature. He didn't want her to think that he had *ulterior* motives. She had joked with him: *Don't worry, Mohammad. I know you aren't going to throw me on the bed and 'have your way with me.' We are going to eat take-out and talk – that's all. After all, I am a farm girl and can take care of myself.* If Sarah had looked closely, she would have seen a blush under Mohammad's five-o'clock shadow.

Sarah had introduced Mohammad to *bowling.* She had taught him how to hold the ball in front of his face – close enough to kiss it if he wanted – and to line it up with the head pin. She had shown him how to bend with his right foot behind his left and swing the ball down with a smooth, straight motion then release it. They had watched as it seemed to go straight, then hesitate as though in deep thought, and swerve into the gutter. He had tried again and again and again until he had finally gotten it. The head pin was struck and the pins scattered into a *strike.* "I *knew* you were a natural," she had laughed. Bowling became *their game!*

Sarah had rearranged the furniture in his studio apartment. She had a natural eye as to how to make his one-room not only functional, but beautiful. Rather, *she* had the eye and *he* had the muscle. She instructed and he did. She would playfully smack him on the shoulder, and laughingly say, *Not there,* **there!** *Now, just an inch more in this direction, that's right. You've got it.* She was an organizer, and he had to admit that her organization of his things made sense. She had him shove the bed along the wall, so it didn't jut out into the room. They had bought colorful pillows to put along the back – and presto, she had created a sitting area with a couch! She *made* colorful curtains to match the pillows. *We, Iowa farm girls, all know how to sew, to cook, to keep house, make jam, muck out a stall, and milk cows. We are not just pretty faces,* she had said as she kissed him lightly on the cheek – it was as if it were a brush of butterfly wings.

Sarah *knew* she loved Mohammad. He was *different* from other boys she had known. There was no doubt that he was handsome and attractive. (She had had fleeting moments when she *almost wished* he would throw her on the bed/couch and *have his way with her.*) He was charming, he was smart, and she had no doubt that he cared about her. There was something about him that was very masculine, but her favorite thing about him was that quality of innocence.

She did realize that there were obstacles: he was foreign; he wanted to eventually return to the Middle East; he was *Moslem*. Her parents would see these as insurmountable obstacles – not just *bumps in the road* or *hurdles to be jumped.*

Her mother was a staunch Methodist. She was a member of the Women's Mission Society; she taught Sunday school; she served at church dinners; she sang in the choir. Her father was very casual about religion. He was a non-practicing Jew. Sarah wondered though how he would *really* feel about her marrying a *Palestinian Moslem*. She was afraid that the fact that she wanted to marry a man named *Mohammad* would make her father remember that *he was Jewish*. She didn't quite know how to tell her folks about Mohammad. She hadn't even mentioned him. When her mother had asked: *Isn't there someone special?* Sarah had lied and said, *No, not really.*

Part of her, in her *rasher* moments, thought that she would marry Mohammad no matter what her parents thought. In her more rational moments she *knew* she wanted her family's approval and blessing. She didn't want to move to the Middle East. She wanted a church wedding, a white dress with a train; she wanted to walk down the aisle with her father; she wanted to see the beaming faces of her family and friends. Though it *really* didn't matter to her, (or so she tried to convince herself) part of her *wished* that Mohammad *wasn't* a Moslem and that he *wasn't* named Mohammad, and that he *didn't* want to live in the Middle East. Part of her wished he was an Iowa farm boy from the neighboring farm named *Jake.*

Even though Mohammad hadn't *spoken* about marrying Sarah; and Sarah hadn't *spoken* about marrying Mohammad – they *knew* that that was what they both wanted; and this was the direction in which the relationship was heading. They were young; they were optimistic; they *chose* to be blind to the pitfalls. They both naively thought that *love could conquer all.* (That was another cliché that Mohammad had picked up and adopted.)

Mohammad had even toyed with the idea of going to the County Court House, having a civil wedding, marrying Sarah *before* her parents, or his, could object; marrying her *before* he returned to the West Bank to renew his permit. Once Sarah was his wife, and he was her husband, the families would *have* to accept, to adjust, to make the best of it. He had learned something from the Israelis, *create facts on the ground.*

One morning he and Sarah walked around the duck pond that was on campus. The pond was very near the *Shakespeare Gardens.* It was early morning and not too many people were about. There were a few swans majestically gliding through the water. It was like a scene on a calendar, Mohammad thought. They were holding hands, their fingers intertwined.

They sat on a bench facing the pond. She slipped her arm through his and interlaced her fingers with his. She laid her head against his shoulder and sighed. They sat in silence, content to be together, content to be in love. The moment was magical.

"You know I love you," Mohammad said. "I think I have probably loved you from the first moment I saw you." He paused. "You know I want to marry you, that I want you to be my wife. I can't imagine a life without you."

Sarah's fingers tightened around Mohammad's. She kissed his shoulder. "I love you too." She smiled. "I *do* want to marry you"...Sarah paused, hesitated, and looked up at Mohammad.

Mohammad saw the questioning look in her eyes. He felt a tightening around his heart.

"It just seems so complicated," she continued. "Our families will not want us to marry foreigners. They will see the cultural differences, the religious differences, and the fact that we come from opposite sides of the world." She paused and looked out at the swans as their gliding sent gentle ripples through the water. "I love you, but I wonder if *love is enough.*"

Mohammad released her hand and put his arm around her shoulders so he could hug her. "I know. Our families will not be happy, *at least at first,* but they will come around. I know my family will love you once they get to know you." He said the words as much to reassure *himself* as to reassure her.

Sarah rested her head on his shoulder and kissed his shirt. "I know that my parents *could* come to love you, *if* they got to know you. But I am afraid that all they will see is: *Palestinian, Moslem, Mohammad.* They won't give themselves a chance to get to know you." Sarah sighed. "I haven't even *mentioned* you to them. How cowardly is that?!" There were tears in Sarah's eyes.

"There *is* a way." Mohammad softly spoke. "We could go to the Court House and have a civil marriage. Once we were married, our families couldn't do anything about it. Oh, they might be angry and threaten to have nothing to do with us, but the truth is: *they love us;* they would eventually come around and accept the situation; in time, I think, they would eventually come to love us."

Sarah squeezed Mohammad's arm. "I *wish* that that would be true." She laughed a bit grimly, "It makes me feel that we are a modern adaptation of Shakespeare's *Romeo and Juliet.* And you *know* how *that* ended: *Romeo and Juliet* dead in the tomb and the parents coming too late to the realization that their children loved each other!" Sarah stopped, too overcome to speak. "I think we are fooling ourselves. I think we are not destined to be together."

"We're not going to end up dead!" Mohammad squeezed her and kissed the top of her head. "We are going to be an exception. My Sitteh Hasna used to say that the people we are *meant to love are written into our hearts.* I *know* that that is true. You have been written into my heart, and I have been written into yours. I believe that Allah will open the minds and hearts of our families." Mohammad hugged her tightly, as her tears gently fell, "I think I *need* to meet your parents." He smiled and jokingly said, "Once they meet me they will just *know* how perfect I am for their daughter."

"Oh, Mohammad," she sadly smiled through her tears, "they will probably *hate you!*"

Chapter 6

Nijmeh and Omar were anticipating Mohammad's return. Khalil and Mansur were anticipating Mohammad's return. The more each had thought about it, the more each agreed with the other that Mohammad *needed* to get married. He would be twenty-three. Yasmeen was eighteen – the five year age difference was perfect. Khalil and Mansur had not met Yasmeen, but from Nijmeh's description she sounded as though she were *just right* for Mohammad. None of them liked the idea of his returning to the States unmarried. He was impressionable and there were too many temptations.

Nijmeh had dictated to Hasna what she wanted to say to Mohammad. Khalil had written to Mohammad. Mansur had written to Mohammad. All three letters arrived on the same day.

When Mohammad went to check his mail box, there were the three letters. It was as though he didn't have to open them to know what was inside. He carried the letters up to his studio apartment. He threw his bag down beside the door; he put on water to make a cup of coffee; took off his shoes and stretched out on the "couch" Sarah had made from his bed.

When the water had boiled, he spooned in a heaping teaspoon of coffee crystals, poured in the water; added a heaping teaspoon of sugar and a heaping teaspoon of Coffee-Mate. Placing the mug on the nightstand, he tore the end off of the first envelope and shook the letter out. It was from his mother.

May the peace and blessing of Allah be upon you my son. Inshallah, you are studying well for your exams. We are counting the days until you return. We are anxiously awaiting your arrival.

I have talked with your father, who also sends his salaams and blessings, and with your brothers Khalil and Mansur. We all are concerned about your welfare and are anxious that you marry this summer before returning to the States.

I think I have found the perfect bride for you. She is eighteen, has completed tawjihi and received very high scores. Her English is excellent. She is an excellent cook and housekeeper and since she is the oldest of six, has had the care of her younger siblings. She is kind and patient, soft spoken and thoughtful.

Added to all these qualities, she is a rare beauty. I have known her since she was a little girl and I think, knowing you as I do, that she is meant for you.

Your father and I would like your permission to speak formally to her family and to ask for her hand in marriage.

May Allah bless you my son. Your loving mother, Nijmeh

There was an added line from his sister, Hasna:

Mohammad, The girl has a wonderful sense of humor. She is beautiful and I know once you see her, you will fall in love with her.

Mohammad slipped the letter back into its envelope and placed it on the nightstand. Taking a sip of the cooling coffee, he opened the second letter. This one was from Mansur:

Habeebee, Mohammad, my brother. Zaleena and the children send their salaams. I know that Yum'ma is writing to you and that Khalil is also sending a letter. We have been talking back and forth on the phone the last several months and all feel that it is time that you got married.

We know how lonely you must be on your own. You will be twenty-three and need to have a wife with you in the States; someone to care for you and share the experiences you are having.

Yum'ma says she has found the perfect girl. Over the years we have all come to realize how really sound our mother's judgment is. She knows each one of us in a very special way, and she wants what is best for us. When she says that she has found a woman who will make a perfect wife for you, we believe she has. Look how happy Hasna, Mona, Manal, Najla and Azeezeh are. It was Yum'ma who really decided that their spouses would be good matches. I know I have been the exception, but if Yum'ma had known Zaleena before, I know she would have picked her for me.

All I am saying is, trust Yum'ma's choice. We are all hoping that you, once you have sat with this girl, will realize Yum'ma's wisdom and agree to get married this summer before you return to the States.

May Allah bless you; our love to you,

Your brother, Mansur.

Once again Mohammad folded the letter and slipped it back into its torn envelope, placing it on top of the one from his mother. He got up and threw the cold coffee into the sink. Returning to the bed, he flopped down and tore open the flap of the third letter. This one was from Khalil:

May Allah be with you, my brother, my son:

*You have probably already received letters from Yum'ma and Mansur, so can be in no doubt about the subject of this letter. We are all in agreement that you **must** get married this summer. We do not like the idea of you being in the States on your own, without a wife. I know you are a good boy, but the temptations that abound on a college campus are many and you are young and alone. We know that many young Arab students become involved with American girls, and we <u>know</u> that you will not be one of them, but still we are concerned. It is good to take precautions.*

Yum'ma has spoken with us about a young woman. From what she has said about this woman, we feel she would be ideal for you. We trust her judgment in these matters. We know that once you meet her, you will see that Yum'ma has made a good choice.

It is our wish, our <u>prayer</u>, that you are married this summer and take her back with you to America. I am prepared to pay the extra expenses necessary for your tickets and housing. And of course, Mansur and I will pay for the wedding, the gold for the bride, and any dowry her parents' *request. You need not be concerned about the financial part.*

I know you will see the wisdom of our decision. We only await your approval before proceeding with the arrangements.

We anticipate your positive response. May Allah bless you and guide you. Your loving brother, Khalil

Mohammad added Khalil's letter to the other two. He put on his shoes, turned out the light, and locked the door behind him. He needed to walk. He needed to think. He needed to see Sarah.

Mohammad seemed to walk aimlessly for over an hour. He looked in the windows of shops; seeing the brightly lit displays, but not *really* seeing them. When he looked in the windows, he saw his own reflection as though he were one of the mannequins. The mannequins stood expressionless, arms rigid, eyes blind, mindless, dressed as the window dresser desired; arranged in the display as the clerk wished. Mohammad thought: *All they need are strings, and they would be like me.* He felt that his mother, Mansur, Hasna, Khalil, all wanted to dress him, turn him, twist him, arrange him in the display their minds had fashioned for him. He might as well be blind, mindless, and expressionless.

He *knew* the very fact he was here was because of Khalil. He owed him. He thought of all the sacrifices his mother and father had made. He owed them. He never doubted that they all loved him and wanted the best for him – the best as they *knew it.* He *knew* they were probably right. He *knew* he shouldn't be thinking about *marrying* Sarah.

He continued to walk down the darkened street, bright only where there were street lights. He thought how the lights illuminated some things, and hid what was in the darkness just beyond the light's reach. Because of the brightness of the lights he couldn't see the stars. He thought that maybe, just maybe, his love for Sarah was like those street lights, preventing him from seeing what was lurking in the darkness, preventing him from also seeing the stars, only allowing him to see the limited area around him, blinding him from all else.

Before he was really aware of it he was in front of Sarah's dorm. It was as though his feet had known where to go, that *they* had done the thinking. He asked the student receptionist at the desk to page *Miss Goldman.*

Sarah was surprised when the receptionist rang her room to tell her she had a visitor. It was almost eleven o'clock. She hastily slipped into jeans, threw on a sweat shirt, and ran a comb through her hair. When she pushed open the door into the reception area, she was not *too* surprised to see Mohammad standing there.

"What's up," she said, kissing him on the cheek. "You need to shave," she smiled rubbing the bristles on his chin.

Mohammad took her hand and said: "Let's go for a walk."

Sarah was about to protest and then she looked into Mohammad's eyes. "Okay."

Sarah slipped her arm through Mohammad's. They walked out into the darkness only dimly illuminated by the occasional street lamp. Mohammad guided her to the bench in front of the ivy-covered classroom building where they always had their morning coffee. There were lamps softly glowing on either side of the building's door; *their* bench stood in shadow.

As they sat, Mohammad took her hand, lacing his fingers with hers. At first he didn't say anything, just held her hand in the darkness.

"What's troubling you, Mohammad?"

He caressed the back of her hand with his thumb. Finally he spoke. "There were three letters in my box when I got back to the flat. There was one from my mother; one from my brother Mansur; and the third from my brother Khalil." Sarah listened, her heart beating a little faster. "They are worried about me." Sarah continued to listen. Mohammad had paused, as though clearing his throat. She could not clearly see his face as it lay in shadow.

"It *seems* they are concerned about me living alone; concerned that I might *give in to temptation.* They want me to get *married* when I return to the West Bank this summer." Mohammad took Sarah's hand and held tightly to it. Raising it to his lips he turned the palm up and kissed it, folding her fingers over the kiss. She could see that his dark eyes were bright with unshed tears.

"I *don't* want them to arrange a marriage for me! I *don't* want my mother *choosing* whom I should marry. My father *didn't* marry the girl who had been chosen for him. My mother *didn't* marry the man her uncles thought she should marry. My brother, Mansur, *didn't* marry an Arab. And, *I am not* going to marry someone the three of them think I should marry – make that *four,"* he added. "My sister, Hasna, also thinks this girl would be *wonderful* for me."

"They have already chosen a girl for you?" Sarah whispered, not trusting the sound of her own voice. "I never even *heard* of arranged marriages before I met you. I can't imagine marrying someone that had been *picked out* for me."

Sarah was silent as she clung to Mohammad's hand, stroking the smattering of dark hairs on the back of his hand with her thumb. Finally she spoke. "This is all really about me, isn't it? Part of you is thinking that your mother, and brothers, and sister are *right*. Aren't you?"

She seemed to be searching for the right words. "They *know* you and *love* you and want what is best for you. They want someone from your own culture, your own background; someone who would automatically know how to be a proper Palestinian wife. I understand that, I really do. They are thinking much like my own parents would think. They are hoping that I marry a boy from the same town, who goes to the same church that my mother goes to, who is a farmer just like my dad." Sarah's tears were silently sliding between the freckles on her cheeks. "No matter how much I tried, I could *never be a Palestinian* wife."

Mohammad released her hand so he could draw her down to his shoulder. "I *don't* want a Palestinian wife," he huskily whispered. "I want you."

Sarah whispered into his shirt, "I know you love me -that you *want me* - but as I said earlier today, *sometimes love isn't enough.*" There was silence between them. Sarah continued. "I want you to be happy. And I am not sure you could be happy in defying your family. You owe them too much; you love them too much; you are partly who you are because of them." She raised her head from his shoulder, and looked thoughtfully into his eyes. They were as moist as hers. "Let's go back. It's getting cold, and we have an exam tomorrow. We both need to get some sleep." she said.

She got up from the bench, still holding onto Mohammad's hand. She bent down and kissed him softly on the lips. "We'll think about this tomorrow." She suddenly laughed, "Remember that film we saw at the college union last week, *Gone with the Wind?* That's a line from the film. How did the rest go?"

Mohammad smiled, "Scarlett O'Hara said, *'I'll think about this tomorrow, if I think about this today I won't be able to stand it. Tomorrow is another day.'*"

Mohammad, holding Sarah's hand, stared out into the night sky. The moon had disappeared behind a cloud, and neither of them could see the stars because of the tears in their eyes.

When Sarah got back to the room, she undressed and slipped beneath the sheets wearing just her underwear. Her roommate was half asleep, but she thought she heard Sarah say, "I love him enough to let him go."

Chapter 7

It was just three days of exams before Spring Break and he had only *seen* Sarah three times. She hadn't been on their bench for morning coffee. They had taken their exams together, but had not studied together, or spoken. Sarah was *avoiding* him! She had managed to duck out of the exam room before he could intercept her and talk to her. He had gone to her dorm, but the receptionist had told him she wasn't in. *Even though he knew she was in.* She was scheduled to go to Iowa for Spring Break and he *had* to see her before she went. He tried phoning her, but she had caller ID and refused to answer. He was desperate. He *had* to talk to her!

Finally he had waylaid her roommate and brow-beaten her into telling him when Sarah was leaving for Iowa. Her roommate, who really liked Mohammad and thought his love for Sarah *tragically romantic,* told him that she was leaving the next morning taking the *Greyhound Bus* to Des Moines.

Mohammad called the *Greyhound Terminal* to see what time the bus for Des Moines left and how much a ticket cost.

With a heavy heart Sarah had handed her ticket to the driver. She had already placed her bag beside the bus so it could be placed in the luggage bin beneath. She took a window seat way in the back. She didn't want to see anyone or talk to anyone. She closed her eyes trying to block out everything. She kept telling herself that she had been *right to avoid Mohammad; that there was no point in talking; that it was right that he marry someone his mother had chosen for him.*

She heard the swishing sound as the driver closed the door. The bus started to back up. Someone moved into the seat next to her, brushing her side with his arm. She instinctively moved closer to the window. He moved closer. Finally, opening her eyes she turned and angrily said, "Do you mind?!"

"Frankly, yes," said the man smiling. "I *do mind.*"

Sarah's mouth dropped open. *It was Mohammad!*

"You didn't *really* think I was going to let you get away without talking to me, did you? I'm going to Iowa with you to meet your parents."

"This is crazy. You *can't* come to Iowa with me!"

Mohammad looked out the window and smugly said, "It appears that *I can.* This bus is going to Des Moines; I have a ticket, and that is where I am going."

"But my parents don't even know you exist."

"Well. I guess they are in for a *pleasant* surprise then. They probably *should* meet their future son-in-law."

"What do you mean *future son-in-law?!* You, my disillusioned friend, are going to go back home and marry the girl your mother has chosen for you. *That's* what you are going to do. They won't *want* to meet you. They'll *hate* you." Sarah was close to exasperated tears. "You're impossible!"

"Ah, yes, but certainly *loveable.*" Mohammad calmly countered.

"There is no hotel in the small town next to the farm. Where do you intend to stay?" Sarah challenged.

"I thought maybe, if worse comes to worse, I'll camp out in a cornfield, or perhaps your father will let me sleep in the barn – you *do* have a barn for all those cows, don't you?"

"What happened to the *shy, awkward* Mohammad? What have you done with him? Of course you can't *really* sleep in the cornfield, or bed down in the hay. You are being absurd. This *isn't* you."

"The town probably does have an all-night truck stop. I can just drink gallons of coffee and snooze in a booth." Mohammad replied.

"I'm going to *pretend* I don't even know you." She threatened.

"Go ahead, see how far it gets you when I walk up and down the street of your small town, going into every shop and asking if they know *Sarah Goldman, that I am her fiancé, Mohammad.*"

A small smile started to twitch at the corners of Sarah's mouth. "You would, wouldn't you?"

Mohammad smiled back and said, "I learned a new cliché that I really like: *all is fair in love and war.* And the way I see it, this is a little bit of both. You, *habeeptee* are going to have to work pretty hard to get rid of me."

Sarah slipped her arm through Mohammad's, interlacing her fingers with his. She kissed his shoulder and said, "There *is* an all-night truck stop just off the inter-state that bypasses the town, but there is also a bed-and-breakfast in town where you can stay until I figure out *how* to introduce you to my family." She leaned her head against his strong shoulder, and before the movement of the bus lulled her to sleep, she whispered into his sleeve, "I'm so glad you came. I love you so much it sometimes hurts."

About a half hour before the bus was scheduled to pull into Des Moines, Sarah woke up. She shook her hair, blinked her eyes and looked out the window. She sighed, and looking at Mohammad said, "I think it is probably better if you spend the night in Des Moines. I change buses here to a local bus. Here's my home phone number," she said taking a scrap of paper and a pen from her purse and scribbling a phone number on it. "Call me tomorrow afternoon and tell me where you are staying, and I'll drive in to pick you up. I need a little time to tell my folks about you. It is better than taking you home with me now, putting you up in a bed-and-breakfast, and having folks speculate who you are. You know how small towns are: *everybody knows everything about everyone.*"

They picked up their bags at the side of the bus and proceeded into the waiting room. Sarah looked in the Yellow Pages for a hotel, wrote down the address and telephone number. "Just take a taxi – they are lined up out front – tell the driver you want to go to this address. I have written down the phone number, it is probably best if *I* call *you* tomorrow. She kissed Mohammad softly on the lips. "It will work out. Just give me some time."

"Okay, but just remember, *you're not getting rid of me. I'm here to stay.*"

Sarah heard the voice on the loudspeaker announce that her bus would be boarding. "That's my bus. I've got to be going. I'll see you tomorrow." She watched Mohammad pass through the heavy glass doors.

She turned to get in line and she was lifted off her feet in a bear hug. A big, blonde giant of a man swung her around and kissed her soundly on the mouth. Sarah struggled and was about to slap his face when she saw who it was. "*Sam!* What are you doing here?"

"Your folks told me you would be arriving in Des Moines this afternoon and I decided to drive in and pick you up. Surprised?" he grinned.

"Surprised isn't quite the word I had in mind."

"Here, give me your bag." He put his other arm around Sarah's shoulders and was carrying on a rather animated one-sided conversation. As they walked out through the heavy glass doors into the late afternoon sun, Sarah saw Mohammad standing there, staring at her.

He had gone out to take a taxi, and had decided he needed to use the restroom first. He had gone back in and *seen* the encounter between Sarah and the big, blonde giant.

Sarah started. She felt her heart drop into her sneakers. She could tell from Mohammad's face that he had seen Sam hugging her and kissing her.

"Sam, there's a friend from school over there. I need to speak to him for a few minutes." She removed herself from Sam's arm and briskly walked over to Mohammad.

"It's *not* what you think. Sam is a boy I knew from school. His parents' farm is adjacent to my parents' farm. We have known each other since we were kids. He thought he would surprise me and pick me up." Mohammad had a flash of Teri Bachman turning up at the airport, of what *his* reaction had been. He knew that Sarah was embarrassed and trying to make excuses.

"Hey, it's okay, Sarah." Mohammad paused, licked his lips, and avoided Sarah's eyes. He looked somewhere over her head. "I am a little surprised that you never mentioned him before. I told you about Teri Bachman, and you never mentioned a friend named Sam."

"I know I should have told you about him. We dated some in high school. It's kind of like your mother finding a girl for you. My parents and Sam's parents would really *like* us to be a couple. But *we are not* – at least on my part, *we're not*. We can't discuss this here in the street. I'll call you tomorrow. *Wait for my call!"*

Sarah wanted to hug him. She wanted to kiss him. She wanted to tell him that she loved him. But she didn't, not in the street, not in front of the *Greyhound Terminal,* and definitely *not* in front of Sam.

"Who was that? Sam asked.

"He is a close friend from college. I'm going to bring him out to the farm tomorrow; he's a foreign student and doesn't really know his way around. I wanted to be sure he knew about taking the taxi to the hotel, how much to pay the taxi driver, that kind of thing."

"You're the same old Sarah, always concerned for the underdog. Though he looks like he could take care of himself; he sure is a big bruiser."

"Yes, he *can* take care of himself, and *no,* he certainly isn't an underdog." Sam was somewhat surprised at the vehemence of her tone.

"Is he your boyfriend? It sounds like he's your boyfriend."

"He's a boy, and he's my friend, and frankly, it is none of your business."

Chapter 8

Mohammad hadn't gotten into the taxi. He had gone back into the terminal. He took a booth in the cafeteria after first paying for a cup of coffee and a not-so-fresh roll. The coffee was hot; he took a sip and scalded his tongue. He needed to think.

He recalled so clearly how *he* had felt when Teri Bachman had surprised him at the airport. He tried to put himself in Sarah's shoes. It was *clear* she had been embarrassed. It was *clear* that the man, Sam, cared a lot about her. He remembered how awkward *he* had felt. He didn't want Sarah to feel *awkward* about him. He didn't *want* her to be embarrassed by him – and he could see where she could be. The advent of Sam had given him a different perspective; perhaps his mother was right: *one should get married to someone from their own* **thob.** He loved Sarah too much to want her to have to choose between her family – her friends – and *him*.

The coffee was finally cool enough to drink. He had put in three packets of sugar, and two packets of powdered milk. After a couple bites of the roll, he carefully wrapped it back up in its cellophane wrapper and put it back on the tray.

He finished his coffee, put the plastic cup on the tray and carrying the tray to the trash, dumped the cup and roll into the can. He placed the tray on top of the trashcan counter.

Going back into the terminal he went up to a free window and asked about a ticket to Chicago with a connection to Lafayette. He was going to go back to Purdue. He paid for the fare and was told the bus would be leaving at 6:30. He took a seat in the waiting area.

Sam had a brand new, red, pick-up. He was obviously quite proud of it. He swung Sarah's suitcase into the bed of the truck and held the door open for her as she had stepped up into the cab. They had driven quite a ways in silence. Sam had tried to make conversation, and Sarah had answered in one-word sentences.

"What's wrong, Sarah? Are you mad that I came to pick you up?" he questioned.

"I don't want you to make a special effort with me, Sam. We are friends, and yes, we dated some in high school, but that is all in the past." Sarah paused and looked out the window. "I *know* your parents and my parents would like to see us being a *couple*, but that isn't going to happen."

"It's that guy back at the terminal, isn't it?" Sam asked. "He's *more* than just a friend you know from school, isn't he?"

Sarah could see the hurt look in his eyes. "I care about him, yes, but it really has nothing to do with you. We were over a long time ago. Long before I met Mohammad."

"What do you think your parents are going to say about a guy named *Mohammad?*" There was mocking bitterness in Sam's tone.

"It really has nothing to do with you."

"We'll see about that! I can just *see* how excited your dad will be that you have a boyfriend who's a *Moslem.*"

"Are you *threatening* me?" Sarah challenged. "What I do with my life is certainly up to me – it *definitely* isn't up to you or to my dad."

They drove the rest of the way in angry silence. Sam drove up the dirt road to her parents' farm. There were neat, fenced-off pastures on each side of the road where cattle lazily grazed. He pulled up in front of a rambling, white clapboard farm house. Sarah's mother rushed through the opened screen door and hugged Sarah.

"Oh, you have finally arrived. I have been pacing and looking at the clock, and out the window, and out the screen door for more than an hour. My, you look good. You are certainly a welcome sight."

Sarah hugged her mother and felt the warmth of her mother's embrace. "There's your dad now coming up from the barn."

Her dad was a bit bent from all the years of farming and lugging heavy milk pails. He hugged Sarah and kissed her on her cheek. Turning he said to Sam, "You're staying for supper, Sam. Emily has prepared Sarah's favorites and there is even fresh apple pie, just out of the oven."

Sam looked at Sarah and grinned, a grin that didn't quite meet his eyes. "I'd be pleased to stay for supper. There is a lot I want to talk to you about. Sarah has a *friend* she wants you to meet."

"A *friend?* Well, why didn't you bring her out to stay at the farm?" Her mother asked.

"It isn't a *her;* it's a *he.*" Sam maliciously added. "He came on the same bus with her from Purdue. His name is *Mohammad.*"

He half expected a reaction from her parents, but was disappointed.

If looks could kill, as the old cliché went, *Sam would have been dead.* At that moment, Sarah realized how much she disliked him. She wished her father hadn't invited him for supper.

"There is a Palestinian student in the same program at Purdue. We have all the same classes and I have helped him get adjusted to the States. He is an agricultural engineering student, like me. He is staying in Des Moines tonight, but I intend to pick him up tomorrow and bring him out to the farm. You'll like him."

"Why of course, we will like any friend of yours." Her mother answered. She looked at Sarah, and then looked at Sam; she could see there was more to the story.

Sarah helped her mother clear the table and put the leftovers away; her mother asked about Mohammad. "Why didn't you just bring your friend out with you from the bus terminal?"

"I wanted to talk to you and dad about him first. I didn't want to just spring Mohammad on you."

"It sounds like this boy is more than just a *friend;* Sam certainly thinks so. I have never seen this side of him – there is *bitterness* in his tone."

"I know you and dad think that Sam would be *perfect* for me. But that was a high school crush, over long ago. He and I have known each other since we were children, but I can't imagine myself married to him – *ever.*"

"And you *can* imagine yourself married to this boy *Mohammad?*" Sarah's mother was insightful and she loved her daughter.

"I don't know. There are times when I *can* imagine Mohammad and me together. There are times when I *can't*. I *know* all the arguments of why it *wouldn't work.*" Sarah said pointing to her head. "But I haven't yet been able to convince my heart."

"It seems we have a lot to talk about." The coffee is ready. Take in these pie plates and I will bring the coffee. Sarah felt hopeful; she thought, *I can really talk to my mother and she will listen and understand.*

Sarah talked long into the night to her mother and father. She told them about Mohammad. She told them about her growing affection for him. She told them about her doubts and misgivings. She told them that she really wanted them to meet him, to meet him with an *open mind.*

Her father had listened. He hadn't said one word. He only watched her face as she talked. It was obvious to him that she was infatuated with this boy – perhaps even *thought* she loved him, but he *hoped* it was *just* infatuation. He didn't believe in inter-cultural marriages. And he certainly didn't want his daughter *marrying a Palestinian – a Moslem named Mohammad.* But of course he didn't express those feelings to Sarah.

He knew his daughter. She would become *defensive* if he registered his objections. He must in subtle ways wean her away from her infatuation. Her mother was anxious to meet the boy who had captured her daughter's heart.

After breakfast the next morning, Sarah called the number of the hotel she had written down. She waited. The reception answered and Sarah asked to be connected to the room of *Mohammad Omar Mansur.* The woman checked the registry and said, "I'm sorry. We have no one by that name staying here. Are you sure you have the right hotel?"

"Thank you." Sarah hung up the phone. Her mother was doing the breakfast dishes. "Mom, Mohammad isn't there. I *know* he has gone back to Purdue. He saw Sam hug me and kiss me at the bus terminal. I *know* that he thinks Sam is my boyfriend." Sarah's eyes were full of tears. "I *know* he is hurt and confused about what he saw. He probably thought it will be easier for me if he just left."

Sarah's dad had come into the kitchen for another cup of coffee before going to the barn. He saw Sarah's face. "What's wrong?"

"She thinks her friend, Mohammad, has gone back to Purdue. He wasn't at the hotel," her mother answered.

"Well, perhaps it is all for the best. Things have a strange way of working out the way they *should.*" Her father replied.

"For *the best*, how can you say that? I *like* Mohammad and I wanted you to get to know him and *like* him too." Sarah was angry. Her *defenses* were up. "If he has gone back to Purdue, then *I'm* going back to Purdue too!"

Under her breath she said, "If you think you can get away from me that easily, you have another think coming!" She went up the stairs, got her suitcase out of the closet and began to toss clothes into it.

Chapter 9

Mohammad had slept on the bus; he was emotionally exhausted, and the motion of the bus reminded him, *so he thought he remembered, but of course he didn't,* of when he used to be rocked in the metal cradle at home. He had changed buses in Cleveland to catch the bus to Lafayette.

Once back in his studio-apartment, he flopped down on the bed that Sarah had transformed into a couch. He could hardly keep his eyes open. He left his clothes on, just removed his shoes, and slipped between the sheets, pulling the bedspread over his head so that just his nose poked through. He slept. He had no dreams – at least none that he remembered. It was as though his mind was *sans* thought, his heart *sans* feeling.

Nijmeh had been thinking about Mohammad all day. It seemed that no matter what she was doing her mind was preoccupied with Mohammad. Kneading the dough for bread, she thought of Mohammad. Pushing carrots through the wire screen that confined the rabbits, she thought of Mohammad. Pouring water on the stone tiles and swishing it out the door with a handle-less broom, she thought of Mohammad. She had always had this uncanny *connection* to her children. She thought that it was *just something unexplainable* that all mothers had. She thought to herself: *the cord may have been cut when the baby pushed into the world, but there was an invisible cord that was never severed – a cord that mystically tied a mother to her child.*

She had finished the mopping. The bread dough needed to rise before it could be shaped and baked. There was time to go and get Hasna and bring her back so she could place a call to Mohammad in America.

Nijmeh had never been able to figure out how to use the phone.

Mohammad finally woke up, His mouth was dry. His teeth felt gritty. He needed to pee. He was hungry.

He took off his wrinkled clothes and threw them in the hamper. He stepped into the shower adjusting the water so it was as hot as he could stand it. He shampooed his curly hair; he soaped the hair on his chest. He soaped his arms and legs. He let the almost scalding water run over him, watching the soap flow from his body and swirl down the drain. He toweled off; rubbing his body vigorously with the soft blue towel that Sarah had bought for him. He brushed his teeth. He scraped the two-day's growth of beard from his cheeks. He ran a comb through his dark curls thinking he should get a haircut.

He slipped into jeans and a black t-shirt with the Arabic character *Handala* on it in red. His sister Mona had sent it to him. He straightened the covers on the couch/bed – Sarah had said *when the room is tidy it looks bigger*. He tied the laces on his Reeboks and was just going out the door when the phone rang.

"Hello." He waited for the response and was happy to hear his mother's voice.

"Mohammad, Mohammad habeebee?"

He spoke to her in Arabic. "*Ai'wa* (yes) *Yum'ma, Mohammad.* You don't need to shout *Yum'ma* I can hear you just as though you are in the same room."

Nijmeh always felt that if she shouted that her voice would carry across the six thousand miles a bit better.

"I have been thinking about you all day, *Yum'ma,* and wanted to hear your voice. *Keyf il-hal* (how is everything)?"

"*Illhumdillah* (thank God), *Yum'ma,* I am fine. How are you and *Yaba,* Issa, Hasna and the boys?"

"We are all fine and they send their *salaams.* Did you get my letter, *Yum'ma?*"

Mohammad hesitated. "I got your letter, *Yum'ma* and one from Mansur and one also from Khalil. I am thinking about what you wrote, and I will be writing to you. I know you want what is best for me. I just need a little time to think. It is a big step," Mohammad tried to laugh, "marriage."

"Think about it, *Yum'ma.* You are almost twenty-three, *habeebee,* when your father was twenty-three he already had five children."

Mohammad *did* laugh. "You can't expect me to be like *Yaba.* I will never be the man he is. My moustache is not *nearly* as impressive as his," he joked.

"It does my heart good to hear you laugh, *habeebee.* I just wanted you to know that we are thinking about you and that we love you. Take care. Everyone here sends their love. *Allah my'ak* (God be with you), *habeebee.*"

"*Allah my'ik, Yum'ma.* Give my *salaams* to everyone."

Mohammad hung-up the phone and thought about how much he really loved his mother, his father, his sisters: Hasna, Mona, Manal, Najla and Azeezeh, and his brothers Khalil and Mansur and Issa. He couldn't imagine purposely hurting them, or disappointing them, or choosing to live a life of which they were not a part. Perhaps he *should* forget Sarah. His head told him so; he just had to convince his heart.

It was ten o'clock Monday morning and Mohammad was still in bed. For the first time, in a really long time, he felt rested. He stretched and yawned and punched the pillow to get it just right. He had just closed his eyes, when there was a rapping on the door. He blinked his eyes open, wondered who it could be, and chose to ignore it. Everyone he knew was on Spring Break; there was no point in going to the door. The person would eventually go away, thinking he was on Spring Break too.

The rapping continued, this time a little more energetically. Finally, saying a mild curse under his breath, he yanked the door open. There standing at the door was a very *angry* Sarah! Mohammad was keenly conscious that he was standing there in just his briefs.

He hurriedly backed away from the door and picking his jeans up off the floor wrestled his legs into them. His face was scarlet under his two-day old beard. Keeping his back to Sarah, he picked a shirt off the floor and pulled it over his head. Finally he turned to look at her. "What are you doing here?"

"Oh, I just thought I would *drop* in and see what you slept in!" Sarah was angry. "What do you *think* I am doing here? Didn't I ask you to wait for my call? No, you decide to get the first bus back to Lafayette."

"I thought it would be better this way." Mohammad offered as a form of excuse.

"Oh, better *is it?* Weren't *you* the one who said it would be difficult to get rid of you? Or am I mistaken? Apparently, all it takes is one scene that is misunderstood."

"Do you want to come in and sit down?" Mohammad asked.

"Oh, I *want* to come in, and *yes,* I want to sit down, but *first* I want to tell you how angry I am with you. How could you just leave like that without talking to me, without letting me know? Who are *you* to decide what I think or how I feel?"

She closed the door behind her with a bang. And before Mohammad knew what was happening, she was in his arms, kissing him on the lips and pressing her body against his. When she finally came up for breath she whispered: "Don't you *ever* do that to me again! Don't you ever just walk away from me and think that it is for *my own good.* I will make it very clear to you what I want and what I don't want. And don't you forget it."

Mohammad smiled. "I guess you want to be here with me."

"*Of course* I want to be with you!"

Chapter 10

Nijmeh sent Issa to Im Najib's with a message. He rapped on the metal door leading to her courtyard and waited. A voice on the other side of the door asked, "*Mean?* (Who is it?)

"Im Najib, it is Issa. *Yum'ma* sent me with a message for you."

The door was opened and there before him stood the most beautiful girl he had ever seen.

"Sitteh (grandmother) said for you to come in. *Ta'fad'dal* (welcome), I am Yasmeen, her granddaughter."

Issa waited by the door for Im Najib. Yasmeen excused herself and went into the little kitchen alcove directly opposite the door. He followed her with his eyes as she disappeared. The butterflies in his stomach were doing a funny dance.

"*Marhaba* (hello), Sitteh," Im Najib said. "Sit down, *ta'fad'dal,* you must have a cup of coffee while you tell me what your mother wants." Issa at first refused, but Im Najib insisted. "Yasmeen has already gone to make coffee, you *must* sit."

Issa sat on the low, thresh-bottomed stool, his back against the warm cement wall. Im Najib sat beside him. "*Im'me* (my mother) wanted me to tell you that Abu Haseeb delivered the *jibneh* (cheese) this morning. He delivered two *ten'a'cat* (tin cans) for her and two *ten'a'cat* for you. She wanted to know if I should bring them over."

"*Habeebee* Sitteh, there is no reason for you to bother. Yasmeen and I will come over and get the cheese."

"It is no bother, Sitteh, I will carry the tins of *jibneh* over for you."

Yasmeen brought the tray of coffee and offered first to Issa and then to her grandmother. She didn't sit with them. It wouldn't have been proper, but when she went back into the alcove kitchen, she *did* glance back at Issa. He was about the handsomest man she had ever seen with his dark auburn curls and blue eyes.

As Issa walked home, he thought that he had seen the face of Yasmeen before. He couldn't quite remember where; then it dawned on him. In the shop where he sold his sketches, there was a huge poster in the window. It was the drawing of a Bedouin tent, there was a camel in the background, a bit of desert reaching toward the mountains towering over the tent, and a beautiful Bedouin girl with dark eyes, heavily lashed, outlined in *kohl*. The girl had her hand raised against the tent rope; she was gazing into the distance. It was the face of Yasmeen.

"What did Im Najib say, *Yum'ma?*"

"She is at home and would send her granddaughter for the cheese, but I told her that I would carry the tins over."

"It is good that Yasmeen is there. She can help her grandmother boil the cheese and get it ready to store in the glass containers. Of course, you must carry the tins over to her."

Issa carried the heavy tins of *jibneh* to Im Najib's. "Thank you, Sitteh." Im Najib said. Issa excused himself, but not before taking one last look at Yasmeen. She also looked at him, and there was just a shadow of a smile about her lips as she walked him to the door and closed the metal gate behind him.

Mohammad and Sarah spent their Spring Break at Purdue. They ate at their favorite Chinese restaurant; they went bowling – at which Mohammad had become quite good; they went for long walks around the lake; down to the river; through the Shakespeare Gardens. They window shopped; they held hands; they *talked*.

Sarah told him all about Sam, about her parents *wanting* her to marry him, or at least someone *like* him; someone who would eventually inherit the farm and keep it going. She told him about talking to her parents and how her mother seemed genuinely sympathetic and wanted to meet him, how her father was not very happy that she had become *infatuated* with a Moslem.

"I don't want to come between you and your family, Sarah," Mohammad said.

"And I don't want to come between *you* and *your* family. We are who we are because of them. One doesn't just marry an individual, one marries a *family*. Your family is important to you, like my family is important to me." Sarah sighed. "The problem is *we love each other*. I *so* wish that *love was enough*."

The street lights and stars were in competition. At times the street lights blinded them to the stars; at times, walking out of the street lamps' glow, the stars were brilliant jewels in the black velvet sky. They had been holding hands. Mohammad raised their joined hands to his lips and kissed the back of her hand.

"We have to convince our parents that we can love each other and still love them. We have to convince them that *love is enough* to encompass us all, to bridge the difference in culture and religion." He paused and looked into Sarah's eyes. "I *know* we can make this work."

Sarah kissed him softly. "I hope so," she murmured against his lips.

That evening, back in Mohammad's studio apartment, they had lain together, fully clothed, on the couch/bed. Their arms and legs were intertwined. They were so close that their hearts almost touched.

When Mohammad felt their kisses becoming more demanding, he rolled away from Sarah and jokingly said, "I think I need to take a cold, cold shower. I *want* so much to *show* you how much I love you, but this is something that I want to happen only after we are married."

Sarah laughed. Her face was flushed. It would have been *so easy* to give in to their feelings. But like Mohammad, she believed this was something *special* that she only wanted to share with the person she married. "I think *I* need to take a cold shower too, but I *don't* think women take cold showers, do they?"

She laughed and Mohammad laughed. The idea of a *woman taking a cold shower* struck them both as hysterically funny. "I think it is time for me to walk you back to your dorm," Mohammad said pulling Sarah up from the bed, "as much as I *want* you to stay!"

"I think that is a *very* good idea, or I just might push you back onto the bed, rip your clothes off and *have my way with you*," Sarah joked. "Then you would no longer *respect* me. I don't want you to think that I am *easy!*" She laughed.

When Mohammad got back from walking Sarah to her dorm, he put the water on for a cup of instant coffee and began a letter to Mansur and Zaleena.

Salam aleikum (Peace be upon you), Mansur and Zaleena. Inshallah this finds you and the children well. I am well, illhumdillah, and am on Spring Break. I think I did well on my exams, inshallah.

I received three letters: one from Yum'ma that Hasna wrote; one from Khalil, and one from you. I have decided that it is best to write you first. I need your advice and have thought, out of anyone, you two would understand.

I have fallen in love with an American girl. This past year we have been in all the same classes. Her name is Sarah. She is funny. She is smart. She is caring. She is thoughtful. I have struggled not to love her, as she has struggled not to love me. We each know all the arguments that are against our being together: different cultures; different religions; different backgrounds; family on opposite sides of the ocean.

I know that Yum'ma has picked out a bride for me. I know that Khalil, Hasna, and you, all feel that I should marry this summer the Palestinian girl that she has chosen. My head says that would be the reasonable choice. But Sarah is in my heart.

Sarah and I both love our families and we don't want our love for each other to cause a break with our families. I know that if you met her, you would love her. She is as right for me, as you two are right for each other. She is nothing like Teri Bachman. Sarah comes from American peasant stock; her father is a farmer.

I need your advice as to how to broach the subject with both Khalil and our parents. Both Sarah and I know there are obstacles to overcome, but we love each other.

I await your response. My salaams to the children and to Khalil (perhaps you can sound him out to see what he thinks – though, of course, I can guess.), God be with you, Your devoted brother, Mohammad

Mohammad read the letter out loud to *hear* how it sounded. He folded it and slipped it into an envelope. Licking the flap he sealed it. He addressed it to: *Mansur Omar Mansur.* He would mail it from the post office tomorrow morning before meeting Sarah for breakfast at *McDonalds.*

That night he slept soundly. He *did* dream. He dreamt of Sarah pressed against him; her arms tight around him; her head resting on his chest.

Chapter 11

As Spring was tip-toeing over the hills and valleys of Palestine leaving footprints of green wherever it stepped, footsteps muddied with wild flowers in vibrant reds, and yellows, in delicate pale blues and pinks, the Occupiers were marching through the West Bank and Gaza trying to stomp out the continuing popular uprising. The Palestinians adjusted to every repressive tactic employed. It seemed the harsher the repression, the stronger the opposition. It seemed to involve the entire populace. The demonstrations no longer primarily consisted of *shabab* (youth); but often included older men, young girls, and women. There was an irrepressible spirit of unity that seemed to buoy the people no matter what the reprisals.

The day after Nijmeh talked to Mohammad on the phone, the international phone lines were cut. One could still call Jordan, but calls to Europe and the States were no longer possible. Any mail sent or received had to first go through Israel. The majority of the letters eventually reached their destination; sometimes letters *never* arrived. Thankfully the telephone and postal service between the States and Jordan were still reliable. This became the only way that Mohammad had to communicate with his family.

Ten days after he had sent it, Mansur and Zaleena received Mohammad's letter. They shared the contents of his letter with Khalil. As Mohammad had anticipated, *Khalil was not happy.*

"It is just as I feared. He thinks he is in love with an American-Christian. We should have thought of this and gotten him married *before* he left for America. He is young; he is alone; he naturally would feel drawn to a young woman." Khalil said.

"He *is* mature, though," Zaleena interjected, "he doesn't want to just *live* with the girl. He *does* want to marry her. And, he is asking for our advice."

"He *wants* us to *agree* with him, to *support* him; to *argue* his case with Im'me and Abou'ee (my father)." Khalil countered. "He is seeing you and Mansur and how well your marriage has worked, and thinks that that will be true for him as well."

"Perhaps *it would work,*" Mansur said. "Zaleena and I are from different cultures, different backgrounds, and yet we are happily married."

"You're happily married because Zaleena is Russian, a *Moslem*, and speaks Arabic. If she had been American, and *Christian*, and spoke no Arabic, it would have been an entirely different story."

Mansur and Zaleena had to agree with him. They *were* sympathetic, but the situations were *only* similar in that Zaleena was not Palestinian.

"We must write to Mohammad and *strongly* counsel against any further involvement with this American girl." Khalil stated.

"But if we *order* him to stop seeing this girl, he may rebel – he is not a child," Zaleena said.

"We should write and tell him that *we do understand; that we are sympathetic;* and *we think he should come here this summer, meet the girl; talk with us and Yum'ma and Yaba before he decides anything,*" Mansur added.

Khalil thought about what Mansur had said. "You are probably right. We need to reassure him that we love him, that we care about him, that we *are* in theory *supportive,* but we want him to take time and to look at the broader issues, hoping that he will see for himself *the folly of marrying an American-Christian.*"

****

Spring meant that Omar and Saji had considerable work to do. There were stone walls to repair; there were gardens to dig; there were weeds and grass to be cleared from around houses. The sun was warm on their backs as they used their short-handled spades; as they hauled stones in the shallow buckets made from old tires; as they raked the grass-and-weed cuttings into piles.

They left for work just after the dawn prayer. They returned from work just at dusk when the call from the mosque was asking people to stop and *remember God.* Saji was still reluctant to go any place without his grandfather. The two brutal beatings he had received, the last which had almost killed him, had left scars of fear on his spirit. He still held his Sido Omar's hand whenever they were in the street. He still held his thoughts in his mind, rarely giving them voice. The words *were there* on his tongue; Omar at times thought he could almost *see* them, yet they remained unuttered.

Omar carried on a one-sided conversation with Saji. He would talk about Saji's aunts: Mona and Manal and their children in California; he would talk about his aunts: Najla and Azeezeh and their children in Bahrain; he would talk about Saji's Uncle Mansur and Uncle Khalil in Amman; he would talk about his Uncle Mohammad studying in America. And Saji would listen, and smile, and squeeze his grandfather's hand, but seldom spoke a word. Omar would smile at Saji and stroking his impressive moustache say: *Besides being one of the finest stone masons in Palestine, Allah also gave me the gift of reading minds. I know just what you are thinking; you don't really need to say anything. But, one day, Sido, you will surprise us and speak; everything in Allah's good time.*

After a light supper Omar and Nijmeh and Issa were sitting in the courtyard. The evening was pleasantly warm. The stars, pinned against the black velvet sky, twinkled in remote grandeur. There was the perfume of jasmine coming from the vine that crept over the courtyard wall. The darkness hid the camp, the occupation, the *intifada* – for a moment one could *imagine* being back in one's village, the family sitting peacefully together on a pleasant spring evening, the air warm and fragrant.

Nijmeh sighed. "I sometimes long for the old days; the days when one's children would marry and stay in the village and not go to live in California, or Bahrain, or Amman. I sometimes long for the days when our sons, May Allah bless them and keep them, would have worked the land like their father and grandfather."

"Ah, but our sons are, *illhumdillah,* better than we are. They can read and write; Mansur is a doctor, Khalil is a lawyer, Mohammad will be an agricultural engineer, and this our youngest," Omar said placing a hand on Issa's shoulder, "will be a businessman and artist. They will not have to toil in the fields, their hands calloused and rough from gripping the hoe, from building stone walls; they will not smell of sheep and goats."

Issa laughed. "*Yaba* you *never* smelled of sheep and goats." And a bit seriously he added, "We, none of us, could *ever* be better than you and *Yum'ma*. It is *because* of you both that we are who we are." They couldn't see his face in the darkness; couldn't see the truth that was so evident in his expression. "I think that you two are probably the smartest people I know."

Nijmeh laughed. "Ah, yes, *I am* one of the smartest women you know. I do know how to cook and clean and preserve olives and *jibneh* and raise chickens and children. But sometimes," she joked, "my children do not recognize how smart I am. They do not listen to the advice I give as I *direct* their lives. Look at your brother, Mohammad. He *wants to think* about getting married this summer. He does not realize that *I* know best."

"Have you already picked out a bride for him, *Yum'ma?*"

"Of course the final choice is his, but I think the perfect wife for him is, and this is just between us, Im Najib's granddaughter, Yasmeen."

Issa felt a blow around his heart. He hadn't dreamed that Yasmeen had been chosen by his mother for *Mohammad*. He *had wanted* to broach the subject with his mother of Yasmeen as a bride for him. Ever since that chance meeting he was thinking more and more about marriage. He was almost twenty-one; thoughts of Yasmeen had crept into his mind and heart. But his mother had already picked her for his much-loved *brother, Mohammad!*

Mansur and Zaleena wrote to Mohammad. They had tried to phrase the letter in such a way that he would not be angry. They had listened to Khalil's comments and concerns, but thought they needed to soft-pedal them. It seemed senseless to rehash the same points. Mohammad knew what the obstacles were.

Mohammad had been anxiously awaiting their letter. Every day, two weeks after he had written them, he checked his mail box to see if their letter was there. Every day he was disappointed. Finally, three weeks after he had written, the long-anticipated letter arrived.

Mohammad took it up to his studio apartment. He tossed his backpack into the corner between the bathroom and the door. He put water on for some instant coffee. Took off his shoes, put an extra pillow behind his back, and placing his feet on the coffee-table that he and Sarah had found on the street one evening, he tore off the end of the envelope and shook the letter out.

It wasn't a very long letter; only one page. It began:

> *Salam aleikum brother,*
>
> *Inshallah this finds you well and that you did well on your exams. Zaleena and I have carefully read your letter – several times in fact. And as you suggested, we did share the contents with Khalil.*
>
> *Though we certainly understand your affection and growing attachment for the American girl of whom you spoke, we can't help but endorse the arguments that you have had with yourself. There is little to be gained from repeating them to you. We are deeply concerned, as your happiness is our primary concern.*
>
> *We know that you look at Zaleena and me and think that a bi-cultural marriage could work. The major difference in our two situations is that Zaleena is Moslem and speaks Arabic. If I had*

attempted to marry an American-Christian, Yum'ma and Yaba would never have agreed.

We strongly encourage you to come home this summer and meet the young woman that Im'me has chosen. God be with you, Mansur

There was a post script at the bottom from Zaleena.

Hamoudeh (nickname for Mohammad),

I know how hard this must be for you. It is difficult to deny what you feel in your heart. The only possible solution I can see, and even then, it will be difficult to persuade your parents and especially your brother, Khalil, is to have the young woman convert to Islam and to begin intensive Arabic. If you can show your parents that Sarah (that is her name, isn't it?) has embraced Islam and is conversational in Arabic, perhaps they can agree to your marrying her. Otherwise, I think you will have to choose between the girl and your family. All my love, Zaleena.

Mohammad folded the letter, slipped it back into the envelope and slid it between the pages of the Quran that was on the table next to his bed. It was as he had thought it would be, maybe a little worse.

The choices seemed clear: he could break off any relationship with Sarah and marry the girl his mother had chosen for him; he could marry Sarah, against his parents' and brothers' approval and be estranged from them; or he could convince Sarah to convert and learn Arabic – the possibility of that seemed as likely as finding an oasis in a desert.

Chapter 12

Sarah asked Mohammad if he had heard from Mansur and Zaleena. Reluctantly, he told her that he had and summarized for her what they had said. Over Szechwan beef, which they shared, and egg rolls at their favorite restaurant *The Chinese Dragon,* they discussed their options.

"I *can't* really believe that in this day-and age marriages are arranged and that you would get married to someone *your mother picked out for you!* I can't believe that you would even think about marrying someone you didn't know." Sarah paused. "I don't want to come between you and your family, but I can't see that they will ever accept the situation as it is. What alternative do you see?"

Mohammad hesitated then said, "Zaleena suggests that you *might* consider learning Arabic and *might* consider converting to Islam." Mohammad waited for the explosion. He looked closely into Sarah's eyes.

"I don't mind learning Arabic and can see myself doing that. But, converting! Would you *want* me to convert?"

"I only know that I don't want to lose you. I don't want to lose my family, but I don't want to lose you more. If converting to Islam, and it only need be on paper, is an alternative, I think it is an option we should consider."

"*We* should consider? I thought *I* was the one who would have to be doing the converting. Would you consider converting to Christianity?" Sarah was getting angry. "If my family said the *only* way we could marry is, say, you became *Methodist,* would you do it?"

Mohammad remained silent as he cut the egg roll on his plate.

"I didn't think you would. How can you even *ask* something like this of me?"

"I can *suggest* it because I love you. Zaleena is only thinking of what might convince my parents and brothers to support our marriage." Mohammad paused. "I don't have to convert to Christianity to lose my family; all I have to do is marry you." Even to Mohammad the words, once out there, sounded cruel. "That *wasn't* what I meant to say. I *want* to marry you. You are the most important thing in my life." He swallowed the lump in his throat. "If the price I have to pay for marrying you is losing my family, I am willing to pay that price."

There were tears in Sarah's eyes as she reached across the table and took Mohammad's hand. "It is too high a price to pay. Marriage should be a joyous occasion for the couple *and* the families. It shouldn't cause so much heartache and pain. It is absurd that formal religion should come between a man and woman who want to marry. "

"Religion, for us, is a way of life. It permeates everything we think and do. It *is* our culture and our traditions and our language. It is who we are; it is who I am."

Sarah looked at Mohammad. She couldn't imagine herself loving someone else as much as she loved him. "I am not making any promises, but I am willing to learn more about Islam, do some *reading*."

Mohammad leaped out of his chair and kissed her, right there over the Szechwan and rice. "That's all I am asking. Just do some reading." He kissed her again and whispered against her lips, "You are wonderful."

That night, after Sarah finally got to sleep she had a dream. In the dream she was standing beside a tent in the desert. She saw Mohammad at a distance. He was riding a camel. In the dream she saw herself. There was a black shawl covering her hair; and across her face – just below the eyes there was a veil of a black gauze-like material. Clinging to her long skirt was a little boy who looked like Mohammad must have looked when he was a toddler. He looked up at her and said something in a language she could not understand.

Sarah awoke with a start. Her heart was beating rapidly. There was a fine film of sweat on her brow. She had, for just a moment, thought that the dream was real and it scared her.

The next morning when they met for coffee on their favorite bench, Mohammad had brought two books for her: *Understanding Islam* and an English translation of the *Quran*. Sarah looked in the bag. "What are you looking for?" Mohammad asked.

"I'm looking for the veil." Sarah half joked.

"Don't worry. No veil, though I might have to have you practice walking ten steps behind me." Mohammad noticed the serious look in Sarah's eyes. "Hey, I'm just joking. I really appreciate your willingness to do some reading. It means more to me than you can imagine. I know it is asking a lot of you."

"You know, my mother is one of the most independent women you could find. So, was my Sitteh – my grandmother. It was these two, strong, independent women who held our family together. They never covered their faces or walked ten paces behind the men in their family. My father always says that my mother is the real backbone of our family. I think part of their strength comes from the fact that they are Moslem women." Mohammad paused and took Sarah's hand. "All I want you to do is to get a glimpse into what has gone into making them who they are or were. I know what the stereotype is: *tent, veil, submission, subservience.* It is really *not* that way at all among Palestinians."

"I am *willing* to read so I can better understand, but don't expect too much of me. I am strong-willed and independent and equal to anyone – especially *equal to you, my fine friend.*" Sarah joked as she poked Mohammad's arm. "I am *willing* to learn more about Islam – about your culture, so I can understand you better – and this is *only* because I love you so much." She said kissing his shoulder.

"And I love you, more than you can imagine." Mohammad replied kissing the top of her blonde hair.

Sarah's dad had finished the morning milking and had driven the cows out to the pasture where they could graze and chew to their heart's content. The hired hand was mucking out the barn and he would go in to help him shortly, but for the moment he wanted to enjoy the morning. He gazed out over the flat countryside. All one could see for miles were acres and acres of field. There wasn't a cloud in the sky. It was a perfect spring morning in rural Iowa.

It *would have been* perfect if he hadn't been worried about Sarah. He was upset that she had decided to return to Purdue after she had been at the farm for *only* two days because she was concerned about that kid, Mohammad. He had tried to persuade her to wait until the end of Spring Break, but she was adamant she would return immediately. She was *one determined* young lady when she got an idea in her head. She was like an old dog he had had, once that dog had a bone to chew, come hell or high water, he gnawed at that bone. Sarah was stubborn and willful and had a mind of her own. She must care an awful lot about that young man to go traipsing back to college to see if he was alright. He was worried that she *cared a damn sight too much.*

He carried his religion lightly – maybe *too lightly* at times. Except for his name, there were times that he forgot he was Jewish. Religion had never been important to him. He had never objected to Emily being in the choir, teaching Sunday school, being a member of the church sewing circle and Missionary Society. If one chose to be religious, that was an entirely personal matter. He considered himself *open-minded* – liberal even, but when he thought of Sarah getting involved with an *Arab Moslem*, he found a conservative vein he didn't even realize he had, rising to the surface. It surprised him that the fact the boy was Moslem reminded him that *he* was Jewish. *Damn.*

When Mansur made his weekly call to check on his parents, Nijmeh asked him if he had heard from Mohammad. He didn't want to lie, so he told her that they had received a letter from him.

"Did he mention about getting married, *Yum'ma?*" Nijmeh asked.

"He said he was still thinking about it?" Mansur had replied.

"Did he say *why* he was still thinking about it, *Yum'ma?*"

Mansur hesitated and then decided to tell her what was in the letter. "It seems he has formed an attachment with an American girl he met at college. He *knows* all the arguments of why such an attachment would not work, but he *thinks* he loves the girl and that he wants to marry her." Mansur waited for his mother's response.

"What did you tell him, *Yum'ma?*"

"Zaleena and I wrote, after talking with Khalil, that he should meet the girl you have picked for him when he returns this summer. But I don't know if he will be convinced or not. He is young; he is far from home; he is in love."

"We should never have allowed him to go to the States unmarried. I should have insisted. It is hard, once the eyes have seen, to convince the heart." Nijmeh said.

Mansur had to smile. "You are thinking of you and *Yaba* aren't you?"

"Yes, your father saw me and once he had seen, his heart could not be convinced how inappropriate I was. And you remember how *forceful* your Sitteh Hasna was; still he defied her." Nijmeh had to laugh. "Mohammad is a lot like his father, *as are you Mansur,* I don't think he will listen to any advice that we give. *You* didn't listen to the advice we gave you, did you!?"

"Perhaps this is Mohammad's *naseeb* (destiny), *Yum'ma.* Perhaps it is written that he marry this American-Christian."

"Perhaps, but we must *still* caution against it, even though he may not listen. *Inshallah* he will realize how difficult this match would be. To be happy, he needs to marry a Palestinian Moslem."

When Nijmeh hung up the phone she thought about what Mansur had said – she thought about *naseeb* (destiny); she firmly believed that *what was meant to happen happened.* She believed that there was always a reason – a *plan* behind the events that occurred. Her faith taught her that one didn't always understand the *reasons,* but that Allah's plans were always right. She knew that she and Omar and Mohammad's siblings would love Mohammad no matter what decision he made. Still, it was their *duty* to make him aware of the obstacles, and Allah, so she believed, would lead him to make the *right* decision. *Perhaps Allah had planted the seed of love for this American-Christian in Mohammad's heart; perhaps it was meant to be.* She *hoped* it wasn't. She did not want to lose him. But if Mohammad's *naseeb* was to marry a foreign Christian, then she would accept that as Allah's will and welcome into her heart a Christian daughter-in-law.

Chapter 13

Beatings, rubber bullets, tear gas and live ammunition punctuated the pages of their lives. Hardly a day went by without demonstrations, rock throwing, burning tires, and reprisals. It didn't seem to be *what* people did, as much as it was *that* they did! The *acts of defiance* were seen as cause enough to beat, to toss canisters of tear gas, to fire rubber bullets and live ammunition.

Nijmeh, Im Najib, and Im Suleiman had been swishing water over the stone step that lead into their courtyards when four boys, about ten years old, raced down the narrow alley. They were being chased by three soldiers. They paused in their sweeping to watch the *game.*

Three of the boys disappeared around the twist in the alley and escaped. Only one child was left. The soldiers grabbed him and started beating him with their truncheons. The child kept trying to mumble something, and was shielding his head with his arms. Nijmeh and the two other women ran into the street and started to argue with the soldiers, trying to shield the boy with their bodies. The soldiers pushed them aside and continued to beat the boy.

Down the alley raced a woman. She was screaming, "Let my boy go! Let him go!" She flung herself at the soldiers, and using her own body, covered that of the frantic child. The soldiers continued to beat, their blows landing on *her.*

Im Najib, shouted at Nijmeh, "That is Fatima; that must be her son, Yaseen!"

Im Najib, Im Suleiman and Nijmeh pleaded with the soldiers. "The boy is *deaf!* The boy can't *speak!* He is *retarded! Stop! Minshan Allah* (for God's sake)*! Stop!"*

It finally seemed to sink into the soldiers what the women were saying. They stopped pummeling the woman and her son.

"He shouldn't throw stones," was all they said as they turned and walked back down the alley.

Nijmeh and Im Najib turned Fatima over. She was bruised and bloodied. "Yaseen, how is Yaseen?" Im Suleiman knelt in the street and turned Yaseen over. He was unconscious. She ran into her house and brought out a basin, some water and a clean rag. The four women hovered over the child; cleaning his wounds, gently chaffing his face.

Gradually he opened his eyes and looked from one face to another. When his eyes finally looked into his mother's he made some guttural sounds and kept patting her face. "*Ma'lash* (its okay)*, habeebee, ma'lash."* Fatima said as she caressed his face and kissed his hand. He couldn't hear the words, but he saw her lips move and felt the touch of her hand.

Fatima looked at her neighbors. "Yaseen doesn't throw stones. He only watches the other boys. He couldn't *hear* when the soldiers told him to stop. I *should* have kept him at home. Why would they beat a child who is deaf, dumb and retarded? Just to look at him, they would have seen that he is *slow."*

Sarah and Mohammad had fallen asleep on the couch/bed in his room. Sarah was the first to stir. She raised her head from where it had been resting on Mohammad's chest and gently shook him awake. "I have to be getting back. It is almost midnight and we have an 8 o'clock class tomorrow."

Mohammad stretched and kissed her lightly on the lips. "I wish I could always wake up like this. It feels so *right.*" Mohammad smiled.

Sarah smoothed an imaginary wrinkle on Mohammad's shirt. "We need to get going. Come on, *my Arab prince,*" she joked, "walk me back."

They walked back, hand-in-hand, not saying anything, content to be together. They didn't talk about the future, or the obstacles, or about Sarah converting. It was a welcome relief to both of them. It seemed that all they had talked about all week was *the problem of his parents, his brothers, and what they wanted.* Sarah wondered where the relationship with Mohammad was ultimately going, but pushed the question into the attic of her mind.

Nijmeh was relating the story of Fatima and her son to Omar and Issa. Omar, sipping the small, hot cup of coffee, observed: "It must be very frustrating for the military to realize that we, Palestinians, are no longer afraid of them. They can beat us, arrest us, and even kill us and we are not deterred. Even our women are not afraid to confront them. Look how you, and Im Najib and Im Suleiman challenged the soldiers today."

He said, turning to Nijmeh, "we no longer cower in our homes. Everywhere they look they see defiance; Palestinian flags flying from electric wires; political slogans spray-painted on shop doors and walls; burning tires in the streets; roads blocked with stones; demonstrations, closures. "

"It is as though the *barrier of fear* erected by the occupiers between them and us no longer exists," added Issa. "They want that barrier back, and are having a hard time rebuilding it. It is hard to control us since we are no longer afraid."

"I think it has probably surprised them that we are rebelling. In 1948 we were like sheep running from the wolf; it took almost forty years, but we are no longer sheep; the yapping of the dogs, and the snarls of the wolf no longer scatter us. We are the *samedeen* – the steadfast."

The political cartoon in Sunday's paper showed a broken wall. The wall was called in Arabic: *the barrier of fear.* On one side were soldiers, fully armed, hastily adding brick upon brick. Behind them flew the Israeli flag. On the other side, children and women in traditional dress were removing the bricks. The soldiers were frowning and making hostile gestures with their guns. The women were smiling calmly and saying: *We are no longer afraid.* A young boy stood in the background waving a Palestinian flag in one hand, a raised stone in the other. The cartoon was signed: *Ibn Omar.*

Mona and Manal were coming to Purdue! They had called on Saturday to inform Mohammad that they had persuaded their husbands to send them for a weekend – only a weekend – to see Mohammad before he went back to the West Bank for the summer. Their mother-in-law had graciously offered to watch the six children – only for a weekend – so the girls could come and see him. They gave Mohammad their flight number, when they would be arriving at the Indianapolis Airport and asked him to meet them.

Mohammad was delighted, but also wondered if Khalil had *instigated* the surprise trip as a way of putting further pressure on him. Unlike the summer before when Teri Bachman had surprised him at the airport, he *wanted* his sisters to meet Sarah, and for Sarah to meet them.

When they met for dinner at the *Chinese Dragon* Mohammad told Sarah, "I have wonderful news; my sisters, Manal and Mona, are coming next weekend for a visit. The timing couldn't be better. They will get a chance to meet you, and you will get to meet them. They are great girls – women, I should say. You will like them, and they will *love* you."

"It sounds like someone has been whispering in their ears – *you better go and see Mohammad; he's become involved with an American!*" Sarah laughed. "You are right about the *timing;* it sounds like your family is calling in the reserves."

Mohammad smiled, "I thought of that too, but I *want* you to meet some of my family. And starting out with Manal and Mona is perfect. We can rent a car, drive up to the airport, pick them up and bring them back here. I'll rent a hotel room for them for the weekend. We can keep the car, take them for drives, take them out to eat, and then take them back to the airport on Sunday. The *four* of us can spend the weekend together."

"They'll want to spend time with you alone. They won't want me tagging along." Sarah said.

"I'll arrange to have time – just the three of us – we can have breakfasts together. I *want* them to know how important you are to me."

"You are more optimistic than I am. Weren't *their* marriages arranged? They are probably not going to be too excited to meet me. Your brothers have probably already *warned* them about me. I am, frankly, a little worried."

Mohammad took her hand, and raising it to his lips, kissed it. "They are going to see how much I love you. And that will be all that is important to them. Plus, *how can they NOT fall in love with you!*"

Sarah tried to smile. "I wonder if *K-mart* carries face veils and head shawls?"

Mohammad laughed. "They are going to love you just the way you are. Though, I *do* suppose you might stand about *ten paces* behind me when we meet them at the airport," he joked with a twinkle in his eyes.

Chapter 14

Summer continued to flirt with spring, and if one *didn't* know it was late April, one would assume it was June. Mohammad and Sarah had taken a blanket, a few containers of Chinese takeout, and gone to lie under the clouds, watch the ducks send out ripples as they glided through the pond, and talk.

Sarah tried to show her skill with chopsticks as she ate Mandarin duck. "Okay, I skimmed through the book you gave me on Islam, and *philosophically* there is nothing I really disagree with. It's *not* Methodism, but it sounds to be morally and ethically very similar. When I read through the social customs involving marriage, it sounded a bit like the Amish – marrying your cousins and all. I didn't see anything about *arranged* marriages."

Mohammad, not as adept with chopsticks as Sarah, was maneuvering the vegetable rice into his mouth with a plastic spoon. "The sexes, except for immediate family members, are kept apart. Boys go to boys' schools; girls go to girls' schools; I suppose it is a way of preventing too much temptation. It is felt that parents best know their own children, and therefore best know who would be a *suitable spouse*. It is primarily a way of protecting girls from the advances of horny males," Mohammad laughed. (He had never used the work *horny* before and thought himself, at least momentarily, quite worldly – quite Western.)

"That's probably the first time you ever used the word *horny*, isn't it?" Sarah joked, poking him with the end of her chopstick. "What's the word in Arabic?"

"I don't think I have ever heard the Arabic word for *horny?*" Mohammad sheepishly smiled.

"So, your parents' marriage was arranged; your grandparents' marriage was arranged; and your brother, Mansur's and sisters' marriages were arranged?"

"In a manner of speaking, my father was only seventeen when he married my fifteen-year old mother. It had been arranged that he marry his cousin, Miriam."

"Like the Amish," Sarah interjected.

"Except unlike the Amish, they had never really *spoken* to each other. They had *seen* each other at family gatherings, but other than seeing each other they didn't have any contact.

"My mother had almost been promised to a widower – who must have been about fifty – who had been a friend of her father's."

"*Fifty*! And she was only fifteen!" I can't believe it."

"My maternal grandfather had died, my mother was the oldest of seven sisters, and they were a burden to their uncles. Though undesirable, it was thought to be prudent." Mohammad paused to maneuver more of the rice into his mouth.

"Then my father saw my mother at the well where she and her sisters had gone to get water. It was love at first sight for him. They had never even spoken!"

"How did your mother feel?" Sarah asked.

"She didn't feel anything; she had never seen him before. She used to joke with us that all she had seen of my father was the wisp of black hair on his big toe. She had never really looked at his face until he lifted her veil with a sword on their wedding night."

"Lifted her veil with a *sword?*"

"It was an old custom that is no longer practiced. It was to show a groom's dominance over his bride. My mother would say that my father put the sword on the floor, told her that *he* thought it was an absurd custom, and comforted her when she wept. She was *so frightened,* and he was *so gentle and understanding* – so my mother said." Mohammed paused, "I think she loved him from that very moment." Mohammad watched the clouds forming shapes in the sky. "Their love story is like a story out of *A Thousand and One Nights.* It produced *ten* children. And, if anything, they love each other more now than they did then."

"So, their marriage really *wasn't arranged* – your father *chose* your mother. What about your brother, Mansur, he is married to a Russian, isn't he? A woman he chose."

"That is why I wrote to Mansur and Zaleena; his wife. I thought if anyone would understand, they would. They were sympathetic, but the big difference is that Zaleena, though she is Russian, is a Moslem and she speaks Arabic."

"The issue really is that I am *not* Moslem, not so much that I am American?"

"That is why I even made the suggestion that you convert." Mohammad pointed to a line of clouds, "That almost looks like a line of camels slowly loping through the desert, doesn't it?"

Sarah had finished the small container of Mandarin duck. She wiped her lips on a paper napkin and laid her head on Mohammad's chest. "Tell me more about your family."

"My Sitteh Hasna was an extraordinary woman. She was short and round and had red hair, blue eyes, and freckles."

"She doesn't sound very Arab." Sarah murmured against his shirt.

"I think she must have been a throwback to some Scottish Crusader." Mohammad smiled into Sarah's hair. "She was a domineering woman and had a temper that went with her red hair. But she was kind and thoughtful and *wise*. I think she would have approved of you, even though she told my brother, Khalil, that she *would die before she saw an American Christian bride cross the threshold.*"

"Again, we are back to the issue of being non-Moslem." Sarah whispered.

Mohammad put his arm around her and squeezed. "Times are changing; my parents know that, my brothers know that, it is probably why they are being so persistent that I marry a Palestinian *Moslem* this summer. They know I am not a child, that I am a man with a mind of my own, that I can't be completely manipulated as they would like. "

"Do you know American girls who have converted? *I am not saying that I will,* I am just *gathering information.*" Sarah said as she raised her head and looked into Mohammad's dark eyes.

"I know a few. Some Palestinian students have brought back American wives. Some of the wives seem to adapt quite well. They learn Arabic; they seem to become absorbed into their adopted families; many convert to Islam and become quite devout." Mohammad pointed, "Look, the camel clouds seemed to have reached a tent."

"Do all the cross-cultural marriages work out?" Sarah asked.

"No, sometimes the American wife finds it too difficult to adjust and eventually the couple divorces; the American wife returns to the States and the man marries a Moslem girl." Mohammad hesitated, "I think that is also a reason why my parents are pushing that I marry a Palestinian Moslem; they don't want me to be hurt, and they don't want the American wife to be hurt."

Sarah also paused, searching for the right words with which to express her thoughts. "I don't think your parents, and brothers, are being dogmatic or irrationally conservative. I think they really care about you, perhaps even care about *me.*"

Mohammad kissed the top of her head and hugged her more closely. "Of course they care about *you!* They know that I could only love someone who was special. They *know* that because I love you, you are someone quite unique." Mohammad swallowed. "Like you always say, they too wonder if *love is enough.* And for them, the idea of an arranged marriage is quite workable. They really believe that people *fall in love* after marriage and the more a couple has in common, the stronger the marriage will be. They worry that we don't have enough in common."

The warmth of the sunny afternoon, the serenity of the ducks gliding through the water; secure in Mohammad's arms, Sarah fell asleep. Mohammad held her close to his heart. He watched the camel train of clouds change and merged and become a mountain. The cloud formation looked like a volcano ready to erupt.

Mohammad had booked his sisters into a *Holiday Inn* near his apartment. He had rented a car and he and Sarah had driven the sixty-five miles from Purdue to the Indianapolis Airport. They arrived in plenty of time to have coffee while they waited.

Mohammad checked the arrivals monitor, and his sisters' plane was scheduled to arrive on time. He and Sarah were waiting at the gate when Manal and Mona arrived. "Do you want me standing, appropriately in back of you?" Sarah joked.

"I want you right here beside me," Mohammad said putting an arm around her shoulders.

It wasn't difficult for Sarah to pick out his sisters. There was a marked family resemblance. The sisters were beautiful and fashionable. Sarah wondered if *all Palestinians were exceptionally good looking.* They seemed to bubble with genuine affection as they hugged Mohammad, both talking at once.

Mohammad pulled Sarah close to him and said, "I want you to meet Sarah. Sarah, I want you to meet my sisters, Manal and Mona." The two girls smiled and shook Sarah's hand. Then Manal leaned in and kissed Sarah on both cheeks, as did Mona.

"We are so happy to meet a friend of Mohammad's."

Mohammad looked at his two sisters and said, "Sarah is *more* than just a friend." Manal and Mona looked at him questioningly, but tactfully said nothing.

On the drive back from Indianapolis, Manal and Mona chattered nonstop. They would occasionally lapse into Arabic and Mohammad would translate for Sarah. Sarah thought to herself: *I really must learn Arabic.*

Mohammad saw his sisters situated in the *Holiday Inn* and told them he and Sarah would be back around six to take them to dinner.

Once they were in their room, Manal said to Mona: "Khalil was right. Mohammad *is* in love. It is written all over his face."

"He just as much *said so*," Mona replied, "when he said that Sarah was *more* than a friend. Khalil was right to suggest they we fly out and assess the situation and *talk* to Mohammad."

"We have to make sure that we have some time alone with him," Manal added. "There are things we need to say to him not in front of Sarah. She seems like such a nice girl, and we don't want her to misunderstand us."

Mohammad and Sarah took his sisters to the *Chinese Dragon* for dinner. The conversation was punctuated with anecdotes about their children, about their husbands, about their mother-in-law. The girls laughed easily. With Mohammad they reminisced about Sitteh Hasna and her *when-I-was-girl-and-not-very-pretty* stories. Sarah loved listening to the stories. She could *almost* picture Sitteh Hasna and Mohammad's family. He obviously came from a very loving family. Sarah told a few stories of her own, about growing up on a dairy farm. Mona laughed and said, "Why, you are a peasant – an *American peasant* – just like us!"

It seemed they talked for hours, but they really didn't. "I probably should take you back to your hotel. I thought we would meet for breakfast, just the three of us, tomorrow morning. Then, Sarah and I have planned a scenic drive for you, then lunch at a posh restaurant, and a *surprise!*" Mohammad said.

He and Sarah drove them back to their hotel and walked them into the lobby. Manal and Mona kissed Mohammad *and* Sarah on both cheeks and thanked them for a lovely evening. "We'll see you about eight tomorrow morning, Mohammad, for breakfast."

"Why don't we say 7:30, so we have plenty of time to talk." Mohammad asked.

"Seven thirty is fine. We'll meet you here in the lobby."

Mohammad drove Sarah back to her dorm. They sat in the car. Mohammad switched the engine off. "I really like your sisters," Sarah said. "It is so obvious how much they love you," she added.

"I can tell that they like you too." Mohammad said as he drew her close and kissed her. Her lips parted beneath his.

"I am glad you are going to meet with them for breakfast. You need to have some time alone together."

"I'll pick you up around noon." Mohammad said as he walked her to her dorm. He kissed her again in the lobby and whispered into her ear. "It's going to be all right, you'll see."

The next morning, promptly at 7:30, Mohammad was in the lobby waiting for his sisters. The girls were only ten minutes late. "I thought we would have breakfast here in the hotel dining room," Mohammad said as he ushered them into the spacious room.

Once they had ordered, the questioning began. "Tell us more about Sarah. It is apparent that you care quite a bit for her and that she cares for you."

"Yes, I do care a lot about Sarah. I *love* her and she loves me."

"What do *Yum'ma* and *Yaba* think about it?"

"You *know* what they think. I suspect that is partially why you are here. Khalil and Mansur must have been talking to you."

Manal smiled. "Yes, it *is* part of the reason we are here, but we also wanted an *excuse to* get away for a weekend. We haven't been away from our husbands or our children since we got married. Mona and I felt we were *due* for a weekend away. So when Khalil suggested it, we jumped at the chance."

"So it was Khalil's suggestion?"

"It was really Amr's suggestion heartily endorsed by Khalil and Mansur; they wanted us to see Sarah first hand and to talk with you face-to-face. There is only so much that can be written in a letter or said over the phone."

"Are you going try and talk me out of marrying Sarah?"

"Khalil did mention that you were talking marriage. And after meeting Sarah, we can understand why. She seems like such a nice girl. She is beautiful and obviously smart, and there is no doubt that she cares for you."

"But," Manal interjected, "she is not Moslem. That is the biggest problem. We all want you to be happy – and after meeting Sarah, Mona and I would want Sarah to be happy. You know what the pitfalls are; we don't need to go over them with you. Marriage is difficult at times, any marriage, and if there is the added stress of different religions and different cultures, sometimes the marriage can't bear the strain and breaks. We wouldn't want that for you or for Sarah."

The waitress came and asked if she could warm their coffee. They nodded. "What if Sarah became Moslem?" Mohammad asked.

"Would you force her to become Moslem just to marry you?"

"No one forces Sarah to do anything," Mohammad smiled. "She is strong-willed, independent, and very much her own person. If she *did* covert it would be because she was convinced. I don't think she would do it *just* to marry me. Sarah has principles and wouldn't fake anything."

"The more I hear about Sarah, the better I like her," Mona smiled. We can easily see why you think you love her."

"I don't *think* I love her, I *do* love her."

"If it is alright with you, Mona and I would like to have breakfast tomorrow *alone* with Sarah; just some *girl time.*"

"You are going to try and convince her to leave me alone, aren't you?"

"I don't think that we are strong enough to do that. She, thankfully, seems to have a mind of her own. It is only fair to you, *and to her,* to tell her what marriage to you might mean. You want her to be informed enough to make an intelligent decision, don't you?"

"I never realized how much you are like *Yum'ma.*" Mohammad said.

Manal and Mona both smiled. "That is really quite a compliment."

Chapter 15

The *special surprise* was the *Tippecanoe Mall* – 110 stores – a shopper's paradise. "I thought you would enjoy seeing this amazing shopping center. It is not quite *Sears*," Mohammad joked, "but it is darn near as nice!"

Manal and Mona were like two little girls being allowed free reign in a toy store. If there was one thing they liked to do, they *liked to shop.* They seemed to have endless energy and wanted to buy *a little something* for their children, their husbands, their mother-in-law, and for themselves. Sarah *also* liked to shop on occasion, so it had been easy for her to get into the spirit of the afternoon.

The four of them had a wonderful day. Mohammad had known exactly what they would have liked to do. He had known it wouldn't be visiting museums, or historical sites, or attending a band concert, or going to the theatre, it would be *shopping.*

They had an early dinner in the mall's food court, having to choose among a multitude of fast food places: Chinese, Mexican, Tai, *Long John Silver's* and the ever popular *McDonald's.* There was even a Lebanese pavilion, and they all decided on Lebanese food. Manal kept remarking to Sarah, "Lebanese food is so much like Palestinian food. Delicious, isn't it!" Sarah would nod her head and smile. She had to admit that it really *was delicious.*

The Mall stayed open until ten, and the girls and Mohammad were among the last to leave. "You had a perfect idea, Hamoudeh. You knew exactly what we would like." Manal said.

"In one of these bags, there are some things that we got for you to take back to *Yum'ma, Yaba,* Issa, Hasna, Imad and their children. I *think* we remembered everyone."

When he drove them back to the *Holiday Inn,* they kissed Mohammad and Sarah on both cheeks. Manal reminded Sarah that they had a date for breakfast the following morning.

"Is eight o'clock good for you?" Mona asked.

"Eight is fine, but are you sure you don't want Mohammad to come along as well?"

Manal gave Sarah a hug, "This is just to be a *girls'* breakfast. Mona and I want to get to know you a bit better."

They said good-night.

Mohammad drove Sarah back to his apartment. "I'll take you home later. We don't have class tomorrow. I want you to come up for a while."

"I'd like that," Sarah smiled.

Sarah put on water for decaffeinated tea. "It's probably a bit too late for coffee." She made two cups of mint tea and placed them on the coffee table that she and Mohammad had found on the curb. She removed her shoes, and drew her legs up under her as she cuddled close to Mohammad.

"I really like your sisters. They are so easy to talk to. They are fun to be around – and what *energy they have when it comes to shopping!"*

"I think it is probably because they almost *never* shopped when they were girls. We were ten and quite poor. There was military occupation, curfews and such. I think they are probably making up for all those years of deprivation – at least when it came to *shopping*. If you asked them, they would probably say they had a pretty good childhood, in spite of all ten of us, plus my parents and grandmother sleeping on the floor in one room." Mohammad laughed. "Oh, Mansur, when he was nineteen, *did* briefly sleep on the daybed. My parents used to joke about how Mansur had an argument with my Sitteh Hasna, trying to convince her that *she* should sleep on the daybed and her replying that *someone of his elevated intelligence – he could read – should sleep on it."*

Sarah kissed his shoulder. "I think you had a pretty good childhood, too. Did you sleep on the floor, even as a baby?"

"No, very briefly I slept in a crude metal cradle. Palestinian babies, at least in the camps, are swaddled – probably like the Prophet Jesus in Biblical times – where all they can move is their head. We don't have central heating, so my Sitteh took me to sleep with her when the cold weather started. I slept with her until I was two. When my ten-year-old brother, Ahmad, was killed, Khalil took it the hardest. Ahmad had shared a pallet with him most of those ten years. Khalil was inconsolable the night that Ahmad was buried, so my Sitteh literally *gave* me to Khalil. She put me in Khalil's arms – Khalil was sixteen at the time, and told him that I was now his to take care of. And from that time, Khalil has been almost like my father." There were tears in Mohammad's eyes.

Sarah wiped away the tears with her finger and kissed him on the cheek. She smiled and said, "I think I am falling in love with your family."

They drank their tea and cuddled. "I am a little scared about having breakfast alone with your sisters."

"Don't be. They will point out to you the downside of marrying me – only because they *like* you. I *know* that sounds funny, but when I questioned them about why they wanted to talk to you alone, Manal told me that they just want to make sure you know what being married to me would mean." Mohammad squeezed Sarah, "They know that I am terribly handsome, smart, and a great catch."

He laughed as Sarah poked him and said, "Oh *please*," and rolled her eyes.

"But they want you to be well aware of the pitfalls before you make a final decision," Mohammad said seriously. "They thought it was wrong of me to even *suggest* to you that you consider converting to Islam *just to marry me.*"

Mohammad looked at the alarm clock on the nightstand. "It's almost one o'clock, and you need to be ready for breakfast by eight. I need to get you home." Sarah's legs were cramped. She stretched and put on her shoes. Mohammad helped her up and held her close as he kissed her. "It is all going to be alright. You just wait and see."

Mohammad dropped Sarah off a little before eight. "I'll be back around 9:30 to pick you all up. There is a bit more sightseeing I'd like to do, then a late lunch, before we need to drive the girls back to Indianapolis to catch their evening flight to LA."

After they had ordered, and the waitress had poured their coffee, Manal started: "Mona and I wanted to have a chance to talk to you without Mohammad. That he loves you is obvious to us. And we think that you love him."

Sarah nodded. "I do love him."

Manal hesitated, "Sometimes love is not enough. Any marriage has its rough spots – I think the only exception I can think of is perhaps our parents' marriage. Sometimes it seems to us that it is a love story out of a fairy tale."

"Our own marriages work," Mona added, "because we and our husbands all had the same expectations. We *expected* that we wouldn't really know each other before being married. We *expected* that love would come later, and thankfully it did. That was the way they were raised, though I expect being raised in the States they probably did do some dating that their mother wasn't aware of," Mona laughed, "and that was the way we were raised. For us it was fine, but for you – that was *not* the way you were brought up. It must all seem very strange to you – the very concept of an *arranged marriage."*

"It *is strange to me.* I didn't realize that those things still happened." Sarah paused, "Do you know anything about the girl that your mother has chosen for Mohammad?"

"Oh, he told you about that? That must have been very difficult to hear." Manal answered. "No, we know nothing about her. My parents have not spoken directly to her family or to her for that matter. And they will not do so until they hear from Mohammad. We *do know* that Im'me (my mother) would only choose a girl whom she thought would make Mohammad happy."

She looked at the tears pooling in Sarah's eyes. Mona took her hand, "*Im'me* hasn't seen you yet. She hasn't seen you and Mohammad together."

"Mohammad probably told you that our parents were a love-match, at least on the part of our father. He saw her and would have no other but her." Manal smiled. "The same is true of

Mansur and Zaleena, though initially our parents were not happy about their decision to marry.

"If you and Mohammad *do* decide to get married, someone will have to give up part of who he or she is. It is hard to live with a foot in two different worlds. It *can* be done, but it won't be easy. Mona and I just want to be sure that you are *aware* that it won't be easy; that it will be a struggle." Manal said. "The way we were raised, it seems that it is always the *women* who have to adjust, to give-up, to make things work. We think that if you and Mohammad *do* decide to get married that *you* may be the one who will have to give up the most. It will probably mean leaving your family; moving thousands of miles away; living in a country where traditions and customs are so different from what you are used to.

"It will take a strong woman to give up, what she will need to give up, in order to marry Mohammad." Manal paused. "Mohammad is charming and handsome and kind and sincere. He is thoughtful, but he *is* an Arab male. Beneath all that he is, there is that *Arab male mentality*. He thinks that ultimately he is right and should be obeyed."

Sarah smiled in spite of herself, "I *have seen* a little of that."

"Mona and I have been raised to *listen* to our father, our brothers, our husbands. We have also learned from our mother how to lovingly *handle* the men in our lives. We just want you to be as aware as you can be about the possible life you will live with Mohammad and the sacrifices you may have to make. Mohammad told us that he even *suggested* to you that you convert to Islam! I can't believe he suggested that. For us, Islam is the answer, but it is naturally the answer for us because we know nothing else. You certainly must not convert unless you are convinced that it is the right thing for you –

certainly not convert *just* to marry Mohammad." Manal was quite adamant. "Mohammad *did* say that you would never adopt something unless you were convinced. I'm glad that that is so."

The waitress brought the check and put it face down on the table. Sarah reached for it, but Manal was too quick. "This is our treat."

Mohammad came into the dining room. "I am so glad we had this talk," Sarah said. "You have given me a lot to think about."

Manal took a slip of paper out of her purse. "I have written down our phone numbers. Call us anytime, just to talk. If you have any questions, Mona and I would be happy to try and answer them."

Impulsively, Sarah hugged them both. "I am so glad that I have met you both."

"Should my ears be burning?" Mohammad asked.

"What does that mean?" Manal questioned.

"It is a new phrase I picked up, it means, should I be concerned that you have been talking about me?"

"Of course we have been talking about you! I was telling Sarah what she needed to do to handle an Arab male! Who knows better how to handle an Arab man than an Arab woman?" she laughed. "*Especially* when the Arab man is a younger brother, and the Arab women are his *older* sisters."

The four of them had a delightful time the rest of the day. Mohammad was so happy that his sisters had had a chance to meet Sarah and that she had had a chance to meet them. The drive to Indianapolis was enjoyable. They chatted, in both English and Arabic; they laughed. Mona and Manal taught Sarah a few Arabic phrases.

Their plane was on time. "We had a wonderful time, Mohammad. It was such a good break for us – not nearly long enough, but certainly water to our thirsty spirits. Thank you." Manal and Mona kissed him on both cheeks and hugged him.

"It was wonderful meeting you, Sarah. We can so easily see why Mohammad loves you." They also kissed her on both cheeks, and as she hugged them, Manal whispered to her, "Remember what we talked about. And *do* call us. Promise?"

"I promise."

Mohammad and Sarah held hands as they watched Mona and Manal pass through the boarding gate. After they disappeared, Mohammad put his arm around Sarah's shoulder. "I am so glad that you got to meet my sisters."

"I am glad I got to meet them too. If anything, meeting them made me feel closer to you!"

As they were passing Gate 36, a woman came up to Mohammad. "Well, well, well, if it isn't Mohammad Omar Mansur. Imagine running into you." It was Teri Bachman.

Chapter 16

Mohammad removed his arm from around Sarah's shoulders, and slipped his hand into hers. Teri noticed the subtle change. "So, fancy meeting you here. What brings you to Indianapolis?" Teri asked. The question was directed at Mohammad, but Teri's eyes raked Sarah from head to toe.

"We were just seeing my sisters off." Mohammad answered.

"Aren't you going to introduce me to your friend?" Teri asked.

"Sarah, this is Teri Bachman. She is a journalist who did an article about the camp last year. Teri, this is my friend, Sarah, we are in the same program at Purdue."

Teri looked down at their clasped hands, the fingers intertwined. She smiled, not a very nice smile. "It seems that you are *more* than friends. I didn't catch your *last* name?"

Sarah replied, "My family name is Goldman."

"*Goldman!* My, my, *you* have grown up, Mohammad, haven't you! Not only did you find an American, but a *Jewish-American* princess. How *happy* your family must be! Bravo! Well done."

"Let's go, Sarah." Mohammad softly said as he guided her around Teri Bachman.

As he passed Teri, she said to him in a stage-whisper, "So are you bopping her, you *prick?*"

Sarah tightened her grasp on Mohammad's hand. "She certainly hates you, doesn't she?" Sarah's next phrase could barely be heard; it was as though she was thinking aloud. "She must have really been in love with you."

Mohammad looked down at Sarah's upturned face. "She is a crude, pushy, opinionated woman. We had coffee, *once,* alone. We wrote a couple of letters. Remember, I told you about her. I was probably a bit flattered – it was my first encounter with a girl who wasn't my sister, mother, or grandmother. She thought there was more to the relationship than there was." Mohammad paused. "I think she *thought* herself in love with me. When she saw that I wasn't in love with her, she felt rejected." Mohammad smiled down at Sarah and chuckled, "I think it was the first time that someone ever gave me *the finger* and called me a *prick.* Mona's thirteen-year old son had to explain to me what a *prick* was and what was meant when someone *gave you the finger."*

Sarah kissed Mohammad's shoulder and whispered, "You *certainly* aren't a prick. And, no matter *what* you did, I would *never* give you *the finger."* Sarah chuckled, "We, Jewish-American princesses, raised Methodists on farms in Iowa have class. You know, it is the very first time I have ever been referred to as *Jewish* and as a *princess;* my parents would find it quite amusing."

Manal and Mona were barely back in California when Manal received a phone call from Khalil.

"Well, what did you find out? Did you meet the girl? Did you talk with Mohammad?"

"Yes, of course. We met Sarah, and we talked to Mohammad," Manal responded. "We found the girl delightful. She is smart; she is beautiful; she obviously loves Mohammad. There is no question that Mohammad loves her. Seeing them together, frankly, reminded us of *Yum'ma* and *Yaba.* We are convinced Mohammad is aware of all the obstacles. Neither Mona nor I felt that he was being ruled entirely by his heart.

"It sounds like you liked the girl." Khalil said.

"We *did* like her. Both Mona and I were glad that we met her. We had imagined her to be completely different. She is wholesome, down-to-earth, engaging. We think that she compliments Mohammad well. She comes from a farming background – just like us, only an *American-peasant.* I think if you met her, Khalil, you would see how truly *right* she seems. We think even Sitteh Hasna, *Allah yer'hum'ha* (God have mercy on her), would approve."

Khalil had his doubts. He understood love and attraction, but he also understood Arab society. If Mohammad married a *foreigner – an American-Christian,* he would be out-of-step with those around him. He realized that there were bi-cultural marriages, especially among the elite – among professionals, that worked. A number of Arab doctors and lawyers had studied abroad and had formed liaisons with women they had met at university. In the circles in which they moved everyone was bilingual, or trilingual; often in these circles the individuals were rather casual about their religion; their children attended private schools and often Arabic was not the language they spoke at home. He could understand how in these situations having a foreign spouse would not matter as much.

This was *not,* however, Mohammad's background. He came from a camp; their parents were illiterate; religion was interwoven into the fabric of who they were; their parents didn't speak English; this girl didn't speak Arabic. He was honest enough with himself to believe that *perhaps* a marriage between them would work *if they remained in America,* but if they came back to the West Bank to live, he didn't see how it could possibly survive the numerous strains they would face. In that kind of setting, marriage *wasn't* just about the couple; marriage was about an extended family; marriage was about society.

Saji and Omar had not gone to work that April morning. Curfew had been called. Sami, Salah and Salam had managed to slip out over a back wall of the camp and had gone to their work in the settlement. Saleem, Imad and Abu Imad had also snuck out and gone to the carpentry shop. They had work to finish on a bedroom suite. They would keep the shutter of the shop closed, so if a patrol came by it would seem that no one was there. Sameer and Sammer had gone to hang out with their Uncle Issa at their grandparents' home. Curfews in the camps, especially in the early morning, were often not strictly enforced. There were always military jeeps at the entrance to the camps, but the soldiers were often reluctant to walk through the winding alleys.

Hasna, Im Imad, and Ayesha, Hasna's daughter-in-law, were making pickles. Saji was helping them. The nine-month-old Imad was sleeping in his metal cradle.

There was a commotion in the street. The women turned from their work as the metal door was kicked open and three soldiers burst into the courtyard. They were wild, waving their rifles, pointing at the women and demanding the *boy who had thrown stones.* They made a grab for Saji!

Hasna, Im Imad and Ayesha threw themselves against the soldiers, turning over the pot of boiling water, breaking the large jar in which they had placed the cucumbers. "He didn't throw stones. He has been here with us!" Hasna screamed at them. "He doesn't speak! He doesn't speak!" She screamed. Im Imad had grasped one of the rifles in her hands and was wrestling with the soldier. Her strength was no match for his. The baby started to wail.

The soldier wrest the rifle from Im Imad and pushed her aside. "We'll teach him to throw stones."

Two of the soldiers grabbed Saji's arms; the third got a strangling grip on his neck. Hasna and Ayesha had each grabbed a soldier by his elbow. The soldiers easily shook them off and pushed them to the floor, threatening them with their rifles. They forced Saji into the alcove kitchen and pushed him against the wall, his head hitting the pots and pans dangling on hooks. Stepping into the front of the doorway, not more than a meter or two away from him, they opened fire pounding his back with rubber bullets. They were panting and sweating and *grinning*.

As abruptly as they had come, they left. The rubber bullets peppered the tiles of the small kitchen. Saji was huddled on the floor. He was unconscious.

Hasna screamed at her daughter-in-law, "Run! Get my father!"

Ayesha peered out the door to see if there was anyone in the street, and then she ran. She was hysterical when she pounded on Omar and Nijmeh's door. "Soldiers have fired rubber bullets at Saji. You must come!"

Omar ran through the street, followed by Nijmeh. They had forced Ayesha to remain at the house with Issa, Sameer and Sammer. "We are old, if the soldiers catch us, what can they do? You stay here until it seems safe to come."

The metal door to Hasna's courtyard was ajar. She was sitting in the alcove kitchen, Saji's head in her lap. Im Imad was trying to console the wailing infant. Omar knelt down beside her and lifted Saji up in his arms. He carried him into the sitting room and placed him on the daybed. Saji had still not regained consciousness.

Nijmeh and Hasna turned him over onto his stomach and peeled off his shirt. His back was a mass of purple bruises. They counted seven, each about the size of the palm of a man's hand. "He needs to have a doctor." Nijmeh said.

Omar had knelt down beside the daybed and taken one of Saji's limp hands in his calloused fist. "I'm here, Sido. I'm here." Omar could barely get the words out his throat was so full of tears. "Why Saji? Why Saji? I promised I would protect him. I promised."

Cool cloths were applied to his back. They gently applied cooling liniment to the bruised flesh. Saji still had not regained consciousness.

When the alley was clear, Ayesha and the boys had rushed to the house. The curfew was surprisingly lifted in the afternoon, and the house was once again filled with family and neighbors. A doctor was brought; Saji was examined; the doctor thought that there had been no internal damage, but he was concerned about the psychological damage. Saji had been beaten twice and now this. He was concerned that he hadn't regained consciousness, but had examined his pupils, and resignedly said that perhaps sleep was the best treatment at the moment.

Saji seemed to be in a sleep from which he would not awaken. It had been decided to not move him but leave him on the daybed. Omar had insisted that they spread a pallet on the floor for him. "I want to be here when he wakes up, *Yaba*. I want him to know that I haven't left him." There were tears in his eyes.

Hasna pressed his shoulder, "I know, *Yaba*. I know. He would want you to be here," she sobbed.

The house finally settled for the night, though no one slept. Nijmeh had gone home with Issa, telling Hasna that she would be back first thing in the morning. Hasna laid her head against Imad's chest and sobbed. "I don't know how much more Saji can take. I don't know how much more *I* can take seeing him brutalized."

Saji's five brothers lay on their pallets. "It should have been one of us, not Saji. It should have been one of us," they murmured. The only one who said nothing was Sami. He rolled over on his pallet so his brothers could not see his face. There were silent tears falling off his chin. "They will pay. I will make them pay." It was to that mantra that he finally fell asleep.

At about three in the morning, there was movement on the daybed. Omar immediately woke up. A hand groped his face, fingered his bushy moustache. "Sido, Sido, are *you* here?"

Omar sprang up and put his arm around his grandson, kissing his cheek. "I'm here, Sido. I'm here. I am so sorry I didn't protect you, *habeebee*. I had promised, and I didn't protect you."

"It wasn't your fault, Sido." Saji paused as though he had just *discovered* something. "Sido, I think the soldiers *shot* the words right out of me. I can talk!"

The house was awakened by Omar's joyous shout. "*Subhan Allah, Subhan Allah,* Saji can talk! Saji can talk!"

Chapter 17

Sarah could see herself married to Mohammad. She could see Manal and Mona as her sisters-in-law. She, however, *couldn't* see herself living in the Middle East, *especially* in the volatile West Bank.

She and Mohammad were sitting on a blanket watching the ducks slowly glide through the water, sending gentle ripples ever expanding into the pond; the ripples breaking as they bumped into water lilies. The water was clear enough to see the ducks' webbed feet propelling them through the water.

Mohammad had received a long distance call from Mansur that morning telling him of the wonderful news that Saji *was talking*. He, of course, had related *how* it had come about. Mohammad was shocked that once again it had been Saji who had been brutalized. Out of all of Hasna's sons, Saji was the gentlest. He had *never* thrown a stone, yet he had been, along with Sameer and Sammer beaten by soldiers; he had been abducted and almost killed by settlers; and now had had rubber bullets fired into his back from close range – *while he was at home!* There was certainly truth in that American adage: *being in the wrong place at the wrong time.*

"Why didn't your nephew speak?" Sarah asked.

Mohammad moved the blade of grass he was chewing to the side of his mouth. "About a year ago, when Saji was on his way home from school with a friend, settlers from a settlement close to the camp were driving by and started taunting them. The boys ran, Saji stumbled, was caught and kidnapped by the settlers."

"Kidnapped?"

"The settlers, American-Jews it turned out, wanted to scare an Arab child. They took Saji into a valley and brutalized him: broke his arms and nose; stomped on his legs; apparently made him think they would rape him with a stick; his pants were torn in the back. He was only eleven. He was found; brought home; but had been so traumatized that he couldn't speak.

Once his arms healed, he had to be taught all over again how to use his hands; how to feed himself; to dress himself; even how to use the bathroom. It was as though he was an infant again learning everything for the first time. He had been so affected by the experience that he never spoke; it was as though he forgot how. He would refuse to leave the house; it was only through my father's persuasion that he reluctantly agreed to finally venture out but *only* with him. "

"Two days ago, Israeli soldiers burst into the house, accused Saji of throwing stones, and fired seven rubber bullets into his back at close range. When Saji regained consciousness, according to Mansur, he *was able to talk!* Saji told my father that *he thought the soldiers had* **scared** *the words out of him. Subhan Allah* (Praise God), it is a miracle. My sister, Hasna, despaired that after this last attack that Saji *would* **never** *speak.*"

Sarah was silent for a moment. "How could anyone do this to a child? It is unbelievable." She paused as she gazed out over the pond, seemingly watching the ducks. "It doesn't sound like a very *safe place* to be. I think I would be scared all the time."

Mohammad took the blade of grass he was chewing out of his mouth. He reached over and touched Sarah's cheek. He gently turned her face so she was looking at him. "I know it *sounds* scary, and at times it *is* scary. Bad things, unimaginable things, happen all over. We have to have faith that ultimately, no matter what happens, we will be alright."

"I suppose so," Sarah said, but the words didn't even sound convincing to *her*. For a moment, gazing at the ducks, Sarah envied them—how *safe* they seemed paddling quietly around the peaceful pond.

Saji's miraculous recovery of speech amazed everyone around him, *especially him!* Though his back was still badly bruised and painful, he seemed to be *smiling* all the time. He would tell whoever was listening: *I now know that whatever happens to me, I will be alright. Allah is watching out for me. You know, I am no longer afraid of the soldiers – what can they possibly do to me that hasn't already happened to me?* He would look at his brothers and add: *I'm glad it didn't happen to one of you. If it had to happen to anyone, I would rather it had been me.*"

Sami would look at his youngest brother, and there would be tears in his eyes. It had been Sami who had carried him home when the settlers had brutalized him; it had been Sami who had taken him to the bathroom when his arms were broken and wiped his butt; it was Sami who could never *forget* or *forgive* what had happened to Saji. Saji would bear the scars for the rest of his life, and so would Sami. There was a bitter resolve that had taken over his heart. He would have revenge, and it would be something that the Israelis would never forget.

As Mohammad lay awake that night, he dreamed and planned. He wanted to convince Sarah to go to the West Bank with him this summer. He wanted her to meet his parents, his family. He wanted them to meet *her*. They would stop off in Amman first; meet Khalil and Mansur, Zaleena and the children. She would see how cosmopolitan Amman was. She would be, rightly, impressed, he thought, with his brothers and Zaleena. They all speak English well, even the children. She wouldn't feel so strange, so *foreign*. He knew she was apprehensive about the Middle East – certainly apprehensive about the West Bank, but that *once* she had actually been there she would see what it was *really* like and it would eliminate some of her fear. Everyone who visited the West Bank fell in love with it. He *knew* that Sarah would too! For the moment, his heart and his head were in total agreement.

Sarah also lay awake that night. She couldn't get out of her mind what Mohammad had told her about his nephew, Saji. She had read articles about the West Bank, and it *sounded* as though there were valid reasons for being apprehensive – *scared even*. She turned over in her mind what Mohammad's sisters had told her: *how she would have to sacrifice more than he would; how she would be the one who would have to give up things that were important to her.* She *knew* her parents would object to her marrying Mohammad. She was a simple, Iowa farm girl, what did she really know about the Middle East? How could she even *contemplate* the possibility of living there? How could she possibly even conceive of raising children there?

Her heart told her that she loved Mohammad and that *anything was possible*. Her head told her: *run!*

Khalil had told Nijmeh what Manal and Mona had said about their visit to Mohammad. He even told her that Manal had said that: *Mohammad and Sarah remind us of Im'me ou Abou'ee.* "Did she really say that, *Yum'ma?*" Nijmeh asked. "It is interesting that she made that comparison. I trust their judgment, yet I worry that they won't be happy together."

"I, too, am worried. But Mohammad is not a child. He is a man who will make up his own mind. I only hope that the girl and her family come to their senses. I pray that her family has more influence over her than we seem to have over Mohammad."

"Everything will be as Allah has written it, *ibnee.*" Nijmeh said.

Mohammad had agreed to meet Sarah at *Starbucks* for their morning coffee. She was already seated at a window table when he got there. She saw him come in the door. *God,* she thought, *how incredibly handsome he is.* He waved and smiled. Coming over to her, he kissed her on both cheeks. She loved his aftershave – clean, fresh, masculine. He had shaved, but there was a distinct shadow to his cheeks that she loved.

"I see you have ordered my favorite coffee," he smiled. He took the lid off and took a tentative sip. "Perfect." He looked at her closely, "You look a little tired. Didn't you sleep well last night?"

"I slept alright, I guess. There were a lot of things running through my mind."

"What kind of things?"

"Oh, I was thinking about your nephew; thinking about what your sisters had said to me; thinking about *us."* Sarah took a sip from her coffee.

"We are *so different* you and I. We come from such *different* worlds. Sitting here now, across the table from you, drinking our coffee, watching the people in the streets, safely in Lafayette, I *believe* that we can be together. Then I think about your nephew being brutalized – not once but three times. I think about how terrible it must be to live in that *constant* uncertainty; that *constant* fear; that at any moment armed soldiers can burst into your home and beat your child. I think about *your* family having already picked out a bride for you; I think about *my* family how upset they would be to know how deeply I love you." Sarah was close to tears. "My heart kept telling me: *you love him; you love him; you love him.* My head kept urging me to *run!"*

Mohammad took both of Sarah's hands in his. For a while he didn't say anything, just held her hands running his thumbs back and forth across her fingers as they clutched his. "I *know* it is scary, *habeeptee.* I don't know what to say to make you believe, *that it will work out; that it will be alright."*

Mohammad changed the topic slightly. He wanted to reinforce for Sarah the positives. "You saw how my sisters were. I can tell that they really *like* you. If they hadn't, they would have been very frank with me and told me so. They *scolded* me for even *suggesting* to you that you consider converting. They like you *just the way you are.* They told me they understand why I love you so."

Sarah smiled though her tears continued to flow.

"When I talked to Mansur on the phone, he said that Khalil had told him that Manal's remark about us was that she and

Mona thought we were like *Im'me ou Abou'ee* --my mother and father. Mansur said that when Khalil told him that, that convinced *him* that we were right for each other." Mohammad squeezed her hands. "We *are* right for each other, Sarah. What can I say to convince you?"

Sarah looked at him through eyes glistening with tears. "You asked me to convert for you. Would you remain in America for me?"

Mohammad continued to hold her hands and to stroke her fingers. He looked at their joined hands. He looked at the tears in her eyes. "I would do *anything* for you. I only ask – I only *suggest* – one thing. Come back to the West Bank with me this summer – *just for a visit*. Meet my family; let them get to know you; and you get to see them in their environment. Come for just *three weeks*." He paused and moistened his lips. "*Just three weeks,* that is all I am suggesting. It will help make things clearer for you – it will help make things clearer for them. Just *think about,* will you?"

"*Of course I will think about.* It is a reasonable request." Sarah smiled and wiped the tears from her cheeks. "It seems a reasonable request to me, though I am not sure that *my parents* will think it is *reasonable at all!* They don't know how deeply I love you, but if I explain it *just right,* they will come around."

"I *don't* ever want to lose you, Sarah," Mohammad said seriously.

"And I *don't* ever want to lose you...You know," Sarah said taking a last sip from her coffee, "I am suddenly famished. Let's go some place and have a *big* breakfast. I feel *so much* better."

Chapter 18

The idea of Sarah visiting Mohammad's family in the West Bank had found fertile soil in both their minds. It made *perfect sense*. Sarah *should* visit the West Bank, get to spend time with his family, and get to know Mohammad in his home environment before committing her life to him. Meanwhile, Mohammad should see how Sarah (and he) reacted outside of the rarified environment of Purdue.

Once the seed had been planted, Mohammad wasted no time in writing to his family. He wrote to Khalil and Mansur, and he wrote to his parents in care of Hasna. He laid before them all the reasons why Sarah's visit was necessary; that she would only be coming for three weeks; and that still left him most of the summer to spend with his parents, and for Sarah to be home with hers. He rationalized that *before any final decision* was reached, he wanted Sarah to meet them, and he wanted them to meet her. As he read the letter back, it sounded *reasonable, rational,* and *mature.* He did add a postscript. He wondered about the sleeping arrangements for Sarah's visit. She obviously couldn't stay with his parents as he and Issa would both be there and it wouldn't be proper; she couldn't stay with Hasna, as she had seven sons and no space; he didn't think it was proper for her to stay, a woman alone, in a hotel; he was very open to suggestions. He wondered if perhaps she could board with Im Najib. She was a neighbor. There were no adult sons at home; and she had been like a sister to Sitteh Hasna.

Sarah called her parents and told them that she was making a surprise visit the next weekend, that there was something really important she wanted to discuss with them. Her mother, of course, inquired as to what was so important that she would come for just a weekend when the summer holiday was only six weeks away. Sarah had been rather cryptic in her reply. *It was not something that she wanted to discuss over the phone. It was something she needed to talk to them about face-to-face.*

When her mother hung up the phone, she turned to Sarah's father and said: "That was Sarah. She is coming for the weekend, next weekend. She says that there is something important that she wants to talk with us about and that it can't wait until the summer break. She didn't want to discuss it over the phone." Her mother was thoughtful as she said, "I wonder what it is about?"

Sarah's dad took the pipe from his mouth, dumped some of the ashes into the ashtray, and laid the pipe down. "You can bet that it has something to do with that Arab boy, Mohammad. She either wants to marry him, or she is pregnant."

Sarah's mother was shocked. "Dave, how can you say this about our daughter?! Of course she isn't *pregnant*! Sarah is *not* that kind of girl. As she went into the kitchen to make coffee, she slapped Dave on the shoulder as she passed him. "The very idea – *pregnant*- I can't believe you even thought that. Shame on you, Dave Goldman!"

Khalil and Mansur had different reactions to Mohammad's letter. Mansur thought that is was a reasonable, rational, mature suggestion. Khalil figured that the *very fact* that he was inviting Sarah to meet his family meant that they had *already* made their decision to marry. In any event, he couldn't think of any reasonable excuse to dissuade Mohammad. So his brothers wrote to him and said that they looked forward to meeting Sarah, as she and Mohammad would be traveling through Amman, and that they hoped they would stay with them for several days. Sarah could stay with Mansur and Zaleena; Mohammad could stay in Khalil's apartment with him,

Im Najib just happened to drop in to see Nijmeh shortly after Hasna had read Mohammad's letter to her parents. Nijmeh was just putting the letter into the pocket under her embroidered breast panel when Hasna opened the door to welcome Im Najib.

"Your timing is perfect, Im Najib. I was just going to make coffee. Hasna brought a letter from Mohammad and has just read it to us. He is coming this summer and bringing a friend." Nijmeh drew up a low stool for Im Najib.

"*Yum'ma* I'll make the coffee. You sit and chat with Im Najib." Hasna said. She looked thoughtfully at her mother as she went into the kitchen alcove to make the coffee.

"Mohammad is bringing a woman he knows from college. She wants to visit the area, and Mohammad suggested that to really see the area she should stay with a family. Of course, she can't stay here, it isn't proper, but he suggested that..."

Before she could even finish, Im Najib said, "If you are willing, and she doesn't mind simple accommodations, she is welcome to stay with me and Abu Najib. I could ask Yasmeen to come and stay with us as well. She speaks English and perhaps the young woman would feel more comfortable with another young woman in the house, especially one who speaks English."

"May Allah preserve you and your family; this is exactly what Mohammad had hoped. He had said in his letter that you were like Sitteh Hasna's sister, *Allah yer'hum'ha,* and such a good friend and neighbor, that he couldn't think of anyone else with whom he would want his friend to stay. She will naturally take all her meals here and spend time with the family. Mohammad wants to show her the sites in Jerusalem and Bethlehem, so it is really only having a place for her to sleep. We really don't want to inconvenience you though."

"Nonsense, of course she must stay with me. After all, *I am* the closest thing you and Abu Mansur have to an aunt. You two are like my own children." She took the steaming coffee cup from Hasna. "This will be such a treat for us – a welcome change from soldiers bursting into the house demanding to know *where the boys are* and asking my granddaughter to spit on me," she laughed. "Yasmeen will be delighted for the chance as well to visit with a foreign woman close to her age, and to practice her English. It couldn't be more perfect."

Hasna saw the thoughtful expression in her mother's eyes.

After Im Najib and Hasna had gone, Nijmeh was thinking about Sarah's proposed visit. She worried about what the neighbors would say about Mohammad bringing a female *friend* home, even if they were students at the same university. There was bound to be speculation. Nijmeh wondered how it was going to be possible for people not to *see* that Mohammad and the girl were *more* than friends from school. People may not say anything to her, but they would certainly be able to *see* the looks and gestures between Mohammad and Sarah, and to jump to the *obvious* conclusion; that Sarah was here to *meet the family.* She visibly sighed as she went about her work.

The unexpected suggestion that Yasmeen stay with Im Najib when Sarah was visiting was a concern. Of course, neither Yasmeen nor Im Najib knew that Nijmeh had *chosen* Yasmeen as a possible bride for Mohammad; thankfully no one knew expect for Omar, Hasna, and their son Issa. Nijmeh told herself: *I must be sure to tell Issa **not** to mention to Mohammad that it is Yasmeen whom I had picked.* Issa would be discreet, but she wished he didn't know about Yasmeen. She thought it would be awkward to have both of these women – the one *she* had chosen and the one Mohammad had chosen – living under the same roof for those three weeks. Mohammad was bound to run into Yasmeen. He *must not* discover that she was the one his mother had picked.

There was, however, a possible *plus* side to the two girls being together. Yasmeen's candid observations of Sarah would be helpful. She would see Sarah outside of the context of the family visits. She would see a more casual, less guarded Sarah. The girl would of course be nervous around the family and want to impress them, but around Yasmeen she would certainly be more herself.

Dave drove his pick-up truck to Des Moines to meet Sarah's bus. Sarah's mom, Emily, had wanted to ride along, but Dave had tactfully suggested that she should stay home and be sure everything was ready for Sarah's visit – her favorite meal cooked and all– since he *wanted a little time* to talk to Sarah *alone*. Emily agreed that it was probably a good idea.

When the *Greyhound Bus* pulled into the Des Moines terminal, Dave was at the gate waiting. Sarah kissed him and gave him a hug. He took her overnight bag and pointed her out the door to where the pick-up was parked.

They didn't say much until they had gotten out of the city limits and were on the open highway.

"So," Dave started, "what's this all about? Your mother said you have something important to talk over with us that couldn't wait."

Sarah shifted in her seat, fiddled with the seat belt, trying to think of *just the right way* to begin.

"I'm thinking of taking a three week vacation as soon as school's out."

"Where are you thinking of going?"

Sarah hesitated, "I want to take a trip to the Middle East." She paused, waiting for her father's reaction.

"Middle East, huh? Are you suddenly interested in religious sites? You wantin' to get in touch with your *Jewish* roots?" He waited. "Wouldn't have anything to do with the young man you brought to visit in the spring, would it?"

Sarah looked at her dad. "The *only* thing Jewish about me, and *you* for that matter, is our *name*. Yes, it *does* have something to do with Mohammad, but I would really rather talk about this with *both* you and Mom."

"You're not pregnant are you?" Dave glanced over at her, and Sarah could see the pain in his eyes.

"Oh, Dad, *of course* I'm not *pregnant* – how could you even have thought such a thing," Sarah said softly and touched his arm. She had wanted to scream at him, tell him how hurt and angry she was that he even thought that, but she saw the pain in his eyes and heard the hurt in his voice.

"You're wanting to marry him, aren't you? This is what this is all about, isn't it?" He kept his eyes on the road; it was easier than looking at this daughter he loved so much. He didn't want her to see the moisture in his eyes.

"I love Mohammad, yes. And he loves me," Sarah said staring straight ahead. "We *know* all the reasons that we *shouldn't* love each other: *different cultures; different religion; the distance between our families whom we love.* Our heads tell us one thing, our hearts a different thing. We *didn't* want to fall in love. It just seemed to happen."

They drove on in silence for quite a while. The towns disappeared and they were seeing more farms, open fields, cows grazing in pastures. "Before we make any *real* decision – and we *haven't slept together if you are worried about that,*" Sarah added, "we think it would be a good idea for me to meet his family, to see where he grew up, to get a firsthand feel for his family and the area. It really *is* reasonable, I think."

Her father didn't say anything. "You, know, Dad, *his* family feels the same way you do. They have been putting pressure on him through phone calls and letters to *not* get involved with an American-Christian. It is really ironic, when you think about it, two different sets of parents from different parts of the world, following different religions, speaking different languages *thinking the same thing:* how *inappropriate* the person that their child has fallen for *is.*"

"Your mother and I want you to be happy...and I *can't* see how marrying an Arab Moslem from the Middle East will ultimately make you happy. There was a catch in his throat when he said: "We don't want to lose you."

Sarah moved over close to him, close enough that their shoulders were touching. She laid her head on her father's shoulder. "I don't want you and Mom to *ever* think you are going to lose me. That's never going to happen," she whispered, "I love you both too much for that.

"It is just possible," she raised her head to smile at her father, "it is just possible that you may even come to *tolerate* the idea of an Arab, Moslem, son-in-law named Mohammed. You could have fathered a daughter who is a living example of assimilation and tolerance; a daughter who has a Jewish father, a Christian mother, and a Moslem husband.

Her father said with a hint of a smile: "Wouldn't that be a real *kick in the pants* to some of the conservative bastards, *pardon my French,* who live around here."

Sarah's weekend with her parents went much better than she had anticipated. It was clear that they weren't *doing somersaults, turning cartwheels,* or *jumping for joy,* but they hadn't *driven her from their door,* laid down any *ultimatums,* or *turned deaf ears* to her arguments. In the end, they had given their permission for her trip to the Middle East. "You're twenty-two and a grown woman and don't need our permission," her father had said.

"I know I don't *need* it, but I *want it.* I love both of you and I don't want to ever make you feel that I don't care what you think or how you feel. We *are family.* I am who I am because of you."

Her father put his arm around her mother and jokingly said, "*Damn,* where did we go wrong, Emily?"

Both her parents took her back to Des Moines to catch the bus. She sat between them in the pick-up. Close enough that she could rub shoulders with them both. It reminded them each of when she was a little girl. She, however, was no longer a little girl with the red bows on her pigtails bouncing when the truck hit a rut in the road; she was a woman about to begin a new adventure, a woman who was going to travel down a road they had never traveled. There would be ruts and bumps in that road, but they *knew* she could *bounce;* they couldn't think of a better word to describe Sarah's resiliency.

Chapter 19

Hope walked on cat feet through Issa's heart when his mother informed him that Mohammad was bringing his *American "friend"* to meet the family. Unlike his parents and older siblings, he hoped that Mohammad was determined to marry this American-Christian; he selfishly felt that this would mean that his mother could eventually ask for Yasmeen *for him!* He had promised his mother he would *not even hint* to Mohammad that Yasmeen had been the girl chosen for him. And he wouldn't.

Sarah had related to Mohammad the details of her weekend visit to her parents; she had even told him that her dad had thought that maybe she was *pregnant!* She had been surprised to see Mohammad blush. He had sheepishly smiled and said, "I suppose that would be *one* way to force our parents to accept our marriage."

Sarah joked with him. "I can see it now. I tell my parents that I am converting to Islam, marrying a Moslem, going to live in the West Bank, and, oh, by the way, I am pregnant. What would have happened if one of your sisters told your parents: *I'm converting to Christianity, marrying an American, going to live in Chicago, and by the way, I am pregnant?*"

Without hesitation Mohammad replied, "They would probably kill her. Not my parents," he quickly added. I can't really see them doing something like that, but my nephews, Hasna's sons, would probably feel obligated to do so for the family's honor."

"I can understand why Arab girls would be *reluctant* to get in a situation where they might become pregnant outside of marriage if *death* was the possible consequence. It's a pretty *powerful* contraceptive! Just so you know," Sarah laughed, taking Mohammad's hand, "my father wouldn't kill you, but he *is* a farmer and has gelded horses; he just might drive up from Des Moines and *cut off the offending pound of flesh.* Shylock was a Jew you know."

Mohammad squeezed Sarah's hand and grinned, "A *horse, and a pound* of flesh, huh? I'm flattered!" It was Sarah's turn to blush.

Mohammad went to the counter and got a refill on their coffee. "I am *so glad* that you are coming with me. I *really* want my family to meet you. I think they will fall in love with you, just like Manal and Mona did. I am glad that you will be able to see the West Bank first hand."

"I am a little nervous –*very nervous,* actually," Sarah said. "It will be hard for me to be *natural* and casual. I'll feel like I'm on *probation;* that I will have to be on my best behavior all the time."

"You are *always* on your best behavior, aren't you?" Mohammad joked, "Or are you performing for me as well?"

"With you, my fine *Arab prince,* I am me."

"Talking about *performing,*" Mohammad said, "there will be a bit of play-acting." He saw the quizzical look in Sarah's eyes. "Oh, not in front of my family; there you must be your wonderful, natural, genuine self. It is in front of the neighbors.

They will speculate as to why I have brought an American *girl* to visit. My parents will have casually told them that I am bringing a *friend* from college to visit, a friend who happens to be a *girl*. They will probably *guess* that you are there to meet the family; that I am serious about you, but it will *not* be acknowledged by my family that that is the reason for your visit; and the neighbors won't *know* for sure."

"So you want me to *act* as though we are school chums?"

"Just in front of the neighbors, *if* they happen to drop in. It's just the way things are done there. People suspect, but don't really *know* until the marriage contract is about to be signed."

"I suppose I *could* refrain from sitting in your lap, wrestling you to the floor, and kissing you in the street." Sarah frowned. "It would be *hard*, but I think I can manage it. Gosh, *give me a break!*"

"Don't be mad. I really don't want you to be any different than what you are. It's kind of like when you didn't want me to come to visit you because of what the neighbors might think."

Sarah softened. "I *do* understand. I just hate the idea of having to pretend in front of some people. I am not ashamed of loving you."

"And I am *not* ashamed of loving you. Perhaps we should just tell everyone that you *have come* to meet my family as we are getting married."

Sarah backtracked some. "No, you are probably right about appearing to be casual friends in front of your family's neighbors – *not* in front of your family, but in front of others, until everything is finally settled."

Hasna had brought her grandson, Imad, over to visit with his great grandmother Nijmeh. As Nijmeh played with him, counted his toes, tickled him under the chin and cooed to him, Hasna brought up the subject of Sarah's visit.

"You know that Mohammad has already decided to marry his American friend."

"I know, *Yum'ma*. Perhaps it is *what is written for him*. We have to be open-minded when we meet this girl, for Mohammad's sake, for the girl's sake. We know that Mohammad would not just pick anyone. This girl must be really special. "

"I know all that, but I still feel that it will be, in the long run, *wrong* for him- *wrong* for them. He has been away for almost a year. He has been alone. He may not be thinking clearly."

"Khalil said when he last phoned, *Yum'ma,* that both Manal and Mona *liked* the girl and could understand how Mohammad fell in love with her. We need to see the girl first hand too. Perhaps we will feel the same. If it is destined to be, if it is Mohammad's *naseeb*, we must be willing and ready to accept the girl into our family as a daughter, and as a sister-in-law."

"I know you are right, but I still wish he would see the wisdom of marrying a Palestinian. Any marriage has its rough patches, *except for you and Yaba's marriage,"* she smiled touching her mother's arm," and sometimes the added strain of *different cultures, different religions, different backgrounds* are rocks in the path over which they may stumble and fall. I don't want that for Mohammad, or for *his friend."*

When they had their usual morning coffee on the bench in front of the classroom building, Mohammad told Sarah that he had already bought their tickets.

"What! You bought *my* ticket! I don't want you buying my ticket."

"Aren't you going to visit my family because *I asked you to come?* Aren't you doing this *for me?*"

"Yes, I mean *no.* Yes, you asked me to come, and I am doing it partially for you, but *no*, I'm not just doing it because you asked, but because I *want to.* It's therefore my decision, and I should pay for my own ticket. To have you pay for the ticket somehow makes me feel *obligated* to you."

"We *are* going to eventually get married, aren't we? Isn't it only a question of *where we will live?*" he asked. "The question is not *if* we love each other or *if* we are going to get married."

Mohammad saw that she was still uncomfortable with the fact that he had bought her ticket. "Okay, I have the money. Every time one of my siblings writes, or whenever Manal or Mona send one of their care packages, they each include a *little something for my pocket.* If it would make you feel more comfortable, *if by some strange twist of fate* we are not destined to be together, you can pay me back for the ticket. You can slip it into my coat pocket as I lay in my coffin, for that's the *only* way that we won't be together; and that is the *only* way I am accepting money for the ticket!"

"You *do* have a stubborn streak, don't you?" Sarah said.

Mohammad laughed, "Perhaps you should change your reference to my *endowments* as being those of a *horse* to being those of a *mule*. Still quite *impressive* but adding the quality of *stubbornness!*"

"Just to put things in perspective for you, my *well-endowed* –so I am assuming – *friend,* the biggest *balls* recorded in science belong to the tsetse fly not an elephant and certainly not a mule. Now, if you were to say you were endowed like a *tsetse fly,* I would be impressed."

Mohammad grinned, "It doesn't *sound* quite the same. I think I will stick to *horse* or *mule.*"

They laughed together. Their decision to speak with Sarah's family and to travel to meet Mohammad's felt like a mutual commitment and had brought a new, more relaxed, more intimate humor to their banter.

Chapter 20

One evening, a week before their scheduled departure to Amman, there was an unwelcome visitor waiting for Sarah when Mohammad walked her back to her dorm. There was only one more exam to take; her personal things had been boxed up, and many of the boxes had already been carried over to Mohammad's flat. He was keeping the flat, had paid in advance the summer rent, and as Sarah didn't want to ship all her things home only to bring them back in the fall, they had decided that it made sense to store them in Mohammad's room.

On their walk back Mohammad had been explaining about how the social customs about engagement and marriage were a little different from what they were in the towns and cities of Palestine. "In the camps, we tend to be a bit more conservative than in the towns and cities. Since there is no dating, parents are careful to keep the negotiations between the families of prospective couples private. There has to be a *formal* agreement before the neighbors really know. The *formal* agreement in most cases means that the couple has *signed* a marriage contract and that they are *legally* married."

"*Legally married?*" Sarah replied.

"Yes, they are married *on paper*. They don't live together until after the wedding, but if they decide *not* to have a wedding, they need to get *divorced* even though they have never lived together as husband and wife."

"In the towns, the couple also doesn't really date, though they may know each other from college or social gatherings. It is somewhat different for Christian couples, so I understand. They make a declaration in front of the two families. They wear wedding bands on their right hands until the official wedding when the bands are worn on their left hands. They don't need to divorce if they decided they do not want to get married, as there has been no contract, but there *is* a bit of a social stigma. There is *no* dating even among Christians until there is an acknowledgment that the couple *intends* to marry."

"It is so different here. I can't imagine any of my friends from high school or college getting *engaged* first and then dating."

Mohammad laughed, "It is *rather* strange when looked at from a Western perspective, but for Palestinians it has worked. I suppose it shows the world that the couple is serious about each other; their intent is to marry.

"What we are doing is very strange by camp standards. For me to bring home a girl, to whom I am not already engaged or married, is a break with tradition. That is why there is this element of *secrecy* about the real reason of your visit." Mohammad raised their clasped hands and kissed Sarah's fingers. "I know you see it as somewhat *deceptive* – but it really is not. Think of it as being *different*, yes, but really a matter of *privacy* until everything has been settled."

Sarah smiled at him and kissed his shoulder. "It is all so strange."

They had entered the lobby of the dorm when they both saw him. It was Sam. He was sitting there, cap in his hands, watching the people as they entered, scanning each face and waiting. When he saw them, he put his cap on, strolled over –

and not looking at Mohammad said to Sarah, "I need to talk to you in private."

"What are you doing here?" Sarah said in shock.

"I ran into your dad at the Feed Store this morning, and he let slip that you were planning a trip with *him,*" he said only nodding in Mohammad's direction. "I need to talk to you alone."

"Sam, you have nothing to say to me that I want to hear. Where I go and with whom has *nothing,* and I emphasize the word *nothing,* to do with you."

He grabbed Sarah's arm and in anger said, "*I've* driven all this way to talk some sense into you. And, *by God,* that's what I am going to do."

Mohammad stepped in front of Sarah and broke Sam's grasp on her arm. "As Sarah said," he spoke, his voice low and barely above a whisper, "she has nothing to say to you."

"Take your hand off me, *Camel jockey,*" this is between Sarah and me."

"*Camel jockey?*" Mohammad was smiling, but Sarah could see the anger in his face. "I've never ridden a camel. Perhaps you should call me a *Rag Head.* I *do* wear a *kuffiyeh* – a rag if you would prefer, in winter."

Sam balled up his fists, "Maybe we should take this outside?"

"Fine by me." Mohammad answered.

Sarah stepped between them. Now she was really angry. "If you two *bulls* can stop snorting and pawing the ground, *I have something to say.*"

First she turned to Mohammad, put her hand on his chest and pressed. "I appreciate you coming to my defense, but I can handle the situation." She kissed him on the cheek and said, "Go over there and sit down. I will be alright. *GO!*"

Then she turned to Sam and unleashed her fury. She poked him repeatedly in the chest with her finger. It was hard enough that it must have hurt.

"How *dare* you come here and *demand* to see me. How *dare* you presume to think that I would listen to anything you had to say about what I do and who I do it with! We were friends in high school. Sure, we dated, that was kids' stuff. But we are *nothing* to each other. The way you are acting, I would not want anything to do with you *even if you were the last man on earth,*–certainly *not* marry you. How *dare* you presume that I don't know what I'm doing, that I need *you,* of all people, to *enlighten* me! What I do concerns me, concerns my family, and concerns Mohammad. *You are not in the picture."*

"But Sarah, he's..." Sam started to stammer.

"*He* is the man I love." Sarah countered before he could finish the sentence. Sarah turned to the few people who were sitting in the lounge, trying *not* to watch the drama, but of course *were* watching. She was really pissed. "I love Mohammad and I am not ashamed to say it," she told the few people who sat in the lobby, challenging them to contradict her.

It started with one hand meeting the palm of another. Then the entire lounge erupted into applause. One of Sarah's friends sitting in the lobby with her date even hollered out, "Way to go, Sarah!"

"*You,*" she turned to Sam, again poking him in the chest, "need to get in your pick-up and go home."

Sam adjusted the brim of his cap, put his hands in his hip pockets, and attempted to swagger as he said, "Well, you're making a *big mistake,* Sarah. I just came here to *point that out to you.* Not my fault that you're too stubborn to listen."

When he was gone, Sarah felt a little weak in the knees. She walked over to where Mohammad was sitting and almost fell into the seat beside him. He took her hand. She laid her head on his shoulder. "That was pretty impressive, I must say," Mohammad said. "Remind me *never* to piss you off."

The night before they were to leave from the Indianapolis Airport to begin their trip to the Middle East, Sarah's folks drove down to Lafayette to take them out to dinner. They had wanted to meet Mohammad earlier, but Sarah had told them that they had finals and perhaps it would be better if they waited until just before they left. It was really partly an excuse. She secretly didn't want them to try to talk her out of going.

They asked Sarah where she would like to eat, and of course, she said *The Chinese Dragon.* It was a little awkward for all of them. Sarah knew that her parents were unhappy about her trip. Mohammad knew that they were prepared not to like him, and he really couldn't blame them. Her parents were *going through the motions,* but it was clear that they wished none of this were happening. They *really* wanted to put Sarah in the front seat of the pick-up, *safely between them,* drive back to the farm, and forget there ever had been someone named Mohammad.

Sarah's mother tried to break the ice. "Tell me something about yourself, Mohammad. Sarah has really said very little about you." Her smile was encouraging. She *did* want to know more about him. She could see that he was startlingly handsome.

She thought to herself that *he looked like a stereotypical prince out of a fairy tale.* She could understand how Sarah could be attracted to him.

"Well, I am the ninth out of ten children. My parents are refugees, Omar and Nijmeh, are their names. My father was a farmer until 1948 when the family lost their land. He now is a day laborer, builds walls, digs gardens – that kind of thing. I have a brother who is a doctor, another brother who is a lawyer, and I am working on a Masters in agricultural engineering. I have two married sisters in California. They came out to meet Sarah," he smiled. "And she won them over," he said smiling at Sarah. "I also have two sisters married to engineers and who live in one of the Arab emirates. My oldest sister lives in the camp. She has seven sons and is a grandmother already. My youngest brother will graduate from college this year. He is studying business, but really wants to be an artist."

"That is quite an impressive family, I must say," Sarah's mother smiled.

"So, you want to marry my daughter?" Sarah's father spoke after taking a drink of water. His voice was gruff, and there was obvious pain in his eyes.

"I love Sarah, sir." Mohammad paused. "I know it must be difficult for you. I imagine it would be difficult for me to see a daughter of ours thinking of marrying someone from such a different background." Mohammad looked earnestly into Dave's face. "I *do* understand how you must feel, but I want you both to know *I love Sarah.* I want her to meet my family, to see the West Bank, before she commits herself to marrying me."

Mohammad took a drink of water to soothe his parched throat. "I know Sarah has told you that *my* family is also worried. They probably have some of the same concerns that you have. That is why it seems important for them to meet Sarah, to get a glimpse into why I love her so much."

He waited for her dad to say something. "My older brothers keep reminding me that one doesn't just marry an individual, but one marries a *family*. As my family is important to me, you are both important to Sarah. And because you are important to Sarah, you are also important to me."

Sarah's mother reached over and touched Mohammad's sleeve. There were tears in her eyes. "Thank you for saying that. We are so concerned that we are losing Sarah."

Mohammad covered her hand with his. "How could you possibly *lose* Sarah? She is your daughter, and she will always be your daughter." Mohammad tried to joke, "The worst that could happen is you would be gaining a Moslem son-in-law."

"That's another problem. You know that I am Jewish? I carry my religion lightly, as did my father and grandfather, but I am Jewish nonetheless," Sarah's father said.

"I know that, Sir. My father always says that the Jews and Arabs are really *cousins* – that if you take out the current politics, you would find that they have much in common and are related. My oldest nephew, who is just about my age, works on a settlement. His crew boss is an Iraqi Jew. Sami says that he keeps forgetting that his boss is Jewish, as he thinks like an Arab, acts like an Arab, and speaks Arabic almost better than Hebrew. When my youngest nephew was hurt by settlers, it was his Jewish crew boss who found him and returned him to the family."

"You seem to have an answer for everything, don't you?" Dave said with just a hint of sarcasm.

"Dad!"

"I know. I know. I am trying awful hard *not* to like Mohammad, but he *isn't making it easy*" said Dave with just a hint of a smile.

The waiter brought their food. It was hot. It was delicious. Over the various dishes they had ordered they talked about trivial things. It seemed they had gotten the *real* conversation out of the way.

Sarah's dad insisted on paying for their dinner, though Mohammad did try to pay. "Please," he said, "allow me to take the check. You are my guests."

"No, son, I got this," Sarah's dad said.

Sarah and Mohammad walked them to where the pick-up was parked. Sarah gave her mom and dad a hug. "I will be fine. I'll be back in three weeks and then we will have the whole summer together." She whispered to her mom and dad in turn, "I'm *so glad* you came to meet Mohammad and to see me off."

Mohammad shook hands with her dad. "Now, you take care of Sarah. I am entrusting you with her."

"You have my word. I know how much you love her, and I want you to know *I* love her too."

When he said good-bye to Sarah's mother, rather than shaking his hand, she hugged him. "I know you will take care of Sarah. I can see how much you love her, and to me *that is the most important thing.*"

Sarah and Mohammad held hands and waved as Dave drove out of the parking lot. "I think you won them over," Sarah said, "even my dad. But then, why *wouldn't* they love you?"

Chapter 21

The *fasten seat belt* sign had gone on; the flight attendants patrolled the aisles to make certain that seat backs were in the full upright position; the curtains between the different cabin classes were pulled back and tied as the plane began its descent into Amman Airport.

Mohammad held Sarah's hand. Her palm was sweaty. She was obviously nervous. She looked at Mohammad and tried to smile. "I am really nervous about meeting your brothers."

Mohammad tightened his grasp on her hand. "It will be fine, you'll see; they will *love* you."

They went through different lines at passport control. Mohammad went through the line for those holding Jordanian passports. Sarah went through the line for tourists. When she got to the window, the man behind the counter looked at her passport, looked at her, asked how long she planned on staying in the area, checked her visa, stamped her passport and motioned her through the gate.

Mohammad met her on the other side. They proceeded to baggage claim and luckily, after a bit of a wait, they saw their suitcases lazily moving along the conveyor belt. They loaded them onto a metal trolley and passed through security. They were not stopped. As they emerged through the swinging doors, Mohammad scanned the crowd looking for Khalil and Mansur. He finally saw them leaning over the barriers looking for him. They grinned and waved.

They had no sooner pushed the trolley through the exit, maneuvering it through the crowd, when Mansur and Khalil grabbed Mohammad in a bear hug and kissed him four times, twice on each cheek. Sarah stood quietly waiting, resting her sweaty palms on the metal handle of the trolley.

"Sarah, these are my brothers, Mansur and Khalil," Mohammad said gesturing first to Mansur and then to Khalil. "This is Sarah."

Mansur and Khalil both shook hands with Sarah. "Welcome to Amman. We have long looked forward to meeting you. Zaleena is anxiously waiting at the flat. She has prepared a welcome dinner for you. Come."

Sarah smiled as she shook their hands. "I can certainly see that you three are brothers. There is such a strong family resemblance. Even if I didn't know who you were, I would have been able to pick you out of the crowd."

Mansur laughed. "Yes, we do look alike. Wait until you meet our father. We all look just like him. He is only seventeen years older than I am and when we are all together folks think he is our older brother. He *is flattered* by the idea." He continued to laugh, "And our mother is only *fifteen* years older than I am and could easily pass as our older sister. You have met Manal and Mona; they look a lot like *Im'me,* though perhaps not quite as beautiful. Mohammad has probably told you about how our parents met at the village well? It is like a fairy tale from *A Thousand and One Nights.*"

Khalil hadn't said much. He had smiled and nodded, but hadn't engaged Sarah in conversation. He thought to himself: *she is beautiful and seems poised. I can understand how Mohammad is captivated. This may be more of a challenge than I had anticipated.*

On the drive to the apartment, it was Mansur who pointed out the sites. He seemed to be keeping up a running commentary. Khalil drove, maneuvering the car easily through the Amman traffic. Sarah thought: *this is really defensive driving; nothing like driving back home.* She sat in back with Mohammad who surreptitiously held her hand, from time-to-time squeezing it reassuringly.

Fourteen-year-old Omar had been standing sentinel at the window waiting to see his uncle's car pull in front of the apartment building. "Mama, they are here," he cried excitedly. Eleven-year-old Nijmeh and nine-year-old Ahmad had also rushed to the window to see their Uncle Mohammad and his American friend. Zaleena pushed the curtains aside, and peering over their heads, got her first glimpse of Sarah.

The door was open and they were all standing in the hall when the elevator stopped. "You see, there is already a welcoming committee ready to greet you," Mansur said as they stepped out of the lift. "I'd like to present my wife, Zaleena, and our children: Omar, Nijmeh, and Ahmad." The children politely came forward, took Sarah's hand, kissed it and raised it to their foreheads. Sarah was touched and bending down kissed each one on both cheeks.

When Zaleena came forward, she hugged Sarah and kissed her. "We have been looking forward to meeting you." She put her arm around Sarah's waist as she ushered her into their flat.

While she was showing Sarah the guestroom, Khalil took Mohammad over to his apartment to get him situated. Mohammad couldn't wait to hear Khalil's first impression of Sarah. As soon as the apartment door was closed he asked. "What do you think of her?"

Khalil hesitated, just a fraction of a second, but Mohammad noticed. "She is lovely. I can see why you are enamored."

"I'm not just *enamored,* Khalil. I love Sarah, and I want to marry her. I am hoping you will love her too."

"Let's just take it slowly. Give us a chance to get to know her. You have known her for almost a year; we have just met her." He smiled at Mohammad and clapped him on the back, "We are open to seeing things your way, *habeebee,* but *do* give us time."

Mohammad hugged Khalil, "I know I am being impatient. It is just that I love her so much, and I love all of you so much, that I *want* you all to love each other."

After Mohammad had gone over to Khalil's for the night, and Mansur had also excused himself as he had to get up early the next day, Zaleena asked Sarah if she would like a cup of warm milk with just a dash of cinnamon on top. "You are probably too exhausted to sleep. The warm milk will help and you and I can visit.

"That sounds great."

Zaleena pulled the curtains open so they could look out the big picture window at the lights of Amman at night. "The city is lovely at night. It seems to *sparkle,* I think." Zaleena drew her legs up under her as she sat on the plush sofa next to Sarah. "We *really* have been looking forward to meeting you. Mohammad has written of little else or talked of little else when his brothers phone him, for months. You have certainly captured his heart, and I can *see* why."

"You are very kind." Sarah paused. "Do you mind if I ask you a rather personal question?"

"But, of course, please ask whatever you want. We Circassians are known for being quiet straight forward; I think you Americans would probably say *blunt.*"

"You are not Palestinian, and yet you and Mansur, from the little I have seen, and from all that Mohammad has said when talking about you, seem very happy together."

"Yes, we have been blessed. We *are* very happy, *illhumdillah.* I think it has been easier for me, because though Russian, I am also Moslem and speak Arabic. I was the one who suggested to Mohammad that you might want to consider converting to Islam. I am sure you will pick up functional Arabic, the real hurdle for his parents will be that you are not Moslem."

"I *have* thought about it. Mohammad gave me some books to read, but I can't just convert on paper in order to marry him."

"Nor should you," Zaleena said. "I can see that you are a woman of integrity. There is much of beauty and simplicity in Islam; it is easy for me to say as I was born a Moslem and never had to make a conscious choice, but even if I had not been, I would like to think I would have found something in it of worth."

"I am really apprehensive about meeting Mohammad's parents. We won't be able to even talk with each other."

"I have never visited his parents in their home either. They came to Amman for a visit. His parents are delightful! You will like them, and I am *sure* that they will like you. *I do, Mansur does,* and the children do." Zaleena rested her hand on Sarah's shoulder. "At first I was concerned when Mohammad began writing about you. He was alone and seemed vulnerable; there are so many temptations in the States for a handsome young man like Mohammad. I was afraid that he would be *seduced* by some college girl, but after meeting you and learning more about you I think you may be perfect for him. Oh, there will still be rocks in your path to step over, but I think that your lives have *really been written together.*"

Sarah felt the tears – tears of happiness – sliding over her curved cheeks. "Thank you," was all she could say.

The three days in Amman went well. Khalil had taken time off, and with Amr, had taken Mohammad and Sarah to see the sites of Petra. The long drive to Petra and back had given them time to talk. It was just casual enough to allow Sarah and Khalil to get to know each other a bit.

While Mohammad and Khalil walked through the ruins of the Nabataean city, Sarah walked along with Amr. "This is historically the site," he said, "where the Prophet Moses, while wandering in the desert, was told by God to strike a rock and water would come forth. A city grew up around the spring that was found here. Petra became a famous trade city."

Sarah marveled at the monastery that had been literally cut from the rock. She had seen pictures of it, but the pictures had not captured the grandeur. "It is amazing! It almost takes my breath away."

Amr smiled. "This must be all so new to you, and probably a bit scary." Sarah looked puzzled. "No, I don't mean scary to see the sites, I mean it must be scary to come to meet Mohammad's family. I imagine you feel as though you are *on trial.*" Amr laughed, "Don't worry. You have made a fabulous first impression. Mohammad is almost like a younger brother to me as well. I can see how much he cares for you, and how much you obviously care for him. The family can *see* that too."

"I want to make the right impression, but I do find it a bit – *daunting* – I can't think of a better word to describe it. Everyone has been so nice here, and I can imagine myself being part of this family, but I am really nervous about going to the West Bank and meeting his parents."

"You will be fine. Just remember that Mohammad and Mansur and Khalil are the men they are because of the parents they had. Their parents must be unique individuals to have raised men like these." There was just a touch of wistfulness in Amr's speech. Sarah had seen the way he looked at Khalil and wondered if she had stumbled onto a secret.

The time flew by. The day of their departure had arrived. Mohammad was to go to the West Bank through the Allenby Bridge, as that was from where he had left. He would go through one bridge. Sarah would have to go to the north and go through the bridge that was the entry point for visitors. Once she was across the bridge, she would take a taxi to Jerusalem. It had been arranged that Mohammad would meet her in Jerusalem at the American Colony.

Khalil and Amr drove Sarah to the northern border crossing. "I really appreciate you going out of your way to do this for me," Sarah had said.

"It is our pleasure. We have enjoyed meeting you. It is good to be able, as they say in America, *to put a face with the name,*" Khalil said. "I know it has been somewhat awkward for you. We *do* appreciate you making the effort to come all this way to meet us."

Sarah hesitated and then decided to ask, "Have I passed inspection?"

"You are certainly straightforward. I like that," Khalil laughed. "You have won over Mansur and Zaleena and the children. There is no doubt about that." He glanced at Amr who was sitting in the front beside him. "And, you have won over Amr here."

"And *you?*" Sarah asked.

"Ah, me, now that is the question, isn't it?" He concentrated on his driving a bit. "Mohammad is more than my brother; he has probably told you how our grandmother, Sitteh Hasna, *Allah yer'hum'ha, gave* him to my care when he was two years old and I was but sixteen. Mohammad became my responsibility. He is like my son." He paused. "I want him to be happy. And after meeting you, I want *you* to be happy. I like you, I really do, but I worry." He looked straight ahead. "I can see that you both love each other. As my sister, Manal said, it *is* like looking at the love that exists between our mother and father. I sincerely *hope* that *love is enough.*"

Chapter 22

Sarah passed through the northern bridge with minimal stress. The Israeli at passport control *did* question her as to why she had chosen to come through Amman and not through Ben Gurion, asked her what she had done in Amman, and what she planned to do in Israel. Sarah had been prepped with the *correct* answers to give. *She had come through Amman as she had wanted to visit the tourist sites of Petra, to see the Roman Amphitheater in Amman, to get a flavor of the Arab Middle East. She wanted to visit the Holocaust Museum, and since she was Christian, she also wanted to visit Bethlehem's Church of the Nativity, the Holy Sepulcher and take a trip to Nazareth.* Her passport was stamped with a three-month visa.

Khalil had told her how much a taxi should cost to Jerusalem. The taxi driver had wanted more, but Sarah told him that she had been told to pay no more than $100, and she would easily find a taxi which would take her for that amount. The driver finally agreed to the price. He dropped her off in front of the American Colony in East Jerusalem.

Sarah went into the reception area, asked where the garden terrace was and if it would be alright to leave her bag with the receptionist. She was directed to a beautiful, enclosed garden where she ordered coffee and waited for Mohammad.

She didn't have to wait too long. She had just finished her second cup of coffee when she saw him weaving his way between the tables. "I see you made it," he beamed. *Illhumdillah* (Praise God). This is my brother, Issa." Sarah shook hands with the handsome young man, and noted that unlike his three older brothers, he had auburn curls and a dusting of freckles across his nose.

"The car is waiting. Shall we go? I can't *wait* for my family to meet you."

Mohammad chatted the whole way to Ramallah. He would point out what he thought were interesting sites. Sarah gazed at the beautiful mountains and the lovely stone houses. As they drove through town she noticed graffiti splashed on walls, clutter along the sides of the streets, dark scorched patches on the road where tires had been burned.

Mohammad had described the camp to her, but it was worse than she had expected. The taxi wove its way through the narrow, twisting alleys, honking the car horn when he turned blindly around a corner. He drove in the one entrance through which vehicles could enter the camp and finally came to a stop before a metal gate identical to all the other metal gates. To the side of the gate something had been written which had been painted over with white paint. The one word that popped into her mind when looking at the camp was *poverty*.

Issa paid the driver. Mohammad got her suitcase out of the trunk and rapped on the metal door. It was immediately opened by a middle-aged woman whom Sarah could only think of as being *the most beautiful woman she had ever seen*. The woman smiled, and said what must have been a greeting, but Sarah couldn't understand what she said. The woman made a wide gesture with her hand, obviously welcoming Sarah in.

"Sarah, this is my mother, Nijmeh. *Yum'ma, ha'dee Sarah.*" Again the woman spoke. She opened her arms, hugged Sarah and kissed her on both cheeks. "My mother wishes you to know that you are welcome," Mohammad said.

Mohammad next presented his father. Mansur was right; the older boys *did* resemble their father. Omar offered his hand and Sarah shook it. He smiled and Sarah could barely see his lips beneath a really impressive moustache. "And this is my sister, Hasna. Hasna speaks a little English."

"You are welcome to our home. We have heard much about you and have wanted to meet you. You are welcome." Hasna said.

"And I have heard much about all of you. I met your sisters Manal and Mona in the States. I must say you all look so remarkably alike." Hasna only smiled, but said nothing.

A wonderful meal had been prepared in their honor. Sarah had been conveniently seated between Mohammad and Issa so both could translate for her. They made a point of including her in the conversation. Mohammad whispered, "You are being especially honored. I had to convince my mother that it was alright for us all to sit together. She had thought that it would somehow be showing disrespect for her and Hasna to sit with you."

"Disrespect? Why?" Sarah asked.

"Usually the women do not sit with guests. They wait until the guests have been served and have left the table before they eat. My mother is treating you as though you are already part of the family."

There *were* moments of awkwardness. The lack of a common language was a problem. There was none of the ease that Sarah had felt with Mansur and Khalil, with Zaleena and Amr. Sarah felt the butterflies fluttering in the pit of her stomach, and for a moment she wondered about the wisdom of coming.

Mohammad looked at her with concern. He didn't take her hand, but he did say to her. "It is going to be alright. Of course, there is going to be this awkwardness at first, but it will pass. You'll see."

"Tell Sarah that she is going to be staying with Im Najib and her granddaughter. That her granddaughter speaks perfect English." Nijmeh said. Nijmeh could also see Sarah's discomfort.

Mohammad translated what his mother had said. "Im Najib was my Sitteh's best friend. She is like an aunt to my mother and father. She lives right across the alley. You will sleep there, but we will spend the majority of our time together. It *is* going to be alright, Sarah. I promise."

The words were barely out of his mouth when there was a rap at the door. Hasna went to open it and greeted Im Najib. She was ushered into the sitting room and introduced to Sarah. Mohammad rose when she came in the room and took her hand, kissed it and raised it to his forehead. Im Najib kissed him on both cheeks.

When she greeted Sarah, just as Nijmeh had done, she hugged her and kissed her on both cheeks and apparently said how glad she was that Sarah had come. Sarah felt as though she were watching a foreign film without subtitles.

The evening wore on. More guests came: Imad and his parents; Hasna's seven sons, her daughter-in-law, Ayesha, with her nine-month-old baby. Sarah had a hard time putting the names with the faces. It seemed that everyone was talking at once. She could hear the sounds, but she couldn't understand the words. Oh, she could tell basically what was going on, but she felt completely out of it. Mohammad had moved across the room to sit with the men. Ayesha moved next to Sarah. "This all must be very confusing to you," she said.

"You speak English!" Sarah said in welcomed relief. "I am *so glad.*"

Ayesha smiled. "It will only be awkward like this today. Mohammad is only sitting with the men this evening because his nephews and Imad and his father are here. They would think it strange if he sat beside you. Though I *know* he wants to sit next to you so you will feel more comfortable."

"Can you tell me everyone's names again?"

"Of course," Ayesha pointed to each of her brothers-in-law and named them. When she got to Saleem, she pointed and said, "This is the oldest brother, Saleem. He is my husband. He and Mohammad are only two years apart." Saleem saw Ayesha pointing to him and smiled.

After the coffee had been served, the guests shuffled their feet and got up to go. Im Najib said to Mohammad, "When you are ready, bring your guest over. We will be waiting."

"You are probably exhausted," Mohammad said to Sarah. "Why don't I take you over to Im Najib's?"

"Alright, I *am* quite tired."

Sarah shook hands with Omar and Nijmeh and bade them good night. Mohammad carried her bag over to Im Najib's. He rapped on the metal door only once and it was opened. Im Najib smiled and welcomed them into her home. Standing right behind her was a lovely dark-haired girl of about eighteen. "This is my granddaughter, Yasmeen," she told Mohammad. "She speaks English very well. I thought that your friend would be more comfortable if there were someone in the house who spoke English."

"Sarah, this is Im Najib's granddaughter, Yasmeen. She speaks English."

Yasmeen came forward and offered her hand to Sarah. "Please, come in. You are most welcome."

Yasmeen turned to Mohammad. "I will take my grandmother inside for a moment so you can say good night to your friend."

So for a brief moment Mohammad and Sarah were alone in Im Najib's courtyard. He took Sarah in his arms and hugged her. She clung to him as he tilted her face up and kissed her. "I'm a little frightened," she murmured.

"I know, *habeeptee,* but I am here. It is going to be alright."

"You promise?" Sarah said, close to tears.

"I promise."

He kissed her again and then called to Im Najib. "Thank you, *Khalti* (Auntie) for taking care of Sarah for me."

"Don't worry, *Khalti,* she will be like one of my own granddaughters."

"I'll see you first thing in the morning, Sarah."

Yasmeen showed Sarah into the guest room. There was a mattress spread on the floor. There were hooks behind the door upon which Sarah could hang her clothes. Right across the narrow hall there was a closet bathroom. "I will be in the bedroom right next door. If you need anything, do not hesitate to ask me." Yasmeen said. She looked at Sarah and went over and gave her a hug. "Don't be uneasy. I know it all must be very strange to you. You will soon get used to us." Sarah hugged her back.

"You have all been so kind, but I really feel like I have stepped into another world. And, frankly, I am a little scared."

Yasmeen smiled at her, "It is natural to be scared at first, as it is all so new. But you will soon see that though we speak a different language, and perhaps live a bit differently than what you are familiar with, we are all basically alike. You will see."

Yasmeen closed the door. Sarah got her nightgown out of her bag. She hung a few things on the hooks behind the door. She went across the hall and used the tiny bathroom. She remembered what Mohammad had said about putting the toilet tissue in the covered can beside the toilet, *not* in the pot. She washed her hands and brushed her teeth. She looked in the cracked mirror and for a moment wished *like Dorothy, in* The Wizard of Oz, *that she were back in Kansas.*

As she lay on the pallet, in this strange house in the camp, the tears began to slowly fall. She turned her face into the hard pillow to muffle her sobs and cried herself to sleep.

Mohammad lay awake. Sleep seemed reluctant to come. He worried about Sarah. He knew that her experience with his family in the camp would be altogether different from the three days she had spent in Amman. He had forgotten *how different* it would be for her. This may not be as easy as he had hoped.

Chapter 23

Neither Mohammad nor Sarah had slept well. When Sarah had finally gotten to sleep, she had almost resolved to change her ticket and return immediately. She felt so out of her element. She had gotten up, smoothed out the cover on the bed, taken a sponge bath, brushed her teeth, combed her hair and gone back into the room to dress. She had listened to see if anyone else was up. She didn't hear anyone so she had waited. Finally, she opened the door quietly and tiptoed down the stairs.

The courtyard was bright with sunshine, and Im Najib was already up and sitting on a stool with her back against the cement wall. She motioned to Sarah to come and join her. Sarah took the low stool that Im Najib offered her. They smiled at each other. Im Najib said something but Sarah could not understand her.

It wasn't long before Yasmeen came out of the kitchen carrying a tray of little glasses with steaming tea in them. "I hope you slept well," she said. "Though probably not so well as it is a strange bed, and a strange place, and you were probably too exhausted from your journey to really sleep. You will sleep better, *inshallah,* this evening."

Sarah thanked her for the tea but didn't quite know how to hold it as the glass was so hot.

"Let the tea sit on the little saucer and cool a bit," Yasmeen said. "You are probably used to having tea in cups. I can get you a cup if you prefer."

"No, that's alright," Sarah said, "this is fine."

Sarah took a small sip. "It's delicious," she said. "What's in it?"

"We boil it with a few mint leaves in it and add a teaspoon of sugar to each glass," Yasmeen said.

"I usually don't take sugar in my tea, but this is really good. I will have to try it like this when I go back to the States."

"You should take a box of little glasses back with you. It will be a novelty for your parents and friends to have tea served this way."

There was a rap on the door. Yasmeen went to open it and stepped aside so Mohammad could enter. Sarah's spirits lifted as soon as she saw him. She wanted to rush over and hug him, but she remembered what he had said about appearing casual - as though they were just friends – in front of the neighbors.

"I hope you slept well. I have a big day planned. I want to take you into Jerusalem to see some of the holy sites, perhaps do a little shopping for your friends and family. I thought I would take you to the YMCA for lunch."

"The *YMCA*? Isn't that a gym?" Sarah asked.

Mohammad had to laugh. "The *YMCA* in Jerusalem has a roof-top restaurant. It is right next to the American Consulate. It is *the place* to go in Jerusalem to eat. You will be surprised. I think you will love it." He continued to chuckle, "Did you really think I was going to take you to a *gym for lunch?!*"

"That sounds great. Let me get my purse," she said.

"Be sure you have your passport with you," Mohammad hollered as Sarah ran up the stone stairs.

"I hope it hasn't been too inconvenient for you having my friend here?" Mohammad asked in Arabic.

"We have enjoyed having her, *Khalti.*" Im Najib replied. Yasmeen had excused herself and gone into the kitchen since Mohammad was there.

Sarah came down the steps and walked over to Mohammad. "How do I say thank you to Im Najib?" she asked.

"Just tell her *shukran, Khalti,*" Mohammad said.

"*Shukran, Khalti,*" Sarah said kissing Im Najib on both cheeks.

"*Af'wan ya bintee, af'wan.*"

"She said that you are welcome and called you daughter."

They walked across the alley to Mohammad's house. "My mother has prepared a little breakfast for us. They have already eaten. She thought we might like to eat alone."

"That was really thoughtful of her. But are you sure it is alright; it isn't *improper?*" Sarah asked.

"Of course, it is alright. My parents know why you are here. There is no one at home at the moment except for my mother. My father has taken my nephew Saji to work with him, and Issa is off running some errands. He will join us in a little while. He has some business to do in Jerusalem so will take the taxi in with us; then we will be on our own."

Sarah found herself relaxing. It was soothing to her troubled spirit to be alone with Mohammad for a bit. In the daylight the fears of the night before did not seem quite so real.

After they had finished eating, Sarah asked Mohammad if he would ask his mother to join them for coffee.

Nijmeh was pleased. She brought three cups and the long handled brass coffee pot in case they would like more.

"Your mother is probably the most beautiful woman I have ever seen. It is hard to think that she has had *ten* children. She *does* look as though she could be your older sister and *not* your mother." Mohammad translated what Sarah had said. Nijmeh blushed and put a rough, reddened hand up to cover her smile.

"I am a *great*-grandmother and certainly old enough to be the mother of ten, but please thank her for the compliment." Mohammad translated for his mother.

Just then Issa returned. "Are you ready to go into the city?" he asked.

"We're ready I think. Are you ready to go, Sarah?"

"Yes." She turned to Nijmeh and said, "*Shukran Khalti,*" as she kissed her on both cheeks. Nijmeh was surprised, but touched.

Issa left Mohammad and Sarah at Damascus Gate. "I'll see you at home. Enjoy your day."

"Where is he off to?" Sarah asked.

"He sells some of his sketches to a man who owns a shop outside New Gate. He wants to see if the sketches he dropped off last month have sold. He has some new drawings he would like to sell.

"Come on. Let me show you the Old City." They climbed down the large stone steps that lead to Damascus Gate. Once inside the wall, the streets were cobblestone and narrow. There seemed to be hundreds of little shops. They would pass a shop and a storekeeper would shout in English to Sarah, "Welcome.

Welcome." Mohammad would ignore them, or frown and say in Arabic, "*Ihna Arab* (We are Arab)." Part of him didn't like the idea that he was seen, because he was walking with Sarah, as not being Arab, even though he certainly *looked* very Arab, or that the shopkeepers were assuming that Sarah had *hired* him as her guide.

They visited the *Holy Sepulcher* then walked to the *Dome of the Rock.* Sarah had a headscarf with her in her purse. Mohammad had told her she needed to cover her hair when walking through the mosque grounds. They stopped in a few shops to pick up some trinkets for friends in the States. Mohammad did not hold her hand. Sarah knew that he wouldn't; he had told her why before they came, but she felt like she *needed* her hand held. She needed a *tangible* connection to Mohammad.

By one o'clock, they were at the YMCA, just up the road from Damascus Gate. It wasn't a tourist hangout, so Mohammad seemed more himself. After they had ordered, he reached across the table and took her hand. "I have missed holding your hand today. I had to keep fighting within myself the impulse to reach over and take your hand."

"I wanted you to hold my hand too. I am feeling a little *vulnerable,* I guess. It was easier in Amman. Your family there is so easy to be around. And they *all speak English.* Here I feel at a real disadvantage. Frankly, last night I wondered why I had come."

"I *know* it isn't easy. I am so *proud* of you for making the effort. I promise we will spend as much time alone as we can."

When the waiter brought the first course, Mohammad released her hand. "This looks good," he smiled.

"It *does* look good. I am hungrier than I thought," Sarah replied. They talked, and for Sarah, it almost felt like they were back at Purdue.

After coffee, they walked back toward Damascus Gate and the taxis. Just opposite the YMCA there was an Armenian Pottery shop. Sarah looked in the window as they passed. "Look at that lovely pitcher, Mohammad. That is something that I think my mother would really like."

"Well, let's go in and look then," he said.

It was a lovely piece of hand painted pottery. They looked at the other things he had in the shop. He also had matching tea cups. "I think I will get this for Mom. She will love it."

"They probably ship to the States. That way you wouldn't have to carry it and be afraid of it breaking." He asked the shopkeeper if they shipped to the States. The shopkeeper took down the address and added the shipping costs to the purchase price.

They got in the backseat of the *service,* (taxi). The driver waited until the car was filled before he took off. Mohammad didn't say anything on the drive back to Ramallah, though he would occasionally press his leg against Sarah's.

The *service* dropped them off in the center of town. They walked back to the camp, keeping a short distance between them. Mohammad pointed out some of the graffiti and translated for Sarah what the slogans said. They came in the back entrance to the camp as it didn't face the main road and there was usually not an Israeli patrol parked there.

He dropped Sarah off at Im Najib's, so she could lie down a bit if she wanted. He told her he would be over later to pick her up. "My sister, Hasna, has invited us for supper," he said.

"I think I *will* take a nap. I didn't sleep much last night and could use one." Sarah smiled. "I'll be waiting for you. I love you."

"I love you too," Mohammad smiled.

When he knocked on the door, Yasmeen opened it. "Did you have a nice day?" she asked.

"I think Sarah would like to rest a bit. We are going to Hasna's for dinner."

When she closed the door as Mohammad left, she turned to Sarah and smiled, "You must be tired. Do go up and have a little rest. I will call you in an hour or so, so you can get ready to go to supper."

Sarah went up and lay down on the pallet. She was asleep as soon as her head hit the hard pillow. She was exhausted. Her sleep was deep and dreamless.

There was a soft rap at the door and a gentle, muffled voice called, "Are you awake, Sarah? It is time to get up and get ready."

Sarah opened her eyes. For a moment she couldn't remember where she was. "Yes, thank you. I'm awake." She yawned and stretched. She got up, put on a long-sleeved print dress, and went across the hall to wash. She looked in the cracked mirror, ran a comb through her hair, and said to the girl looking back at her, *I can do this! I can do this!*

She slipped into her purse three silk scarves that she had brought for Hasna, her daughter-in-law, and for Im Imad. At promptly five o'clock Mohammad came for her. He said to her, once they were in the street, "You look lovely." He caught himself reaching for her hand and pulled back.

At Hasna's, Mohammad, Abu Mansur, Issa, Abu Imad, Imad and his seven sons ate first. While they were eating, Sarah sat in the sitting room with Ayesha and the baby. "You probably find this strange as well," Ayesha said, "the men eating alone and before the women. It is just the way we are. In America, doesn't your mother serve your father and brothers before she eats?"

"My mother *does* make sure that my father's plate is filled first," she laughed, "but we all sit together to eat."

"Even when you have guests you all sit together?" Ayesha asked.

When the men came into the sitting room, Ayesha picked up the baby and steered Sarah out of the room. As Sarah passed Mohammad, he looked quickly around to see if he was being observed, and when he saw that he wasn't, he *winked.*

The plates and serving dishes had been cleared away and new plates set for the women; new serving dishes heaped with hot food were placed on the table. The women gossiped and chatted. Both Hasna and Ayesha were good about translating for Sarah. They asked Sarah what she had seen in the Old City. She told them about the sites they had visited and about buying the Armenian pottery set for her mother.

After the meal, Hasna told Sarah that they could all go into the sitting room for coffee. The men sat on one side and the women sat on the other. The men seemed to be doing most of the talking and the women seemed to be doing most of the listening. Sarah tried to see some humor in the situation, but couldn't.

As they got up to leave, Sarah gave the three scarves to Hasna. "I brought something from America for you, for your mother-in-law and Ayesha. It is just something small to thank you for your hospitality."

"This really wasn't necessary. Thank you." Hasna said kissing her on both cheeks.

They walked back together: Mohammad, his parents, Issa and Sarah. "Why don't you invite Sarah in for a cup of tea before she goes over to Im Najib's?" Nijmeh said to Mohammad in Arabic.

"My mother thinks you should come in for a cup of tea before you go over to Im Najib's. I think you should come in for tea too."

"Okay, I'd like that," Sarah smiled.

Omar and Issa excused themselves and went into the sitting room to watch a soccer game on the TV. Mohammad and Sarah sat under the stars. The smell of jasmine was heavy in the air. Nijmeh had gone into the kitchen to prepare thc tea. Mohammad and Sarah had a few moments alone. "You know, Sarah. I love you more each day that passes." He looked up at the stars. "I am so thankful that you have come to meet my family. It means so much to me." When he saw that no one was around, he reached for her hand and pressed it to his lips. "I love you so much. Never forget that."

"I love you too, more than there are stars in the sky," she whispered.

Chapter 24

Sarah slept better, though not as well as she would have slept at home. At first it had been the persistent buzzing of a mosquito in her left ear. She would swing at it with her hand, and it would retreat, and then come back to buzz again. *It must like foreign blood,* Sarah thought. And then it had been the call to prayer blaring over the loudspeaker. *It isn't even light yet,* Sarah grumbled to herself. Sleeping on the floor made her feel like she was *camping out.* She thought wistfully of the lovely guest room at Mansur's: a comfortable bed with an innerspring mattress, a mahogany armoire, a private bathroom with pink blossoms on the shower curtain and pink fluffy towels hanging on the polished brass towel rack. She really *didn't mind* the simplicity; it was just that she was struck by the *contrast.*

She finally gave up. She thought, *Okay, the mosquito has won this round, but we'll see who wins tomorrow: the mosquito, the blaring loudspeaker, or me!* She went into the tiny bathroom. Yasmeen had called it a *closet bathroom.* It really was like a closet. She could literally sit on the pot, wash her hands in the sink, and take a shower at the same time if she wanted to. Yasmeen had explained to her that there was a shower attachment beside the toilet and a drain in the floor, that there was no actual *shower stall. I suppose it is quite practical,* Sarah thought, *I can take a shower and clean the bathroom all at the same time.* She hadn't quite anticipated the rather *unusual* bathroom conditions. She had seen campers at home that had better bathrooms.

When she dressed and went downstairs Mohammad was already waiting. He was chatting with Im Najib. Yasmeen was nowhere to be seen.

"Good morning, Sarah. I hope you slept better last night. My mother has breakfast waiting for us."

"I did sleep much better. Thank you. Just let me get my purse and I will be ready to go." When she came back down she thanked Im Najib, using her two word Arabic vocabulary and kissed her on both cheeks.

Over breakfast, again Nijmeh gave them some time alone and Mohammad outlined the plan for the day.

"Since it is Friday, I want to go to services at the mosque. My mother said that Yasmeen has offered to take you to meet her family while I am there. Then in the afternoon, I thought I would take you to see Bethlehem. You can visit the *Church of the Nativity, Shepherd's Field,* and do some shopping. Bethlehem is known for its olive wood carvings and its mother-of-pearl work. There is also, so I understand, an order of Catholic Nuns that make earthenware nativity sets. In the evening, I have invited my parents and Issa to go out to dinner. There is a well-known garden restaurant in Ramallah that serves excellent, typically Arabic, food. I think you will enjoy it. How does that sound?"

"It sounds like you have put a lot of thought into it. You have but to *lead, and I have but to follow."*

"You're not angry are you?" Mohammad asked with concern.

Sarah smiled, "No, I am just joking with you. It is really very thoughtful of you to have planned all these activities."

While Mohammad went to noon prayers with his father and brother, Yasmeen took Sarah to meet her family. "I know you are probably tired of seeing yet more new faces. But my mother has heard a lot about you from my grandmother and has implored me to bring you over. We won't stay long. There is something I want to show you though."

Yasmeen's mother, again like Mohammad's mother, looked like she could have been Yasmeen's sister and not her mother. "Was your mother married at *twelve?*" Sarah whispered. "She looks so *young!*"

Yasmeen whispered back, "She was almost fourteen when she was married; and almost fifteen when she had me. It is wonderful having a young mother; we really are like sisters much of the time."

Yasmeen's mother insisted they sit for coffee. Through Yasmeen she asked Sarah about her own family, about what she had seen so far, about *how well* she knew Mohammad. Sarah carefully replied, when answering about Mohammad, that they had classes together and were in the same program at university. She didn't lie, but she didn't elaborate.

"Sit here just a moment, Sarah. There is something I want to get from my room to show you." It literally was only about two minutes and Yasmeen was back with a bundle in her arms. The bundle was carefully covered with a piece of white sheet.

She laid the bundle in Sarah's lap and pulled the sheet away. There in her lap lay a beautiful embroidered dress. The material was soft red velvet. Sarah picked the dress up and shook it out. It was breathtakingly beautiful. The side panels of the dress were in green satin. The breast plate was heavily embroidered in threads of gold and green. The panels and sleeves were connected to the main body of the dress with bands of multicolored threads. Sarah had never seen anything like it.

"It is the most beautiful dress I have ever seen." Sarah said.

"I thought perhaps you would like to try it on, and then we could go to a photo studio in the camp and have your picture taken in it. The picture would be something for you to have to remember your visit to Palestine. My mother had this dress made for me for my *henneh.*" Yasmeen said.

"What is a *henneh?*" Sarah asked.

"The day before a girl is to be married, her female relatives, those of her husband-to-be, and her female friends have a party. At the party there is singing and dancing and the women paint the bride's hands with *henna*. Small packets of *henna* are also given to each of the guests. For that party a dress such as this is worn."

"But this is for your wedding," Sarah protested, "I mustn't wear it and have my picture taken in it!"

"Of course, you must. I insist!" Yasmeen replied. It didn't take much persuasion. Sarah slipped the lovely dress over her clothes. Yasmeen tied around her waist a wide belt made from striped silk. Yasmeen's mother brought out of her bedroom an embroidered cap and a white shawl. "My mother wants you to wear her embroidered cap and head shawl when you have your picture taken. You will look like a traditional Palestinian bride!"

Yasmeen's mother said, "*Shu'hada?* (What's this?) *Hadee bint bit'gen'en.*"

Yasmeen laughed as she turned Sarah around to face her mother. "My mother says that you are so beautiful that you would drive someone out of his mind."

Yasmeen was true to her word. She had spoken to a photographer the day before, he happened to be her uncle, and he had agreed to open his shop, even though it was Friday, to take the foreign girl's picture. Sarah was carefully set in a chair; the dress was artfully arranged about her. Yasmeen fiddled with the embroidered cap and shawl so it was just right. The photographer tilted Sarah's head just the way he wanted it. He had Yasmeen tell her to *only give a suggestion of a smile.* He took several shots.

Yasmeen made tea on the primus while her uncle developed the film. The backdoor of his shop opened into a tiny garden. Sarah and Yasmeen sat there, enjoying the sun, drinking their tea, while Yasmeen's uncle worked. "He usually makes people come back. But I told him we were in a hurry. I think I am his favorite niece, so he is doing me a favor." Yasmeen laughed.

"I have read about arranged marriages, and if you don't mind me asking, why aren't you married?"

"Have you been talking to my mother?" Yasmeen laughed. "She has been pushing me to get married since I passed my government exam; she had turned down any offers that came before I was eighteen, *and there were offers,"* Yasmeen laughed, "using the excuse that I was *too young.* But there is something about being *eighteen* that spells *spinster* to my mother. Considering that by the time *she* was eighteen she already had *two* children, I can understand her concern."

"Don't you want to go on to college?"

"Oh, I thought about it. But when I looked at it realistically, my *life* is going to be spent as a wife and mother. And that is really alright. I just have to wait for *Mister Right,* or more accurately, for *Mister Right's mother* to speak to my mother, and presto," Yasmeen snapped her fingers, "I will be married."

When she went to get more tea, her uncle was just coming out of the darkroom. He showed Yasmeen the prints he had made of Sarah. Sarah looked beautiful. "I have made six prints for her," he told Yasmeen in Arabic. "Please ask her if it is alright that I also make a larger print to frame and put in the shop window. I think people passing would be intrigued to see an obviously American looking girl in traditional Palestinian costume.

Yasmeen showed the prints to Sarah. Even Sarah thought that she looked like a model in a magazine. Yasmeen asked her if it was alright for her uncle to display an enlargement of the photo in his shop window. Sarah readily agreed. He had been so kind to take the pictures, how could she refuse his request. Sarah offered to pay for the photos, but he insisted that it was a gift. He put the prints into an envelope and Sarah slipped the envelope into her purse.

As she was walking back to Im Najib's with Yasmeen, Yasmeen slipped her arm through Sarah's. "It is such a welcome treat having you visit. I feel like I have an American *sister.*"

"What an incredibly kind thing to say." They walked on in companionable silence for a few paces, then Sarah said, "You are such a kind person, and *beautiful;* I'm sure many mothers are hoping to arrange for you to marry their sons." As they walked on, arm in arm, a thought like that proverbial *lightning bolt* struck Sara's heart: *Yasmeen had been chosen for Mohammad!* She *knew it was true;* it was as though the hand of God, Himself, had written it in bold letters across the sky for her to read!

On the taxi ride to Bethlehem, Sarah was quiet. She politely nodded or replied in one-syllable words when Mohammad pointed something out. She was lost in thought: *Yasmeen is meant for Mohammad. Yasmeen and Mohammad make perfect sense.*

"Hey, where are you?" Mohammad teased. "You seem a million miles away."

"I was just thinking; that's all. Sorry."

Bethlehem was built on hills. One was either climbing up or slowly going down. *The Church of the Nativity* was, she supposed, interesting if you liked old churches. It was interesting to learn that the main door was so low that one had to bend to get in. Apparently, as the guide told them, *it was done to prevent soldiers riding into the church on their horses.* The church was built, again according to the guide, over the *exact* spot where the baby Jesus had been born. It didn't look anything like the manger stall that Sarah had seen in Sunday school pamphlets. She was not impressed, though she did nod appropriately.

She walked through the shops with Mohammad looking at the olive wood carvings and picked up a few crosses as gifts for her aunts. The mother-of-pearl items didn't really appeal to her. They somehow seemed too gaudy. When they went to the small shop run by Catholic nuns, she did buy several earthenware nativity sets of *Mary, Joseph and the baby Jesus.* They were small, would be easy to carry, and would make nice Christmas gifts.

They took a taxi out to *Shepherd's Field*, but Sarah thought: *you've seen one field; you've seen them all.* She couldn't envision a choir of heavenly hosts singing *Joy to the World.* Throughout the day the same thought kept swimming through her head: *Yasmeen would be perfect for Mohammad. Yasmeen would be perfect for Mohammad.*

*If Yasmeen hadn't been chosen for Mohammad, she should have been. Damn, **I'd** even choose her for him,* Sarah thought.

"Hey," Mohammad waved his hand in front of Sarah's face, "there you go again. What are you thinking about, Sarah? You have been distracted all day and I wanted this trip to be special for you."

"I was thinking about Yasmeen and what a wonderful girl she is. I had such a good time with her this morning. She even told me that I was like her *American sister.* Wasn't that a thoughtful, generous thing to say?" There were tears threatening to fall in Sarah's eyes.

Mohammad looked in her eyes. "Sarah, you are close to tears! What is it, *habeeptee?* Has someone said something to offend you?" Mohammad was almost angry. "If they have…"

"No, everyone has been especially nice. I guess I am still a little tired. I wonder if Hasna and your mother would be willing to talk to me. I have some *girl-stuff* I would like to know from your mother. Hasna could translate for us. You think that would be okay?"

"*Girl-stuff?*" Mohammad asked.

"Yes, my Arab prince." Sarah tried to sound as though she was teasing. "There are a few things about you that only a mother would know."

"I'm sure it will be alright. I'll arrange it, but are you *sure* you don't want me there to do the translating?"

"I'm *perfectly* sure."

Chapter 25

Sarah carefully repacked her bag. She laid on the pallet the things she had brought for Mohammad's father and mother and brother, Issa. She hadn't known quite what to bring. She had purchased from an art store in Lafayette a box of different colored charcoals for Issa, along with two sketch pads. She hadn't known quite what to get for his mother. She had bought an assortment of silk head scarves and a fancy lace tablecloth; for his father twelve Irish linen handkerchiefs and a leather chain purse like her grandfather had once used. She hadn't known about Yasmeen then, known that she would be staying with her that is, but she laid on the pallet several pair of new panty hose still in their cellophane packets, a silk kimono that Sarah had never worn, but had bought especially for the trip, and of course, a silk headscarf. For Im Najib she brought a set a blue bath towels.

Sarah had written the name of the intended recipient on the top of each neat pile. She added one last item, an envelope addressed to Mohammad. All that was in it was the professional photograph of her in Yasmeen's traditional dress. On the back she had simply written: *With all my love always, Sarah.*

She wasn't quite sure what she was going to do; she was only resolved that she couldn't stay. If she couldn't change her ticket, she would book a tour to the Galilee in the north, perhaps to Gaza in the south, and book herself into a Jerusalem hotel for the two or three days before she was ticketed to leave from Tel Aviv. She was a big girl, after all, perfectly capable of taking advantage of the remainder of her *vacation* alone. She was thankful that she and Mohammad had planned her itinerary so that she wouldn't have to go back to Amman.

Mohammad arranged with his mother and Hasna that she would have time alone with them that afternoon. He and Issa were going to visit some old school friends who lived in the camp. His father would still be at work. The three women would have the house to themselves so they could *talk over their girl stuff,* he had joked.

Sarah spread the light bedspread over the piles on the pallet and closed her suitcase. She went into the small bathroom, looked at her reflection in the cracked mirror, and wished *like Dorothy* that she could *just click the heels of her slippers together and she would be back on the farm.*

It has been like a story she thought, *but all stories come to an end.* Sarah sighed, moistened her lips, patted her hair into place and went down the stone stairs.

Mohammad was already waiting. Like the day before, he was chatting with Im Najib, and Yasmeen was nowhere in sight. *It probably wasn't really proper for her to sit with Mohammad,* Sarah thought, *at least not at the moment.*

Mohammad got up and smiled when he saw her. "Hasna is already at the house. I must say that she is curious about what this *girl stuff* may be about." Sarah only smiled.

In the short walk across the alley Mohammad asked her, "Sarah, are you all right?" There was concern in his voice.

"Of course, I am all right. I want to find out from your mother things that you would *never* tell me," she joked. "I want to find out as much about you as I can."

"Okay, but take whatever my mother tells you with *a grain of sand,* as you Americans say."

"It's with a grain of *salt,* my learned friend, *salt* not *sand,* though perhaps since we *are* in the Middle East, a grain of *sand* is a more appropriate reference."

There were three low stools already arranged in a circle around a small table. It was in a sunny part of the courtyard and the smell of jasmine hung heavily in the air. An array of geraniums in vibrant reds and pinks spilled out of the cans arranged against the top of the cement wall. In a rustic way the spot was really quite lovely.

Mohammad and Issa left almost immediately. Sarah sat on one of the low stools, Nijmeh opposite her, and waited while Hasna fixed the tea. When Hasna had placed the tray of tea on the low table, Sarah began.

She cleared her throat and turning to Hasna said, "Please tell your mother how really grateful I am for her hospitality, especially with her agreeing to talk with me this afternoon." She waited while Hasna translated what she had said. "I know that it hasn't been easy for her, for all of you for that matter, to have Mohammad insist that you meet me." Again she waited as Hasna put her words into Arabic.

Nijmeh kept looking from Hasna to Sarah. "Mohammad had told me that his mother had already chosen a bride for him, and that she had hoped that he would get married this summer." Hasna looked at Sarah and started to protest. "Please, tell your mother what I said." Hasna did. "I know I am not the woman you would have chosen for him."

Nijmeh listened, this time she heard what Hasna said, but she only looked at Sarah. "I know that Mohammad has no idea who that woman is, but I think I do." Sarah paused, angry with the tears she felt pooling in her eyes. "The woman I think you have chosen is Yasmeen. And if it isn't, *it should be!*" Sarah's lips trembled as she said it. "I think Yasmeen would be *perfect* for Mohammad. I can see them being very happy together." Hasna translated the words and then put her hands in her lap. She looked thoughtfully at her mother; she didn't look at Sarah.

Nijmeh finally spoke. She said in Arabic to Hasna, "Translate exactly what I say, *bintee,* word-for-word. Do not interrupt or add your own opinion." Hasna only looked at her mother and nodded.

"Yes, you are right, my daughter. Yasmeen *is* the girl that I had thought would make Mohammad a good wife." She waited for Hasna to tell Sarah what she had said. "You are also right, my daughter, that neither Mohammad, nor Im Najib, nor Yasmeen knows anything about it." She paused to give time for Hasna to translate.

"Yasmeen is a wonderful girl, as you have seen for yourself. She has many qualities that would make her an ideal wife for Mohammad."

Hasna was about to interrupt, but Nijmeh shook her head and said, "Only translate, *bintee.*" She did.

"Mothers know their sons, and I thought I knew Mohammad and what would be best for him." She waited. "I *did not.* I have seen the way that you look at Mohammad and the way that he looks at you." She waited, looking only at Sarah's face. "I believe that Allah writes into our hearts the individuals we are meant to love." Again she waited. "I think that Allah has written Mohammad into your heart and you into his."

The tears that had pooled in Sarah's eyes were gently falling. Hasna was also wiping tears from her eyes. "Khalil has told me that he worried that *love is not enough.* Mohammad has told me that you, also, have wondered if *love is enough."* There was the pause as Hasna put Nijmeh's words into English. "My daughter, you must believe that *love **is** enough.* After seeing you and Mohammad together, I know it is. Yasmeen, with all her wonderful qualities, would not be *you.* And it is *you* that Mohammad loves."

Hasna translated, but did add her own opinion. "You see how wise my mother is!"

Nijmeh spread her arms wide and with her hands motioned for Sarah to come and hug her. Sarah did. Sarah sobbed on Nijmeh's shoulder. Nijmeh patted her back and said soothingly into her hair words that Sarah could not understand, but whose meaning she could *feel.* "You will make my son a wonderful wife, *bintee,* a wonderful wife."

Nijmeh looked at Hasna, "Tell her, *Yum'ma,* that she must dry her tears. We don't want Mohammad returning and finding her eyes swollen. He will think that I have beaten her," she laughed. Hasna translated and then she too went over and hugged Sarah.

Mohammad was shocked when he returned with Issa. There sitting on the stone tiles of the courtyard were his mother, his sister, *and* Sarah. They were sorting through lentils and laughing. Hasna looked up and said to him in Arabic, "I have been translating one of Sitteh Hasna's *when-I-was-a-girl-and-not-very-pretty* stories for Sarah. It is so funny to *hear* them in English. She turned to Sarah, "How is my English, Sarah? I translate pretty good, don't I?"

Sarah poked her arm and said, "I translate pretty *well*, not pretty *good*," she laughed and Hasna laughed with her.

"*Wain ku'nit enta, habeebee?* (Where have you been, my love?)" Sarah stumbled as she fractured the words. She looked at Nijmeh, "*Hada muz'boot?* (Is that right?)"

"*Muz'boot, bintee, muz'boot.*"

Sarah looked at Mohammad with a twinkle in her eye. "I have been practicing that phrase for over an hour. How did I do?" He just shook his head, but his smile literally reached from one ear to the other.

That evening he walked Sarah across the alley to Im Najib's. He paused in the empty alley before Im Najib's door. He took Sarah's hands in his. "What happened? I can't believe the change. It is like someone has lifted a dark cloak from around your shoulders."

"I just needed to talk over some *girl stuff* with your mother. She told me something about you that only a mother would know." Sarah laughed as she looked up and down the alley and gave Mohammad a quick kiss on the lips.

That evening, Mohammad sat with his mother and father and Issa. They were half watching the comic antics of the Lebanese comedian *Ghawar*. Out of the blue, Nijmeh said, "*Yum'ma*, your father and I think that you and Sarah should proceed with *katb el-kitab* (the signing of the marriage contract) before she returns to America. Mohammad literally dropped the glass of tea he was holding.

"You want us to become officially *engaged*?"

"Of course, isn't that why you have brought her to meet us? Hasna helped me call Khalil and Mansur this evening, and they are in agreement, even Khalil."

Issa had brought a handle-less broom and dustpan and was in the process of sweeping up Mohammad's broken tea glass. He looked up and grinned, "It *is* what you want, isn't it!"

 "Yes, of course, but..." Mohammad was stammering, "I don't know if it is what Sarah wants."

Nijmeh looked like an English cliché that Mohammad had once heard about *a cat that swallowed a canary.* "I think she will agree, *Yum'ma,* but you, of course, must ask her tomorrow."

"What *did* happen here this afternoon? Sarah is changed. You are changed. Did you cast some magic spell?"

Nijmeh smiled as she cracked some *bizer,* (watermelon seeds) with her teeth. "She asked me some questions about you. I gave her the answers that only a mother would know, but they happened to be just the answers she *needed* to hear."

Chapter 26

Mohammad's long eye lashes hardly dusted his cheeks all night. He couldn't *believe* that his parents, even Khalil, thought that he and Sarah should get *engaged! Katb el-kitab* in the Islamic world meant that they were *legally married,* not just engaged as the West looked at engagement. He couldn't *wait* to hear what Sarah thought.

Sarah, unlike Mohammad, had slept the sleep of the dead. She had been so tense and exhausted by her visit that she had hardly slept at all. But after her talk with Mohammad's mother, this wonderful feeling of *peace* had washed over her allowing her mind to finally be at rest.

That night she didn't *hear* the mosquitoes buzzing in her ear; that night she was not awakened by the loudspeaker calling the faithful to prayer; she didn't hear, at first, Yasmeen rapping on her door telling her that Mohammad was downstairs waiting for her.

She stretched, raising her arms high above her head, arching her toes. Throwing off the light blanket, she got up, went across the hall to wash, brush her teeth, and run a brush through her hair. Back in the room she rummaged in her suitcase and shook out an ankle-length skirt. She dressed and went down the stairs to see Mohammad. She couldn't believe how truly *happy* she felt.

As the two previous mornings, Mohammad was in casual conversation with Im Najib, and Yasmeen was not present. Mohammad looked up at her and beamed. "It's about time you got up! I have been enjoying coffee with *Khalti* Im Najib for over half an hour.

"I slept really well. I think it is the first *real* sleep I have had since I arrived," Sarah smiled.

"*Yallah, ya bintee,* come and have your coffee," Im Najib said pulling a low stool out for Sarah.

"*Shu'kran, Khalti,*" Sarah said. She looked at Mohammad and winked at his pleased expression that she was using an Arabic phrase.

When they finished their coffee, it was Sarah who took the tray into the kitchen saying, "I want to say good morning to Yasmeen before we go."

Sarah put the tray on the counter and hugged Yasmeen. Yasmeen smiled and hugged her back, "You seem so much better today. I am so glad."

"I feel better, thank you." Sarah said. "I am sure that Mohammad has our day planned. I must get going. I will see you later." Sarah kissed Yasmeen on both cheeks.

Once she and Mohammad were out in the alley, he couldn't wait to tell her his news. "Let's take a walk," he suggested. "I have something I want to discuss with you in private."

There weren't many people in the street. Mohammad had never really walked with her through the camp before, and Sarah was a little surprised that he had chosen to do so now. The shops were just beginning to open. As they passed the photo shop of Yasmeen's uncle, he was just pushing up the iron grate that covered his window.

He recognized Sarah, and of course knew Mohammad. He called them over. He pointed to the framed portrait of Sarah in his shop window. Mohammad looked, and then *looked again.* "It's a picture of *you!* You are dressed as a Palestinian bride!"

Sarah laughed. "It was Yasmeen's idea. She wanted me to try on her dress and to come to her uncle's to have my picture taken. She thought it would be a nice memento of my visit to Palestine. We did it that afternoon when you went to the mosque with your father and brother. Do you like it?"

"You are beautiful. You *almost* look Palestinian." Mohammad paused, "Though I am not so sure that I want others looking at your picture," he laughed.

"It was Yasmeen's uncle's suggestion. He thought it would be good for business. It *does* make people stop and look in his window."

"She *is* beautiful, *ibnee* (son). If I were you, I wouldn't let such a beauty get away," Yasmeen's uncle said in a good natured way to Mohammad in Arabic.

Mohammad smiled at him and responded in Arabic, "Perhaps I won't."

As they walked on Sarah asked, "What was that all about?"

"Oh, he was just commenting on how beautiful you were and advising me *not let you* get away. That's what I want to talk to you about. Mohammad automatically reached for Sarah's hand, then thought better of it.

"I don't know what you said to my mother yesterday, but when we were talking last night she suggested that you and I become engaged." Mohammad waited for Sarah's response.

"She said that she had called my brothers in Amman and that they also had agreed that we should proceed with *katb el-kitab* before you return to the States. Remember I told you about this. It is a formal contract that basically means we are *legally married* in the eyes of Islam."

"Your mother *and* brothers suggested this?"

"Yes, you don't have to convert. We would meet with the Imam of the mosque. The contract would be drawn up, signed by us, and witnessed. There would be a small family gathering. We would exchange wedding bands, which we would wear on our right hands until we were *actually* married."

Sarah looked at the excitement and eagerness and hope she saw in his eyes. "Are you asking me to *marry you?* Wouldn't you be happier with a nice, Palestinian bride?" she teased.

"I told you before that the only woman I am ever going to marry is *you!*"

"In that case, my Arab prince, *I accept!*"

It took some convincing to persuade the Imam to draw up a wedding contract. He was not comfortable with the idea that there were no male representatives from Sarah's family. He was not comfortable with the fact that Sarah was, for all he knew, an American tourist wanting to get married to an Arab. He looked at her passport and noted her age. He listened to what Mohammad said as to how he and the girl had known each other for over a year, and that her parents knew that they wanted to get married.

Mohammad also argued that she had come *specifically* to meet his family with the eventual intention of marrying him. The

Imam listened to what Abu Mansur had to say. He listened to the opinions of Abu Imad and Imad. Finally he was convinced, in spite of his *strong* reservations, because he knew and liked and respected Abu Mansur, Abu Imad and Imad, (who had agreed to act as proxy for Sarah's father).

The contract was drawn up. The Imam came to the house that evening. He first asked to meet with Sarah privately, but in the presence of Nijmeh. Hasna was also present to translate. He asked Sarah if she *had been forced to agree to the marriage or if she was marrying of her own free will.* Sarah affirmed that she was not being forced, and that she had made the decision of her own free will. The Imam was satisfied.

In the presence of Omar, Abu Imad, Imad, Issa, Nijmeh and Hasna, he gave a short message directed to Mohammad and Sarah on the *duties* and *responsibilities* of a husband and wife in a marriage. He asked Mohammad if he understood. Mohammad nodded. The Imam then asked Sarah, through Hasna, if she had understood. Sarah nodded.

The Imam then read the contract and asked Mohammad and Sarah to sign. Then he asked Imad to sign as proxy for Sarah's father. Issa and Abu Imad also signed as witnesses; Omar made his mark.

The *fatiha* (the opening prayer from the Quran) was said to conclude the simple ceremony. Sarah watched the men with their outstretched hands raised in prayer. She watched them as they concluded the prayer and wiped their hands over their faces. There was a simple, touching beauty about it, she thought.

Mohammad slipped a simple silver band onto Sarah's right ring finger. She slipped a matching silver band onto

Mohammad's right ring finger. Mohammad kissed her on both cheeks.

The Imam smiled and said, *Ma'bruk inshallah bit'hen'new* (Congratulations, God willing they will be happy and blessed). Nijmeh and Hasna served a fruit drink to the guests.

There still needed to be the traditional wedding party, but for all practical purpose they were already husband and wife! Sarah found it an interesting, though puzzling, concept. She was legally married to Mohammad, but she would stay in one house and he in another until the traditional wedding celebration had taken place. *It certainly wouldn't have been that way in America,* she thought.

Two days after the signing of the contract, Issa approached his mother. "*Yum'ma,* there is something I want to ask you."

"What is it, *Yum'ma?* "

"*Yum'ma,* now that Mohammad is married. I wonder..." Issa hesitated as he organized the words. "I would like to marry Yasmeen." He had rushed it, but he finally got the words out.

Nijmeh was so stunned that she had to sit down. "You want me to go and ask for Yasmeen's hand for *you, Yum'ma?*"

"Yes. Ever since I saw her that day when I took the *jibneh* over, I have thought of nothing else. I kept quiet as I knew that you had chosen her for Mohammad. But now that Mohammad is engaged, I can tell you that *I would like to marry Yasmeen.*"

Nijmeh smiled recalling a conversation that Omar must have had with Sitteh Hasna over forty years ago: *I have seen...I want to marry.* She thought to herself: *he is old enough to get married; Yasmeen would make a wonderful daughter-in-law, and better she come to us than go to some other household; there is ample room for them to live here.* Finally she said to Issa, "I will speak to your father and brothers."

Within a matter of *two days* it had been settled. It had been mind-boggling to Sarah to realize that everything had been decided so quickly. Khalil and Mansur had readily agreed to Nijmeh's suggestion. They offered to send money to pay for the gold to be purchased for the bride and to pay for the wedding itself.

Nijmeh first approached Im Najib, and then went with her to see Yasmeen's mother. (Im Najib and her daughter had secretly *hoped* that Nijmeh would ask for Yasmeen's hand for one of her sons.) Yasmeen's mother had then talked with Yasmeen. Yasmeen was happy at the prospect. She too had *seen* Issa when he had brought the *jibneh* to her grandmother's. She liked what she had seen, and she liked what she knew about him and his family.

Omar, Imad, Mohammad and Issa went to officially ask for Yasmeen's hand from her father and uncles. Yasmeen and Issa were allowed to sit alone together for an hour. At the end of the hour, Yasmeen's mother asked her if she would be willing to marry Issa. Her mother took Yasmeen's reply to her husband. Of course, it had all been a matter of formality. Both parties already *knew* before they had come that the proposal would be accepted.

Her father and uncles smiled at the delegation that had come. "*Elf mab'ruk* (a thousand congratulations). We are honored to give our daughter to your son."

That evening, Yasmeen came into Sarah's bedroom. She sat on the pallet on the floor and hugged Sarah. "Now we are truly sisters!" she beamed.

Sarah and Mohammad had specifically gone to the post office in East Jerusalem to make a collect call to her parents. The international phone service to the West Bank had been cut. One was still able to call Amman but not Europe or the US. Sarah wanted to inform her parents about the engagement. She was going to wait until she saw them to tell them that *an engagement* in Islam was *really marriage.*

They had figured the time difference; if they called at 2 in the afternoon, it would be about 7 in the morning in Iowa. It had seemed to take quite a while to connect. Just when Sarah had about given up hope, she heard her mother on the line being asked by the operator if she would accept a call from a *Sarah Goldman.*

As soon as her mother got on the line, her first words were, "Sarah, are you alright? Where are you?"

"I'm fine, Mom. I am in Jerusalem. We have to call from a pay phone as there is no long distance service to the States at the house. How are you?"

"We're fine and anxiously awaiting your return. I hope the vacation is going well."

"That's the reason I am calling. Mom, Mohammad and I got engaged!"

There was a pause on the other end. Sarah, for a moment, thought that she had been disconnected. "Mom? Mom? Are you there?"

"Yes, dear, I'm here. I am frankly at a loss for words. I thought you were going in order to meet Mohammad's family. I had no idea that you were going to get engaged! This is rather *sudden,* isn't it?"

"It just seemed to happen."

"When are you planning to get married?" Her mother asked.

"We'll talk about that when I see you. I was just so excited about our news that I couldn't wait to tell you!"

"Don't you think you should have waited a bit? It just seems a bit *rushed* to me?" She paused, waiting for some response from Sarah.

"I should be home in about ten days. I *want* you and dad to be happy for us, Mom. *Please* be happy for us." Sarah waited for her mother to speak.

Finally Sarah said, "I can't wait to see you and dad. Give him my love. I love you."

It sounded as though the line had gone dead. Finally, there was her mother's voice at the other end, "We love you too, dear. Good-bye."

"How did your mom take it?" Mohammad asked.

"It came as a shock to her. She didn't expect us to get engaged *ten days* after we had just seen her and Dad."

Mohammad held Sarah's hand as they left the post office. He felt comfortable holding her hand, as they were now officially betrothed. There were a lot of Israeli couples walking hand-in-hand in the street. It felt *so right, so natural.* As soon as they got to the bottom of the hill and were in Arab Jerusalem,

Mohammad smiled, and gave Sarah's hand a squeeze before he released it.

"When we are back in Purdue," Mohammad grinned, "I wonder if we should think about going to the courthouse and getting an American wedding license as well."

"Isn't the document we signed legal in the States?" Sarah asked.

"Yes, it *is* a recognized legal marriage in the States as it is a contract which we both have signed. There is sometimes a problem with a student visa if the student marries abroad. It is probably better to get an American marriage license as well. "Besides," Mohammad grinned, "I *like* the idea of marrying you *twice!* We will be tied together so strongly that nothing will be able to untangle the knot."

Chapter 27

Sarah had expected the West Bank to be *different*. She had anticipated that there would be demonstrations, road blocks, and curfews. The two weeks she had been in the camp had been calm. She had seen occasional jeeps of soldiers, and of course there was the graffiti everywhere. She had seen a few, rather ragged Palestinian flags dangling from electric wires, but nothing of the violence she had read about, seen on TV in the States, or heard about in the stories that Mohammad told. Here she was sipping her morning coffee with Im Najib and Yasmeen, enjoying the sunny morning and the heavy scent of jasmine, waiting for Mohammad. They had planned another visit to Jerusalem.

The thoughts no sooner had formed in her head when she heard a vehicle racing down the street and mumbled shouts coming from a loud speaker. Yasmeen went to the door and peered out. "Curfew has been called," she said.

"Curfew?" Sarah asked.

"It is routine," Yasmeen replied resuming her seat on the low stool and picking up her coffee cup. "I have been surprised that we haven't had a day of curfew since you arrived. You must bring good luck," Yasmeen smiled. "Often it is called in the morning and then lifted in the afternoon. Sometimes it is called in the morning and not lifted for a couple of days."

"Aren't you concerned?" Sarah asked. *I wish Mohammad were here*, she thought.

"We have really gotten used to it. And frankly," Yasmeen laughed, "I am glad to be here with Sitteh and not at home having to entertain my siblings."

"It will be an opportunity for me to teach you how to make *ma'loubeh*. Mohammad will slip over later to see you, but in the meantime, you can have your first lesson in Arabic cooking. After all, you *now* have a *Palestinian husband* who is used to eating *ma'loubeh!*"

Sarah was a good cook. She had been raised on a farm and all farm women, *so her mother kept telling her*, knew how to: cook, bake, can, make jam, and sew their own clothes. She thought to herself: *I was all packed ready to leave, and now I am taking a lesson in Arabic cooking. Amazing.*

Yasmeen poked her shoulder. "What were you thinking about?"

"I was just thinking about how a few days ago I was packing and today I am going to learn how to make Palestinian dishes *just like my husband's mother makes, inshallah.*"

"*Inshallah*, huh? I see you have added another Arabic word to your vocabulary." Yasmeen teased. "In no time, you will speak Arabic better than me."

Sarah had gotten a pad and pen from her purse. She wrote down all the ingredients that went into making *ma'loubeh* and the order they went into the pan. It was a *one-dish* meal. The meat was browned with onions. Yasmeen had called the small chunks of beef *bird heads* because the chunks were about the size of a robin's head.

Separately, she had browned in hot olive oil broken pieces of cauliflower. She would take them out of the hot oil and place them in a strainer. On top of the browned meat and onions, which Yasmeen had seasoned with: salt, pepper, cinnamon, nutmeg, and allspice, she placed slices of potato and diced carrots.

When all the cauliflower pieces were browned and had drained, she placed them on top of the potatoes and carrots. Finally, she added three cups of washed rice. Over it all, she poured boiling water, just enough to cover the rice. She turned the flame on the primus very low and covered the pot.

"That's all there is to it," she told Sarah. "It is done when all the water has been absorbed. It is then allowed to set. We wrap the pot in a blanket to keep it hot until dinner. When it is served, we turn the pot upside down on a serving tray and add a garnish of browned pine nuts or almond slivers. It is delicious. Everyone loves *ma'loubeh.*"

There was a soft rap at the door. "That is probably Mohammad," Yasmeen said as she went to open the door.

"Are you going to sit with us today?" Sarah asked.

"Of course, now that I am going to marry his brother, Issa, it is okay for me to sit with him. We are practically brother and sister now. Before it would not have been proper, as he was unmarried and I had not been spoken for. Now we are, technically, related."

Sarah impulsively hugged her. "I am so glad! It made *no sense* to me at all that you always had to leave the room when Mohammad came over."

Mohammad kissed Sarah on both cheeks. "You are getting to experience your first curfew. I was worried that you might be scared."

"I probably would have been a little uneasy if it weren't for Yasmeen" Sarah said trying to minimize her real fear. "She has assured me that it is perfectly normal and has even used the *forced togetherness* to give me a lesson in Arabic cooking." Sarah's eyes twinkled as she told Mohammad, "I think I will be able to make *ma'loubeh* for you when we are back at Purdue." As she took his arm she whispered, "I *am* so glad you are here! I *was* a little uneasy."

"Maybe I should give Yasmeen a list of *all* my favorite dishes, so if this curfew goes on for a few days, you can compile your own book of recipes and she can give you first-hand instruction," Mohammad laughed. "Now if she can also show you how to bake Arabic bread and do Palestinian cross-stitch, I think your three weeks in Palestine will have been *very well spent.*"

"And, what am *I* getting out of this deal?" Sarah joked.

"Why, that should be *obvious, habeeptee. You* have acquired a handsome, sophisticated, good-natured *husband – me!*" Mohammad bowed. "Not *every* farm girl from Iowa is able to capture the heart of a handsome Arab sheikh*!* Ah, if I only had a camel to whisk you away to my tent in the desert, then I would *demonstrate* how richly blessed you truly are."

By this time, both Sarah and Yasmeen were laughing. "Let me make some tea," Yasmeen said. "After a *story* like that, we need something to drink."

Mohammad spent most of the day with Sarah; Yasmeen had persuaded him to stay for lunch to sample the *ma'loubeh* that Sarah had helped make. He gave the proper *compliments* and joked that he thought *he could taste the difference – that it was obvious an Iowa farm girl had observed the procedure.*

After lunch they snuck across the alley to have coffee with Omar, Nijmeh and Issa. Then Issa went back with them so the three of them could visit with Yasmeen and Im Najib. (Abu Najib had used the pretext of Sarah's staying with them to go and stay with his daughter, Yasmeen's mother. He had said that he wanted time to enjoy his other grandchildren, and he didn't want to be the only cock in the hen house.)

Sarah had brought up further questions she had about the *katb el-Kitab.* The words had been read to her before she signed, but she wasn't clear how it differed from a marriage license – a permission to marry. Mohammad was saying they were legally married, so it was really a marriage certificate, not a license.

"The contract is a marriage license *and* the marriage certificate. It is both a religious and governmental document. Its main purpose is to allow the man and woman to *go out alone together-* to get to know each other. They aren't *dating,* as they are already married, though they don't yet live together. No one can object to them sitting alone or going out together without a chaperone, as they are already husband and wife. It is really a way of protecting a girl's honor." Mohammad explained it a couple different ways, repeating himself somewhat, in order to try and show how the contract was *both* a license *and* a certificate.

"The man commits himself to the woman in front of his family and hers. The contract is binding. In some contracts, financial terms are stated. In ours, as you heard, money was not mentioned."

"Financial terms?" Sarah asked, puzzled.

"For example, the weddings are all paid for by the groom and his family, unlike in the States where the bride's family pays for the wedding. Here, the bride pays nothing. It may be written in the contract that the groom agrees to pay, for example, $1500 to the bride to buy clothes for the wedding and gold. It may also be stated that he will pay a certain amount of money for furniture for the house. The contract usually lists an amount he will pay to the bride if there is a divorce. This is all decided by the *bride's* family. Her father will make certain demands on her behalf. This is especially true if the bride is not related to the groom. Her father wants to look out for her interests if she is marrying a stranger."

"Sometimes it is a matter of *show*. The bride's family will ask for a large amount of money so they can tell the neighbors *'we demanded so much for our daughter'*, and the groom's father will be exceptionally generous so he can tell the neighbors, *'money is no object to us, we gave more than they asked,'*" Issa added.

"In the past women had few rights and were uneducated. They had almost no money that was their own. There was no insurance. They were completely dependent on the males in their lives. Financial terms were written into the contract to give *her* some financial security. At the time, it was quite a progressive idea. Women in Europe were often just chattel, while women in the East had this gift of gold and money that was legally theirs; their husbands couldn't touch it," Mohammad explained.

"Why were there no financial terms in the contract I signed?" Sarah questioned. "Is it because I am American? It sounds like I am getting *no* gold, *no* clothing allowance, *no* money for furniture; and if you divorce me, all I get is a handshake." Sarah tried not to sound upset.

Mohammad and Issa both laughed. "There were no financial stipulations in our contract. Not because you are American, *habeeptee.* Everything I have is yours." Mohammad smiled. "Khalil and Mansur were – *are* - perfectly willing to supply any funds we need. They are planning to subsidize our expenses at Purdue until we are employed. They even suggested that you buy gold. But since you never wear any jewelry, I didn't see the need to write an amount for gold in the contract. We aren't having a wedding celebration here, so there is no need to buy a trousseau. We still have another year of university and will be living in Purdue, so no need for a furniture allowance. And, I *never* plan to *divorce* you, so no need for money to be set aside for an eventuality that will never happen."

"I see you had this all figured out, oh *Arab sheikh.* How fortunate for you that I signed the contract *before* I learned that I could have made some money on the deal. What if by some strange, unforeseen twist of fate, *I* decide to *divorce* you?"

"There *is* that *handshake...*" Mohammad grinned. "Though, seriously, everything I have or will have is yours. If you ever wanted to divorce me, you could have everything. I wouldn't need it, for without you I wouldn't want to live."

Sarah heard sincerity in his tone and was touched. She reached over and kissed him on the cheek. "I am *never* going to divorce you. You are stuck with me for life. Though, it *does* seem as though you got a really *good* deal financially," she teased.

Sarah turned to Yasmeen and smiling said, "There is a lesson to be learned here, Yasmeen. Be sure that *you* have written into your contract an amount for gold and trousseau; an amount for furniture, and a *substantial sum* in case of divorce!"

The curfew was lifted the following morning. Again a jeep sped down the street, the soldier mumbling into the loudspeaker. Yasmeen had to listen carefully, as the accented Arabic could have been: *movement is permitted,* or *movement is forbidden.* The Arabic words for *permitted* and *forbidden* sounded quite similar when mumbled by a non-Arabic speaker through a bullhorn.

Issa and Yasmeen had hoped to have their wedding before Sarah went back to the States. But it didn't look as though that would be possible. There was just not enough time. The Imam had come to Yasmeen's home perform the official *katb el-kitab* (writing of the document/book). The contract was drawn up and signed (She had joked with Sarah later that she had made certain that the appropriate, though modest, financial obligations had been listed.) She was now legally married to Issa.

Nijmeh and Omar had suggested that since Sarah was only with them for another few days, that they have a combined engagement party for *both* couples. The party would naturally be low-key because of the *intifada* (the uprising) out of respect for those affected by the almost daily arrests, injuries and deaths around the country, but it would be a chance to celebrate and to announce to the neighbors the two unions.

It sounded like a good plan.

That night as Mohammad lay on his pallet, thinking of how it had all worked out even better than he had hoped, he was suddenly hit with an *alternate* thought: *what if the combined party was the engagement party for Issa and Yasmeen, and the* **wedding** *for him and Sarah! It would be the same guests; his parents and two of his siblings would be present; they had* *already signed the contract; all they lacked was the actual* **public** *ceremony.* He could hardly wait for morning when he could present the idea to Sarah and his parents.

Chapter 28

Mohammad wanted to talk over his brainstorm with Sarah *before* he talked to his parents. He *knew* she would want her parents present at her wedding. He *knew* she probably had dreamed of a white wedding dress and a church wedding. She was leaving within a few days, and it probably was a bit too much to spring on her at the last minute. *If* she did go along with the idea, they would only be together two nights before she had to leave for the States – not much of a honeymoon.

He had thought a perfect place for them to discuss his idea privately would be over lunch at the American Colony in Jerusalem. The garden at the Colony was quite picturesque, and he thought it would provide *just the right atmosphere.*

"I have a surprise for you, Sarah," he told her when he picked her up. "I'm taking you out to lunch in Jerusalem today. I'm not going to tell you where. I have something really special I want to get your opinion on. That is also part of the surprise."

On the *service* ride into Jerusalem, Sarah kept trying to get him to tell her *where* they were going and *what* he wanted to talk with her about. He wouldn't budge. He just smiled and said, "You'll see all in good time."

They got out of the *service* in front of the American Colony.

"Isn't this a bit too expensive, Mohammad? I wanted to have lunch here the afternoon I arrived while I was waiting for you. I looked at the prices, and the only thing on the menu I could afford was *coffee!*" she joked." It was more expensive than *Starbuck's, McDonald's, Long John Silver's* and *The Chinese*

Dragon combined. It is really a bit out of our league. What you pay for lunch here, we could eat out every night for two weeks at Purdue."

"I told you it was a surprise. It is just the *right* place for what I wish to talk to you about," Mohammad grinned.

They were seated at a round table for two in the lovely garden. The waiter gave them menus and said he would be back in a few minutes to take their orders.

"Order whatever you want. I think I am going to have the mixed-grill plate." Mohammad said.

Sarah decided to order the mixed grill platter as well. When the waiter returned Mohammad gave them their order and also requested a selection of Arabic salads and dips along with a dish of *kubbeh, sambousik, and sfeeha* as appetizers.

The waiter in no time had spread the appetizers before them; filled their water glasses, and had asked if they wished American coffee with their meal. They didn't.

"So, what did you want to discuss with me that needed this ambience?" Sarah asked.

"What does *ambience* mean?"

"It means *atmosphere, setting, surrounding,*" Sarah smiled.

"I just want to run this by you to see what you think. You know that my parents have suggested that we have a combined engagement party for the neighbors and family before you leave. We have all agreed that it is a good idea," Mohammad said.

Sarah nodded and smiled, waiting for him to go on.

"As I lay awake unable to sleep last night, I had a *brain storm*. What would you think if it was an engagement party for Issa and Yasmeen and a *wedding* party for you and me?"

Mohammad studied Sarah's face.

"You need to give me some time to think about this. I had always assumed that I would have a *church* wedding, wear a white wedding dress with a long train, be given away by my father; all those things that girls dream about when they are little playing with *Barbie* and *Ken.*"

"I know." Mohammad said, "That's why I want your opinion. This ceremony is really just a *reception* of sorts. Lots of weddings in the camp are very simple because of the *intifada*. Many brides choose *not* to wear a white wedding dress; the family chooses *not* to rent a hall or have a banquet; everything is really low-key. But it would mean that we could begin *living together as husband and wife.*"

"I would really like that, but we would be together only a couple of nights before I had to return to the States. It would probably be *harder* actually married to you and leaving, than leaving when we are just *engaged*. Does that make sense?"

"Of course it *makes sense*. I have thought about that, too. It is just, *we are here; we are married; my parents and two of my siblings and their families would be present;* and I want desperately to be *married to you!*"

"It seems an awful lot to spring on my parents. *Hi, Mom and Dad. I had a great three weeks. Oh, by the way, Mohammad and I got married.* It *doesn't* sound like something I would do. The Sarah they know *is* strong-willed, independent, with a mind of her own. They know that once I have made up my mind there is no changing it; *that's the way they raised me.*"

She smiled. "I suppose I was a difficult child to rear, being as willful and as stubborn as I am. They would expect *me* to choose the man I married. They *hoped* I would naturally choose someone like Sam, but they knew it was always going to be *my* choice. But to travel to the Middle East on a three-week trip and to get married while there? That *doesn't* sound like me."

"We *could* also plan a wedding reception at your home in Iowa. It would be a chance for you and your family to invite your relatives and friends. You could even wear a white dress, and we could have a justice of the peace perform a civil ceremony at the reception. It wouldn't be a church wedding. I feel sorry about that. You realize a church official *couldn't* marry us because I am Moslem, but to have a civil ceremony would be a good idea. It is a good idea to be legally wed in both countries. When a Palestinian marries an American in the States, when they come back to the Old Country they have to have the document translated into Arabic and stamped by the religious court. I *know* it doesn't make much sense."

Sarah smiled. "Of course, I *realize* that. I have no problem with a civil ceremony. In fact, I rather like the idea of having a wedding reception at the farm. I don't need to wear a white wedding dress or have a church wedding. That was a little girl's fantasy, I am a grown woman now, and I am already *married* to the man I love." Sarah reached over and put her hand in Mohammad's. "I *would* like to have some kind of ceremony for my parents' sake. I know we don't really need to get married again, but I think they would feel better about the marriage if they actually *saw* a justice of the peace *marry* us. I don't think they would feel that a Moslem wedding was..." Sarah searched for the word, "*real*. I understand your reasons for the reception here being our wedding ceremony. Though it is still puzzling to me *why*, since we are legally married, we need the ceremony before we can live together as man and wife."

"Tradition," Mohammad said, "It is purely tradition. There *has* to be a public ceremony for the *sake of the neighbors.* If there isn't this *public announcement* of our union, the neighbors would wonder why?" Mohammad smiled, "Even in the West, there are certain social traditions that are followed – some of which really make no sense at all."

Sarah smiled and gave her consent. "I bow to your reasoning, though I do think you have an ulterior motive, my *Arab sheikh;* you are thinking about that camel and tent in the desert where you can *impress* me with how much you love me."

Mohammad grinned. "Ah, yes, *there is that!"* He placed a small piece of grilled lamb into his mouth. "I think you will be quite *impressed!"*

"I *do* have one condition though," Sarah said dipping a bit of bread in the hot Turkish salad. "When we have finished lunch, I want you to take me to the Old City to find a *used,* traditionally embroidered, Palestinian dress that I can wear for my *wedding.* I don't want something new. I want something that has been worn before and has *a bit of history* to it."

"You have a deal!"

When they had gone to visit the Holy Sites the first week Sarah was there, she had noticed the numerous shops selling old traditional Palestinian dresses. She couldn't avoid seeing them. They hung on suspended rods above dozens of shops, gently dancing in the breeze, sometimes brushing against the heads of tourists passing in the street.

Thankfully, the Old City shops were small and close together. One twisted street had over twenty small shops on it; all were selling versions of the same thing. They must have glanced into ten shops. Nothing seemed to catch Sarah's eye. Finally, in the eleventh shop, though it seemed like the twentieth shop to Mohammad, Sarah explained to the shopkeeper *exactly* what she wanted. "I want something old, but in good condition. I want something that would have been worn for a wedding in the past."

The shopkeeper had showed her a variety of dresses, none of which caught her eye, when Sarah saw an exquisite dress hanging on the wall behind his head! It was made of variegated strips of velvet. The breast plate was not cross-stitch but couching – cords of orange, red, green and yellow silk secured to the fabric with gold thread. There were two panels of orange and green silk that ran the length of both sides of the skirt. The same couching was also on these pieces. The sleeves tapered down to points. The top of the sleeves had the same orange and green silk attached. The dress was breathtaking. It was a *real museum* piece, Sarah thought.

"That is *exactly* what I want," Sarah said pointing to the dress.

The shopkeeper smiled, looking fondly at the dress. "Unfortunately, that dress is not for sale. It is over forty years old. I bought it in 1948 from a refugee woman. I paid very little for it, certainly not what the dress was worth. I had just opened my shop, didn't have much business; money was very *dear* in those days, and many women were selling pieces like this in order to support their families. I felt badly that I couldn't pay the woman more."

"How much do you want for the dress?" Mohammad asked. "It reminds me of my mother's wedding dress."

"Oh, I *don't know* that I could ever sell it. I have had it on display for over forty years. There have been offers, but I just can't seem to part with it."

"How *much* would you take for it, *Ammie?* (uncle)

"I'm sorry, *Ammie,* the dress is not for sale. Perhaps I can interest you in another dress."

"Thank you, but no. After we have seen this dress, no other dress would seem right."

Mohammad and Sarah still lingered, not wanting to go, hoping the shopkeeper would change his mind.

"I can see how much you really want this dress. You seem like such a nice couple, but I really can't part with it. It has this almost mystical hold over me," he said looking lovingly at the dress.

"I can still see the face of the woman who sold it to me. She wasn't very old – perhaps fifteen or sixteen. She had a young child with her, a baby really, and was obviously pregnant. She was very beautiful. I was just a young man at the time." he chuckled. "She had said that her husband had not wanted her to part with the dress – it had been her wedding dress you see, but they needed the money. You see, she and her husband had lost their home and all their family in the massacre of Deir Yassin. Perhaps you have read about the massacre?"

The shopkeeper looked at Mohammad and saw tears in his eyes. "Are you not well!? I am sorry if I have said something to upset you."

Mohammad could hardly get the words out. "The woman you just described is my *mother."*

"*Your mother!* It can't be!"

"My mother used to tell the story about her wedding dress. It was one of the few things they carried out of Deir Yassin. She told how my father didn't want her to sell it, but that she had insisted as they needed the money so badly. My oldest brother would have been about eight months old and she was already pregnant with my sister, Hasna."

The shopkeeper, himself, was also close to tears. It was just a fantastic tale, but it *had to be true*. "Wait a moment, there is something else I must show you." He went into the back of the shop and came out with a Japanese wedding shawl. It had once been white, but had aged to a mellow off-white. The embroidered flowers were still bright red. The fringe was still heavy around it. "Your mother also brought in with the dress this shawl. I assume it must have been her wedding shawl. I am ashamed to remember; I gave her only half a dinar for it."

The shopkeeper folded the dress and shawl and wrapped them in brown paper. "Please return these to your mother. It seems only *right* that after forty years they be given to her son and his bride. *Subhan Allah;* how strange the workings of God. For forty years, I have refused to sell this dress – though I have had many offers. And today you walk into my shop, ask about a dress with a bit of history, and it is almost as though I was *lead* to tell you the story about this dress."

"Please, you *must allow* me to pay you for the dress," Mohammad said.

"I should say *not*. Allah has brought you to my shop. This is *His doing;* I could *never* accept money. Today I am only an instrument of Allah. Please, *ibnee,* (my son) take it. I am only returning to you what is rightfully yours. May the peace and blessing of Allah be upon you both."

Mohammad and Sarah were stunned. They couldn't believe what had just happened. Sarah had her wedding dress – the *same* dress that Nijmeh had worn when she married Omar.

"We must return this to your mother." Sarah said. "She will be shocked."

That evening, after they had had a light supper and were all sitting in the sitting room (even Yasmeen was there) watching an Egyptian film starring Omar Sharif and Fatin Hamama about the Deir Yassin massacre, Mohammad told them the story just as the shopkeeper had told it to them.

Mohammad looked over at his mother, and at his father, and at his brother, Issa, at Yasmeen, as he told the unbelievable tale. There was shocked disbelief in their faces, tears in their eyes.

"For over forty years the man refused to sell the dress and shawl." Sarah place the package in Mohammad's lap then watched him unwrap it. He spread out Nijmeh's beautiful wedding dress and head shawl.

"When he knew the dress was yours, *Yum'ma,* he refused to take any money for it. He said he had been entrusted by Allah to care for it, and now he was returning it to its rightful home."

Mohammad got up and placed the velvet mass in Nijmeh's lap. She stroked the soft fabric as her tears flowed. "I never thought I would ever see this dress again. I can still remember when my mother, sisters and your Sitteh Hasna, *Allah yer hum'him,* went to Bethlehem to buy it. I only wore it twice: once on my wedding day, and once when we had our picture taken." Nijmeh looked at the framed photo over the daybed.

"When we first came to live in the camp, and were still sleeping in tents, this used to be the mattress for Mansur. He slept in my wedding chest, you know. I can remember nursing him and thinking how *pretty* he looked wrapped up in this shawl. It was a lifetime ago." She paused to wipe the tears from her eyes.

"And now it is to be the wedding dress for my ninth child's bride! How fitting, *Subhan Allah.*"

Chapter 29

Nijmeh couldn't get over the return of her wedding *thob. It is a miracle,* she thought. It was hard to imagine that the shopkeeper had not sold the dress in all those years, but then she had heard of similar, unbelievable stories.

When she had worked in the city, the woman for whom she worked had told her a true story that had happened to the woman's aunt. Her aunt had to leave her home in a suburb of Jerusalem in 1948. Before leaving the house, she had put all of her gold and the family silver in a large glass jar used to store *jibneh* (cheese). Her husband had taken the jar and buried it in the backyard beneath an olive tree in the hopes of retrieving it when they returned. Their home was taken and they were not allowed to go back.

In 1967 when the borders were open between the West Bank and Israel, the woman went to see the house she had left. The house had been turned into a restaurant, as had the two houses on either side of it. The woman went in to have tea. She sat at a table in the back where there was a window overlooking the garden. The olive tree was still there.

Two days later, she returned late at night with an Arab taxi driver and a priest from the Latin Church. The restaurants were closed. There was no one in the streets. The woman had persuaded the taxi driver that she would pay him well to dig around the olive tree where her husband had buried the jar of valuables twenty years before.

The man dug. It didn't take him long to uncover a burlap-wrapped jar! He handed the jar to the woman, quickly filled in the hole, and they hastily returned to Ramallah.

The woman paid him handsomely for his night's work.

Accompanied by the priest, she took the burlap-wrapped jar into the house. On the kitchen table she carefully uncovered it. It was a miracle that the jar was not broken. It wasn't even cracked. She lifted out a linen bundle. Inside was the family silverware: knives, forks, dessert spoons, teaspoons, and serving spoons. Next she took out a cloth pouch; it was the kind of pouch that women put yogurt in to make *lebaneh*. She emptied the contents of the pouch onto the kitchen table. There were gold rings and bracelets, a pearl necklace, diamond earbobs, a ruby broach, and the diamond engagement ring her husband had given her. For twenty years the valuables had lay buried under the olive tree!

It had not been too hard for Nijmeh to believe that the shopkeeper had returned the dress and had refused to take any money for it. She thought *he must be a devout Moslem*. There was a belief taught in Islam that individuals were *entrusted* with certain things by God, that it was *haram* – a shame to receive financial benefit from something with which one had been entrusted. They would receive *spiritual* blessing, but to have taken money would have broken trust with God.

She also saw it as a blessing on the marriage of Mohammad and Sarah; proof that Allah had blessed their marriage by returning the dress to them. It was *written* that an American-Christian daughter-in-law would continue the *story of the dress.*

The combined party was scheduled for three days before Sarah was to leave. Friends and neighbors had been told by word-of-mouth that they were invited to the engagement of Issa and Yasmeen, and the wedding of Mohammad and Sarah.

The party was to be held in the reception rooms of the mosque, as Omar and Nijmeh's home was too small for such a gathering. The men would gather in the one room. They would be served soft drinks, sweets, and coffee. The women would gather in the larger hall where there would be dancing. It was in this hall that Issa and Yasmeen would sit at one raised table, and Mohammad and Sarah would sit at a second.

Half way through the ceremony, Issa and Mohammad would go into the men's room to shake hands with the men and receive congratulations. The male guests, if they wished, would slip an envelope of money into Mohammad's suit coat pocket as he was the bridegroom, and this was his wedding celebration. In the women's room a decorated donation box had been placed at the entrance where women guests could drop a small money gift for the bride and groom if they wished.

For the celebration Yasmeen would wear her beautiful embroidered dress. The dress in which Sarah had had her picture taken. Sarah would wear Nijmeh's wedding *thob* and Japanese shawl. Nijmeh had bought a meter (yard) of Damascus silk and made a belt for Sarah to wear. Both women would be stunning.

The day before the wedding Yasmeen had instructed Sarah in Arabic dancing. She had put a tape of Arabic wedding music in the cassette player and shown her how to move her hands and hips and feet. She had joked with Sarah that at no time was she actually to *touch* Mohammad, unless he grasped her hands above their heads and moved with her in a circle, moving their clasped hands back and forth as they danced. She had also told her that she would be *expected* to dance alone in a circle surrounded by dancing and clapping women who would yodel good wishes to the newlyweds. *It will be fun,* she said.

As Sarah slipped the beautiful velvet *thob* over her head and smoothed the folds of the skirt, she thought: *tonight I will be a bride; tonight I will actually be a wife.* It sent shivers down her spine to think of it. She found herself trembling. It was suppose to be the happiest day of her life. Yet, she was a little apprehensive, a little scared; she wished her parents were present.

There was a soft knock on the bedroom door, "Sarah, it is Yasmeen, may I come in?"

"Yes, please do."

Yasmeen looked breath-taking in her embroidered dress. "You look like an exotic Bedouin beauty," Sarah said, kissing her on both cheeks. "I don't quite know how to tie this belt," she said, handing the wide silk belt to Yasmeen.

Yasmeen wound it around Sarah's waist; tied the long ties and tucked them beneath the silk at the back so they could not be seen. She held Sarah's hands out and turned her around so she could get a good look at her. "You are beautiful."

Yasmeen picked the Japanese shawl off the pallet and draped it over Sarah's head. "When you get up to dance, you can take the shawl off so it doesn't keep slipping off your head," she said.

Im Najib called up the stairs, "Come, my daughters, your bridegrooms are here."

Sarah and Yasmeen walked down the stairs side-by-side. In the courtyard below waited Mohammad and Issa; they looked handsome in their dark blue suits. Nijmeh and Hasna were also there as were Yasmeen's mother and aunts. As soon as they saw the brides the women chanted wedding blessings, waved colorful handkerchiefs in their hands and did their *Ah'ee's* raising a hand to their opened mouths as they moved their tongues back and forth and ululated in joy.

Sarah put her arm through Mohammad's; *how handsome he is,* she thought. She could feel the strength of his arm as she rested her trembling hand on his jacket sleeve. Yasmeen put her arm through Issa's. The four of them walked the short distance to the mosque as the women from the family walked behind them clapping and chanting and ululating.

Sarah almost felt like she was in a foreign film. It felt so strange to her. It didn't seem right that everyone around her was speaking Arabic at *her* wedding. She *wanted* to marry Mohammad- there was certainly no *doubt* about that, but this wasn't how she imagined her wedding would be.

In the women's reception hall there was a large raised platform. Side-by-side on the dais two small tables, two chairs behind each, had been placed. Mohammad and Sarah sat behind the one table, Issa and Yasmeen behind the other.

The room soon filled with women and girls. *It is like a flower garden,* Sarah thought, to see all the colorful embroidered dresses that some of the women wore. A boombox played Arabic music tapes. The women got up to dance, moving back and forth; their feet shuffling to the beat of the music. Sarah couldn't help but feel that she was an *observer,* that this wasn't really *her* wedding.

Nijmeh, Hasna, and Ayesha, as they were the closest female relatives of the grooms, were at the center of the dancing. Hasna and Ayesha came and got Sarah and Yasmeen to dance with them. The women guests formed a circle around Nijmeh and her daughters-n-law as the three of them danced together. Sarah felt awkward as she tried to mimic the shuffling steps of the women. She wished she were dancing with *Mohammad*, not with these *women* whom she barely knew.

Into the circle Hasna and Ayesha stepped, joining hands with Yasmeen and Sarah and Nijmeh. The linking of their hands was symbolic of the tie that now bound these women together; a mother and her *daughters*. Sarah understood the symbolism; it had been one of the things that Yasmeen had explained to her; yet part of her felt that she was wearing a costume; merely an actor in a play.

The circle of clapping, dancing women got larger as more and more women and girls joined the circle. Nijmeh went to the dais and pulled her two sons down. They too joined the inner circle, each one dancing with his bride; shuffling feet, swaying hips, hands waving above their heads.

Mohammad was grinning broadly. He was happy, in fact, he *felt over the moon*, to quote a cliché he had once heard. Every time his eyes met Sarah's, she could see the *joy* – the *passion!*

Nijmeh went to each couple, and joining her hands with theirs, raised them above their heads and danced in a circle with each. Again symbolic of how these *two* were linked to her: she the mother; they her children.

Omar, along with Imad and his seven sons, came into the women's hall. As soon as they entered the hall, Yasmeen took Sarah's hand and they returned to the dais. Sarah felt strange to be excluded. Again she felt like an *outsider* not a *participant*.

Yasmeen had told her that weddings were very gender-oriented; that it really was the *groom's* wedding. Sarah had been puzzled by Yasmeen's explanation and frankly a little unhappy about it.

As his grown nephews entered the circle, Issa bent down so they could place Mohammad on his shoulders! Mohammad was the *bridegroom;* this was *his* wedding and his brother must show him honor.

Issa smiled and joked, sweating as he moved about the circle dancing with Mohammad balanced on his shoulders. Their nephews Saleem and Sami kept their hands raised ready to balance Mohammad on Issa's shoulders if he should start to fall.

Mohammad wrapped his legs under Issa's arms. He raised his own hands above his head and began to snap his fingers to the rhythm of the music. He grinned from ear-to-ear, the sweat beading on his forehead and stinging his eyes. His married nephew, Saleem, noticing the sweat dripping off Mohammad's chin, shouted above the clapping, loud enough for Mohammad to hear, "The *real sweating* comes tonight, *Khali* (uncle)," he grinned.

Nijmeh, Hasna, and Ayesha joined the men of their family and also danced around the groom.

Sarah kept whispering to Yasmeen that it was like *nothing* she had ever seen before. *American weddings in Iowa are quite tame compared to this,* she sighed, *and more romantic!*

After fifteen minutes or so, the boys helped Mohammad down from Issa's shoulders, kissed him on both cheeks, congratulated him, and with the other male members of the family left the hall.

The dancing continued until about nine o'clock. Mohammad and Issa had gone into the men's hall to shake hands with the men and receive their congratulations. A few of the male guests had slipped envelopes into Mohammad's suit pocket.

Sarah had sat, *unsmiling,* next to Yasmeen. Yasmeen had warned her about *smiling.* She had explained that if Sarah smiled people would think she was *too eager* to get married. When Sarah had commented that Mohammad was grinning the entire time, Yasmeen said, "Of course. He is *expected* to smile; he is *expected* to appear eager – to be anticipating tonight when he will be *powerful* and prove he is a man. For him it is the *night of the entrance* – I think that is how it would be translated."

It seemed somehow *deceptive* to Sarah. *She* was happy to be marrying Mohammad, and she would have liked to have shown that – at least by smiling. She didn't want to *appear* sad when she *wasn't* sad, though she could *understand* how brides in the past, *marrying complete strangers,* would have been sad – probably terrified. And as far as it being *the night of the entrance* – she would probably have been amused if she hadn't found the phrase crude.

As the party was winding down, the female guests came up to congratulate Sarah and Mohammad; many standing beside them as the photographer, Yasmeen's uncle, snapped a photo. He took photos of everyone it seemed: Sarah and Mohammad with Issa and Yasmeen; Sarah and Mohammad with Im and Abu Najib; Sarah and Mohammad with Imad and Hasna and their sevens sons; Sarah and Mohammad with Saleem and Ayesha and their baby; Sarah and Mohammad with Yasmeen's mother and father and siblings. He had, *thankfully,* Sarah thought, *even* taken a few photos of just Sarah and

Mohammad in their wedding finery. *After all it was their wedding!*

In one photo she was facing Mohammad; his hands were around her waist; hers were resting on his chest. After the flash went off, Mohammad smiled down at her and whispered, "You can't imagine how happy I am! You are now *really* my wife!" Sarah could almost picture a photo of her in Nijmeh's wedding dress framed behind the daybed in Nijmeh's sitting room.

All the guests had gone except for Mohammad's family. The photographer posed them together for a family photo. Mohammad and Sarah were at the center. Next to her was Nijmeh, Omar stood next to Mohammad; Issa stood at his father's right; Hasna to her mother's left. The photographer took several shots.

When he was finished with them, Nijmeh turned to Sarah and gathered her into her arms. Sarah couldn't understand the words, but she could *understand* the love. When she looked into her mother-in-law's eyes, she saw that they were moist with unshed tears. Nijmeh smiled and hugged Sarah again. Sarah began to have a warm feeling inside; she began to feel that this really had been *her* wedding too.

When Mohammad and Sarah came out of the hall there was a taxi waiting. Mohammad bent down and kissed her. "You can't imagine how truly *blessed* I feel. How fortunate I am that you consented to be my wife. I must have really done something extraordinary for Allah to have rewarded me with you." Mohammad opened the door and smiled at Sarah. "I have a surprise for you, *habeeptee.*"

Before Sarah got into the backseat, Yasmeen came up to her and gave her a warm embrace. As she hugged her she whispered into her ear, "I am so glad that we are truly sisters now. You are a beautiful bride. This has been like a romance that one sees in films," she laughed.

Sarah slid across the backseat to give Mohammad room to slip in beside her. He reached over and kissed her. "I wanted our first night together to be special. I have booked a room at the American Colony for just this one night. Tomorrow, we will return as husband and wife to my parents' home."

"But we had talked about this. I thought we had agreed to spend our wedding night at your parents'. I need to pack *something* for tonight. I don't even have a change of clothes."

"That has all been taken care of. Yasmeen packed an overnight bag for you and put in it everything she thought you would want and need. It is already in the trunk of the car along with my overnight bag."

When they checked into the American Colony, it was obvious to the guests in the lobby that they were newlyweds. One American tourist with bleached blonde hair came up to Sarah and commented on her lovely dress.

"I know it must seem a bit forward to you, but I just have to tell you what a beautiful dress this is. You must be newlyweds," she gushed. "You have that look about you. You two look like you have stepped out of a storybook or off a movie screen." She patted Sarah's velvet sleeve. "My congratulations to you both; may you have many, many years of happiness."

Mohammad had reserved the *honeymoon* suite. It was spacious, a combination of modern and quaint.

"This room is lovely, Mohammad. I really had felt a little uncomfortable about spending our wedding night at your parents'. I am glad that you thought of this. Thank you."

Mohammad kissed her. "Why don't you get undressed," he whispered. "You'll find everything you need in the bag Yasmeen prepared.

Sarah took the overnight bag into the spacious bathroom. She removed the heavy velvet dress and hung it on the hanger that conveniently dangled from the hook on the bathroom door. She opened the overnight bag, and there she found a white satin nightdress that Yasmeen must have purchased for her. She stepped out of her slip and put on the satin nightdress. It slithered in silky softness around her. She ran a comb through her hair and took the small bottle of perfume she found in the cosmetic bag and put a dab behind each ear, and, as an afterthought, between her breasts. She opened the door and switched off the light.

A mixture of emotions moved through her mind and made her heart race: *excitement, anticipation, fear,* and thankfully *peace.* She thought of those nights in Purdue when she had lay in Mohammad's arms, wanting *more,* yet being *cautious, guarded;* her body yearning for intimacy; her mind telling her *not yet.*

As she gently pulled the bathroom door closed, she thought: *how right this all is. It is right that I be here in this quaint hotel, in this foreign city, six thousand miles from the farm; it is right because Mohammad is here and I am his wife.*

Mohammad was already in bed. There was only the soft glow of the lamp on the desk to illumine the room. Mohammad pulled the covers back and smiled. She slipped between the cool sheets and moved into his naked embrace.

Chapter 30

Morning had come too soon, so it seemed to Sarah. She was *pleasantly* exhausted. The wedding night had been all she had expected *and* more. Mohammad had been powerful, yet tender; aggressive, yet thoughtful. She wondered where he had *learned* to be such a good lover. She smiled to remember how *impressed* she had been!

She lay on her side; Mohammad was spooned against her. She felt the softness of his hairy chest against her back; the strength of the arm, corded with muscle beneath the black hair that was thrown protectively, yet *possessively,* across her. His soft breathing was warm against the nape of her neck.

As she stirred, his arm tightened around her. "Where do you think you're going?" He sleepily murmured.

"I need to use the bathroom." As she slipped out of his embrace, she spoke out loud, "Now where is my nightgown?"

Mohammad partially opened his eyes and looked through the heavy screen of long lashes. "You don't *need* your nightgown, *habeeptee.* I *prefer* you without, my little *hourieh."*

Sarah blushed.

"Use the restroom and then come back to bed. It is too early to get up." Mohammad said as he rolled over.

It was close to the two o'clock check out time before Mohammad and Sarah stirred from the room. They carried their overnight bags into the lobby and Mohammad paid the bill. They asked the desk clerk to phone for a taxi.

There was to be a family dinner at four in honor of the newlyweds and Issa and Yasmeen.

As the taxi drove toward Ramallah, Sarah and Mohammad felt blissful. Neither one knew, now that they had experienced this new intimacy, how they would bear to be separated for the entire summer.

Mohammad, holding Sarah's hand and sitting as close to her as possible, impulsively said: "I know we haven't discussed it, but I am going to buy a ticket and come to the States next week. I *can't* spend the entire summer away from you. Perhaps we can take a summer course. The apartment is paid for through the summer. We can, temporarily, make do with the cramped space while we look for a bigger flat." The words just spilled out of him; he had been struck by a moment of panic at the thought of being separated from Sarah even for a night, certainly not for an *entire summer!*

Sarah squeezed his hand and rested her head on his shoulder. "I *love the idea!* Everything has happened so fast. We didn't expect to get married this summer. We didn't even consider the *possibility*. And *now* we are, unbelievably, *married!* I don't want to be separated from you either. If I didn't already have a non-refundable return ticket, I would change it and wait with you so we could go together. Do change your ticket and come as soon as you can."

"The week apart will give you a chance to spend some time with your parents and *ease* them into the fact that they have an Arab son-in-law." Mohammad smiled. "You can discuss with them the idea of having a *wedding reception* for us, so they can announce our marriage to your family and friends."

222

"I was sorry that Khalil, Mansur, and Zaleena could not be here." Sarah said.

"It *was* unfortunate. They certainly would have come if they had been granted permits. Both Khalil and Mansur had their identity cards taken away by the Israelis. They both had stayed outside the West Bank beyond their permits. It is why I have to come back every year to renew mine; I don't want to lose it as they lost theirs.

"As Jordanians, they are not allowed into the West Bank. Occasionally exceptions are made for a *day,* but only if a son or daughter is coming to attend his father or mother's funeral. It is absurd; before 1967 people from Ramallah used to drive to Amman for lunch and be home in time for supper. Now it is often a seven or eight hour trip across the bridge. Palestinians, who do not have Israeli ID cards, cannot come at all."

"I am sorry that we didn't think about my returning to the States through Amman. I would have loved to have seen them again." Sarah paused. "They really felt *like family.*"

"They are family," Mohammad smiled.

The taxi drove through the back entrance of the camp and wove its way through the serpentine alleys until it came to a stop in front of Omar and Nijmeh's door. Mohammad paid the fare and got their overnight bags out of the trunk.

When he rapped on the door it was immediately opened by Omar. He smiled broadly and welcomed his son and his son's wife. Mohammad kissed his hand and raised it to his forehead. Sarah, though it felt unnatural, also kissed his hand and raised it to her head. Omar smiled and drew his hand back. "That is not necessary, my daughter." He said in Arabic.

Nijmeh came out of the kitchen wiping her hands on her apron. She soundly kissed both Mohammad and Sarah on both cheeks and hugged them. Hasna also came out of the kitchen and kissed and embraced them both.

She told them in English, for Sarah's benefit, that Imad and her sons were already in the sitting room and that Mohammad should go on in. Yasmeen came over from setting the table and also hugged and kissed Sarah. "Come with me she said. I want to show you to your room. I have already taken the liberty of moving your things over this morning."

Yasmeen took Sarah up to a small bedroom in which two pallets had been spread on the floor and pushed together. In the corner stood Sarah's suitcase and a basket in which were all the gifts she had laid out for the family.

"How was it?" Yasmeen asked shyly. "Were you scared?"

Sarah looked at the concern in Yasmeen's face. She hugged her and said, "It is wonderful. You will see for yourself. There was an initial moment or two of pain, but he was tender and gentle. There is nothing to be afraid of."

Sarah could see the relief in Yasmeen's face. "I hope it wasn't *improper* for me to ask?"

Sarah smiled, "Of course not, after all we *are* sisters now."

There were lots of people at the dinner: Imad and his seven sons; Yasmeen's father and three younger brothers; her grandfather, Abu Najib; and of course Issa, Mohammad, and Omar.

Sarah still found it strange that the men ate first and *alone* and that the women had to wait for the *second sitting.* She sat with the women and *listened* to their chatter, understanding only that which Yasmeen translated for her. (Hasna and Ayesha were busy helping Nijmeh serve the men.) She wished that it was possible to *see* subtitles when the women spoke, or that she had one of those little earphones in her ear and someone was feeding into it simultaneous translation. She was officially *part of the family,* but she still *felt completely* foreign.

After both groups had eaten and had fruit and coffee, the neighbors began to arrive. The men sat in the courtyard and the women sat in the sitting room. Thoughtfully, either Ayesha, or Hasna, or Yasmeen sat next to her, but Sarah still felt on the periphery of all that was happening.

The last guests finally left at about eight o'clock in the evening. Mohammad took Sarah's hand and smiling at his family, made their excuses and led her up to their room.

"This has been an ordeal for you," he said kissing her. "I am sorry that we didn't even sit together. It is not as I would have wished it. I should have booked another night at the American Colony, but my folks were dead set on having this dinner. And since you are leaving the day after tomorrow, I didn't see how we could get out of it."

"It was a little hard on me, but I *do* understand. Yasmeen, and Ayesha and your sister, Hasna, were thoughtful enough to be sure that one of them was sitting next to me all the time to translate. But it is a relief that we can be alone now." Sarah sighed resting her head on Mohammad's shoulder.

He held her in his arms and kissed her as he lowered her to the pallet. "You can't *imagine* how much I love you," he whispered as he began to unbutton her blouse.

Mohammad was unable to get a permit to go to the airport with her. He was told when he went to the Military Headquarters to apply, that permits were issued *only* to those Palestinians actually traveling and for a specific flight. He would have to prove that he was flying and present a copy of his ticket. Even then, the permit would only be issued for a specific time frame, usually four hours before the plane was scheduled to take off. Sarah would have no problem traveling as she was an American, and she had a three-month tourist visa stamped in her passport.

He felt badly that he couldn't accompany her to the airport and see her off. He had wished that he was traveling with her or that they had thought in the States to have her return through Amman, then Khalil and Mansur could have gone with her to the airport.

Sarah tried to reassure him that she was, after all, a big girl and that she could take care of herself. She would fly straight from Tel Aviv to New York. In New York she would change planes, taking a domestic flight to Indianapolis. Her parents would meet her there and drive her back to the farm.

It was hard saying good-bye to Yasmeen. A special bond had grown between them in those three short weeks. Sarah had grown relatively close to Issa, Hasna, and Ayesha as well; she thought it was probably because they all spoke English. She cared about Nijmeh and Omar and of course Im Najib, but there *was* the barrier of language. She knew that once she became conversationally fluent that barrier would no longer exist. (And Sarah was *determined* to learn Arabic!)

The parting with Mohammad was painful. The taxi arrived at five in the afternoon. Her suitcases were placed in the trunk.

Nijmeh had insisted that she take the wedding *thob* and shawl with her. Sarah had folded them very carefully and squeezed them into her hand luggage. She didn't want to risk them getting lost.

She clung to Mohammad and sobbed on his shoulder. "I will be coming soon, *habeeptee*. Before you even know it, I will be with you. Be sure to call Mansur or Khalil as soon as you arrive, and they will phone me to let me know. No matter what the time, *be sure to phone."*

He was trying not to cry and found it difficult to get the words he wanted to say past the lump in his throat. "Are you sure you have your passport and your ticket? I put Khalil's and Mansur's phone numbers in your purse. If there is any emergency at all, *call them!"*

"I will. I'll be fine. I'll be sure to call as soon as I get to New York, and then I'll call again from the farm."

The driver he had hired kept looking at his watch and gesturing to Mohammad. He was getting impatient. "It's time for you to go, *habeeptee*." Mohammad kissed her on both cheeks wiping her tears away with his thumb. "Remember how much I love you!"

"I love you, too!" Sarah said as she got in the backseat of the taxi.

As the taxi wound its way down the narrow alley, Sarah kept looking out the back window until Mohammad vanished from sight. Mohammad stood there until he could no longer see the taxi. His heart felt heavy. She had only been gone two minutes and he already missed her!

Thankfully, Sarah sailed through security. They looked at her passport and saw that she had visited in Amman before coming to Israel, and that she had only come for three weeks. They asked her where she had been. She said: Jerusalem and Bethlehem where she had visited the holy sites. They asked her where she had stayed, and she said that she had stayed at the American Colony.

Sarah stuck with plain, unembroidered answers. They asked, since her name was Sarah Goldman, if she were Jewish. She said that her father was Jewish, but her mother was Christian. The Israeli security woman felt through her open bag, turning over the first layer of clothing, not really looking. She closed the suitcase, handed Sarah her passport, and told her to have a pleasant trip.

The direct flight was long, but Sarah slept most of the way. The last week had been exhausting, and she welcomed the rest. She was awakened by a stewardess when the food was served. After eating, Sarah would doze again.

Luckily when she arrived in New York, she breezed through passport control. Her suitcase was one of the first that spilled out of the shoot onto the conveyor belt. She had three hours to make her connecting flight. She took the shuttle to the domestic airline, checked in, had her bag weighed and tagged, and proceeded to the gate.

She still had an hour and a half to spare. She put several dollar bills into a change machine and got a pocketful of quarters. There was a bank of pay phones on the wall opposite the gate from which she would be departing. She dialed the international operator and gave Khalil's number in Amman. The woman placed the call and as it was ringing told Sarah how much money to deposit.

It only rang twice when she heard Khalil's voice on the other end. "Hello, Khalil? This is Sarah. I just arrived in New York and am about to board the plane for Indianapolis. I had a very easy trip. I wasn't detained at all in Tel Aviv. My luggage arrived, and everything has gone like clock- work. Please call Mohammad and assure him that I have arrived safely and the trip went well."

"Of course, Sarah, I am so glad you had a good trip. I will phone Mohammad immediately. Please phone when you reach home. I will be awaiting your call."

"Khalil, be sure to tell Mohammad that I love him and miss him." Sarah said.

"That will be the *first* thing I tell him, Sarah. You can count on that." Sarah could hear the smile in his voice. "Good-bye, Sarah, *Allah my'ik.*"

"*Allah my'ak enta,* Khalil. (God go with you too, Khalil)" Sarah was proud that she could speak one complete sentence in Arabic. And that she could use it *correctly!*

Chapter 31

Sara looked out the window. It was a bright, sunny day. She could see the tops of houses as they descended; some had swimming pools in the backyard and neat, tidy gardens. The flaps on the wings went up; she could hear the swish as the wheels descended, and then there was a brief trembling as the wheels hit the tarmac and the plane began to slow.

Again the pilot's voice on the intercom reminded them to remain in their seats with their seat belts fastened until the plane had come to a complete stop and the *fasten seat belt* sign had gone off.

Sarah was *excited* and a tad *apprehensive*. She was excited about seeing her parents, a little apprehensive about breaking the news to them that she was married. It had been a long trip, even though it had gone exceptionally well. She was exhausted; she *missed* Mohammad.

Overhead compartments were opened; passengers were retrieving their carry on luggage impatient for the line to move so they could disembark.

As she went through the open door, pulling her one carry-on, the other weighing heavily on her shoulder, she saw her parents in the crowd at the gate. When they spotted her they smiled and waved. Her dad came forward, hugged her, took the heavy bag off her shoulder and the handle of the carry-on she was pulling from her. "I'll get these," he said.

Her mother hugged her and kissed her on the cheek. "We are so glad you're back. My goodness, we have certainly missed you. You must be exhausted. You must tell us all about your trip." She chattered on, not giving Sarah a chance to answer. Her parents moved her down the long corridor, following the signs to *Baggage Claim* and to the outside doors leading to the parking lot.

Her bags were already taking their lazy ride on the conveyor belt. She spotted them just as they passed through the leather flaps into the back only to emerge again a few moments later to continue their circle.

Her father handed her the shoulder bag and grabbed her two bags as they came within range of his arms. He unsnapped the cover that covered the handles, pulled them up and proceeded to drag the bags on their squeaky wheels through the glass doors into the parking lot.

He had driven the station wagon instead of the pick-up. Sarah's bags were stowed in the back. She got in the backseat, moved the pillow that her mother had obviously brought, and slid in. She leaned again the backseat in such a way that she could stretch out her legs. "Ah, it feels so good to finally be able to stretch my legs." Sarah sighed.

"We brought the station wagon, and I threw in a pillow, thinking you would be more comfortable and that you probably might like to snooze. It is a long drive back to the farm," her mother said.

"Thanks, Mom. You think of everything."

Once they had maneuvered through the city traffic and turned onto the inter-state, her mother asked about the trip. "Tell us about your three weeks. What did you see? What did you do?" She skirted around the call and the engagement. Sarah had thought that that would be the *first* thing her mother would want to know about.

"We did a little sightseeing. Mohammad took me to Bethlehem and Jerusalem. When we were in Amman, his brother Khalil and Khalil's friend took us to a fantastic tourist site – *Petra*. He also took us to an old Roman Amphitheater in the center of Amman."

Sarah stopped and questioned: "Aren't you going to ask me about Mohammad's family, the West Bank, the *engagement?*"

"Yes, the *engagement*. We *were* surprised that you decided to get *engaged*. We thought you were going to see where Mohammad's family lived; meet them, come back here and think about it this summer *before* you decided. We hadn't realized that things had progressed to this point."

"What *did* you think of Mohammad's family and where they live?" Her father asked. "You obviously must have liked them and the area a lot to be *talked* into getting engaged."

"I wasn't *talked* into anything." Sarah bristled just a bit. "At first, I found everything so *strange...* so *foreign*. I couldn't communicate with his parents; they don't speak any English. His oldest sister, and youngest brother still live in the camp and they both speak English. They would do a lot of translating for me, but of course it wasn't the same as being able to actually have a *conversation*. It was more like *answering questions*. I did find that frustrating at times.

"I stayed with a neighbor of theirs, an older woman who was a good friend of Mohammad's grandmother. She also didn't speak any English, but she had asked her granddaughter-Yasmeen is her name - to stay with me during those three weeks. Yasmeen is a lovely person. Her English is excellent and she explained a lot of the things I didn't understand." Sarah paused. "She is now more than a friend; she is like a sister.

"The camp where Mohammad's family lives is very crowded. Their home is very small and simple, but bright and *homey*. At first, I found the obvious poverty of the camp depressing, but once I met individuals and saw their homes, I came away with a completely different picture. The people are generous and kind – and in spite of a military presence and graffiti on the walls and the dirt in the streets – their homes beyond the alley gate are clean and orderly and *colorful* – there are flowering plants in rusty containers everywhere. There is genuine *warmth* about the folks I met."

Sarah laughed, "Mohammad's mother scours her aluminum pots and trays with soap and *steel wool* until you can *see* your reflection in them. They are almost like mirrors! She washes the stone tiles in her courtyard *every* day *by throwing* soapy water on them and swishing the water out the door with a broom that doesn't have a handle. She is *barefooted* and she tucks the hem of her long skirt into her belt. It is quite a picture!"

Sarah's mother had turned so she could face Sarah. "What is Mohammad's mother like? She apparently is a good housekeeper. Is she a good cook?

"Nijmeh – that is his mother's name – is an amazing woman. She has raised ten children; she worked as a cleaning woman for years until her older sons insisted she stop as they were old enough to support the family." Sarah interrupted her tale. "Her two older sons are quite well off. The oldest is a doctor in Amman; the next is a lawyer.

"Anyway, Mohammad's mother seems to do everything really *well* and almost effortlessly – or so it seemed to me. She could prepare a banquet; entertain guests; and always have time to sit and have coffee. She makes anyone who comes to the door *feel welcome.* She never seems to be too busy. I really *liked* that part of Palestinian culture."

"Having worked so hard and had ten children, she must look quite old and worn out," her mother said. "Life is often very hard on women. I can remember stories your great grandmother used to tell..."

"Mohammad's mother had her first baby when she was only *fifteen*; Mohammad's father was only *seventeen* – they were teenagers. If you could see his parents, you would think that they were both Mohammad's older brother and sister. Mohammad looks very much like his father. His mother is one of the most beautiful women I have ever seen."

"Mohammad's parents must come from good stock," her mother smiled. "There is certainly something to be said for good *genes.*"

Sarah's father had listened in silence, but he wasn't to be deterred. "What made you decide to get engaged? It seems *rushed* to your mother and me."

He looked at the gas gauge, glanced at the clock on the dashboard and said, "We're coming up to a service area. I need to fill up the tank, and we should probably stop for coffee anyway. Stretch our legs a bit. Over coffee you can tell us what convinced you to get engaged."

Sarah reached over the front seat and rubbed her dad's shoulder. "Okay, Dad, over coffee you will hear the *whole story.*"

Mohammad had had a long conversation on the phone with Khalil. Khalil had called him, as he had promised Sarah, to tell him that she had arrived safely in New York. The call had gotten Mohammad out of bed. He hadn't been sleeping; he had been waiting for the phone to ring. He missed Sarah.

Mohammad joked a little with Khalil on the phone. "The plan was that I would come home and get married this summer. Well, I have done that – and in just *three weeks too!* See, I *do* listen to my older brothers and parents."

Khalil joked back, "It seemed to me that we were all *recommending* that you get married to a *Palestinian* girl that *Im'me* had picked out. You didn't quite do that, did you?"

"I didn't go against anyone's wishes. You liked her; Mansur and Zaleena liked her; *Im'me ou Abou'ee* liked her. It could be interpreted that I married the girl you all *chose* for me." Mohammad chuckled.

"I suppose there are several ways of interpreting the situation. How does the fact that you are now married change your plans for the summer?" Khalil asked.

"That's what I want to talk to you about. I want to return to Purdue next week. I have come back and renewed my exit permit. I will be back in time to sign up for a mid-summer course. Sarah and I can look for an apartment, but the real reason is: *I miss Sarah and want to be with her.*" Mohammad waited for Khalil's response.

"It *does* make sense that you return early. Of course you and Sarah must be together. I will arrange for the ticket. I will check with the travel agent to see when the first available flights are. It is a busy time of year, and not always easy to find a seat, but I will look around. Amr also has a friend who is a travel agent. We'll see what we can do. Work on your permit to cross the bridge. When you get the permit, come right away. Hopefully, you'll be able to spend a few days with us here in Amman."

"I don't know how to thank you. You are always there for me, Khalil. *May Allah give you rest and blessing.*"

"Just a small matter of business," Khalil said. "I will have transferred to your bank in Purdue funds for your summer course, the fall tuition, and money for rent on a flat and for your living expenses. I will continue to support you and Sarah until you graduate next summer and find a job."

Mohammad expected this, but still the generosity left him speechless. "I really don't know what to say. It is so very *generous.*"

"You are my *brother* and my *son, habeebi.* This is not just my *wajib* – my duty; it is my pleasure." Khalil replied.

"*Inshallah* I will see you within the week. *Allah my'ak.*"

"*Allah my'ak ib'nee.*" (God be with you my son)

Sarah sat in the booth opposite her parents. She toyed with her coffee cup, not really sure how to tell them that she was *married* and not just engaged.

"I know that the engagement seems a bit *rushed and rash,* as you said, Dad. It really isn't when you think that Mohammad and I have known each other a year. You have known since Spring Break that I love Mohammad and that I was hoping that we would get married. We have talked about the different obstacles, but you have known how determined I was to see if this could possibly work." Sarah paused and took a drink from her coffee.

"It just felt *right* to get engaged when we did. I really like his family, especially his two brothers in Amman, and his brother's wife. I could *see* myself being part of his family." Sarah took another sip of coffee.

"It seems that in Islam there is a marriage contract. It is sort of a combination of a wedding license and wedding certificate. The couple isn't allowed to go out together alone – *to date* – unless this contract has been signed by the couple."

"So you *signed* such a contract?" her father asked.

"I did. I wanted to. I am committed to the relationship and it seemed the logical thing to do.

"Anyway, and more importantly, the contract makes us legally *married* -in the Middle East that is. If the engagement were to be broken, we would have to get divorced."

"So, I am to understand that in the Middle East you are not only engaged, but you are *married?!* I am shocked. How could you have signed such a document?" her father said angrily. "You must have been out of your mind!"

"Now Dave, calm down a bit and let Sarah explain." Her mother said.

"I *wasn't* out of my mind. You know how clear-headed I am. You know I would never sign anything, *do* anything without thinking it through. I am not a child. I am a grown woman." Sarah found herself raising her voice. She took a deep breath.

"The contract means we are married *on paper*, but tradition doesn't allow couples to live together as husband and wife until there is a formal, public ceremony. Mohammad's younger brother, Issa, got engaged to the girl I told you about – Yasmeen. Omar and Nijmeh, Mohammad's parents wanted to have a combined party to announce the engagements of their two sons." Sarah paused, took another sip of coffee – noticed how cold it was and gestured to the waitress.

"Mohammad and I talked it over. Since we were already *legally* married on paper; since we are committed to the relationship, we decided to have the party announce our *wedding*. Mohammad and I were married four days ago."

In spite of the noise in the restaurant, Sarah thought she could hear a *pin drop.* Her mother's jaw dropped. Her father just stared at her, slid out of the booth and left without a word.

"I know this has come as somewhat of a shock. But..."

"Don't say another word," her mother said. "I don't want to say anything to you right now for fear I will say something that we will both regret." She could see Dave sitting in the parked car outside the restaurant. "Your father is sitting in the car. Let's go."

On the rest of the drive from the service area to the farm, not one word was said. When Sarah opened her mouth to speak, her father switched on the radio and turned the volume up. Her mother looked at her and pressed a finger to her lips gesturing to Sarah that she should keep still.

Sarah hadn't expected this reaction. They knew she had gotten engaged; they knew she would eventually be getting married; she couldn't understand why they were so angry. It was the first time she could remember them *refusing* to speak to her. There had been arguments in the past – heated arguments –

they had never given her the *silent treatment. What will they do when Mohammad turns up here next week?*

Chapter 32

Sarah thought that by morning things would have smoothed out somewhat between her and her parents. She had slept surprisingly well. She probably had been more exhausted than she had thought. The room was washed in sunshine when she finally awoke. She looked at the small alarm clock on the nightstand and was shocked to see it was close to *three in the afternoon!*

She was bleary-eyed as she went across the hall to the bathroom. She took a shower, brushed her teeth, and combed her hair. Back in her room, she rummaged around in her dresser drawer and pulled out a pair of well-worn jeans. She put on a red-checked blouse and worked her feet into scuffed sneakers. She smoothed the covers on the bed, pulled the bedspread up over them and tucked the spread under and over the pillows.

When she went into the kitchen, her mother was not there. The kitchen chairs were neatly pushed under the round kitchen table. There wasn't a dish in the sink; the glass pot on the coffee-maker stood clean and empty. Sarah got a coffee filter out of the cupboard next to the coffee-maker, placed it in the plastic top, scooped in the appropriate scoops of coffee, poured water in the back, closed the lid, switched the coffee-maker on and watched the slow drip, drip, drip of the coffee. She wondered where her mom was.

She looked at the wall clock over the refrigerator. It said 3:30. She thought about the time difference between there and Amman. It would be about 10:30 PM in Amman. It wasn't too late to call Khalil or Mansur and to tell them that she had arrived.

She went upstairs to get their phone numbers out of her purse.

She dialed the series of numbers she needed to get an international line and to call directly. She paced back and forth between the stairs and the hall desk. Finally, on about the tenth ring, Mansur picked up the phone.

"Hello, Mansur? This is Sarah."

"Sarah, how wonderful it is to hear your voice. I gather you are home. How was the last leg of your trip?"

"Everything is fine. I got in last night, but was too exhausted to call and thought it would be too late to call anyway. I just wanted you to know that I had arrived and to ask you to please contact Mohammad."

"Sarah, are you all right? You sound as if there is something wrong?" There was concern in Mansur's voice.

"No, no. I am just tired. The trip was more exhausting than I thought it would be. I will call again in a few days to find out Mohammad's travel plans. Give my love to Zaleena and the children. And of course remember me to Khalil." Sarah was close to tears.

"Of course, and we all send our love. Do give our greetings to your parents."

"I will. Thanks. *Allah my'ak.*"

"*Allah my'ik, Sarah.*"

When he got off the phone he was frowning. "What's wrong, Mansur?" Zaleena asked.

"That was Sarah. She has arrived home, *illhumdillah,* and wants me to call Mohammad. He looked at Zaleena. "She *said* that she was fine; but she didn't *sound* fine."

"You better call Mohammad. He will be waiting to hear that she has arrived. He probably thought that she would have phoned hours ago."

Mohammad picked up the receiver on the second ring. *"Salam aleikum,"* he said.

"Aleikum salam, Mohammad. This is Mansur."

"Mansur, you've heard from Sarah?"

"Yes, she just phoned. She has arrived at the farm. Said the journey was a bit more tiring than she thought it would be. She sends her love and wants to know about your travel plans. She said she would phone in a few days."

"How did she *sound?*" Mohammad asked.

"She sounded tired. We really didn't talk very long." Mansur hedged.

"Did she sound all right?" Mohammad asked with concern.

"I guess she sounded mostly *tired.* She really has had an exhausting three weeks. Do you have her home phone number written down? I'll have Zaleena give her a call tomorrow."

"It's here in my billfold; hold on a minute." Mohammad took the slip of notebook paper out of his billfold and read the number off to Mansur. "Did you get that?"

Mansur read the number back to him. "Don't worry *habeebee;* I am sure she is just tired. I'll have Zaleena call her and then will call you. Give our love to *Im'me ou Abou'ee* and Issa."

"I will. Thanks. *Allah my'ak.*"

"Good night, brother."

Mohammad replaced the receiver in its cradle. He stood in the doorway into the sitting room and said good night to his parents and Issa.

His mother asked if the call was from Mansur or Khalil and if they had called to say that Sarah had arrived. He told her it was, and she had.

Mohammad slowly went up the stone stairs. He didn't turn on the one naked light bulb that dangled from the center of the room. He got undressed in the dark. Moonlight filtered through the slates of the metal shutter over the window. He lay sleepless for a long time; he was worried about Sarah.

Sarah poured herself a cup of coffee and went to the porch. She sat on the first step and leaned her back against the railing. *It is so peaceful here* she thought. *I wished I **felt** peaceful inside! I can't believe that Mom and Dad are taking it this way!*

About four o'clock her mom and dad drove up in the pick-up. Her dad pulled up in front of the house to let her mom off, and then drove down to the barn. He glanced at Sarah, but turned his head and stepped on the gas.

Her mother came up the walk carrying two bags of groceries. Sarah went to take one of the bags from her. "Here, give me that," she said.

"I can manage." That was all her mother said.

Sarah was hurt and Sarah was *angry*.

She slammed the screen door as she followed her mother into the kitchen. "I can't believe that you and Dad are acting this way! If I were sixteen and pregnant and had run off with the neighbor boy, okay. I would understand you being angry. But, *I am twenty-four, not sixteen. I am not pregnant. I did not run off.* You know I love Mohammad; you knew I was going specifically to meet his family with the idea that he and I would marry. I wanted to explain about the engagement/marriage contract when I saw you. It wasn't something I could explain over the phone." Sarah had raised her voice.

"We should *at least* talk about it. This *silent treatment* isn't going to get us anywhere!"

"You *want to talk about it!* Fine, let's talk." Her mother was also angry.

"You tell us a couple of months ago that you have fallen in love with a Palestinian Moslem. You come home for Spring Break and stay *two* nights because you have to go back and see this boy. We want to come down to meet him, and you tell us *you are too busy* with exams. We drive down and have dinner with you, and you tell us you are going to the Middle East for three weeks to meet his family."

"But..." Sarah tried to interrupt.

"No, let me finish." Her mother slammed a kitchen cupboard door. "Then you call us last week to say you are *engaged* and tell us in the car last night that you are *not* just engaged, but *married!*" Her mother paused and licked the spittle from the corner of her mouth.

"And you sit there *expecting* us to say '*Oh, how nice, dear. We are really happy for you*'" She stared unsmilingly at Sarah. "Well, *it isn't nice*, and *we aren't happy!* She got a pan out of a lower cupboard and slammed it down on the counter.

"You got married without even *thinking* about us. Did it even enter your mind that *I* have dreamed of planning your wedding since you were a little girl? Did you even think how hurt your dad would be? I have always dreamed of your father giving you away, but your wedding day has come and gone, and *we* weren't even there!" Her mother wiped angry tears from her eyes. "You have *always* had to have your own way, haven't you?"

Sarah looked at her mother with tears in her eyes.

"I didn't purposely fall in love with a Palestinian Moslem to make you unhappy. I didn't plot and plan and think: *Oh, this will really piss off Mom and Dad.* I fell in love with Mohammad. It just happened." Sarah stopped to wipe the tears from her eyes. "And I'm *glad* it happened. I can't imagine being married to anyone else. I am *sorry* that you and Dad feel the way you do, but I am *not sorry* that Mohammad and I are married."

She got up from the table. "I knew there would be some issues. I knew that our parents would rather we married someone else – someone from the same culture, same religion, same background. But it *wasn't* meant to be. It was meant that Mohammad and I be together." Sarah paused.

"I am married, Mom. I am no longer *just* your daughter. I am a *wife,* and. whether or not you accept that is up to you and Dad."

Her mother just stared at her and said nothing.

"It is a bit ironic." Sarah sadly smiled, "I had packed my bags and was ready to come home a week after I arrived there. Even *I thought* Mohammad *would* be happier married to a Palestinian. I had even *thought* I knew the girl he should marry. I asked to speak alone with his mother and sister. His sister, so she could translate for his mother and me." Sarah wiped the tears that were falling with the back of her hand.

"I told his mother that I thought Mohammad should marry a Palestinian. I told her that I was leaving. You know what she said?" By this time Sarah was crying.

"She said that I was right, *except for the fact that Mohammad didn't love a Palestinian. He loved me.* She went on to say that she thought *God* had written Mohammad's name in my heart, and that *God* had written my name in Mohammad's heart. Imagine, his mother who had every reason to wish me gone, said that!" Sarah wiped her nose with the back of her hand and then ran her hand down the sides of her jeans.

"Mohammad had told her that I had said to him: *sometimes love isn't enough.* She said that his older brother, Khalil, had also told her that: *sometimes love isn't enough.* You see, *his* family didn't want me to marry Mohammad either. But his mother looked me right in the face; she took both of my hands in hers; she instructed Mohammad's sister to translate word-for-word. She said, *'My daughter, you must believe that **love is enough.'** And I *know* that that is true."

"You seem to care *more* about what this peasant woman says, than you do about me. *Love is enough* sounds like a line from that film – what was it called? *Love Story* – that's it, with Ali McGraw. Doesn't her husband in the film say: *love means never having to say you are sorry?* *Love is enough* could be a line from that script. Both lines are a bunch of *crap.*" Her mother's anger just kept spilling out of her mouth.

"You are *not* Ali McGraw, my fine girl. This is *not* a film; this is your life, and this is your dad's and *my* life. I can't believe you have been so uncaring about us."

Sarah's dad had come in the front door and had stood in the hall listening. The two women had been unaware of his presence. He finally entered the kitchen and said, "That's enough, Emily. I think Sarah has gotten the point that we are angry."

"No, it is *not* enough! She needs to hear the harsh truth." Her mother turned and looked directly at Sarah.

"How do you expect to live? How is *Mohammad* going to support you? Since he isn't a legal resident, he probably can't be employed. Where are you going to live? You still have one more year of grad school. Are you just assuming that your dad and I will continue to pay your tuition?"

"Emily, *stop!* That is enough. Listen to what you are saying. You have already said things you will regret," Dave went over to her and put his arms around her.

"I *know* I have said some things that I shouldn't have said. But *she* has made me so angry. She hasn't thought of us at all. I *am* angry because I am *so hurt.*" She quietly cried on Dave's shoulder.

"What are we going to tell the neighbors," she softly sobbed into his chest.

"This is foolish of me, I know." Emily said drying her eyes with the hem of her apron.

She turned to where Sarah had been sitting at the table. "I have probably said..." She didn't finish her sentence. The chair was empty. Sarah had gone.

Chapter 33

Sarah's mother stood at the foot of the stairs and called, "Sarah, dinner is on the table." She waited for a response. There was none. Again she called, this time raising her voice. **"Sarah, dinner is ready. Are you coming?"** Again there was no reply.

Finally, Emily went up the stairs and knocked on Sarah's bedroom door. "Sarah, are you sleeping? Didn't you hear me call? Dinner is ready." When she got no answer she opened the bedroom door. The room was empty.

For a moment it felt as though her heart had plummeted to the floor. *Sarah was gone!*

"Dave, Dave," she shouted. "Sarah is not in her room!"

Dave came to the foot of the stairs. "What do you mean she is not in her room?"

"She's *not* here! She's left! Emily shouted as she hurried down the stairs. "What has that girl gone and done now? There was anger and worry in Emily's voice.

Sarah had walked three miles across the fields to her Aunt Martha's and Uncle Ken's farm. Uncle Ken was her father's brother, and Aunt Martha was her mother's sister. Their farm bordered that of her parents'. It was just dusk when Sarah knocked on the kitchen screen door.

"Why, Sarah, what are you doing here?" her Aunt Martha asked. "We're just sitting down to supper. Come in. Come in." She held the screen door open so Sarah could pass into the kitchen.

"We knew your folks had gone to pick you up yesterday, but hadn't expected to see you so soon. We thought you would be sleeping the day away," her aunt laughed. "My, it is good to see you," she said giving Sarah a warm hug.

Sarah tightened her arms around her aunt and began to cry. "Sarah, love, what's wrong?"

"It's a long story, Aunt Martha. I really need to talk to someone." Sarah said brokenly.

"Well, you have come to the right place. You sit right down here and tell us all about it," her aunt said pulling out a kitchen chair for her. Uncle Ken leaned over and kissed her on the cheek. "Now, if that little brother of mine has been out-of-sorts with my girl, I'll go right over and kick his butt."

Sarah smiled through her tears and shook her head no. Sarah's uncle and aunt were childless, and they had always had a special place in their hearts for Sarah, and she for them.

Sarah told them everything. She told them about her marriage to Mohammad; she told them about her parents' reaction; she told them what she had said, and what her mother had said. They listened without interruption. Her aunt's lips did form a grim line, and her eyes danced in fury when Sarah related what her mother had said, but she kept silent.

When Sarah was finished, her aunt took her hand and looking over at her Uncle Ken said, "For the time being, love, you are staying right here with us. Isn't that right, Ken?"

"You're damn right, that's *right.*"

"Now, for the time being I don't want you to think any more about it. You must be starved," her Aunt Martha said as she placed a plate before Sarah. "Now, you just help yourself. I'm going to call your mother and tell her where you are. She'll be worried, *and it serves her right,*" she said under her breath.

Emily was just ready to pick up the phone and call Martha to see if they had seen Sarah, when the phone rang.

"Hello, Martha? I was just going to call you. Sarah is missing!"

"She's not missing, Emily. She's here sitting at the supper table having dinner with us."

Martha interrupted Emily as she started to say, "Well, there are some things you need to know..."

"Sarah told us what happened. I think for the time being, it is best to just let it all be. Sarah is exhausted – physically and *emotionally.* Ken and I have invited her to spend a few days with us. I'll be over after supper to pick up a few of her things."

"Now, see here, Martha. Sarah should be home, here, with us. I'll send Dave over to pick her up in about an hour or so."

"No, Emily, don't do that. The best thing at the moment is to give her some time. She needs time to get things sorted out in her mind. *And so do you and Dave.* You need to let her be for the moment."

"I don't feel good about this, but I guess for a *couple* of nights it will *have* to be alright."

Martha went back into the kitchen and sat down. "Well, that's taken care of. You are going to spend some time with us. I'll go over after supper and pick up a few of your things. You just tell me what you want me to bring." Martha smiled and patted Sarah's hand. "It's all going to work out; you'll see."

Dave and Emily had just sat down to their cold dinner when the phone rang. "Everything is already cold, *thanks to Sarah,*" her mother grumbled, "and now there's the phone!"

"Yes. Yes. This is the Goldman residence. Speak up, we have a poor connection."

"No, Sarah is not here at the moment. Who is calling, please?"

"I'm sorry. I should have introduced myself first. This is Zaleena, Mohammad's sister-in-law. I am calling from Amman to speak with Sarah."

"Sarah is staying with her aunt for a couple of days." Emily replied coldly.

"Oh, I see. Would you mind giving me a number where I can reach her?"

Emily reluctantly gave her Martha's phone number.

"Thank you so much. When you do see Sarah, be sure to give her our love. Please accept my apologies for disturbing you at your dinner time."

When Zaleena hung up the phone she looked thoughtfully at Mansur. "I think things are not well with Sarah. Her mother sounded quite cold on the phone. Sarah is not there. She is spending a few days with her aunt. That is strange; is it not? She just got home, and is already staying with her aunt."

"Did you get her aunt's phone number?" Mansur asked. "We should speak to her before we call Mohammad."

"Who was on the phone?" Dave asked when Emily came back into the kitchen.

"Can you believe it? It was one of Mohammad's sisters-in-law wanting to talk to Sarah. She was calling all the way from Jordan. When I told her Sarah wasn't here, she asked for Martha's phone number. I wished I hadn't given her Martha's number, but I thought it would be a bigger story if I didn't."

Zaleena *did* call Sarah. They had a long conversation on the phone. Zaleena listened and only interrupted to ask a few questions for clarification or to give verbal affirmation.

Mansur was standing beside her as she talked. He watched her face. Zaleena was intent and focused. He couldn't hear what Sarah was saying. All he could hear were Zaleena's: *Yes, I see. Of course, I understand;* and *yes, you are right.*

When she finally replaced the receiver in its cradle, he asked, "So, what has happened?"

"Sarah's family is *very upset* about the marriage. In anger, and I imagine in great hurt, her mother has said some very unkind things. Things I am sure she will regret when she has had time to think. Sarah is staying with her aunt and uncle. She doesn't want to be at her parents' home at the moment. And it is probably better that she isn't."

"Mohammad should be with her. It isn't right that she should be facing this alone." Mansur said.

Early the next morning, Sarah was awakened by a soft rap on the bedroom door. "Sarah, love, you have a call from Jordan."

Sarah rubbed the sleep from her eyes, threw on a robe, and in bare feet ran down the stairs. She picked up the receiver and was surprised to hear Khalil's voice.

"Sarah? Good morning. I apologize for calling so early; I probably got you out of bed."

"That's alright. I am surprised that you are calling; I just spoke to Zaleena last night. Is Mohammad alright?"

"Yes, he is fine. I just got off the phone with him. He sends his love and wishes he could be with you. He feels badly that he is not there. The earliest seat I could find him is not for another ten days. He *is* on stand-by, so hopefully, there will be a cancellation, and he will get an earlier flight. In any event, he is coming to Amman, *inshallah,* tomorrow and you will be able to talk to him directly."

"Thank you, Khalil. It makes me feel much better that I will be able to actually *talk* to him, to *hear* his voice. You have all been so kind." Sarah was close to tears.

"Zaleena has shared with me some of the things which you told her. It has been a difficult time for you. I am so sorry that things are not going well with your parents. If there is anything I can do, please let me know."

"Thank you, that's very kind. I hadn't realized how deeply I had hurt them. I *am* trying to understand their feelings, but it is hard to *forget* words once they are spoken. You can't take back the words that you have said. You can understand, and perhaps *forgive,* but one almost never *forgets.*"

Khalil paused. He had heard what Sarah had said. Inside he agreed with her. "This will all work out, Sarah. And I *do* want you to know that you have another family which cares about you. You are *not* alone."

"I appreciate that. Thank you, Khalil.

"God be with you, *habeeptee*."

Sarah felt more at peace than she had in days. She had the unquestioning support of her uncle and aunt. She had the unwavering support of Mohammad's family – especially that of Khalil and Mansur. She would be able to talk to Mohammad tomorrow, and *inshallah,* be with him in ten days. Even though it was raining heavily outside, inside she felt the rising of the sun.

Chapter 34

In addition to the clothes she had asked her aunt to bring, she had also asked for the unpacked carry-on that held Nijmeh's wedding dress – *her* wedding dress. It was perhaps a foolish whim, but she wanted to be able to *see* the dress, to see it felt a little like *seeing* Mohammad and Nijmeh and Mansur and Yasmeen – she couldn't quite explain it, even to herself. For her, it was a *tangible* reminder of the world into which she had stepped.

She unpacked it and hung it on the back of the bedroom door. She wanted to be able to see it when she lay in bed. She knew it was silly, but that world seemed so far away at the moment; she *needed* this visible connection.

It was hanging there when her aunt brought in fresh towels. "My gracious," she exclaimed, "what a *beautiful* dress. Where did you get it?"

"It's my wedding dress. It was the same dress that Mohammad's mother wore when she got married." Sarah told her the story of the dress.

"What an amazing story. This is a real treasure. It will be something for you to hand down to your daughters."

"You make it sound like everything *will* be okay. That everything *will* work out." Sarah sighed.

"Of course it will, love. Your mom and dad will come around. They love you. Once the first grandchild arrives, why it will be like none of this ever happened."

"There is a *long* way to go between now and *that* first grandchild." Sarah smiled.

Aunt Martha sat down on the bed, smoothing an imaginary wrinkle she thought she saw in the quilt. "Come sit beside me, love. Life is kind of like this quilt. I pieced the different bits together long after we were married. There are pieces from the aprons my mother wore; there are triangles cut from some of the dresses your mother and I had as girls; this square of silk is from a vest your grandfather used to wear – *only on Sundays;* these white satin pieces are from the christening gowns of the little ones your Uncle Ken and I lost. Every piece reminds me of someone. Each piece by itself is just a bit of cut fabric, but when arranged together and quilted –it's like a picture."

Aunt Martha paused and took Sarah's hand. "Life is like that, love. It is bits and pieces. Sometimes there is great happiness and joy; sometimes there is sadness and grief. At times the happiness seems so momentary; it seems to flash by before we even have time to blink. At times the sadness and grief seem so unending, so unbearable, that we can't imagine ever being happy again. But *we are happy again.* Everything passes and we survive.

"You know, love, when you and Mohammad move into your first home in Purdue, I want you to take this quilt with you. I can't think of anyone I would rather see have it."

Sarah threw her arms around her aunt's ample frame. "I love you so much, Aunt Martha."

"I love you too, Sarah, always remember that!"

The second night of Sarah's visit to her aunt and uncle's, Martha and Ken drove over to see Emily and Dave.

"You take Dave out to the barn and talk to him like a *Dutch Uncle.* I'll take Emily into the kitchen and do the same," Martha said as their pick-up lumbered down the dirt drive. "I can understand their hurt and anger, but *what is done is done.* If they don't want to lose Sarah, they need to come 'round and accept the situation with good grace."

Dave and Emily were sitting in rockers on the front porch when Ken and Martha arrived. "Is Sarah not with you?" Emily asked. "I thought you were bringing her back."

"No, Sarah has decided to stay a few more days. She is going to help me can pears and peaches tomorrow." Martha said.

"Why don't you show me that new calf you bought?" Ken said to Dave.

"All right," he mumbled as he got out of the rocker, came down the wooden steps, and joined his brother as he walked toward the barn.

"I suppose you would like a cup of coffee?" Emily said getting up and walking ahead of Martha into the house. "Let's go sit in the kitchen. It is obvious that you have a *lecture* to deliver."

As Ken and Dave peered over the stall where the new heifer calf stood, Dave said, "You might as well say what you've come to say."

"You know, Dave, sometimes you need a good, swift kick in the pants. You have a lovely daughter there. She is smart and capable and has a good head on her shoulders. Okay, so she got married and you weren't there. And she married an Arab Moslem, not someone you would have picked for her, but it's *her life,* not exactly yours. If you don't want to *lose* her, you gotta accept what you can't change. She loves this guy, and she loves you. But, if you force her to *choose,* she is going to *choose her husband.* That is just the way life is – the way life has always been. Doesn't it say in the Torah some place where a *woman leaves her mother and father and clings to her husband?*"

"Since when do you know what is, or isn't, in the Torah. You are about as religious as I am; which means you are not religious at all."

"I just threw that in to see if you were listening." Ken said slapping his brother on the back. "But seriously, don't force Sarah to be in a position where she has to choose between her parents and her husband. It isn't fair to her, and it's sure-as-hell not fair to you and Emily."

"She's *already* made her choice. She has *made her bed,* let her lie in it."

"I'm real sorry to hear you say that." Ken said. "Just so you know Martha and I are going to stand with Sarah."

"That is up to you, but I want you to know it will be a wedge between you and me."

"I am real sorry to hear that. You are my brother and I love you, but if you force me to choose between you and Sarah, I choose Sarah."

The two brothers walked silently back to Ken's pick-up. "Why don't you tell Martha that I am ready to go? I'll wait here in the truck."

Dave went into the house only nodding at his brother. He went into the kitchen, "Martha, Ken is already in the truck waiting for you."

"Isn't he coming in for a cup of coffee and a piece of pie?" Emily asked.

"He wants to get back." Dave said. "He's waiting, Martha."

Martha pushed her chair out from under the table. She looked at her sister and said, "You take to heart what I said."

"And you can tell Sarah what *I* said," Emily bristled.

Martha left without a further word. As she lifted her ample bulk into the pick-up and shut the door, she turned to Ken and said. "By the look on your face, you had about as much luck as I did."

"They have dug their heels in and want the impossible. I don't think they realize what is at stake. Do they really think that by *punishing* Sarah that she will divorce Mohammad and come crawling back to them? They are being so stubborn and stiff-necked about this. They have lived with Sarah for almost twenty-four years, and it is as though they don't know her at all." Ken said.

"Dave told me that '*Sarah has made her bed and let her lie in it*'. I can't believe that he said that!"

"Emily told me the very same thing. They are going to lose their daughter, mark my words, if they haven't *already* lost her."

"Dave did tell me that if we chose to side with Sarah it would be a wedge between us. I would hate to have that happen."

"Emily told me basically the same thing. She was angry with me for allowing Sarah to stay with us. She said that if Sarah was still under her roof, she would have been able to talk *sense* into her; that by allowing Sarah to stay with us, I was *condoning* what she had done. She was talking like Sarah had committed a *crime.*"

They got home and parked the pick-up in front of the garage. The light was on in the kitchen and Sarah had made fresh coffee. She smiled as they came in, and then saw the expressions on their faces.

"It didn't go very well, did it?"

"Not as we would have wished, love, but I am hopeful that they will come around. Now, don't you fret; it will all work out. You'll see." Martha gave Sarah a hug. "My, that coffee smells good. And I have fresh rhubarb pie to go with it," she said setting dessert plates and forks on the table.

Before she went up to bed, her Uncle Ken stopped her at the foot of the stairs. "I know your mom said some things she didn't mean about the fall and college and tuition and such." Her uncle looked a little embarrassed. "I just want you to know that you don't need to worry about maybe not having the money to go back to school. *You'll have the money.* I just want you to know that I will see to it." There were tears in Sarah's eyes as she hugged her uncle.

"I don't know what I would do if I didn't have you and Aunt Martha."

"Well, you *do* have us. Now just you *remember* that. Now get up to bed; you must be exhausted." As he turned to go into the living room, Sarah noticed that there were tears in his eyes as well.

Chapter 35

Sarah hadn't seen or talked to her parents in over a week. Her Aunt Martha had talked on the phone to her mother several times, but each time her mother had said, "*Sarah knows where we are. It is up to her to come to us.*"

"It is easy to see that you got your stubbornness *legitimately!*" her Aunt Martha had smiled. "My goodness, Emily can be awful unyielding at times." She saw the distressed look in Sarah's eyes. "Don't worry, love, she'll come around. She always does eventually."

"I don't think she will, this time. I think she has dug her heels in and won't be budged. I really don't know what she and Dad expect me to do?"

Sarah had been helping her Aunt Martha can peaches and pears for two days. It was soothing to her spirit to do this very homey activity. Her Aunt Martha was such a warm and loving person. She had never heard her say one critical thing about anyone. They had just put the last of the jars in the canner when the phone rang.

"I'll get it Aunt Martha."

Sarah picked up the phone and said: "*Goldman Residence.*"

"Sarah, *habeeptee,* is that you!"

"Mohammad! Mohammad! I can't believe it is you. How wonderful it is to hear your voice!"

"*Habeeptee,* it is wonderful to hear your voice, too. I just arrived in Amman. In fact I just came in the door. I couldn't wait to call you. *Inshallah* things are better between you and your folks."

"They are pretty much the same. I haven't seen them or heard from them in over a week. I have been staying here with my aunt and uncle. They have been wonderful through all this."

"I am so sorry, Sarah. If I had known it was going to be like this I wouldn't have suggested we get married this summer. We should have waited and included your parents."

"Please, *don't be sorry.* I am *glad* that we got married. I feel badly that my folks are so upset, but I am not upset that we got married. Even knowing what I know now, I still would have married you. When are you coming?"

"Amr has a friend who is a travel agent. His friend was able to find me a seat on a flight that leaves on Friday. I should be in Indianapolis Saturday afternoon. The flight is scheduled to arrive at three."

"*This Friday!* I can't wait to see you!"

"I'll call you again tomorrow at this time. I love you.

"I love you, too."

Sarah hung up the phone and sat down on the second step of the stairs. *Mohammad would be here in four days. Four days.* She had a lot to do.

"That was Mohammad on the phone, Aunt Martha. He is arriving in Indianapolis on Friday! Do you think that Uncle Ken could drive me down to Indianapolis and then take us on to Purdue?"

"Well, of course he can. But don't you want to bring Mohammad back here? He's got to see your folks sometime, and probably the sooner you get it over with the better. He is certainly welcome to stay here. Then when you two are ready to go to Purdue, why of course, Uncle Ken will take you." Her Aunt Martha paused.

"Don't you think you ought to go and see your folks and tell them that Mohammad is coming for a couple of days, and then you'll be going to Purdue?"

"I don't think they will want to see Mohammad. They are still so angry and hurt."

"These peaches need another thirty minutes on the fire. How about I drive you over to your folks in about a half hour? I know they would appreciate that you made the first step. They love you, Sarah, in spite of all their words and *cantankerousness.*" Martha saw that she was still hesitant. "Do it for me, love."

"Okay, Aunt Martha, you're right; I should be the one to take the first step."

Forty-five minutes later, Martha dropped Sarah off in front of the house. "It's probably better if you go in by yourself, love. I'll come in if you would rather I did, but I think your folks would probably like to see you without me around."

Sarah leaned over and kissed her aunt. "You're right. It's better if I go in alone. Would you mind coming back for me in about an hour?"

"Sure. I'll be sitting here in this old pick-up, waiting for you. I'll even put on a clean apron," her Aunt Martha laughed.

Sarah walked up the front steps and paused. She didn't know if she should just walk right in, or if she should *knock*. She thought it was strange that she even *thought* about knocking. She decided she would do neither. She looked in the screen door and hollered, "Anybody home?"

Her mother came out of the kitchen drying her wet hands on her apron. She was surprised to see Sarah.

"Why are you standing at the door? Aren't you going to come in?"

"I felt awkward about just walking in. Kind of funny that I should feel that way, isn't it?" It was more of a statement than a question.

"Is Dad here? There is something I wanted to talk over with you two?"

"He's down at the barn. He should be up shortly."

"Why don't you sit here on the porch? I'll go and make some coffee."

"I can make it, Mom."

"No, I'll do it. You just sit here and wait for your father." Her mother seemed cool and reserved. Sarah could tell that she was still angry, yet she did seem pleased that Sarah was there.

It wasn't long until she saw her father coming up from the barn. She thought he looked a little more stooped. Then she smiled to herself: *It had only been a **week** since she had seen him.*

He didn't come in the front but went in the kitchen door. He hadn't seen Sarah sitting on the porch. Sarah could hear their muffled conversation but couldn't make out what they were saying.

Finally, her mother came out carrying a tray of coffee mugs. Her father was right behind her.

"Sarah" was all he said.

Her parents sat in the two rockers on either side of her. "What did you want to talk to us about, Sarah?" her mother asked.

"I had a call from Mohammad today. He is arriving in Indianapolis on Saturday and would like to come out to the farm for a couple of days. He would like to see you."

She waited for her parents to say something. They said nothing.

"We had talked, before I came, about having a reception here at the farm for family and friends; a way to announce our marriage. Mohammad has even suggested that it might be nice to have a justice of the peace marry us here. That way we would also have an American marriage certificate and you could see me get married. He knows how important it would be to you, *to me,* to have a ceremony here."

Again she waited expectantly. Her parents said nothing.

"A day or so after the ceremony, we could go back to Purdue. Mohammad has paid the rent on his apartment through the summer. It is small, but will be fine until we find a bigger flat."

Again they said nothing. They sipped their coffee and rocked.

"Aren't you going to *say* anything?" Sarah asked. She could feel the tears pooling in her eyes.

"What do you want us to say?" her mother asked. "Do you want us to say how great it would be to have a party here, *after* you chose to exclude us? Do you want us to *welcome* Mohammad here after he has almost *destroyed* our family, and taken our daughter from us?" Sarah's mother began to dab at her eyes as she rocked and looked the *victim.*

"I'm ashamed of you, Sarah. I never thought I would live to see the day that I would say that *I'm ashamed of my own daughter.* If *only* you had married a nice boy like Sam. But no, you had to go and marry an Arab Moslem."

"So, what do you want me to do? Do you want me to divorce Mohammad? Do you want me to come back here and marry Sam? What *exactly* do you want from me? Do you want an apology? *I am sorry for hurting you.* I apologize for that. Do you want me to apologize for not marrying someone like Sam? *I am sorry I couldn't marry a man who fit your expectations.* I apologize for that, too. Do you want me to apologize for marrying Mohammad? That I can't do. I love Mohammad. *I am sorry* that you feel the way you do about him. I didn't marry him to *spite* you, if that is what you are thinking."

Sarah was weary. She had tried, and she realized nothing she said – at least for the moment – would alter what her parents felt.

She put her coffee mug on the tray. "Thanks for the coffee."

"Uncle Ken will drive me down to Indianapolis on Friday to pick up Mohammad. There is no point in us coming back here, since you don't want to see him. I'll have Uncle Ken drive us on to Purdue. There are some things that I would like to take from my room – clothes, books, that kind of thing. Unless you would rather I took nothing?"

"Take whatever you want," her father said. "Just phone ahead so your mother and I are not here."

"Dad, I don't want it to end this way. *Please!*"

"You've made your choice. So be it." He turned his back on Sarah and walked into the dark hallway.

Sarah looked at her mother. "Mom, it can't end this way. I love you and Dad. *Please* don't let it end this way."

"You've made your bed, Sarah, now you have to lie in it."

Some of the old Sarah was there in her reply. "You are so right, Mom. I *have* made my own bed, and I *will* lie in it, thankfully, there will be an Arab Moslem named Mohammad lying there with me."

Chapter 36

Sarah's aunt drove her over to the farm to pack-up the things she wanted from her room. Martha had called her sister the day before to say that they were coming over and to ask when would be a convenient time. The conversation had not gone well.

Emily had said that tomorrow would be fine between noon and two. She and Dave were going into town to shop and would be having lunch at *McDonald's* anyway. She had added: *Be sure you are gone by two.*

Martha was the older of the two sisters, and *the one with the most common sense* she thought. She told Emily that she was being: *stubborn, unreasonable, pig-headed, obstinate, closed-minded and cantankerous* – all the synonyms she could think of to describe Emily's character at that moment. Emily slammed the receiver down but not before Martha *thought* she heard: *this is also your fault.*

Martha loved her sister, but there were times when she thought that no matter how old Emily was she needed her skirt lifted and a razor strap applied to her backside.

Sarah and her aunt arrived at the farm a little after twelve. Her dad's pick-up truck was gone. There was a note taped to the screen. *Please leave your key on the hall table.* It was unsigned.

Sarah turned to her aunt, "I guess it couldn't be any clearer, could it? I am no longer welcome here."

Martha hugged her. "Well, love, you always have a home with Uncle Ken and me. Your mom and dad will come around. Why one time, when we were girls, Emily didn't speak to me for six months." Aunt Martha chuckled, "She thought she was punishing me, but it was like a *holiday.*"

Martha had picked-up boxes at the grocery store. She and Sarah packed away Sarah's childhood.

It took them a little over an hour to strip the room of all reminders of Sarah. The desk drawers were empty. The dresser drawers were empty. In the closet only naked hangers hung. There was nothing on the shelves or on the top of the dresser and desk.

Sarah opened the two windows, just a little, so the afternoon breeze could flow through the room and carry out with it the remaining *scent* of Sarah.

When she and Martha put the last of the boxes in the pick-up bed, Sarah went back into the house and put her key on the table in the hall beside the phone. She did not leave a note. As Martha drove down the dirt drive that lead to the road, Sarah turned one last time and looked at the house in which she had been raised. The tears rolled silently down her cheeks.

Martha reached over and patted her hand. "Don't worry, love, you'll be back. This is just a bend in your road."

"I didn't want it to end this way. I *really* thought that they would love me enough to accept my marriage. I *never* thought there would come a time when they *didn't want to even see me.*"

Martha didn't say anything. Oh, she could have mouthed platitudes, but she *knew* Emily as Ken *knew* Dave; they were narrow-minded and stubborn; they had seen Sarah's marriage to Mohammad as a *betrayal* of them and what they stood for. In her heart she doubted if they would *ever come around.*

When they got back to her uncle's and aunt's, Sarah sorted through the boxes. She put aside those things she would take to Purdue; the rest of the things she neatly packed in the boxes, folded the tops down, and wrote with a felt-tipped pen what was in each box. There were shelves in the garage where she could store her boxes.

In the guestroom, she repacked her two suitcases. She took the photo of her folks out of its frame and slipped the picture into her Bible. She never actually *read* her Bible, but she did keep it on the nightstand next to her bed. The picture was secreted among the pages of a book she never opened.

Her Aunt Martha came into the guestroom. She had a hammer with her. "What's the hammer for?" Sarah asked.

"I want to take down this single bed and move the double bed from the other spare room into here. This room is so bright and sunny. There is a view of the pond and the woods from that window. It's a much nicer room than the spare room. I think it is the perfect room for you and Mohammad when you come to visit on holidays. This is going to be *your* room, Sarah. And here," she said, placing it on the dresser, "is a key to the front door."

Sarah went over to her aunt and wrapped her arms around her aunt. "I don't know what to say."

"Why there is *nothing* to say; this is your home for as long as you want, love."

Nijmeh and Omar were relieved that Mohammad was married. *Marriage added stability and maturity to a man. A man needed a wife to care for him, to hold him in the night.* Omar, one night just before Mohammad left, had said to Nijmeh as she lay securely in his arms, "No matter how old we men get, we never outgrow the need of a woman's arms about us. At first it is our mother's arms cradling us, as we grow she is always there to hug us and to reassure us that everything is alright. Then, if we are blessed, we marry a woman who also cradles us in her arms and tells us that *everything is going to be alright.*" He smiled down at Nijmeh. "I don't know what I would have done if you had not come into my life. You are my security, my *life.*"

Nijmeh reached up and kissed him on the lips. "*You* are my security and life." Nijmeh settled her head against Omar's chest. "I am so glad that Mohammad now has Sarah and that Issa and Yasmeen will be together. "

Mohammad's bags were packed and he was anxious to go. It had been fortunate that Amr was able to arrange for a ticket. He *really is* like another brother, Mohammad thought.

Saying good-bye to his parents had not been so difficult this time. Not for him; not for them. They all were glad that he was joining his *wife.* Nijmeh and Omar would not worry so much about him now as he would have Sarah with him. Having Sarah in the States *waiting* for him meant in some ways that he was not *leaving home* but that he was *going home.*

His short visit with Khalil and Mansur and Zaleena had gone well. He noticed a marked change in Khalil regarding Sarah. It seemed that once Mohammad and Sarah were married, Khalil automatically assumed that he had a new sister-in-law to love. Because he loved Mohammad, this love seemed to splash over and include Sarah.

Uncle Ken had decided to drive his station wagon to Indianapolis and then on to Purdue. It had plenty of space in the back for Sarah's suitcases and boxes, and there would be ample room for Mohammad's baggage as well. He had thought of taking the pick-up, but Martha had joked that there wouldn't be room in the pick-up for her *and* Mohammad and that she *definitely* wanted to go and meet him.

Uncle Ken pulled the station wagon into the airport parking lot, just as Mohammad's flight flashed *Arrived* on the notice board. It was perfect timing. They had no sooner walked down the long corridor to the gate when passengers started filing through the arrival door.

Mohammad must have been about the fifteenth person to exit through the gate. He scanned the faces of those in the crowd looking for sight of Sarah. Aunt Martha poked Sarah when she saw a tall, darkly handsome man with curly black hair look their way. "Is that Mohammad?"

"Mohammad! Mohammad! Over here!" Sarah screamed.

As soon as he had cleared the barriers, he dropped his bags as Sarah flew into his arms. He lifted her off the floor and swung her around, kissing her in front of the crowd. "Sarah, *habeeptee!*"

Sarah looked into his face and kissed him again. "I'm so glad you are here," she murmured against his lips.

Finally, he set her down, but held tightly to her hand. "I want you to meet my Aunt Martha and Uncle Ken."

Mohammad nodded politely and shook Ken's hand. "Don't think you are going to shake *my* hand," laughed Aunt Martha as she grabbed Mohammad in a bear hug and kissed him soundly on the cheek. "It isn't every day that I get to hug and kiss a handsome *young* man," she said as she winked at Ken.

"Here, let me take your bag, son. You just wrap your arm around our girl there. She's been missing you like a one-armed painter misses his arm" Mohammad looked confused at first; he didn't quite understand the metaphor, but then he smiled as it dawned on him what Uncle Ken meant.

They walked to *Baggage Claim* to retrieve Mohammad's suitcases. When the bags finally began their slow meandering on the conveyor belt, Sarah was a bit surprised at how *large* they were. "Did you have to pay extra weight? Those are huge. You are certainly bringing back more than you went with."

"Most of what is inside those two bags are wedding gifts from Khalil, Mansur, Zaleena and Amr. *Im'me* also sent some things she thought you might need *in order to take care of me properly,*" he laughed. "I think all that is in them that is mine is a change of clothes and an extra pair of shorts.

"You can't imagine how *happy I am to see you!*" he said as he bent down and kissed her again.

"I guess I'll need that arm of yours after all," Uncle Ken laughed. "You have too many darn bags for one man to carry."

"Of course, Sir," Mohammad smiled removing his arm from around Sarah's shoulders.

"You don't need to call me *Sir;* I'm your *Uncle Ken.*"

"And I'm your *Aunt Martha;* every *little bit* of me," she laughed spreading her arms to show her hefty frame.

Ken didn't know how he had managed to squeeze Mohammad's extra large suitcases into the back of the station wagon, but he did. It was an hour's drive to Purdue. Ken pulled into a *Cracker Barrel* restaurant. "Probably time we get a little something to eat," he said.

They found a round table that overlooked the parking lot. "Order what you want;" Ken said, "it's my treat."

While they waited for their order they drank fresh lemonade and munched on bread sticks. Mohammad and Sarah sat side-by-side so they could still hold hands.

"You are certainly a handsome fellah, if you don't mind me saying so," Aunt Martha grinned. "It's a good thing Ken found me before I laid eyes on you. If I was a hundred pounds lighter and thirty years younger, I would have given Sarah a run for her money," she laughed.

Mohammad blushed. He wasn't used to this kind of banter, especially from a woman who was old enough to be his mother.

They talked about his trip; they asked questions about his family; they all tactfully did *not* mention Sarah's parents.

Mohammad found himself relaxing with Sarah's uncle and aunt. It was hard for him to believe that this man was her father's brother, and this woman was her mother's sister. They seemed to have an entirely different attitude toward him and toward his marriage to Sarah than her parents did.

"Sarah said you'll be looking for a new apartment. You'll probably have to rent a new place just to hold all the stuff that is in the back of the station wagon," Ken laughed.

"I've already paid the summer rent for the studio apartment I live in," Mohammad replied. "We'll be able to make do with that while we look for a bigger place. I'm used to sleeping in cramped quarters," he smiled. "When I was a kid, my mother, father, grandmother and nine siblings all slept in the same room."

"How did you fit that many beds into one room?" Aunt Martha asked.

"We didn't *have* beds. We slept on thin pallets that were spread on the floor at night. During the day they were stacked in an alcove over which a curtain was drawn. That one room was the bedroom at night and the sitting room during the day."

"Where did that many people sit to eat? You must have had to have a huge table."

"Nope, there was no table. During the warm weather we ate in the courtyard. My mother would lay a huge straw mat on the floor and put the food on that. Then we would all sit on the *floor* around the mat and eat. When we were done, my mother would hang the mat on the courtyard wall."

"Where did you put the little ones? I gather you didn't have highchairs." Aunt Martha was really curious about the different living situation.

"That's one of the great things of a big family. There was always a ready lap for a little one to sit in while he or she ate. I always sat in my brother, Khalil's, lap. There is fourteen years between us. I also shared the same pallet with him. My Sitteh – grandmother -- felt that a little one should be put in the care of an older one. I, of course, had my mother and father, but I also had Khalil. He was my surrogate father. He still is more like a father to me than a brother."

"You make me envious of large families. Ken and I never had any children. Oh, we had a couple of little ones, but they died in infancy. He and his brother are the only siblings in his family, and Sarah's mom and I were the only two kids in our family."

"I'm sorry about your babies dying in infancy." Mohammad paused and touched Aunt Martha's hand, "You two are certainly like parents to Sarah, and I have a feeling," he smiled, "that you are going to be like parents to me as well."

"Well, if we are all done here, we should hit the road and see this studio apartment of yours." Mohammad reached for the check, but Ken beat him to it. "I told you this is my treat."

When all the suitcases and boxes had been piled in the room, there was hardly any space to walk. Sarah had left her boxes there when she had vacated her dorm room, and with all the additional boxes and suitcases it was almost impossible to see the floor!

Martha was an organizer. "The first thing to do is empty the boxes and fill up the cupboards and drawers with things you really need. If you don't need it, put it back in a box and Ken and I will take it back to the farm. Go through the books and keep only those you think you will use."

"You have way too many clothes. Put in the dresser and hang in the closest only those things you'll actually wear. Things you only wear occasionally, things for special occasions, pack into one suitcase and we'll put the suitcase on a shelf in the closet. You only need *four* bath towels, the rest I'll take back to the farm. We'll also take back the empty suitcases. When you move into a new flat, Ken and I will drive back down, bring the suitcases and boxes and help you move."

Within two hours the flat was organized and tidy. It was hard to imagine where Martha had placed all the stuff, though a good portion of it *was* in the back of the station wagon.

Sarah put her hands on her hips and surveyed the room. "It's manageable. I can see living here for a couple of months."

Mohammad chuckled, "We even have room for about *five* kids."

Ken looked at his watch, "Well, Martha, I think it is time we were heading back. There is still a long drive ahead of us and these kids will be wanting to get to bed," he said with his eyes twinkling.

Sarah and Mohammad walked Ken and Martha to their car. "Now, you take care of our girl, son," Ken said patting Mohammad on the back. "And you take care of our boy, here," he said to Sarah hugging her.

Aunt Martha also hugged the young couple. "Now, if you want *anything, anything* at all, just pick up the phone and call.

"I don't know how to thank you for all you have done," Sarah said brokenly. When she hugged her aunt she whispered into her aunt's ear. "I wish Mom and Dad could be happy for me, too. It breaks my heart."

"It is going to *work out yet*, love, you'll see." Aunt Martha whispered back. She released Sarah and smiled at Mohammad.

Mohammad and Sarah stood and waved as Ken pulled out of the parking lot.

"I really like your uncle and aunt," Mohammad said.

"It is *obvious* that they are really taken with you, too." Sarah laughed.

They went up to their studio apartment. It looked neat and tidy and *homey.*

Mohammad removed the pillows from the back of the bed that they had made into a couch. He pulled back the cover. They had not turned on the light. There was just the soft glow from the nightlight in the bathroom.

They seemed to melt together. Sarah slowly unbuttoned his shirt; he unbuttoned her blouse and slipped it off her shoulders. As he lowered her to the bed he whispered, "I have missed you so much, my love."

Chapter 37

Mohammad and Sarah looked at the married-student housing at Purdue Village. A lot of foreign students and their families lived in this *global village* – that's what the brochure that they had picked up at the student housing office said. There were sixteen units to each building. The one-bedroom flats had a fully-functional kitchen at the end of a large sitting room. There was a bath with shower (no tub). Behind louvered doors, opposite the bathroom sink, there was a full washer and dryer. The bedroom had a huge closet that took up one wall. The flat was unfurnished. It was just a little more than what Mohammad had been paying for his studio apartment; probably, they thought, because his studio apartment was fully furnished and this was unfurnished.

When Sarah talked to her aunt, she told her that they had found an apartment that was within their price range. The only problem was that it was unfurnished.

"Unfurnished? Why that is no problem at all. This old house has furniture just begging to be used. There is furniture in the attic; and more in the barn; and I have so much stuff that I dust every week that I would be *glad* to have *you* dust. I'll take a walk through the house, attic and barn and call you back to tell you what you can have. You and Mohammad go right ahead and rent that apartment."

They did.

When Martha called back, she read off the list: "There's an antique double bed with matching dresser that used to belong to your Grandmother Wellman; your Uncle Ken picked up a new mattress from *Value City;* there's a round oak pedestal table with three matching chairs; an old-fashioned library desk and chair; and two bookshelves that I found stored in the barn. I have put together two boxes of kitchen items for you: pots, pans, dishes, silverware, glasses, cups; that kind of thing. I think that is everything except for a living room suite. Hold on, your uncle is trying to tell me something."

Sarah could hear her uncle talking to her aunt in the background. "Sarah, love, your uncle said he saw a sturdy-looking living room suite on sale at *Value City.* They also had a sofa that pulls out to make a bed, an overstuffed chair in a contrasting fabric, and two end tables. He wants this to be a *flat-warming* gift from him." She heard her aunt laugh. "Who ever heard of a *flat-warming* gift? House-warming, yes, but *flat-warming?*

"When would you like us to bring the things down?

"No, your uncle *insists* that he is paying for the mattress and living room suite. He won't listen to any argument. He can be stubborn when he wants to be. So when can you move in?

"Okay, we'll be down in two weeks. You can put the kettle on!" her aunt laughed.

When she got off the phone, Sarah was laughing. "It seems that Aunt Martha and Uncle Ken are going to *furnish* our apartment!"

"You're kidding?" Mohammad said. "Aren't they going a bit overboard? We could probably pick-up things in used furniture places or off the street, like we did that coffee-table."

"I know. It does make more sense for us to find our own things here. I think they are over compensating because of the way Mom and Dad are acting. I didn't want to say that we would find our own things here. They are being so kind and I don't want to hurt their feelings."

"You're right. They have already been so kind and generous with us; they really don't need to be doing this, but I *can* understand the motivation." Mohammad was remembering that the day after they had left, he had found in the kitchen cupboard, next to the filtered coffee tin, an envelope with a thousand dollars in it. Scribbled on the back of the envelope were the words: *A small wedding gift. Just to help you get started. Love, Aunt Martha and Uncle Ken.*

Emily had been sitting on the front porch shelling peas when the post man delivered the box. "This has come all the way from Jerusalem," he said placing it on the top step. "It's been about two months on route. It's a pretty sturdy wooden box ."

"Thanks for dropping it off," Emily said.

It was still sitting there on the top step when Dave came up from the barn. "What's this?" he asked.

"Must be something Sarah had sent to us from Jerusalem." Emily continued to rock and shell peas.

"Aren't you going to open it?"

"No, take it to the attic or to the barn. I don't want to ever see it." There were tears in her eyes as she rocked and shelled peas.

Yasmeen and Issa were married the end of August. They had a quiet, rather subdued celebration due to the *intifada*. There had been almost two weeks of curfew in the camp. The stone throwing and demonstrations had increased. Twice settlers from the nearby settlements had raided the camp: breaking car windows, shooting holes in water tanks; tossing tear gas canisters into courtyards. Saleem and Ayesha's toddler, Imad, had been rushed to the hospital with a respiratory ailment resulting from tear gas inhalation.

Yasmeen had remarked to Issa that she *was so thankful that all these things hadn't happened while Sarah was visiting.*

Yasmeen, like Nijmeh when she had been a bride, slipped easily into her in-law's family. She had been surprised on her wedding night to find that Issa had ordered a beautiful, custom made bedroom suite. They wouldn't be sleeping on the floor as she had expected. Imad and Abu Imad and Saleem had made the suite. When Issa went to pay them for it, they had insisted that it was their *wedding gift*. Finally, after much argument, they had agreed to take the cost of the materials but insisted that they would take nothing for their labor.

Hopefully, by the end of August, schools and universities would open. The Israelis were not sure if they would allow schools to open. It was a dilemma for them: was it better to have students *in* school and thus *not* in the streets or *out of school* and free to be in the streets? The problem with them being *in* school was that school was a natural place to assemble for demonstrations.

Yasmeen had been surprised when Issa had suggested that she enroll as a freshman. "I know you want to go on to college. And I *want* you to go on. I don't want you just sitting home."

Nijmeh had also insisted that she should enroll. "*Binti,* a woman should be educated. I can't read or write, and the only work I could find to help my family was to clean other peoples' houses. You are bright. You should go on to school. It is the wish of your husband; and" Nijmeh added smiling, "it is the wish of your mother-in-law! And you *know* that a good daughter-in-law always listens to her *mother-in-law.*"

Uncle Ken hitched a small U-haul to the back of his loaded pick-up and drove down to Purdue. When the furniture and boxes had been unloaded and carried into the flat, Mohammad went with him to return the U-haul to the U-haul place in Lafayette. They then went to Mohammad's studio apartment and loaded the bed of the pick-up with the boxes and suitcases that were to be transferred to the new flat. The only piece of furniture they had was the coffee table that he and Sarah had found sitting on the curb waiting for the garbage van.

When they got back to the flat, *drill-sergeant* Aunt Martha had been hard at work. Aunt Martha's beautiful patch-work quilt covered the already made-up bed. The dresser had been strategically placed, and there was a rocker (that Aunt Martha said she had no place for) in the corner.

The *Value City* living room set had been artfully arranged and a crocheted afghan (again, something that Aunt Martha said she had no use for, but had been only *gathering moths in a drawer*) was *casually* thrown over the back of the Scottish-plaid over-stuffed chair. It looked like an ad for living room furniture one saw in magazines.

The oak pedestal table was in place; the three chairs pushed under it. The old-fashioned desk had been placed under the one window in the living room.

Mohammad couldn't believe that this had all happened within two hours. "Did you wave a magic wand? I can't believe all you have done." Mohammad marveled.

Sarah smiled. "When Aunt Martha goes into overdrive, nothing stops her. All the dishes and pots and pans are put away, and the kettle is boiling on the stove for coffee."

"*Amazing!* All I can say is *amazing!*" Mohammad said.

Sarah opened the refrigerator. "She stocked the refrigerator and," Sarah pulled open the louvered door on the pantry closet, "the pantry. She even gave us some of the canned peaches and pears we put up this summer."

"*Unbelievable!* I guess I can say another word than *amazing!*" Mohammad smiled as he gave Aunt Martha a hug. "It *is* a good thing I didn't see you first!" he joked.

They all hauled the boxes and suitcases out of the pick-up into the flat. Within no time, Martha and Sarah had everything put in drawers, placed on bookshelves, and hung in closets.

Finally, they all sat and had a cup of coffee and some of the cookies that Aunt Martha had baked the day before.

Mohammad put his feet up on the coffee table and sighed. "Home. You have transformed this empty apartment into *home.* I don't know how to thank you."

"Oh, I almost forgot. There is another small gift for you in the truck. I'll be right back." Uncle Ken came back into the apartment carrying a small box. He gave it to Mohammad to open.

Mohammad pried the stapled flaps open and pulled out a small, portable TV. "I know you'll both be studying most of the time, but I thought you might like to relax a bit, now and then, and watch a movie or something. It's small, but I thought you might like it."

Sarah bounded out of the chair and gave him a big hug. "You have thought of everything. It's just the right size. It's perfect. It will even save us money; we won't need to pay to go and see a film. We can just sit here in our pajamas,"

"Who wears pajamas?" Mohammad grinned.

"As I was saying," Sarah resumed first sticking her tongue out at Mohammad, "we can just sit here in our pajamas- those of us who *wear* pajamas- and eat popcorn that we have popped ourselves and enjoy a film."

"Before we head back, I'd like to take you out to dinner," Uncle Ken said.

"Oh, no you don't. Not this time. *This time* you and Aunt Martha will be our guests. We are going to take you to our favorite restaurant *The Chinese Dragon*. I hope you all like Chinese," Mohammad said.

Aunt Martha laughed, "Just look at me. Do I look like a woman who turns down *any kind* of food? I like to think of myself as quite *cosmopolitan* when it comes to eating."

Later that night, after Uncle Ken and Aunt Martha had started back to the farm, Mohammad and Sarah stood in the middle of their new flat. "It is really beautiful," Mohammad said. "It doesn't look like a student flat; it looks like a real home."

Sarah put her arm around his waist and leaned against his shoulder. "It *is* a real home."

Mohammad leaned down and kissed her on top of the head. "You know, with a place *this* size, we probably have room for *six* kids."

Sarah poked him in the ribs and laughingly said, "Dream on, my Arab *sheikh,* dream on!"

Chapter 38

Mohammad and Sarah decided to go to the Court House in Indianapolis and get an official American marriage license. There were no vows to be said; it meant filling out an application, paying the $18, and signing the document in front of a judge. All they needed were picture IDs and two witnesses.

Sarah's former roommate had a VW bug and offered to drive them to Indianapolis. Her roommate's boyfriend would go along as the second witness.

It was such an easy procedure. It really wasn't a ceremony; it was merely paperwork. They did have to wait in line a bit, but when it was their turn the judge looked over the application, glanced at their IDs, had them and the witnesses sign on the dotted line, congratulated them and said: *You are now Mr. and Mrs. Mohammad Omar Mansur.* That was it.

On the way back to Purdue, Sarah's roommate pulled into a Mall that had a *Sears.* "You have to have a photo to commemorate your civil ceremony," she joked.

"We are *wearing jeans* and sports shirts!" Sarah protested.

"Perfect," her roommate laughed. "Jeans somehow seem quite *appropriate* for a Court House wedding."

"*My* jeans and sports shirt are *new,*" Mohammad grinned. "I think I look quite debonair."

"*You,*" Sarah laughed, "would think you were quite debonair in boxer shorts and socks!"

"I don't think you can pose in boxer shorts and socks at *Sears,*" her roommate's boyfriend added.

They couldn't help laughing as the photographer tried to pose them. He finally got them situated where Sarah was sitting between Mohammad's legs. Mohammad's arms were around her. His shirt was unbuttoned just enough to show the top of his hairy chest. He had joked with Sarah that it was an *Arab thing.* All Arab men, he said, left the first two buttons of their shirts unbuttoned. Sarah had only rolled her eyes. His chin rested slightly on her curls. They smiled into the camera.

Her roommate dropped them off in front of the building complex that housed their flat. When they got to their second floor apartment, Mohammad opened the door and before Sarah could enter, he whisked her up into his arms and carried her over the threshold.

"I saw this in a movie once," he had joked. "Isn't this what American bridegrooms do?"

Sarah kissed him and smiled. "Yes, you have your traditions and we, Americans, do have a few of our own."

Mohammad set her down. He was laughing. "What's tickling you?" Sarah asked poking him playfully in the ribs.

"Oh, I was just thinking about different customs. Zaleena was telling me that among the Circassians a bridegroom sweeps down into the girl's village on his horse; he scoops her up and basically kidnaps her. He *then* negotiates with her parents. You were so lucky that my mother wasn't sitting outside the bedroom door at the American Colony waiting for the *stained sheet!*"

"What do you mean, *waiting for the stained sheet?*" Sarah asked incredulously.

"Years ago, it was the *custom* for the mother-in-law to wait outside the bedroom door for the marriage to be consummated. Once it had been, her son would hand his mother the stained sheet. She would then hang it on the line for the neighbors to see – proof that the bride had been a virgin."

"And, if there *was* no show?" Sarah asked.

"Then the bridegroom, if he really loved the bride, would make a small cut in his leg and *stain the sheet* himself."

"Would you have cut your leg for me?" Sarah teased.

"I would have cut *both* legs and *both* arms for you?" Mohammad joked kissing her.

"Now that we are officially married, *twice,* we should open our wedding gifts."

They had purposely left the suitcase containing the presents Khalil and Mansur and Zaleena had sent unopened. Sarah had wanted to open the suitcase, but Mohammad had wanted to keep the presents as a surprise until they had had their civil ceremony. *Anticipation is half the fun of presents* he had said. So, Sarah had waited.

Mohammad dragged the heavy suitcase out from under the antique bed. He dragged it into the living room and told Sarah to open it.

"I'm anxious to see what they have sent! **I** haven't seen their gifts yet, either. Zaleena insisted on packing the presents herself and made me swear that I wouldn't open the suitcase until you were present."

Sarah unbuckled the straps and unzipped the suitcase. She threw the lid back. The suitcase was bursting with presents. On the top, neatly folded, was a small, silk rug. There was a note attached to it. *This rug is from the Caucasus region of Russia. Circassian brides must take to their new homes a hand-woven prayer rug.*

Sarah unfolded the rug and spread it out. It was beautiful. It was woven in crimson and blue threads. The center border was made of twists and turns that looked like braids. The two braids were crowned with a large arrow. "The rug should be placed on the floor so that arrow points east toward Mecca," Mohammad explained.

Sarah folded it and placed it on the sofa behind her. Next she took out four embroidered pillow shams. A note was also pinned to them. *Palestinians are known for their cross-stitch embroidery. These four pillow covers were done by refugee women. I hope they will fit the décor of your home.*

Sarah held them out for Mohammad to see. The shams were full of embroidery. Like the rug, the silk used was crimson and blue. They had obviously been chosen to compliment the colors in the rug.

Beneath the rug and pillow shams, a brass tray had been wedged. It was alive with Arabic calligraphy that had been etched into its surface. Again there was a note of explanation from Zaleena. *This tray and the wooden stand you will find beneath it come from Damascus. The calligraphy that runs along its edge is a line from the Quran wishing health and blessings on the household in which this tray rests. It will, inshallah, add a bit of the Orient to your home.*

Mohammad reached into the suitcase and took out the wooden legs. He unfolded them and Sarah set the tray on top. "It is beautiful." Sarah said. "It reminds me of a similar tray-table that your brother, Mansur, has in his sitting room. They have been so generous with us!"

Sarah reached into the bag again and drew out a small chamois bag. The note attached said, *For Sarah from Khalil.*

Sarah opened the bag and spilled the contents into her lap. There were three gold bracelets. Two were quite thin, and obviously a pair. The third looked like twisted gold. At the end of each twist was a flat, pear-shaped form. When the bracelet was placed on a woman's arm, the twists could be squeezed close so that the flat, pear-shaped forms touched.

Sarah slipped it on her wrist and pressed the twists closed. It was exquisite! She looked up at Mohammad and there were tears in her eyes. "It is all too much," she said. "These gold bracelets must have cost a fortune."

Mohammad smiled. "Every Palestinian bride must have gold bracelets. It is Khalil's way of welcoming you to the family."

Mohammad reached in and handed Sarah another gift. This one was a black jeweler's box. The note attached read: *For Sarah from Mansur.*

Sarah lifted the lid and there, resting on its satin lining, was a heavy gold chain and a pair of diamond earrings. The tears slowly ran down Sarah's cheeks. She wiped them away with the back of her hand. "I'll have to get my ears pierced," she laughed brokenly.

There were still *more* gifts. There was a lovely green table cloth covered with gold embroidery. The note attached read: *Damascus is also known for its machine-worked table covers. The work is done by hand. The woman turns the fabric on a sewing machine, creating with the turns the embroidered design.*

Sarah placed the table cloth on the sofa beside the silk prayer rug and cross-stitch pillow covers.

Mohammad handed her a small carton. She opened it and found six crystal tea glasses with six glass saucers. He handed her another box. When she opened it she found six Arabic coffee cups and saucers.

At the bottom of the suitcase, wrapped in a white *dish-dash* (traditional Arab men's garb) and white *kuffiyeh,* was a small brass serving tray. The note attached said. *The dish-dash and kuffiyeh are from Mecca and are for Mohammad. The brass tray is to use when you serve tea or coffee to your guests.* It was signed *Amr.*

Mohammad unwrapped the tray and shook out the *dish-dash.* He smiled and said to Sarah, "This is like the *dish-dash* that my father wears. We should go and have our picture taken with me wearing this, and you wearing my mother's wedding *thob.*

When the tray was unwrapped, an envelope fell on the floor. Mohammad read what was written on the envelope in Arabic. It said: *Congratulations. Inshallah you have a hundred years together.* It was signed *Amr.* Inside Mohammad counted ten new, crisp one hundred dollar bills.

Mohammad and Sarah looked at the wealth spread before them. They didn't know what to say. His family had been overly generous.

"I am speechless," Sarah said. "Everything is perfect, but way *too much."*

Sarah started to cry. Mohammad went over and sat beside her on the floor. He put his arms around her and drew her head down to his shoulder.

"What's wrong, *habeeptee?*"

"I am just thinking how wonderful your family has been about this, and how absolutely *horrid* my parents have been. Your family didn't *want* me to marry you; yet once we decided they *accepted* and *welcomed* me into the family. I so wanted Mom and Dad to *accept* and *welcome* you into our family. I never thought that they would turn me out and not *even want to see me.*"

Mohammad just held her close and murmured endearments into her hair. There wasn't much he could say to ease her hurt.

"Your folks will probably come around in time. It *is* asking a lot to force an Arab Moslem son-in-law on them."

"No more than asking your family to accept an American Christian daughter-n-law!"

"Your Aunt Martha and Uncle Dave have been supportive. In fact, they have been *more than supportive.* Just look around, *all of this* is thanks to them. When you think about it, we have a lot to be thankful for."

Sarah smiled and kissed Mohammad's cheek. "I know," she said drying her tears. "It is just that I *wish* so much that things were different with my parents."

"Didn't your Aunt Martha say that things would be different *once the first grandchild arrives?*" Mohammad joked. "Maybe we should be working on that grandchild?"

"You think *this* is the answer to everything."

"If it isn't; *it should be!*"

Chapter 39

The summer course they had signed up for was time-consuming and distracting. A lot had to be crammed into the three weeks. It was quite intensive, but interesting. Both Sarah and Mohammad were good students, and it was a plus that they could discuss the course with each other and read to the other the required papers. Aside from two required papers, the course was based on class attendance and one big exam at the end.

They had discovered that they worked better *living together*. They felt that they would both ace the course.

There was to be a three-week break between the summer course and the fall term. Aunt Martha had suggested that they come to the farm for those three weeks. Sarah was hesitant. She was bound to run into her parents; and the folks in town had probably *heard* that she was married and that her parents had, basically, thrown her out. It was an awkward situation.

She had mentioned this when she talked to Aunt Martha. "I know it will be awkward, love, but the sooner it is faced the better. I was thinking of having a small celebration for you here, but to invite folks here puts *them* in an awkward position. I know the majority of the folks would *like* to come and offer their congratulations. Why, they have known you since you were a little girl. I suspect," she laughed, "that some folks are curious to see Mohammad. Not many have seen an Arab Moslem before. But even though they are probably *dying* to meet him and *wanting* to see you, they probably don't want to be seen as *taking sides.*"

"So, what's the solution? I don't want to be tense all the time that we are staying with you. I don't want it to be hard on Mohammad. I *would* like to have something there for my friends and family, but I don't see how that is possible with Mom and Dad being the way they are."

"Let Uncle Ken and I go and talk to your folks once more. I'm not promising anything, but I'll sound them out to see how they would feel about us hosting a small gathering here."

"I don't think they'll be willing for you to do that. It would just make more *obvious* the fact that they are unhappy about the marriage."

"It doesn't hurt to try. What's your mom going to do? I'm bigger than her. *Lordy*, I'm bigger than almost anybody," Aunt Martha laughed. "She can't push me around. Oh, she can give me a tongue-lashing, but I can give as good as I get. Leave it to me."

That evening, Ken and Martha went to see Emily and Dave. It was just dusk when they drove their beat-up truck up their dirt drive and parked in front of the house. Dave and Emily were sitting on the front porch rocking.

"Nice evening, isn't it?" Ken remarked.

"What do you two want?" Dave asked.

"Is that anyway to greet your brother and sister-in-law? We came to sit a spell." Ken said.

"You came *to tell us* something, not to sit a spell. So, you might as well spill it while you are standing and be on your way."

"I'm too heavy to stand here when there is a vacant rocker just beckoning me to *sit.*" Martha said. She ignored Dave and sat down and began to rock.

Ken sat on the top step and leaned his back against the porch's pillar.

"I guess you can't take a hint," Dave said as he shifted in his rocker.

"Now, Dave, I don't want to have to wrestle you in the yard. I'd really hate to whip you in front of your wife. But keep pushing me, and by God, I will."

"I talked to Sarah today, and she asked about you." Martha said.

There was no reply.

"She and Mohammad have a three-week break between the summer course they're taking and the fall term. I invited them to come and stay with us. Sarah doesn't feel comfortable doing that. She thinks it would upset you two." Martha continued to rock.

"What Sarah does is of no consequence to us," Emily answered. "She can do as she pleases, just like she has always done."

"I can see I should have brought Dad's old razor strap and given you a good tanning. For a grown woman, you sure do act childish sometimes," Martha said.

"If I had a daughter like Sarah I would go to the moon to get whatever would make her happy. I wouldn't toss her out the door and refuse to see her. Shame on you, Emily, and you,

Dave; you shouldn't be treating your only daughter in such a fashion." Martha bristled.

"This is *our* affair, but I can see you have made it yours!" Dave spat. "You always did put your nose in where it wasn't wanted."

"That may be" Martha calmly said. "I always *was* a bit bossy. Wasn't I, Ken?"

"I'm going to *boss* some more, since I am so good at it. I want to have a little wedding party for Sarah and Mohammad; invite some of the town's folk; some of the neighbors. Nothing fancy, just a barbeque in the yard. Now, Sarah seems to think that you two won't like that idea and that it will make it too *obvious* to the neighbors that you are unhappy about her marriage – that you have basically thrown her out."

"I can't believe you would even *suggest* having a party to celebrate her wedding!" Emily protested.

"There is a solution, you know? You and Dave could have the party here, where it should be; this way the neighbors won't know how you really feel and will just think what they have heard is only unfounded *rumor.*"

"Sarah and her *Arab* husband *are not* welcome here," Emily said. "And if you two host a party for them, it will be like *hanging our dirty laundry* in front of the whole town."

"Sarah and her husband won't be the *only* ones not welcome around here," Dave added.

"Well, I've said my piece," Martha said shifting her weight out of the rocker. "I think it is time we were getting home, Ken."

Emily couldn't resist asking, "What are you going to do?"

"Me? Why, I'm going to barbeque some chicken and beef steaks; I'm going to bake some rhubarb pies; make some of Grandma Wellman's potato salad and coleslaw," Martha looked directly at Emily, "and I'm going to pin some dirty laundry on the line."

Martha called Sarah when she got home.

"It was just as you expected, love, but I want you to come anyway, and I'm going to throw you a wedding party. This old town *needs* to be shaken up a bit. If folks come, fine; if they don't come that is fine, too. We're going to have a party whether it is just the four of us or the whole dang town."

Sarah and Mohammad took the *Greyhound Bus* to Des Moines where Uncle Ken picked them up. Aunt Martha had stayed home to be sure dinner was ready for them when they arrived. Sarah and Mohammad wanted to see Martha and Ken; they wanted to have a holiday at the farm before the fall term began, but they were unhappy about being so close to Sarah's parents, *knowing* her parents did not want to see them. They were uncomfortable about having a celebration that was forcing people to take sides. A wedding celebration *shouldn't* be that way. It should be a time of joy and happiness.

After dinner, Mohammad asked Uncle Ken to show him around the farm. Sarah had helped Aunt Martha with the dishes and said, "I think I'll take a walk around the edge of the pond. It's almost sundown and the sky is beautiful."

"Don't be long, love. We'll have pie on the porch when you get back."

The pond wasn't too far from the house. Martha, looking out her kitchen window, had a good view of the pond. There were a flock of geese meandering around it. *It looks like a picture on a calendar,* Martha thought.

Sarah was watching the ducks swim lazily in the pond, when she was grabbed from behind! At first she thought it was Mohammad. She smiled and turned, "What do you think you're doing. You scared me!" It wasn't Mohammad. It was Sam!

"I've been waiting for you. Your dad told me you were coming here with your *Camel Jockey.*" Sam started to pull her toward the woods. Sarah struggled.

"Let me go! What do you think you're doing?"

"I'm going to do what I have wanted to do for years. I have loved you since we were in our teens; I still love you." There were unshed tears in his eyes. He lowered his face and started to kiss her neck.

Sarah felt the panic in her stomach. She forced herself to relax. They had just reached the edge of the woods when Sarah fought her repulsion and kissed him. He let go of her arms for just a moment and started to unbuckle his belt.

Sarah swallowed the vomit that had risen in her throat. She reached down into his briefs, cupped his balls in an iron fist and *squeezed.* As he yelled, she dug her fingernails into his balls. His erection quickly faded. She twisted his balls as though she would rip them from his body. He bent over and began to vomit. He was in obvious pain.

"You ever try that again," she hissed, "I will rip off your sorry balls and feed them to the geese."

Sam raised his head to protest when he saw Aunt Martha standing there with a tire iron. She had seen him drag Sarah toward the woods and had gotten a tire iron out of the bed of the truck and raced down to the pond.

"His puny balls wouldn't be much food for my geese. I say we just kill him, chop up his body and feed it to the pigs." Aunt Martha wasn't smiling.

"I'm...I'm sorry," he stammered. "I don't know what came over me. I'm *really* sorry, Sarah." Sam looked embarrassed and sick. He pulled up his pants, and fastened his zipper and belt. He backed away from Martha and Sarah. "Please don't tell my folks. My dad would kill me."

"That's good to know," Martha said. "He'll have to stand in line. There will be me, and Ken, and of course the *Camel Jockey*. Have you heard what they do to men who mess with their wives?"

He shook his head.

"Better that you don't know; it would scare the shit right out of you," Martha said grimly.

Sam backed into the woods, then turned and ran.

"That was good thinking squeezing his balls like that," Aunt Martha said. "He sure didn't expect that."

"I knew he was stronger than me, but I also knew that if I made him *think* that I liked it that I could grab him at his weakest spot. I hated it. I almost threw up myself."

"You did good, love. You did good."

"Let's not say anything to Mohammad or Uncle Ken."

"This is just between you and me, love."

As they walked back to the house they ran into Mohammad and Ken. Ken noticed the tire iron in Martha's hand. "What are you doing with a tire iron?"

"Oh, I thought I saw a fox lurking in the woods watching my geese."

"What were you going to do, brain him with the tire iron?" Ken laughed.

"Some foxes *need* braining."

Chapter 40

"I think I'll skip the pie, Aunt Martha. I'm feeling all-in. I think I'll call it a night and go on up." Sarah hugged her aunt and said, "Thanks for *everything.*"

"Aren't you feeling well, *habeeptee?* You look like you are running a little fever." Mohammad felt her forehead. "You seem cool enough, but your cheeks are flushed."

"I'm just tired I think: changing apartments, the summer course, the trip here. I think it has finally caught up to me a bit. A little rest and I'll be fine. There's nothing to worry about. You stay and have some pie." She patted him on the chest.

"Okay, but I'll be up shortly."

Mohammad watched her as she went in and up the stairs. "Do you think she is alright, Aunt Martha? I don't like the way she looks."

"She'll be fine. She just needs a good, long sleep in a comfortable bed. Now, you just sit down here and talk with Ken while I go in and get that pie."

As Aunt Martha went into the hall, she looked up the stairs and frowned. *I feel like punching somebody, and I think I'll start with Dave and Emily and then drive on over to Sam's.*

"That was delicious pie, Aunt Martha."

"Would you like another piece?"

Mohammad shook his head no and patted his stomach. "If I have another piece, Sarah will divorce me and get married to that neighbor boy her parents wanted her to marry," Mohammad joked. "I know it is early, but I think I will turn in, too."

"You get a good sleep, son. We'll see you in the morning," Uncle Ken said.

As soon as Mohammad had gone upstairs, Martha took off her apron and draped it over the back of the porch rocker. "I'm going to run over to see Emily and Dave," she said to Ken.

"They *don't* want to see you. No point in stirring up trouble." Ken said.

"I frankly don't care if they want to see me or not. I'm in the *mood* for stirring up some trouble!" Martha stooped and picked-up the tire iron she had laid beside the front steps.

"What's that for?"

"You never know, I might find something or *someone* I want to brain," she answered.

When Mohammad tie-toed in the bedroom it seemed that Sarah was already asleep. Mohammad went into the bathroom; brushed his teeth, washed his hands and hung his clothes on the bathroom hook. In just his boxers, he slid between the cool sheets, spooning himself against the sleeping Sarah.

When she felt Mohammad slip into bed and snuggle close to her, Sarah turned and lay her head on his chest. She wept, wetting the hairs on his chest with her tears. "Sarah, what's wrong, *habeeptee!*" Mohammad asked in alarm.

"Just hold me, please, just hold me," she wept.

Mohammad tightened his arms around her; resting his chin against the top of her head. "What's wrong?" he whispered. "Tell me what's wrong?"

"I'll be alright; I just need you to hold me."

Mohammad held her. Her weeping finally ceased and she fell into an exhausted sleep. For a long time he lay awake, staring into the darkness, wondering what had caused Sarah such grief, until he, too, fell into a restless sleep.

The lights were on in the living room when Martha parked the truck in front of Dave and Emily's gate. She didn't bother to knock; she walked in the front door and right into the living room.

Dave and Emily were watching TV and looked up in surprise.

"We heard a car drive up, and I was just getting up to see who it could be," Emily said. "How dare you just walk right in without even knocking or calling *hello* through the screen door; the very idea, who do you think you are?"

"Emily, *shut up*! If I hear *one* word from you, or from *you, Dave,* I'm going to start breaking up your furniture with this tire iron."

Dave and Emily looked at her as though she had lost her mind. Dave picked up the remote and turned the volume up on the TV. "There's nothing you have to say that we want to hear"

Martha walked over to the TV and smashed the screen with the tire iron. "Now you know I mean business," she said.

"Have you lost your mind!?" Dave roared.

"You listen to what I have come to say or I'll break *more* than the TV."

They sat in stunned silence, convinced that Martha had *gone mad.*

"Did you tell that boy, Sam, that Sarah was staying at our place with her '*Camel Jockey*' husband? I think that is the phrase he used to describe Mohammad?"

"I might have said something to him to that effect," Dave mumbled. "Why?"

"Well, that *upstanding* boy, whom you have been trying to push on Sarah all these years, came to pay her a visit. You want to know what that, *well-brought up, good Christian, salt-of-the-earth* boy did?" Martha was so angry that she couldn't speak. She kept hitting the palm of her hand with the tire iron.

"Sarah was out watching the sun set over the pond. That nice *Christian* boy," Martha said sarcastically, "grabbed her and dragged her into the woods. I saw them from the window over the sink. I snatched up this tire iron from the truck and flew through the field like I was being chased by the devil himself." Martha stopped again to gain control as she glared at Dave and Emily.

Dave and Emily sat there in shock. Dave's face got red and he curled his hands into fists. Emily had tears in her eyes.

"I shouldn't have worried. Your girl, Sarah, can take care of herself. She had a vise-like grip on his balls and was twisting them so hard that he was bent over in pain and vomiting his guts out. I heard her shout at him that if he tried anything like that again she would rip them off and feed them to my geese.

"By the time he had straightened up, I was standing there ready to brain him with this here tire iron. He begged me not to tell his dad, as his dad would kill him. I told him that his dad would have to stand in line!"

By this time, Emily's tears were flowing and she kept wiping them away with the edge of her apron. The veins at the side of Dave's head were throbbing.

"I'm really pissed, *pardon my French,* at *you two;* sitting here all *injured like,* not caring one bit for your daughter. Saying to Ken and me that *what Sarah does is none of your concern.* Bull. You may not have intended to, but you gave that prick, Sam, the notion that since Sarah had married a *Camel Jockey* that she was *easy* and would welcome being raped by a good old, American, red-blooded farm boy like him!"

Martha paused and brought the tire iron down on the stand beside Dave's chair, splintering the wood and sending shards of a glass ashtray across the living room rug. "Are you hearing what I am saying? Sarah was almost *raped* tonight by that neighbor boy. The same neighbor boy whom you thought was so *right* for her. He doesn't hold a candle to Mohammad!"

Dave and Emily sat there shocked and speechless.

"Now you *think* about what I have said. That girl loves you and you better start showing that *you love her.*"

"Martha, I don't..." Emily started to explain, but Martha interrupted her.

"I *know* you wouldn't have wanted this to happen. But you have given the impression that you think that Sarah marrying an Arab Moslem is wrong. You have given the impression that Mohammad is somehow *inferior* to the local farm boys. You have let it be known that you have thrown Sarah out and that you don't care what happens to her. You haven't stood behind your daughter as you should."

Martha walked to the front door and turned. "I'm sorry about the TV and side table. My anger got the best of me. Nobody knows about what Sam tried to do. Sarah made me promise I wouldn't tell Ken or Mohammad. She said nothing about not telling you."

Dave walked to the pick-up with her. "I don't know what to say or what to think."

"The words will come to you after you have thought it through. You and Emily will figure out the *right* thing to do."

Dave said looking intently into Martha's eyes. "You're not going home right away, are you?"

"Nope, I have one more visit to make. She raised the tire iron so Dave could see it. "I need to see a father about his son."

Chapter 41

Martha had gone to a one-room school with Sam's parents. In fact, his dad had had a schoolboy crush on her when she was thirteen, willowy, with black eyes that snapped and brown braids whose ends were *perfect* for dunking into inkwells – at least Sam's dad used to think so. His mother, Betty, when she and Martha were in their later adolescence, had been her best friend. Sam had *obviously* not realized the connection that Martha had with his parents.

His parents were sitting on the porch swing enjoying the warm summer night. They were surprised and pleased to see Martha get out of the truck and walk up the walk.

"This *is* a nice surprise," Sam's mother said getting up from the swing and giving Martha a hug. "Have you lost weight?" she joked. "Why didn't you bring Ken with you?"

"It's really not a social call, I'm afraid."

"Sit down, Martha, take a load off your feet," Sam's dad said. "Is that a *tire iron* you've got there?"

Martha sat down and placed the tire iron across her lap. "I thought I just might need it. Is your son here?"

"He's in watching TV," Betty said.

"Would you mind calling him?"

"Sam! *Sam*, get out here, we have company," his dad hollered.

"What's this all about, Martha?"

"I'd rather say when Sam is present."

When Sam saw who was sitting in the porch chair, he blanched. "Mrs. Goldman," he stammered.

"Sit down, boy, Mrs. Goldman has something she wants us *all* to hear," his dad ordered.

"It seems your son here thought he could *have his way* with my niece, Sarah."

"What?" Betty gasped. His dad just glared at him.

"He was over at our place this evening, hiding like a fox in the woods down by our pond. Sarah took a little stroll down by the pond after supper. I was just wiping out the sink and happened to glance out the kitchen window."

"Mrs. Goldman, *please...*" Sam stammered.

"You, shut your mouth," his father ordered. "Go on, Martha, we're listening."

"He grabbed our Sarah and dragged her to the edge of the woods. By the time I got there, his jeans were around his ankles; he was throwing-up all over his boots, and Sarah was about to rip his balls off."

Both of Sam's parents glared at their son, barely able to control their rage.

"I told Sarah that we should *just kill him and feed his worthless flesh to the pigs.* Oh, he apologized and said *he didn't know what came over him,* and begged me not to tell you. He thought you would kill him. I told him that you would have to stand in line."

"He's our son. Betty and I get *first* dibs on killing him." Sam's dad said.

"What do you have to say for yourself, Sam," his mother asked; her face was red with anger.

"I know what I tried to do was wrong. I am really sorry about it; I guess I just went crazy thinking about Sarah married to an Arab."

"Crazy enough to try and *rape* her?" his dad said trying to hold in his anger.

"It wasn't *rape,* dad, Sarah *wanted* me. When we went into the woods, she kissed me like she really wanted me."

Martha interrupted. "He's right. Sarah *did* kiss him. She knew he was stronger than she was. She knew he could overpower her if she struggled, so she forced herself to be calm so he would release her arms."

Sam's parents looked Martha in the eyes. "We apologize for our son, Martha. You have every right to be angry. We're glad you came to us and didn't go to the sheriff."

"Sarah doesn't want anyone to know, though I did stop by to see Dave and Emily. Martha sheepishly smiled, "I used this tire iron on their TV and one of their end tables. I was so angry I needed to break something."

"You should have used your tire iron on Sam" Betty said. "I am so ashamed of him."

"Mom!"

"You hush your mouth. I'll deal with you later," his mother said.

"I'll deal with him right now. Get yourself down to the barn and wait for me," his dad spat at him.

"Dad, please!" Sam said his lips quivering. He was trying not to cry.

Martha saw his trembling, and for just a fraction of a moment she felt a little sorry for him. Then she thought of Sarah and what he had attempted to do, and any sympathy she had momentarily felt for him vanished.

"We're obliged to you, Martha," Betty said. "I am so terribly ashamed and so sorry. Please, when you can talk to Sarah alone apologize for us. Give her our assurance that Sam will *never* do anything like this again."

"He won't be *able to*," his father said grimly.

Sarah had been restless all night. She had cried and murmured in her sleep. Mohammad couldn't make out clearly what she was saying. He did hear the words: *Sam, geese, and vomit.* Mohammad had held her all night. It seemed to calm her. He didn't want to move for fear of disturbing her, consequently he couldn't feel the arm on which she had lain all night.

The roosters were just heralding the dawn of a new day when Sarah awoke. She blinked her eyes. Her head was resting against Mohammad's chest. She looked up, and he was awake. He smiled at her and kissed the top of her nose.

"You're awake. Did you get any rest at all last night?" He asked. "You talked a lot in your sleep, *habeeptee;* just ramblings, nothing that I could really understand."

"I'm much better now, though I do feel like I have been run over by a *Mack Truck*. I feel I could sleep all day."

"Why don't you? We're on vacation. You can stay in bed all day if you want." Mohammad said.

"I *would* like one thing," she blushed.

"What is that, *habeeptee?* You have but to ask. I am at your command," Mohammad smiled rubbing her chin with his thumb.

"Love me. I need you to *love me*," Sarah said as she moved on top of him and slipped her tongue between his lips.

When Mohammad came downstairs later for breakfast, he was whistling. "You certainly are chipper this morning," Aunt Martha commented as she poured him a cup of coffee.

"It's already been a great morning," he grinned.

"Isn't Sarah coming down?" she asked.

"She didn't rest much last night, so she is going to have a bit of a lie in this morning. When I came out of the bathroom after showering and dressing, she was already asleep."

"Rest is the best thing for her," Aunt Martha said sitting down beside Mohammad and passing him the scrambled eggs.

"Something must have happened last night. All night long she kept mumbling: *Sam, vomit, and feeding geese.*"

"You know how dreams are. Sometimes they are just scraps of disconnected memories. Sarah was down feeding my geese last night. It is natural that she would think of that boy, Sam. He is probably linked to her memories of being back in the area."

Aunt Martha hedged around the truth. She had promised Sarah she wouldn't say anything to Mohammad. She knew *if* she did tell him or Ken, they would go down to have it out with Sam.

"Where's Uncle Ken?"

"He's down at the barn. He is driving to the feed store in town and was wondering if you'd like to ride along. He wants to introduce you to some of his cronies."

"I'd like that. Sarah is probably going to be sleeping most of the morning anyway."

"Well, when you finish your breakfast, go down to the barn and see Ken."

As they drove into town, Uncle Ken pointed out things he thought would be of interest to Mohammad. "Now, that little brick building over there is the one-room school house that Martha and I and Sarah's folks attended when we were kids. It's no longer used as a school. The township sold it some years back and it has been turned into a mini-museum. It now houses the Historical Society.

"That building over there is the Grange."

"What's a grange?" Mohammad asked.

"Well, most folks around here are farmers. In the past the Grange was kind of the meeting place. There would be box socials there; community dinners; square dances every month.

Sometimes they would have speakers. The grange had a baseball team. Almost all of whatever social activities we had were held at the Grange."

"*Box socials? Square dances?* I don't know what those are?"

Well, used to be that the ladies of the Grange would pack a lunch in a box. There would be an auctioneer who would auction off the boxes. Young fellas would bid on the box of the girl they liked. If he had the highest bid, then the girl who made the box lunch would have to eat with him. I used to spend a lot of money bidding on the boxes that Martha made! That woman can sure cook!" Ken laughed.

"A square dance is a country dance. It's kind of like a *folk* dance. They used to be called *barn dances* because they were..."

"Held in *barns*," Mohammad grinned as he completed the sentence.

"Here's the feed store. Like the Grange used to be, it is kind of the congregating place for farmers. Come on in; I want to introduce you to some of the guys."

There were a group of men just hanging around *shooting the breeze*. "Hi, Nat, I'd like you to meet my nephew, Mohammad."

A short, muscular man in a plaid shirt and with a well-trimmed white beard shook Mohammad's hand. "I didn't know you had a nephew named Mohammad, Ken?

"Yup, I do. This is my niece, Sarah's, husband. He comes all the way from Jerusalem. He and Sarah are visiting for a couple of weeks."

"Pleased to meet you, Mohammad."

"Carl, I'd like you to meet my nephew, Mohammad."

"Mohammad, I am pleased to meet you." Carl was a tall, spare man who must have been in his late sixties. "You *don't* look much like Ken. You're a darn sight nicer looking than he will ever be. You must be a nephew on his mother's side." He laughed.

"This is my friend, Max, Mohammad. He and I were in school together."

"Mohammad, I'm glad to make your acquaintance. I had heard Sarah had married and have been curious as heck to meet you. You are nothing like I had pictured."

"You probably pictured someone with a black beard, wearing flowing robes, with a white scarf covering his head." Mohammad smiled.

"Something like that," Max grinned, "only I *think* in my picture you were riding a camel."

"Iowa was too far to bring my camel," Mohammad joked.

Mohammad was enjoying the banter.

"Well, we need to be getting along. I just wanted to introduce Mohammad to you fine folks. We're going to be hosting a barbeque Sunday afternoon so folks get a chance to see Sarah and meet Mohammad. Be sure to bring your families and come on over."

"Is Martha making her famous rhubarb pie?" Carl asked.

"I think that's on the menu."

"You can count me in."

As they were going out to the truck, they literally bumped into Dave.

Mohammad offered his hand. "We didn't expect to bump into you, Sir."

Dave saw the men in the feed store looking at him. He saw Ken looking at him. Finally, reluctantly, he briefly shook Mohammad's hand. He said nothing to him, merely nodded his head.

Mohammad slid onto the cracked leather seat. Ken turned to him with a twinkle in his eye. As he turned the key and pumped the gas, he said, "Well, he didn't spit in your eye," he chuckled, "or wipe his hand on his trousers after shaking hands with you. I call that *progress.*"

Chapter 42

All day, whenever the phone rang, Martha thought *for sure* it would be Emily. The phone had practically rung off the hook all day. The word that there was going to be a Sunday-Barbeque at their place had spread. Ken had only mentioned it to three old cronies of his at the feed store, and before three in the afternoon, Martha must have had a dozen phone calls from folks saying they would be coming.

When a few neighbor women had asked why Dave and Emily weren't hosting the barbeque at their place, Martha lied. She told them it was a *combined affair* and that she had *insisted* that *she* and Ken be allowed to have it at *their* place. *We do have the pond stocked with fish, and the kids can fish; it will be great for the kids, and if the water is warm enough they can swim in it, too.* When she got off the phone after telling a boldfaced lie, she would sigh and say, *Surprising how easy lying is.*

Sarah slept past breakfast and past lunch, and Martha was on the porch having her afternoon coffee when she finally came downstairs.

She came out onto the porch and gave her aunt a kiss.

"Why I was just about to go up and shake the sheets to see if you were still breathing," Martha laughed. "I *must say* you do look better, love."

"I feel much better. Where's Mohammad?"

"Oh, he is still out in the barn with your Uncle Ken. Those two have really hit it off. I'm *so glad*. Your Uncle Ken was just saying to me last night that having Mohammad here is like having a *son* around." Aunt Martha took a sip from her coffee.

"He was wondering if we could *adopt* Mohammad; he thought *Mohammad Goldman* had a certain *ring to it,*" Martha laughed. "Go get yourself a cup of coffee and come and sit with me, or let me heat up some lunch for you," Martha said putting her hands on the arms of the rocker ready to hoist herself up.

"No, all I want is coffee. I can wait for supper. You sit right where you are," Sarah said.

Sarah brought back a cup of coffee and curled up on the porch swing.

"I did go and see your parents last night and told them about Sam. They were shocked and angry. They feel really bad about what happened."

"Not bad enough to call though or come over," Sarah said in a small voice.

"Give 'em time, love." Martha finished her coffee and set the cup on the stand beside the rocker. "I *did* use the tire iron on their TV and the end table next to your dad's chair," Martha chuckled. "I think they were afraid I was going to use it on one of them."

"Did you also go to talk to Sam's parents?" Sarah asked.

"Of course, I went to school with Betty and Ben. We have been good friends since we were children. I *knew* they would want me to tell them and that once they knew they would deal with him. Betty asked me to apologize to you and to *assure* you that nothing like that will ever happen again." Martha paused. "She even told me that I *should have used the tire iron on him,* she was that angry."

"I'm glad you didn't tell Mohammad or Uncle Ken. You *didn't* tell them did you? Not even Uncle Ken?"

"No, love, I promised you I wouldn't and I didn't. But I *did* want to take care of the situation; I couldn't just sit by and let that young fella get away with what he tried to do."

"I heard you telling someone on the phone that the barbeque on Sunday is a *combined affair.*"

"Yep, I lied. Even though your mom is being stubborn and pigheaded and *selfish,* she is still my sister. If she and your dad don't show up, I'll have to think up another *plausible* story.

Dave had driven to the Mall on the outskirts of town and bought a new TV and end table. He had been mulling over all day what Martha had said about Sam. He couldn't believe that Sam would have tried something like that with Sarah. He felt a twinge of guilt over what he had said to him: *calling Mohammad a Camel Jockey, saying that Sarah had lowered herself by marrying him; saying that he wished Sarah had married someone like him.* Even though in his *heart of hearts* that was the way he felt.

The plain and simple truth was Dave *didn't* like Mohammad and blamed him for the change in Sarah. He wished he had refused to shake his hand when he had run into him at the Feed Store, but there were all those guys inside staring at him, waiting to see what he would do.

That evening at supper, he discussed with Emily what they should do about the barbeque. "The guys in the Feed Store were telling me that they were going to the barbeque on Sunday out at Ken and Martha's. They didn't come right out and ask, but I could tell they were wondering why we weren't hosting the party."

"Let 'em wonder. It's none of their business. They wouldn't be wondering if *their* daughter had married an Arab Moslem. They would be as angry as we are," Emily said heaping a spoonful of mashed potatoes onto Dave's plate.

"Oh, I'm shocked and upset with what Sam tried to do, but as angry as I am, I can't help but think nothing like this would have happened if Sarah had married *one of her own kind*. Instead, she throws herself away on a *Mohammad*. Pass me the peas."

"Well, she has certainly been *brainwashed* by this guy. She's not the girl we knew. I ran into him at the Feed Store this morning. Ken had taken him to *meet* some of the guys who hang out there. He was introducing him as his *nephew*. Imagine. *His nephew!* Mohammad offered to shake hands with me. I didn't want to, but Nat and Carl and Max were all looking to see what I would do; so I felt forced."

"I hope you washed your hands afterwards," Emily said. "The very *thought* of him touching our Sarah makes me almost sick to my stomach. I read some place where Moslems can have *four* wives! He probably already has a couple more wives at home. He is most likely just *using* Sarah, so he can stay in the States. She is being naïve."

"I thought she was such a smart girl, but she has made a very foolish choice," Dave said. "And her coming back here, staying with Ken and Martha, agreeing to their having a *party* for them in honor of the marriage; it is like she is *throwing it all in our face.*"

Just then the hall phone rang. "I'll get it, Dave. You sit there and finish your dinner."

"Hello, Melissa? Why yes, we are all fine. How are you and Matt and the children?"

"You heard what? Where did you hear that? I see. I am afraid you have heard incorrectly. Yes, Sarah and her husband *are* staying with Ken and Martha, but we are not co-hosting a Sunday barbeque. This is something that Martha and Sarah cooked-up."

Yes, I'll see you at choir practice tomorrow. Good-bye."

"Who was that?" Dave asked.

"It was Melissa Collier. She heard from her husband, who had run into Carl McCommons, that *we* were co-hosting the Sunday barbeque out at Ken and Martha's. I set her straight and told her that it was entirely something that Martha and Sarah had cooked-up."

"There is bound to be a lot of gossip now. We'll have to come right out and say that we don't approve of Sarah's marriage," Dave said taking another spoon of mashed potatoes.

"Sometimes you just have to take the bull by the horns and come right out and take a stand. What Sarah has done is *wrong.* Even though she is our daughter, we have to show our neighbors and friends that we in no way support what she has done. The Good Book says: *if your hand offends you, cut it off; if your eye offends you, pluck it out.* I think it is my *Christian* duty, as painful as it is, to cast my own daughter out." At that moment, Emily felt she was being a true Christian martyr. There were tears of righteous indignation pooling in her eyes.

"I can't believe that she would marry a *Palestinian* knowing that I am *Jewish.*" Dave added. "She has completely forgotten her roots." He *had* conveniently forgotten that *he remembered* he was Jewish *only* after he learned of Sarah's interest in Mohammad. If Emily could be a martyr, so could he.

The reality of Sarah almost being raped had been buried under how her marriage to an Arab Moslem had affected *them.*

At choir practice the next evening, Emily wore, along with her blue polka dot dress, an air of martyrdom. When asked about Sarah and her Arab husband, Emily would sigh and say: *Yes, unfortunately it is true. She met this boy in college, and well, seemed to fall head-over-heels for him. You know how headstrong Sarah has always been. We tried to reason with her, but she has always been so strong-willed. She didn't listen to us and against our wishes married him in a* **Moslem** *ceremony. I really don't know if it is even* **legal.**

When she was asked about Sarah and her husband staying with Ken and Martha and about the Sunday barbeque there, Emily had sighed again and replied: *Why, of course, you must all do what you think best, but Dave and I are not going. To go would be to condone their marriage, and, of course, we could* **never condone** *such a match. Sarah has thrown herself away. Though I am her mother and love her dearly, I feel it is my Christian duty to take a stand, much as it pains me. Sarah has made her bed and sadly, she will have to lie in it.*

Emily looked around and was *surprised* that she didn't see much, if any, sympathy.

Martha had been on the phone all week inviting folks to the barbeque. "We're not just relying on those three old cronies of Ken's to pass the word," she had joked to Sarah.

She had told everyone: *It is just a casual afternoon get together in honor of Sarah and Mohammad's wedding. I'm not sending out invitations; I want folks to feel free to just drop by; so do pass the word along to whomever you think might like to see Sarah. And please no gifts.*

Practically the *entire town* turned out for the Sunday barbeque! Most came out of a genuine wish to see Sarah, to congratulate her on her marriage and to meet her handsome, rather exotic-looking husband. Some came out of curiosity to see for themselves what had caused the rift between Dave and Emily and their only daughter. A few came as spies for Emily.

Everyone brought *presents,* in spite of being told *no presents* and the short notice. The dining room table was *laden* with gaily wrapped wedding gifts. Mohammad remarked to Sarah, "I have never seen so many gifts at one time. We tend to give money gifts not actual *presents* unless the presents are from really close family – like Khalil and Mansur. Here it seems that even casual friends bring a present. We will have to have Uncle Ken drive us back to school in his truck!"

Mohammad would shake a box and hold it up to his ear as though expecting to *hear* it say what it was. "You are like a kid," Sarah laughed. "You would think it was Christmas morning."

"I *never* had a Christmas morning, remember?" Mohammad joked. "Let me enjoy this new experience. Maybe, even though I am Moslem, we can *do* Christmas. I like this idea of getting packages to open."

"You, my handsome man, are really a little boy at heart," Sarah smiled.

Mohammad bent down and kissed her. "That's part of my irresistible charm: a *boy* during the day, a *virile man* at night."

"Oh, brother," Sarah rolled her eyes. "Give me a break."

The barbeque was a huge success. Mohammad *loved* the hayride! He, of course, had never even *heard* of a hayride and was like a little kid lying in the hay beside Sarah looking up at the clouds. He remarked to her *that those same cloud camels were heading toward fluffy tents just like they were in Purdue.*

The food was wonderful: corn on the cob, barbeque chicken, tender steaks off the grill that you could cut with a fork, potato salad, coleslaw, fresh garden tomatoes plump and red and still warm from the sun, and, of course, there was Martha's famous rhubarb pie. She had opted not to have a wedding cake.

They couldn't have *ordered* better weather. It was hot enough for the kids to frolic in the pond. There was joyous shouting and laughing as they splashed each other, chased one another around the pond trying to push each other in. Some of the men and boys had organized a soft ball game in the field next to the house. There was the sound of a wooden bat connecting to leather; the whistle of the ball as it sailed through the air; the shouts of the men: *Catch it! Catch It! Throw it here!* The cheers and groans when a player slid into first and the umpire waved his arms and hollered *Safe.* Mohammad was fascinated.

The women had taken chairs out and sat in the walnut grove. They were close enough to watch the game and hear the laughter and shouts of the children swimming in the pond, yet far enough away that they could gossip, drink another cup of coffee, or have another glass of homemade lemonade. There was enough shade that the infants who were present could doze peacefully. Everyone seemed to be having a *really good time.*

Martha, picking up some of the used paper plates, glanced over at the men playing soft ball, the kids frolicking in the pond, the women gossiping in the grove, the babies sleeping under the shade of a walnut tree, the unhitched hay wagon parked next to the barn, and thought: *It's like a Norman Rockwell painting.*

The town's people seemed to have really taken to Mohammad. They found him charming. He was easy to talk to. Oh, he had a slight accent when he spoke English, but many of their parents had been immigrants and had spoken with an accent, too. It was obvious that he was in love with Sarah, and that Sarah was in love with him. Those woman, who had been present at the Methodist Choir practice and had heard Emily's speech, could not understand *why* she felt the way she did. They thought that her son-in-law was engaging; that Sarah had certainly *not* thrown herself away, and, they even *envied* her somewhat for the *bed she had made for herself and the person she had chosen to lie in it with!*

Only two people had mentioned to Sarah that they were sorry her mother and dad were not there. They were keenly interested in her reaction. They had been sent specifically by Emily to observe the party and to ask Sarah that specific question.

Sarah only smiled. "Yes, I *am sorry* that Mom and Dad decided not to come. It would have made me happy to have had them there. When you talk to my mother, please tell her that Mohammad and I really *missed* them."

Sarah turned and began speaking to the next guests who had come up to her to offer their congratulations.

Sam's mother, Betty, came up to Sarah had hugged her. "I am so sorry about that unfortunate incident," she whispered.

"Yes, it was unfortunate," Sarah nodded, smiling weakly.

That evening, as Sarah and Mohammad finally lay together in bed, Mohammad said, "It was such a wonderful party! This was a part of America I never knew existed. Amazing! The people are just like the people back home. Everyone was *so* nice...so *accepting.* I am glad that your aunt and uncle insisted on having the party. I had a *great time,* especially the hayride! I wanted the people you knew and grew up with to be able to celebrate our marriage. It feels as though the wedding is now complete."

"It would have been complete if Mom and Dad had come. I don't think they will ever be reconciled to our marriage. It hurt that they weren't here."

"I know," Mohammad said drawing Sarah's head down to his chest, "for your sake, I wished they had been here, too." Mohammad rubbed her back and kissed the top of her head. "I didn't see your friend Sam at the party."

"He probably felt funny about coming." Sarah knew that *feeling funny* wasn't the reason he had not come, but she didn't want Mohammad to ever find out the real reason. "We had been friends in high school then lost touch. I went on to college; he went into the Marines for four years. I guess when he got back he thought about rekindling a relationship with me. Mom used to write that he would stop by and ask about me, and when I would talk to Dad on the phone, he would sometimes say that Sam had stopped by." Sarah paused and ran her fingers through the curly hair covering Mohammad's chest. "I think he became *obsessed* with the idea that we would eventually get together; that's probably why he showed up at the dorm last year. It probably drove him *crazy* when he learned that I had married an Arab. I think I remember Mom writing that he had been stationed in the Middle East." Sarah sighed. "Anyway, I really don't want to talk about him." Sarah let out a gentle sigh that gently moved those hairs on Mohammad's chest directly below her nose. "I so *hoped* that Mom and Dad would have come."

On the next farm over, Emily also lay awake. She had been surprised and hurt that practically the whole town had gone to the barbeque. The spies she had sent had reported to her what Sarah had said. *Sarah had wished she and Dave had been there!* Part of Emily *wished* she had been there too.

Chapter 43

Hasna brought over a large manila envelope from Mohammad! She carried it into the sitting room where Nijmeh and Omar, along with Issa and Yasmeen, were watching an Egyptian movie with Fatin Hamama and Omar Sharif. Hasna glanced at the screen – she *loved* Omar Sharif.

"This came from Mohammad and Sarah," she said laying the large envelope in Nijmeh's lap. Nijmeh asked what the big red print on the side said.

"It says: DO NOT BEND PICTURES, *Mart Ammie*" Yasmeen read.

Nijmeh ran a finger under the glued flap and pulled out two pieces of cardboard taped together. With the tip of a fingernail she sliced through the tab and lifted the cardboard apart. A series of photos tumbled into her lap, along with two letters. One was addressed to Nijmeh and Omar, the other to Yasmeen.

There was a large photo of Mohammad and Sarah wearing jeans and sport shirts. They were grinning into the camera. On the back was written in Arabic: *This was taken at Sears just after we got our American marriage certificate.* There were two smaller prints, one had written on the back: *For Hasna and Imad,* the other: *For Issa and Yasmeen.*

There was a large studio photo of Mohammad wearing a *dish-dash* with a *kuffiyeh* on his head. Sarah was wearing Nijmeh's wedding *thob* and Japanese shawl. They looked very sober in the picture. On the back was written: *We asked to be photographed unsmiling. We wanted it to look just like the picture of Yum'ma and Yaba!*

Nijmeh, looking at the photo, passed it to Omar. "Look *habeebee*. Mohammad looks just like you, *ma'shallah*. Shame on him; telling the photographer to take them unsmiling so the photo would look just like us." She joked. There were also two small prints for Hasna and Issa.

"You must frame this and hang it on the wall right next to your wedding photo," Hasna laughed. "Mohammad *does* look like *Yaba*, but maybe *Yaba* is just a little more handsome," she smiled lovingly at Omar.

"*Shukran, binti.* (Thank you, daughter) I think it must be my impressive moustache that makes the difference," he said stroking his untrimmed moustache with a twinkle in his eye. "When Mohammad has a moustache like mine, you will think that we are *twins!*"

Issa burst out laughing, and Yasmeen covered her giggles. "Maybe like *brothers, Yaba*, but twins?"

There were a series of snapshots obviously taken at a family gathering. Yasmeen read what was written on the back of each one. "This one is of the wedding reception that was held at Sarah's aunt and uncle's; this one is Sarah and Mohammad with her Uncle Ken and Aunt Martha; this one is of Mohammad and Sarah on a hayride; this one reads: *these are our wedding presents."* Yasmeen passed the snapshots around.

"Where's Mohammad with the presents?" Nijmeh asked." I don't see him."

"There he is, *Mart Ammie;* you can just see his head peeking above the pile of presents."

There was a snapshot of men playing a game in a field, of women sitting under the trees, a cute one of a baby sleeping in a basket.

"Is there no picture of Sarah's parents?" Nijmeh asked.

Yasmeen looked through the snapshots again and read what was on the back of each one. "I don't see any photo of Sarah's parents."

Omar looked at Nijmeh, "Our son's in-laws are still not accepting their marriage."

"*Inshallah* they will come to see what a good husband Mohammad is. It can't be easy for them to have an Arab son-in-law who is Moslem," Nijmeh sighed.

Nijmeh turned to Yasmeen and said, "*Habeeptee*, read the letter that Mohammad sent to us."

Yasmeen read what Mohammad had written about the picnic, about their new apartment, about how kind and generous Sarah's uncle and aunt were, about how happy he and Sarah were.

Nijmeh listened to the words and after every description would say, *Illhumdillah* or *Nush'kur'Allah* (Praise God).

When Yasmeen read Mohammad's description of the hayride, Nijmeh said, "*Subhan Allah,* people sit in a wagon covered with hay and go for a ride!"

"*Illhumdillah,* Mohammad sounds happy," Omar said.

Mohammad had closed the letter praying that they all were well and asking to be remembered to everyone. He asked God's blessing on them all and said that Sarah joined him in sending their love.

Yasmeen handed the letter to Nijmeh, and as she did with all the letters she received from her children, she tucked it into the pocket under her embroidered breast panel so her *heart could read the words.*

As Yasmeen started to read the letter that she had received from Sarah, Nijmeh put her hand over the letter and smiled at Yasmeen, "*La, ya binti,* this is a letter between sisters-in-law; it is meant only for your eyes."

Yasmeen touched Nijmeh's cheek and tucked the letter into her pocket.

Later that night, when she and Issa were sitting in bed, the pillows propped behind their backs, she picked up Sarah's letter from the nightstand and began to read its contents to Issa.

Dearest Yasmeen,

I hope this finds you both well and as happy as Mohammad and I are! It is wonderful being married, as I am sure you two know!

You have seen the photos of the wonderful wedding celebration that my aunt and uncle had for us. Mohammad was like a little boy; he was so excited about everything. Happily, everyone seemed to really like Mohammad, but then how could they not help but like him! My Uncle Ken, who is my father's brother, keeps calling Mohammad his 'nephew' and when speaking to

Mohammad he calls him 'son'. Mohammad is touched by how kind my uncle is. It is obvious to all of us how much he has come to care for Mohammad, and I think, Mohammad for him. I am so glad. (Mohammad has 'fallen in love' with Aunt Martha and keeps joking with her that it was lucky for me that he didn't see Aunt Martha first!)

The only down side is my parents. They have practically disowned me. They didn't come to the party. The three weeks we spent in my hometown, I didn't see my parents once. Mohammad ran into my dad by accident, and Dad was very cold. He didn't even speak to him! It has made me sad. I didn't dream that my parents would react this way. My Aunt Martha, who is my mother's sister, keeps telling me to 'give it time.' I guess that is all I can do.

Aunt Martha believes that once we have a child my parents will come around. Mohammad loves the idea and keeps suggesting that we should have a baby! I am not sure about his motivation!! He loves the idea of working on making a baby. He jokes that it is hard work, but work he is willing to do!

Do let me know if there is anything I can send to you, to Mohammad's parents, or to Hasna and her family. I am more than happy to shop for you and to send a big box!

My love to you and Issa, Sarah

"What a nice letter," Yasmeen said as she folded the letter and put it back on the nightstand.

"It isn't so nice that Sarah's parents are refusing to have anything to do with her. It must be terribly hard on her," Issa added.

"I will write her tomorrow," Yasmeen said.

"Are you going to tell her our news?" Issa grinned.

"It's a bit early. I will wait until I have completed three months," Yasmeen smiled.

"I'm *pleased* that I will be a father before Mohammad. It hasn't been easy being the youngest. Whatever I did, everyone else in the family had already done before me. But *this time* I beat Mohammad!" He pounded his puffed-out chest. "Me Tarzan," he joked. He had recently seen an old *Tarzan and the Jungle* film on TV and had picked up the line.

"I suppose that makes me *Jane?*" Yasmeen smiled kissing him on the lips. She had also seen the film. Yasmeen suddenly laughed out loud.

"What are you laughing at?" Issa questioned stroking her long, unbound hair.

"I was just thinking of that Arabic proverb about *'even a monkey in his mother's eyes looks like a gazelle'*. What if our baby looks like *Cheetah!?*"

It struck them both so funny that they were rolling on the bed in laughter. They laughed so hard that they were gasping for breath.

Omar and Nijmeh, on their pallet in the next room, smiled at each other as they listened to Issa and Yasmeen's laughter. "Do you remember when we were first married and laughed like that? How we tried to suppress our laughter so we wouldn't disturb your parents?"

"What I remember most," Omar said, "is being forced to keep quiet, so we wouldn't wake my mother and our sleeping children when we made love."

"There *is* something to be said about finally having a room of our own, isn't there?" Nijmeh said. She smiled tenderly, and kissed him.

The months since the summer wedding celebration slipped by for Mohammad and Sarah; days punctuated with lectures, field trips, term papers and exams. School dominated their days and many of their nights as they pulled *all-nighters;* time was devoted to gathering the documents necessary for Mohammad's application for a green card.

During their three weeks on the farm, they had started the application process for an adjustment of Mohammad's visa status from student to that of a permanent resident. Sarah had written and gotten the application and necessary information from the Office of Immigration before they came to the farm. There was a list of things they would need to support being granted the status of *permanent resident:* photocopies of her birth certificate or passport; a photocopy of their American marriage license; notarized affidavits from individuals who would testify to their marital status; photographs of them at family gatherings, as well as professional photographs of them as a couple, proof that they had a joint bank account; photocopies of letters addressed to them as a couple; a photocopy of a rental agreement on which both of their names appeared, and a notarized letter of financial support from an American citizen who would guarantee the financial support of the applicant if needed. It was something like co-signing for a car.

When Sarah had been explaining this to Mohammad in front of Uncle Ken and Aunt Martha at dinner one evening, Uncle Ken had piped up, "I will be happy to sign such an affidavit. There is no mortgage on the farm; I have piles of money in the bank," he joked. "If it would help, I will gladly *adopt* Mohammad!" It was then that Mohammad started jokingly calling Uncle Ken *Pop.*

In the five months since their August holiday at the farm, Sarah had heard nothing from her parents. She did get bits and pieces of their news from Aunt Martha when she regularly called every Thursday night. When she questioned Aunt Martha about whether or not her parents had changed their minds, she always got the same answer: *Just give it time, love, they will eventually come around.* Sarah doubted it.

They received a letter from the Immigration Office in December giving them a date for their interview regarding Mohammad's application for a green card: March 19th in Indianapolis. At that time, they were to present all the necessary documents. Sarah wrote the date on the wall calendar in the kitchen and circled it in red.

The last Thursday before the Christmas Break, the phone rang.

"That will be Aunt Martha," Sarah said to Mohammad as she took a tray of cookies out of the oven. He only smiled and nodded. He was engrossed in a boxing match on the TV. "Turn down the volume, please, *habeebee.*"

"Hello, Aunt Martha? We were expecting your call. I just took a tray of oatmeal cookies out of the oven. You and Uncle Ken should drop in for cookies and coffee," she joked.

"Don't tempt me, love. If your Uncle Ken wasn't snoozing in front of the boxing match on TV, I'd prod him into getting in the pick-up and driving down," she laughed. "I hope you kids are planning to spend your Christmas break with us. Mohammad should see a typical Iowa winter, and you should have your first Christmas as a married couple here with us."

"We'd love to come, but it is awkward with Mom and Dad being the way they are. This will be the first Christmas I haven't spent with them."

"All the more reason that you come; you need to spend Christmas with family. You remember how excited Mohammad was with the hayride; just imagine those dark eyes glowing when he sees our Christmas tree and all those *presents!*"

Sarah laughed. "You're right." Hold on just a moment while I ask Mohammad.

"Mohammad, Aunt Martha has invited us to the farm for Christmas."

"Great! All I have to do is put a clean pair of boxers in my coat pocket and I'm *good to go!*"

"Mohammad can't wait to come, Aunt Martha. He says he will put a clean pair of boxers in his pocket and will be *all packed.*"

"You gotta love that boy! When can we expect you?"

"Our last exam is on Wednesday; Christmas is on Sunday; I'd like to be at the farm early to help you make Christmas cookies, and Mohammad should have the experience of going out into the woods with Uncle Ken to cut a tree. I will call *Greyhound* and see if there is a bus to Des Moines Wednesday afternoon. I'll give you a call. *Can't wait to see you!*"

"I'll be awaiting your call. I'm going right up and putting clean sheets on your bed. I'm *so excited* that you and Mohammad are coming. This will be the best Christmas we have had in a long time. Talk to you soon, love."

Sarah took over a plate of cookies and a glass of milk to Mohammad. He was sitting on the floor with his back against the sofa absorbed in the match. Sarah sat on the floor beside him. She slipped her arm through his and watched the match.

With his free hand he ate cookies and sipped milk. The underdog, according to Mohammad, got in a lucky punch and sent the *favorite* spinning. His mouth piece flew out of his mouth; he took a couple of drunken dance steps, and slammed into the canvas. The referee slapped the canvas, counted to ten, waved his arms and shouted: *out.* "What a great match! I love it when the underdog wins," Mohammad mumbled around the cookie he was eating.

Sarah got up; took the empty plate and glass into the kitchen; rinsed them off; dried her hands on the towel hanging from the handle of the oven; and turned out the kitchen light.

"Are you coming to bed?" she asked.

"Yeah, I just want to run down to the lobby and slip this letter to Khalil into the box so it goes out tomorrow."

When Mohammad got back from the lobby, the apartment was dark except for a soft light coming from the bedroom. When he went into the bedroom there were candles burning on the antique dresser and on each nightstand. His side of the bed was turned down and there was a book with a red bow around it on his pillow. Sarah was already in bed. She was wearing the satin nightdress that Yasmeen had given her for their honeymoon, not the usual flannel nightgown she had taken to wearing since it had gotten cold.

"What's all this? He asked surprised.

"You'll see," she smiled. "Come to bed."

It didn't take long for Mohammad to get ready for bed. Off came the jeans, off came the flannel sweatshirt, and presto *he was ready.*

He picked up the paperback book off his pillow and slipped off the red ribbon. He read the title: *Doctor Spock's Baby and Child Care.* At first he was puzzled – *Doctor Spock's Baby and Child Care?* Sarah could almost *see* that proverbial light bulb going on over his head.

"A *baby?!* We're going to have a *baby!*" He practically leaped into bed. He gathered Sarah into his arms. "*You're pregnant! You're pregnant!*"

"Yes, *I know,*" she smiled. "I went to the maternity clinic today and saw the doctor. Everything is fine. It seems all of your *hard work,* my Arab *sheik,* has finally paid off."

"When is our *son* due!"

"*Son?* Maybe the baby is a *daughter,*" Sarah laughed.

"All the men in our family father boys first; it is in our genes," he boasted. "My grandmother had a boy first – in fact she had *six* boys; my father had a boy first; Mansur had a boy first. Of course, our first will be a boy!"

"Our *son,*" Sarah said, deciding to humor him, "is due in July."

"July! That means you have known for almost two months," Mohammad said counting to nine on his fingers. "Why didn't you tell me?"

"I wanted to be completely sure. I was worried I might be like my mother; she mis-carried her first two babies. I wanted to be sure the baby and I were alright before telling you. The doctor at the clinic assured me that everything is fine. In fact, the doctor said that I *was built to have many babies.*"

Mohammad chuckled, "Everyone says that I am *just* like my father, and he fathered *ten!*"

"We'll have to *see* about the *ten,*" Sarah laughed. Kissing his chest, she laid her head in its familiar resting place.

"A *son!* I am going to be the father of a *son!* Mohammad sighed contentedly and kissed the top of Sarah's head. "I already know his name. He shall be called *Khalil.*"

Chapter 44

The stores were packed with Christmas shoppers. Sarah and Mohammad had braved the mobs to do a bit of Christmas shopping for Ken and Martha. Mohammad was intrigued by all the decorations, the music, the hoards of shoppers.

He said to Sarah, "It is almost like *Ramadan* shopping in the Old Country. We have strings of colored lights crisscrossing the streets; there are so many people in the street that you can hardly move. Hundreds of items are displayed on the sidewalk; men with handcarts of goods are everywhere. In some parking lots the cars are not allowed to park. For two days people can't park in town. In the parking lots dozens of tables are set-up and there are portable racks with all kinds of clothes swinging from them. All that is missing is the music!"

He insisted that they walk through the *baby section* of *Sears, Penny's,* and *Macy's.* He bought a six-month size romper in blue and white that said: *Daddy's boy!*

"What's if *he* is a *she?*" Sarah teased.

"I *know* it's a boy. I'm the father of *boys!* He grinned and mockingly pounded his chest.

"Didn't you tell me that your mother was the oldest of *seven girls?*" Sarah continued to tease.

"The men in our family inherit their *potency,*" he grinned, from the paternal side, not the maternal side. *The baby is a boy;* end of discussion."

They picked out gifts that they thought Aunt Martha and Uncle Ken would like. They went to the gift-wrap department to have them swathed in colorful Christmas paper and tied with huge red and green bows.

"I wonder if I should get a gift for my folks and leave it with Aunt Martha to give to them?" she asked Mohammad.

"It would be the thoughtful thing to do, but they probably would feel awkward about it. Remember what your Aunt Martha said about the pottery you sent from Jerusalem. They didn't even open the box."

"You're right. But it's *Christmas* and the first time in twenty-four years that I haven't spent it with my folks."

Mohammad put his arm around her and gave her a hug. He kissed the top of her red wool tam. "I know. I *wish* it were different, too."

The bus ride to Des Moines was long. The bus was crowded with students on holiday. Mohammad and Sarah were lucky to find seats together at the back.

The roads had been plowed, but there was a steady downfall of snow that made the driving slow. It was lovely to look at but a challenge through which to drive.

The bus was a half hour late getting into Des Moines. Only Uncle Ken was there to meet him. He had planned to bring Martha and drive the station wagon, but with all the snow they had decided that the pick-up was probably a better choice. He had shovels in the bed of the truck and a sack of sand. He had thrown a tarpaulin into the back to shield the bag of sand from the snow and to cover the kids' suitcases.

It was coming down pretty heavily when they drove out of the parking lot at the terminal. "There's a thermos of hot coffee and paper cups on the shelf behind the seats," Uncle Ken said. "Your Aunt Martha also put some sandwiches and cookies into a sack. It is better to keep driving and not stop. The snow will slow us down a bit even though the roads are plowed."

The snow *did* slow them down. It had taken an hour longer than Sarah had thought it would take. They even had to get out and do a little shoveling before the truck could get up the drive to the house. The snowplow had passed and had pushed the snow from the dirt road across the driveway closing the entrance.

Uncle Ken and Mohammad shoveled while Sarah kept the motor running and the cab warm. "It's probably the first time you ever shoveled snow, son."

Mohammad grinned, "I did shovel snow once in the Old Country, but I had to use a *dustpan*. We never get snow like this, and we don't have shovels."

Aunt Martha was standing on the front porch when the pick-up pulled into the driveway. She had a wool shawl wrapped around her shoulders. "You kids must be frozen! Come on in where it is warm. Supper's ready; you must be starved."

She hugged them both brushing the snow off Mohammad's shoulders.

The house was warm and inviting. Mohammad took note of the miniature wreaths with their electric *candles* that hung in each window. There was a colorful green table cloth with red poinsettias printed on it covering the dining room table. Aunt Martha had woven a string of colored lights around the banister of the stairs. "The house looks like one of the Christmas cards that Sarah bought." Mohammad said.

Dinner was delicious: homemade onion soup, roast beef, bake potatoes, candied carrots, applesauce, and homemade rolls. "I made pecan pie for dessert, so save room," Aunt Martha said.

"Aren't you going to tell them?" Mohammad asked Sarah. He was grinning from ear-to-ear.

"Tell us what? You look like the cat that swallowed the canary," she said to Mohammad.

Sarah looked lovingly, yet teasingly, at Mohammad.

"You go ahead and tell them. There will be no peace until you get it out."

"We're going to have a *son!*" Mohammad beamed.

Aunt Martha bounded out of her chair and soundly kissed them both. "Why this is the best Christmas present ever! "

Uncle Ken pounded Mohammad on the back, "Way to go, son; I'm proud of you."

Sarah laughed and said, "Well, it seems that *all* the work was Mohammad's. Why didn't anyone say, *Way to go, Sarah?*"

"Way to go, Sarah. I was just getting around to you!" Uncle Ken laughed.

"So, you are going to have a *son?!*" Aunt Martha smiled.

"I *have* tried to explain to Mohammad that it is just as likely that we will have a daughter, but he doesn't seem to understand the concept," Sarah said playfully poking Mohammad.

"Of course I understand the concept. It is the *male* who determines the sex of the baby. I took Biology 101. I have tried to explain to Sarah," he said directing his statement to Martha and Ken, "that the men in my family *always* father boys first. It is impossible that the first baby be a girl."

Both Ken and Martha and Sarah broke out laughing. "You might be pleasantly surprised to find yourself the exception," Aunt Martha said.

"Nope, as sure as the sun rises in the morning and sets in the evening, *our* first is a boy."

Uncle Ken patted him on the back, "You stick with that belief, son. I'm with you; I think it is a boy, too."

"You said your *first,*" Aunt Martha quizzed, "how many are you planning to have?"

"Well, everyone says that I am exactly like my father, and he had *ten,* so...," he looked at Sarah teasingly, "I think I am good for at least *nine.*"

"You may have to acquire *three* more wives if you are planning on nine," Sarah teased back.

Mohammad and Sarah slept well that night. Aunt Martha had put extra blankets on the bed and had folded a knitted afghan at the foot as an extra weight to keep their feet warm.

The morning was bright, and the reflection of the sun off the snow was almost blinding. After a hearty breakfast, Uncle Ken said, "Come on, Mohammad, you and I are going into the woods to get a Christmas tree. I have a pair of boots you can wear, an old coat, and a pair of heavy gloves. Here's a wool cap for your head."

"Sarah and I are going to bake Christmas cookies this morning," Aunt Martha said. "You men go out and chop a good-size tree. I want it tall enough to almost touch the ceiling."

Mohammad and Ken trudged through the snow. In some places the drifts were way above the top of their boots. They finally found the *perfect* tree. It looked to be about eight feet tall. The branches circled it in *perfect* symmetry; it didn't take long for Uncle Ken to chop through the trunk. The tree fell giving off a swishing sound as its branches kissed the snow-cushioned earth.

The *real* job was dragging the tree back over the snow to the house. Walking into the woods had been a little tiring; lifting their booted-feet through the snow. Walking out of the woods, dragging a protesting tree was exhausting. Sweat dampened the hair under their wool caps; their snot ran over their lips before it could be wiped away with a gloved hand; the snow that had fallen in the top of their boots had melted and made their socks wet. Mohammad wasn't so sure that he liked the new *experience* of chopping down a Christmas tree.

When they reached the house they stood the tree against it and with a broom swept the snow off the branches.

"Let's let it dry a bit in the sun before we take it in the house, son. I'm ready to get into some dry clothes and drink a pot of hot coffee!" Uncle Ken laughed.

"I'm right behind you, *Pop.*"

A plastic cloth covered the dining room table and it was laden with cut-out Christmas cookies. Sarah and Aunt Martha were chatting as they frosted the cookies and added colored sprinkles. Christmas music played on the radio.

"Did you get a nice tree?" Aunt Martha asked as she turned to look at them. "You look frozen. Get out of those wet clothes and come sit in front of the fire. I have hot chocolate on the stove."

There was a healthy fire in the fireplace in the living room. When Mohammad came back downstairs in dry clothes, Uncle Ken was already sitting in a rocker with his feet stretched out toward the blaze. He looked over at Mohammad and smiled, "Here, son, this rocker is just waiting for you. Stretch out your legs and warm your toes."

Sarah placed a small table between them and on the table set two mugs of hot chocolate with tiny marshmallows melting on the top. She placed a plate of frosted Christmas cookies between the mugs.

Mohammad sighed as he looked at Sarah's feet.

"Why are you looking at my feet?" Sarah questioned.

"I heard a new English phrase the other day," he grinned. "Something about a wife being 'barefoot and pregnant'; I was just checking to see if you had shoes on."

Sarah messed up his curls, then she slapped him playfully on the side of the head.

After lunch Ken and Mohammad put up the tree. Aunt Martha and Sarah wound strings of lights among the branches.

Colorful glass balls and crystal angels dangled from bent bobby pins. Miniature birds were clipped on the tips of some branches. Aunt Martha handed Mohammad a handful of silver icicles to drape over the branches. On the very tip of the tree, Uncle Ken placed a golden-haired angel in a pink gossamer gown.

Martha and Mohammad and Sarah stood back as Uncle Ken plugged in the lights. It was like the picture of a miracle. Sarah nudged Aunt Martha to look at Mohammad. The lights were reflected in his dark eyes. His mouth was slightly open. He looked in awe at the tree. "*Subhan Allah,* I have *never* seen *anything* like it."

Uncle Ken had planned a surprise for Mohammad. After the supper dishes had been done and the kitchen tidied, he said to them, "I'm going out to the barn for a few minutes. You three get on your coats, hats, and gloves. I have a surprise for you."

About ten minutes later they heard the jingling of bells. Sarah looked out the living room window and gasped. "It's a *sleigh!* Uncle Ken has brought out the *sleigh.*" She was like a little girl again. The last time she had ridden in her uncle's sleigh, she had been about twelve.

"Mohammad," she excitedly cried, "we're going on a sleigh ride!"

Mohammad had no idea what a sleigh ride was, but if it was anything like a hayride, he knew he was in for a treat.

In front of the house was a two-seated sleigh. It was drawn by two horses which had been decorated with bells. Every time they shook their heads and snorted, the bells rang. They were the same horses that had drawn the hay wagon the past summer.

"You and Sarah sit in the back," Uncle Ken said as he covered their laps with an old quilt. "Martha, you get in front with me."

When they were all situated, he clucked to the horses and they took off at a fast clip. The sky was bright with stars. The snow was crisp under the horses' feet. The sleigh slid over the snow as a skater glides across the ice. Uncle Ken drove around the woods; he drove around the frozen pond; he drove over the open field where the men had played soft ball the previous summer; he drove to the outskirts of the village before he turned the horses toward home.

Mohammad had his arm around Sarah; his gloved hand held her shoulder. She rested her head in its red tam against his shoulder. They felt content. They felt happy. It was wonderful.

When they got back to the barn, Ken turned and said to Mohammad, "Well, how did you like your first sleigh ride?"

"I can't describe it, *Pop,* I've never experienced anything like it. I don't know how to thank you."

Aunt Martha asked Sarah if she and Mohammad would be interested in attending the Christmas Eve service at the Methodist Church.

"I don't think it would be something that Mohammad would be interested in. And besides, Mom is bound to be there. It would be awkward for her and awkward for me."

Ken doesn't go to the service, so Mohammad can stay home with him. But, you always liked the Christmas Eve service with the carol singing and all. We could go a bit late and sit in back. You wouldn't have to talk to your mother. I hate the idea that you have to worry about running into her. I know it is awkward; just think about it, love."

Sarah *did* think about it. There were moments when she felt she would go; other moments when she felt she couldn't. She talked it over with Mohammad. He was no help. She listened to what he had to say, but she ultimately knew that the decision had to be hers.

She decided that she would go with Aunt Martha, only if they went late and left before the service was over. She had decided that she wasn't going to purposely *avoid* doing things because she might run into her parents. She was willing to see them; they had been the ones who were purposely avoiding her.

Christmas Eve was lovely. The roads were clear, and the blanket of snow covering the fields was virgin pure except for a few places where one could see the footprints of rabbits.

Martha and Sarah slipped into a back pew just before the choir was seated. Sarah saw her mother, but thought she was sitting where her mother could not see her. The congregation was singing *O Come All Ye Faithful*. Martha and Sarah shared a hymn book. It was during the singing of *O Little Town of Bethlehem* that Sarah looked up and saw her mother staring at her. Her mother wasn't singing. She was just glaring at her. The words to the carol died in Sarah's throat.

Some of the women in the congregation saw Emily staring and turned to see what she was staring that. They saw Sarah and nudged each other whispering, "Sarah's here."

Sarah felt her cheeks getting red and tears threatening to fall. She turned to Martha. "I want to go Aunt Martha." The tears were already spilling out of her eyes.

Martha looked at the choir and saw Emily staring at them. Emily's mouth was in a grim line. If eyes could actually speak, they would be screaming at Martha.

"Let's go, love. I never dreamed it would be like this."

They quickly slipped out of the pew and left the church. When they were outside Sarah began to really cry. "I can't believe she is being this way. She's *my mother!* Did you see her eyes? She hates me."

"I know, love. It sure seems that way, doesn't it. Come on, let's go home."

They drove back to the farmhouse in silence. Sarah cried most of the way back. When she went in the front door she went directly upstairs.

Mohammad and Ken looked up questioningly. "It was pretty bad. Emily was hateful. Sarah is pretty upset."

Before the words were out of her mouth, Mohammad was on his feet and bounding up the stairs.

Sarah had taken off her clothes and left them on the floor. She had pulled a flannel nightgown over her head and had gone to bed. She had the covers drawn up to her chin.

Mohammad stripped and got into bed with her. He pulled her onto his chest. Her body shook with the weight of her weeping. He just held her; there wasn't much else he could do. He wished that he had the magic of Aladdin and could make it all go away, but he didn't have any magic, and he couldn't make the pain disappear.

Finally her weeping became gentle crying; the gentle crying became occasional sniffs. Her arms tightened around

Mohammad, and she said brokenly, "I am so glad that I have you, and Aunt Martha and Uncle Ken."

"And don't forget the little one who swims beneath your heart," Mohammad whispered.

"You have Aunt Martha, Uncle Ken, Khalil, Mansur, Zaleena, Yasmeen, Issa, Hasna, Mona and Manal, *Yum'ma* and *Yaba* – so many people who care about you and love you. I know it isn't the same as your mom and dad. I wish I could change that, but I can't."

"I know that there are people who love me, and I am grateful." Sarah paused."I am so glad that I have *you*. You are the most important person in my life."

"I'll always be here, Sarah. You can count on that. I love you more than you can imagine."

"More than *all the stars in the sky?*" she asked through her tears, smiling slightly

"*More* than all the stars in the sky; all the sand on the beach; all the rain drops in the ocean; all the grain of wheat in a silo; all the snowflakes in a snow drift, all..."

"I *get the idea,*" she laughed. "I love you, too."

Chapter 45

It looked like God had put the farm in a mixing bowl and was sifting flour over it. The snow had gently drifted around the outbuildings making them look like divinity candy with its whipped frosty peaks. There was about an inch or two of snow on the clotheslines. It was beautiful.

Cranberry muffins were in the oven and the batter for pancakes was ready. The table looked pretty she thought – quite *Christmassy*. She had found a holiday tablecloth at *K-mart;* the pattern of red holly berries nestled among green leaves was festive. Christmas music played in the background.

It was a new experience for Martha and Ken to have *kids* in the house on Christmas morning. The holidays had always been secretly hard for them. Holidays were created for *children*, and the greatest sadness in their lives had been that they were childless. As she beat the milk into the eggs, she smiled to herself. *Sarah and Mohammad are like our own kids. Thank you, God* she said softly so only He could hear.

"Merry Christmas, Aunt Martha!" A sleepy Sarah said as she hugged her aunt. "I thought I could sleep 'til noon then I remembered: *It's Christmas!*"

Mohammad was right behind Sarah. He put his arms around Aunt Martha and laid his head on her shoulder. "I could smell the coffee and the aroma of something wonderful. Sarah is so *lucky* that I didn't meet you first," he joked as he gave her a kiss on the cheek.

Uncle Ken came into the kitchen. Sarah stood on tip toes and kissed him. "Merry Christmas, Uncle Ken. Oh, your cheeks are cold! Where have you been?"

"I went out to the barn to check on the stock. It is sure pretty out, but dang cold!"

Mohammad came up and gave him a hug. Uncle Ken patted him awkwardly on the back. "I keep forgetting that I am in America, *Pop*," Mohammad explained. "At home we always hug our father and uncles and brothers and school chums. I keep forgetting that men don't usually do that here."

"Well, it's kind of a *nice* custom, son," Uncle Ken said patting Mohammad on the shoulder.

Sarah smiled, "You would have *really* been surprised if Mohammad had kissed your hand and raised it to his forehead; that's what he does when he greets his father at home."

As they sat down at the table, Martha said, "Let's join hands; I just want to say a little prayer of thanks. *Thank you, Father, for the food that is before us and for the love that is around this table. Thank you especially for Mohammad and Sarah. Amen.*"

It was a wonderful country breakfast. There was everything imaginable on the table: pancakes, cranberry muffins, scrambled eggs, homemade jam, date-n-nut bread, cinnamon buns, a fruit cup and coffee. Mohammad looked at the feast before him and didn't know where to begin!

Before he took a bite of muffin he mumbled something to himself. "What did you just say?" Aunt Martha asked.

"I was thanking God," Mohammad smiled. "Moslems always thank God for the first bite. There is always this realization that everything comes from Allah."

"What a nice way of thinking," Aunt Martha said.

The four of them had a leisurely breakfast. There was too much food, but Mohammad and Ken seemed determined to finish all that was on the table. Finally, Uncle Ken loosened his belt and said, "I don't know about you, son, but I don't think I have room for anything more – *unless I put it in my shirt pocket!*"

Martha and Sarah cleared the table and did the dishes. Uncle Ken *did* offer to dry, and Aunt Martha hit him with a dishtowel, "Since when do you dry dishes? You're just trying to impress Mohammad!"

Mohammad grinned, "I never even *offer* to dry dishes. Thankfully, Arab men don't even know what a dishtowel looks like. We are raised that there are *women's jobs* and there are *men's jobs.*"

Sarah went up to him and poked him in the ribs. "Mohammad, I would like you to meet *dishtowel. Dishtowel,* Mohammad. Now that you have been properly introduced," she said. "DRY!"

"*Only* because it is Christmas, and you must make sure *never* to mention this to my father or brothers," he laughed.

"Well, if Mohammad can dry, I suppose I can dry. Give me a dishtowel," Uncle Ken said.

In no time the dishes were washed, dried, and put away. The four of them went into the living room.

Mohammad remarked again that it looked like one of Sarah's Christmas cards. The lights on the tree flickered off and on; the reflection of the flames from the fireplace was mirrored in the glass balls on the tree. The golden-haired angel in her pink gossamer gown looked down benignly on the scene. There were two felt stockings hanging from the mantel. Mohammad went up to look. On the one was embroidered *Sarah,* or the other *Mohammad.*

"What are these for?" he asked.

Uncle Ken sat in his recliner and said, "It's an old American tradition that originated in Holland or England. Kids would hang one of their own stockings on the back of a chair Christmas Eve. If they were *really* good, Old Saint Nick would put small presents in their stocking. If they were *really* bad he would leave a stick or a piece of coal. It's become part of the holiday to hang Christmas stockings over the fireplace."

"This is the very first year that Uncle Ken and I have had stockings hanging on the mantel," Aunt Martha smiled. "It's wonderful to have *kids* in the house.

"Sarah, pass out the presents, love."

She handed the first to Uncle Ken. He read the card: *To Uncle Ken, Love Sarah and Mohammad.*

"Now what could this be?" he said ripping the paper off the box. He lifted out a red plaid hunter's cap with ear flaps, a pair of fleece-lined gloves, and a red plaid scarf. "Why this is just what I was needing," he smiled. "I'll look quite debonair going out to the barn and pitching hay. Thank you."

Next, she handed a package to Aunt Martha. "*To Aunt Martha with love from Sarah and Mohammad,* she read. She took her time opening the package, neatly loosening the tape and slipping the box out of the paper. "Why, isn't this just perfect," she said removing the tissue paper to reveal a fire-engine red bathrobe and a bottle of *4711* perfume. "Thank you. I'm going to look nice and *smell* nice," she laughed.

Then, Sara handed a package to Mohammad. He turned the card over and read: *To our dear Mohammad with much love, Aunt Martha and "Pop"*. He tore the colorful paper off the box and opened it. There lay a blue plaid flannel shirt, a blue wool stocking cap, and two pairs of blue socks. He got up off the floor and went and kissed Aunt Martha on the cheek. "Thank you." He went over and jokingly, though lovingly, kissed Uncle Ken's hand and raised it to his forehead. "Thanks, *Pop.*"

"You haven't opened anything yet, *habeeptee*. You open a present now," Mohammad said.

Sarah took a colorful box tied with a huge red ribbon out from under the tree. It was to Sara from Aunt Martha and Uncle Ken. The box had been wrapped so that once the ribbon was slipped off, the lid lifted off. She didn't have to tear the paper. Inside was a Norwegian-style sweater, a pair of fur-lined slippers, and a black furry cap. "Thank you so much," she smiled at her uncle and aunt.

"There's one more box there, Sarah – there, in back – that's it," Aunt Martha said.

Sarah read the tag to see who it was for. It said simply, *Baby*.

"Mohammad, come over and sit beside me. This is for our baby." There were tears in Sarah's eyes.

Mohammad sat beside her on the floor as she tore the Santa Claus paper off the box. Inside there were a number of small packages. There were little undershirts, kimonos, sleepers with feet, receiving blankets, cloth diapers and little cloth hats.

"We thought you could use a few things for the baby," Aunt Martha said. "There should be one more thing in the bottom of the box."

They looked in. Sarah pulled out a little blue sweatshirt that had printed on it: *I'm Baba's Baby.* She held it out so Mohammad could see it.

Mohammad laughed, "This is perfect. I can just see our *son,* or *daughter,*" he said smiling at Sarah, "wearing this. Though I am *gratified* to see the sweatshirt is *blue,*" he said winking at Uncle Ken.

Uncle Ken and Mohammad were on the porch *roof* shoveling snow; Sarah and Aunt Martha were having a second cup of coffee in the kitchen when the phone rang.

"I'll get it, love, you finish your coffee."

"Merry Christmas, the Goldman Residence."

"I can't believe you had the audacity to bring Sarah to the Christmas Eve service or that she had the nerve to come. You *knew* I would be in the choir! You can't imagine how *embarrassing* it was for me. Why, everyone kept looking around to see who I was staring at. They know that we don't speak to Sarah. It was bad enough that you invited her and her husband for the holiday but to *throw it in my face* like that? Why, I don't know that I will *ever* forgive you, Martha. I was so *humiliated!*"

Martha gently hung up the phone. She hadn't said anything.

"Who was it, Aunt Martha?" Sarah asked.

"It was no one we know, love."

Sarah and Mohammad had decided before they came to leave New Year's Day. They wanted to have some time in Purdue before school resumed. They had gotten a list of possible employers from the school Placement Office. They wanted to go over the listings and see if they were interested in applying for any of the positions.

In five months, they would graduate and have to find employment and move out of student housing. There was Mohammad's hearing on his application for permanent-residence in March and a baby on the way. There were a lot of things to work out; a lot of plans to make.

Martha and Ken were determined that Sarah and Mohammad would have a great time the remaining week. Uncle Ken and Mohammad wrestled an old toboggan down from the rafters in the barn.

"I haven't used this toboggan since I was a kid," Uncle Ken said. "Let's dust her off and wax her up good."

They pulled the toboggan to the top of a hill. Ken braced his boots against the curved bow and grabbed the rope in gloved hands. "Now, you get on behind me, son. Be sure your feet are on the board and hang tight to the rope that runs along the side."

The toboggan teetered a bit and then *plunged* down the hill, raced across the snow, bumped over snow-covered rocks, and finally dumped them in a snow drift. They lay there with snow in their mouths and eyes laughing so hard that the tears which fell froze on their cheeks.

"That was some ride. I think I have the hang of it now!" Uncle Ken laughed. "Let's see if we can convince Martha and Sarah to take a ride."

It didn't take much persuasion. Uncle Ken was in front, *controlling* the direction; Aunt Martha was behind him, *I'll be a good cushion for Sarah,* she had said; finally with Sarah safely wedged in between Martha and Mohammad, they took off.

The toboggan plummeted down the hill. It twisted and turned and bumped and bounced bringing shrieks of laughter from the four as it raced over the snow. Finally, it came to a *smooth* stop at the bottom of the hill, gently slid and turned itself around, so the bow was facing the hill.

"Are you game to try again?" Uncle Ken asked.

They were. All afternoon they raced down the hill. Ken and Mohammad pulling the toboggan to the top while Aunt Martha and Sarah walked arm-and-arm up the hill.

Some evenings, they ate popcorn and drank hot chocolate in front of the fire while they talked. Some evenings, they watched the Christmas specials on TV while munching on Christmas cookies and drinking hot cider. *Every* evening, they enjoyed being together. They were *family.*

The day before they left, Uncle Ken convinced them to try ice skating. "The pond is frozen over. I could drive a team of horses across it and it would hold. I think that Mohammad should experience the pleasure of *skating."*

The four of them went down to the pond a little before sunset. He and Mohammad had cleared the snow away with snow shovels. The surface underneath was like polished glass. Uncle Ken had retrieved from the barn two pairs of old skates that had belonged to him and David when they were young men.

"Why, you haven't worn these skates since Jesus was a boy!" Aunt Martha remarked.

"They're still as good as new," Uncle Ken protested. "I sharpened the blades real good. See?" he said holding a blade out for Martha to inspect.

He tied on a pair of skates, and Sarah helped Mohammad into a pair. She and Aunt Martha had decided that their role was that of *observer* and *encourager*.

Mohammad got gingerly to his feet. He teetered; he tottered; he fell. "Try again," Uncle Ken said holding him steady with his arm.

Mohammad tried again. He couldn't seem to get the hang of it. Once again, he fell on the hard ice.

Once more, with arms spread out like a tight-rope walker, his body bent almost in half, he took two *gliding* steps and fell flat on his face against the ice.

"Oh, that smarts," he said rubbing his red cheek.

"Here, let me kiss it and make it all better," Sarah teased.

Mohammad removed his skates. "I don't think skating is my thing. I am better at riding a camel," he joked.

"You have never been on the back of a camel your whole life," Sarah laughed.

"Please, don't disillusion your aunt and uncle. I want them to maintain this image of me as a skilled camel rider," Mohammad said in mock seriousness.

"I *don't* think they *have that image* of you, *habeebee.*"

New Year's Eve was spent quietly at home. Martha had made eggnog without the rum. She had laid out cheese and crackers, and, of course, there were still tins of Christmas cookies. They managed to keep their eyes open long enough to see the ball drop in *Times Square.*

"May it be a blessed year for one and all," Uncle Ken said, raising his glass of eggnog. "Happy New Year," they said to each other, their glasses clinking together.

New Year's Day, Ken and Martha drove Sarah and Mohammad to the *Greyhound Terminal* in Des Moines. The roads were clear and there wasn't much traffic. They made good time.

The bus was not crowded. As they stood at the side of the bus they hugged each other.

"We had a wonderful time," Sarah said. "You really went out of your way to make it special."

"*You* two made it special for us! It has been the best Christmas we have had in years."

Uncle Ken initiated the hug with Mohammad. "You take care, son. We love you," he whispered.

"We love you, too, *Pop.*"

As they stepped up into the bus, Aunt Martha hollered, "I'll talk to you on Thursday. Have a safe trip back. We love you."

Sarah and Mohammad took a seat at the back where there was more leg room. They looked out the window and waved to Martha and Ken.

"I sure do love your aunt and uncle," Mohammad said.

"And they love you," Sarah said kissing Mohammad's shoulder.

"I was really touched that they got the baby this," Mohammad said pulling out of his backpack the little blue sweatshirt that said, "*I'm Baba's Baby.*"

Chapter 46

Sarah called her aunt as soon as they got home to thank her again for the lovely ten days. Before she hung up she said: "When, and if, you talk to Mom please don't say anything about the baby."

"Of course, love, I won't."

Mohammad had heard what she said on the phone. He came up and put his arms around her and leaned his chin against her head. He didn't say anything; he just held her.

Both Manal *and* Mona called that evening. "Where have you two been? We have been trying to reach you for days."

"We went to Sarah's aunt and uncle's for part of the break," Mohammad told them in Arabic. "We had a wonderful time. They are really *very* nice people. We went on a *sleigh ride* and tobogganing and..." Mohammad had to stop and explain to his sisters what a *sleigh* and *toboggan* were. "Sarah's uncle tried to teach me to *skate on ice.*"

Mohammad switched to English as Sarah had come into the room. "And, we have really exciting news to tell you." He paused to add a touch of expectation and drama. "We're going to have a *baby!*"

Sarah could hear the *trilling* of his sisters. "Put Sarah on the phone!"

"Sarah, *habeeptee,* what exciting news! How far along are you? Manal and I are going right out this afternoon and buying yarn! Don't buy a thing for the baby; *we* will send everything!"

Sarah tried to protest, but she knew her words were falling on deaf ears. "Put Mohammad on the phone, *habeeptee,* and you take good care of yourself. We love you!"

"Mohammad, so you are going to be a *Baba!* Issa and Yasmeen are only going to have you beat by a month or so! Have you told Khalil and Mansur?"

"I'm going to tell them when they call. *Don't* you girls tell them first! Promise!"

"We promise, but you better *hope* that they call you before they call us!" Manal laughed.

Sarah was pouring the coffee when Mohammad hung up the phone. She handed him a mug. "It's kind of ironic, isn't it?" she said sitting beside him and taking a sip of her coffee. A little while ago I am telling Aunt Martha *not* to mention that I am pregnant to Mom because I know she would be *angry,* and your sisters are already on their way to the Mall to buy yarn to begin knitting things for our baby because they *are so happy.*"

Mohammad rested his hand on her thigh and said nothing.

Mohammad told Khalil and Mansur before their sisters did, and Khalil called Nijmeh and Omar to tell them the good news.

When Nijmeh was relating the news to Issa and Yasmeen, Issa had grinned and said, "*Illhumdillah,* at least we will have beaten them by two months, *inshallah.*"

He had stroked his newly grown auburn moustache and smiled at Omar. "I think it *does* have something to do with a moustache," he laughed. Yasmeen hit him on the side of the leg and blushed.

Nijmeh picked up the almost finished blanket she was knitting for Issa and Yasmeen's baby, "I must finish this tonight, so I can begin a new blanket for Mohammad and Sarah's little one. Babies are such a blessing," she smiled as her fingers seem to make the needles fly.

Mohammad and Sarah had gone through the list of job opportunities for those holding a Masters in Agricultural Engineering. There were opportunities for agricultural scientists, plant and soil scientists, poultry scientists, and experts in water management. There were numerous consulting jobs available and the estimated salaries were impressive.

The best paying jobs seemed to be those offered by the Federal government. There were also job opportunities listed by state. The biggest paying jobs were in California; based on salary, Iowa was third.

Mohammad was also interested in jobs in the Arab Emirates. There were numerous opportunities. One could apply for a job in any of the Emirates through the Department of Agricultural and Consumer Economics. An address was given. The jobs in the Middle East seemed to center around water usage, irrigation, and the management of fruit and vegetable farms. Mohammad had an advantage in that he spoke Arabic, was a Moslem, and there were practically *no* Arabs with a Masters degree in Agricultural Engineering.

Where they went would partially be determined by what happened during his interview in March with the Immigration Office. Once he had a green card, unless he worked for an American agency with work in the Middle East, he would need to be in the States for three years.

There was the question of whether or not Sarah would work now that there would be a baby, *inshallah*. There *were* part time teaching jobs in agricultural engineering; there were part time research jobs, and most of the consulting jobs were for limited time frames. There was a lot to think about.

They had decided that they would apply for jobs in California as Mona and Manal were there. They would also apply for jobs in the Arab Emirates. An advantage to this, Mohammad said: "Najla and Azeezeh live in the Emirates. It is good to be around family, especially with a little one coming." Sarah agreed. They had also decided to apply for a job in Iowa.

Sarah said, "The more applications we send out the more bases we cover; the more bases we cover the better chance we have of being able to *pick-and-choose.*

They had gone over the list of documents they would need to present at Mohammad's immigration hearing. Sarah was an organizer. She had gotten an accordion folder and had labeled the tabs for each pocket. She checked off the list: family photos of her and Mohammad together, check; photocopy of her passport, check; photocopy of their marriage license, check; a copy of their joint bank statement, check; a copy of their rental agreement with both names on the contract, check; an affidavit of financial support from Uncle Ken, check; and a copy of a statement from the University Clinic saying that *Mrs. Mohammad Omar Mansur* (aka Sarah Goldman) *was pregnant.*

They had to prove that they were officially married and living together – that it wasn't a *scam*.

Winter in the West Bank was often interrupted with summer-like days; days when one was deluded into thinking it was spring. It was on such a day that Omar and Saji had gone for a walk in the hills. There was no work to be done at the moment, no walls to repair, no gardens to dig, no olives to be picked.

They had walked over the terraced hills hand-in-hand. Saji, though almost fourteen, still held onto Omar's hand when they went for walks. He was talking now, *illhumdillah,* but the scars of his beatings still lingered in his mind and made him *reluctant* to be outdoors without his grandfather.

They had reached the very top of a hill and stopped. The view was fantastic: gently sloping hills over which olive trees seemed to climb; bare mountain tops crowned with brush and scraggly, stunted pines; stone walls winding through the trees as they slithered over a hill top and disappeared.

They sat side-by-side against a stone wall; Omar took the lunch that Nijmeh had packed out of the basket. He handed Saji a loaf of pita bread stuffed with slivers of goat cheese and sliced cucumber. He took one for himself.

The sun felt good after the days of rain and cold. "*Subhan Allah,* what a perfect day it is, Sido." Omar stretched out his sandaled feet and leaned back against the stone wall.

"Look, Sido," Omar pointed up at the clouds. "There is a string of cloud-camels heading for that oasis. That looks like a tent, doesn't it?"

Saji looked at where his grandfather was pointing. He smiled and nodded his head in agreement.

"I suspect that those cloud-camels can even reach your *Khalto* Mona and *Khalto* Manal and *Khalo* Mohammad in America," Omar laughed.

"*Sido*," Saji smiled, "they can't possibly float all the way to America!"

"Everything is possible with Allah, Sido." Omar smiled putting an arm around his grandson.

"When I was a boy about your age, I used to go to the mountains with my father and brothers on a day just like this – a summer day in the midst of winter. My mother – your Sitteh Hasna, *Allah yer'hum'ha,* - would pack us a basket lunch. We would eat and laugh, and my brothers and I would chase each other over the hills. My father would say that we were *like baby goats skipping, jumping, and butting our heads into one another.* You see, Sido, our younger brothers would come running toward us older brothers and laughingly *butt* their heads into our stomachs; they were begging to be tickled and tackled." Omar paused as he looked into the distance.

"Does it make you sad to think of your brothers Sido?"

Omar smiled at his grandson. "No, Saji, in my mind they are always young and happy. At times, when I look at your uncles; Mansur, Khalil, Mohammad and Issa – I can *picture* how my brothers would look if they had lived. In some ways, *illhumdillah,* they *do* continue to live through your uncles – and *even* through *you* and your brothers, Sido." Omar said as he ruffled Saji's curls.

"Do my mother and aunts look like Sitteh Nijmeh's sisters?

"Yes, Sido, they do." Omar answered. "The Quran teaches that it is a blessing to die young. When one dies young, he is spared the trials and heartaches that naturally come with a long life. Like my brothers, in my memory your grandmother's sisters continue to be lovely young girls. I can still see them, a trail of sisters each a year younger than the one before her, barefoot, earthen water jugs balanced on their heads, winding their way up the stony path from the well. I can still see Ida's face – she was the youngest – turning to smile at me."

Omar paused and looked into the distance as though back through time; he was *seeing* that line of sisters coming from the well; he could *hear* himself stammering to Nijmeh, *I am Omar*; he could see Ida's smile.

"And now, Sido, I am an old man with *twenty-seven* grandchildren, a *great grandson,* and two more grandchildren on the way, *ma'shallah."* Omar chuckled.

Chapter 47

When Sarah felt the baby's first butterfly fluttering, she had gone to the phone to call her mother, but called Aunt Martha instead. As the baby grew and swam beneath her heart, her thoughts were constantly turning toward her mother and father. Many times Mohammad would see her go to the phone, hesitate, and then dial Aunt Martha's number.

He had suggested to her once that perhaps she *should* call her mother. *She won't want to hear from me,* Sarah had said. She had gone into the bedroom to lie down.

While she was resting, Mohammad called Martha.

"Aunt Martha, I'm worried about Sarah. I know she wants to speak to her mother, to tell her about the baby, to ask her advice. It is tearing her up."

"I know, love. I have tried to talk to Emily about making-up with Sarah. I have argued with her; I have appealed to her *Christian charity;* I have told her that *God* would want her to forgive. She chooses to be deaf to reason. She even *blames* me. She says that if I hadn't been so understanding and accepting, Sarah would have been home long ago."

"*Without her Arab husband, right?*" Mohammad stated completing the unsaid.

"She didn't come out and say just that, but I suspect that is what she really means. If she would give herself a chance to know you, she would love you like Uncle Ken and I do!"

"What are we going to do to make things better for Sarah?" Mohammad asked.

"I *could* tell Emily about the baby, but I have given Sarah my word that I wouldn't. I think Emily would feel differently if she *knew* there was a baby on the way. Love, why don't you have Sarah call me when she gets up from her nap? I'll ask her again about telling her mom."

"Thanks, Aunt Martha. Give *Pop* our love."

Sarah was standing in the bedroom door as Mohammad hung up the phone.

"I was just talking to Aunt Martha. I am worried about you, *habeeptee.* I know you must want to talk to your mom. It isn't right that she isn't talking to you." He walked over and put his arms around Sarah. She laid her head on his shoulder.

"That's *just* the way it is," she sighed. "I *would* like to talk to her and tell her about the baby. I *want* her to be excited for me, but I know she won't be. I have you, and Aunt Martha and Uncle Ken, and your sisters and brothers and parents. *All of you* are excited about the baby; that will just have to be enough." Sarah smiled up at him and kissed his cheek. "It *really is* enough, *habeebee.*" Her head told her it was true, but in *her heart* she knew it wasn't.

"Aunt Martha wants you to give her a call," Mohammad said.

"I'll call her this evening."

Over supper Emily was talking to Dave about Sarah. "You just wait and see; the next thing we hear will be that Sarah is *pregnant!* I find the very *thought* repulsive. I won't be able to hold my head up in town. Bad enough that she has gone and married a Moslem Arab, but to then go and have his *children!"*

"It's bound to happen, Emily," Dave said. "We have to accept the fact that Sarah is married to an Arab, and she is probably going to have half-Moslem babies."

"I am not going to acknowledge any Moslem Arab grandchild!" There was bitterness in Emily's voice. "If she does have a child, let Martha and Ken be the *grandparents.* The only way I will ever be reconciled to Sarah is *if* she divorces her husband. *If,* by chance, there is a child, she can give the child to *him."*

Dave looked long at Emily. He hadn't realized how truly *hard* and unreasonable she had become. He wasn't happy about Sarah's marriage, but *what was done was done.* He could never see himself turning his back on a grandchild, even if that grandchild was half-Arab.

Sarah *did* call Martha in the evening. They had a long talk. Martha stated all the arguments for telling Emily about the baby. Sarah stated all the arguments why she didn't want Emily told.

"I *know* Mom, so do you, Aunt Martha. She *wouldn't* be happy about the news. She would just see it as one more way that I was defying her. Dad might be a bit different, but he won't take a stand against Mom." Sarah paused. "He could have called during these months, but he hasn't called once. He didn't even call when there was that terrible incident with Sam."

"I know, love. I thought maybe you would feel better talking to your mom about the baby, but I can see that she probably wouldn't be happy about the news. Emily sometimes gets a thought in her head that can't be shaken by reason, love, or the *Almighty Himself!* She does *cut off her nose to spite her face.* She *should* be thrilled with the news, but she would probably see it as a slap in the face. You know, love, I think when she actually *sees* that grandchild, why, her heart will just *melt.*"

"That might be true if her heart was made of *ice,* but I think when it comes to Mohammad and me, her heart is made of *stone.*"

Mona, Manal, and Martha were diametrically opposite of Emily. Almost every week something arrived for the baby. Sarah had emptied the two bottom drawers in the antique dresser to accommodate everything that was sent. Mona had been *true to her word;* Sarah didn't *need* to buy a thing. That, however, didn't stop her and Mohammad from walking hand-in-hand through *every* baby department in *every* store in and around Purdue!

They couldn't resist buying; the things were just so cute and tempting, so they bought things to send to Issa and Yasmeen's expected baby.

Neither Mohammad nor Sarah slept well the night before his scheduled interview with the Immigration officials. They needn't have worried; they had all the documentation on the list and more. They had included a transcript of Mohammad's grades and a character reference from his graduate adviser in the accordion folder. Sarah's former roommate and her boyfriend had volunteered to drive them to Indianapolis.

There were two immigration officials who conducted the interview. They were very pleasant and interviewed Mohammad and Sarah together. They looked thoughtfully through all the documentation that was presented and applauded Sarah for *being so organized.* They only asked a *few* questions about their plans once they graduated. Mohammad had asked that if he were granted permanent residence status, if that meant that he could not travel to see his parents for three years? He was told no, he could still go on limited visits to see his parents. He only need inform the immigration office, during the first three years, of his intention and proposed length of stay. Mohammad also asked if he would be allowed to go to the Middle East if he were to be employed by an American company, and they *sent* him there. He was told yes, but the office of immigration would have to approve the work to see if it fit within the legal parameters of *being technically* employed in the States, though *actually* living and working abroad. He must *not* stay outside the continental United States a full year. He must come back to the States for *visits* within the year. Again, this would depend on whether or not his working abroad was approved.

The immigration officials kept the accordion folder that Sarah and Mohammad had prepared. They smiled and said that *they knew they were concerned about whether or not Mohammad's application had been approved. As far as they could see, he had fulfilled all the requirements and would receive his green card within six weeks.* The woman official smiled at Sarah when she shook her hand and joked: "Including photos of the two of you on a toboggan with your aunt and being **obviously** pregnant was a nice touch!"

When they got back to Purdue, Sarah and Mohammad went to the *Chinese Dragon* to celebrate. Mohammad was on his way to becoming an American citizen!

That evening, they had called Aunt Martha and Uncle Ken to tell them the good news.

"Why, that is wonderful. I am so happy that Mohammad got approved!" Aunt Martha said.

"I was just going to pick-up the phone and ask how the interview had gone. There is another thing I wanted to talk to you about," Aunt Martha seemed to hesitate.

"What is it? You sound kind of funny." Sarah said.

"Your dad had a minor stroke. But he is fine," Aunt Martha hastened to say. "He has been put on a special diet; the dosage of his blood pressure medicine has been increased, and he has to cut down on some of his activities. The doctors have assured him that he will be fine if he takes care.

Sarah was close to tears. "Do you think I should come up to see him?"

"I asked him that, love, when your mother was out of the room. He said that he thought *it wouldn't be a good idea seeing how your mother was being the way she was.* He did say though that *he wouldn't mind a letter from you sent to us.* He asked me when I talked to you to *give you his love.*"

Sarah started crying and handed the phone to Mohammad.

"What's wrong, Aunt Martha!" he asked with one arm around a weeping Sarah. She repeated to him what she had told Sarah.

"Do you think we should come up?"

Aunt Martha hesitated. "I don't think it would be a good idea. Dave would probably like to see Sarah, but Emily would cause a scene and it would be hard on Dave. The doctor is an old family friend and knows about the estrangement. He said he didn't think the stress would be good for Dave. I'm sorry. I'll keep you informed, and *do* have Sarah write to him in care of us."

Mohammad promised that he would.

Martha hung up the phone and went in to sit by Ken. "I didn't have the heart to tell them what Emily said. She *blames* Sarah and Mohammad for Dave's stroke. She really believes that if it hadn't been for the estrangement, Dave would be fine."

"She *needs* someone to blame, and she sure as hell doesn't want to blame herself*!*" Ken added.

Chapter 48

Sarah labored over a short note to her father. She would write something, chew on the end of the pen, tear up what she had written and start again. It took her over an hour to write a short note. (Mohammad had *timed her!*) She had no sooner put it in an envelope and addressed it, when Mohammad scooped it out of her hand and was out the door. "I'm mailing this *before* you have time to reconsider!"

That Thursday when Aunt Martha called, the first thing that Sarah asked was, "Did dad get the letter?"

"Yes, love, he did. He is getting out and about now; he is going to the barn doing some of the chores, he drives down to the Feed Store, runs errands in town, that kind of thing. He *just happened* to stop in the day the letter arrived. He hasn't *just dropped by* in months."

"And the letter?" Sarah prompted.

"Sorry, love, I got sidetracked there," Aunt Martha apologized. "The first thing he asked was if I had gotten a letter for him. I told him I had.

"I had him sit at the kitchen table and read the letter while I *dusted* the furniture in the dining room," Aunt Martha laughed. "I wanted him to be alone when he read it."

Martha could almost *see* Sarah's grateful smile.

"Anyway, when I went back into the kitchen to slice him a piece of pie and pour him some coffee; he was putting your letter in his old leather wallet and wiping his eyes. He made some excuse about having an *allergy* that made his eyes water. I told him that I knew I was a fool but that I *wasn't that big a fool.*"

"Thanks, Aunt Martha," Sarah said and Martha could *hear* the tears.

Mohammad had been watching Sarah's face as she talked to Aunt Martha.

When she replaced the receiver and turned to him, he said, "Your dad got the letter didn't he?"

"Yes, he got the letter, and he *cried,*" Sarah said, crying herself.

Mohammad had her in his arms before she could get a Kleenex out of the box on the counter to wipe her nose. "I'm so glad, *habeeptee;* I'm so glad."

Sarah hadn't expected her dad to write; but she kind of thought that he might call. He didn't.

It had been three weeks since she had sent him the note and she had heard nothing from him.

Mohammad kept reminding her that *at least it had been a beginning – a break in the wall.* She would smile and rest her hand on her ever-growing tummy and whisper, "Don't you *ever* worry, little one, I'm going to *love* you no matter what, even *if you marry a Moslem like your Baba.*" She would look at Mohammad and grin. "He or *she* should be so *lucky!*"

Sarah and Mohammad were sitting having lunch at the round antique table from Aunt Martha's barn when the doorbell rang. "I'll get it, *habeeptee,* I'm already up."

Mohammad went to the door and opened it. He was stunned and just stood there.

"Who is it, Mohammad?" Sarah asked pushing herself away from the table.

"Sarah, it's...it's your dad." Mohammad stammered.

Sarah's legs gave out and she sat down hard on the chair.

"Come in, Sir," Mohammad said as he rushed over to Sarah.

"Are you okay, *habeeptee?*"

"Help me up. I feel kind of weak in the knees."

Mohammad steadied her as she got up. Her dad was standing just inside the flat.

He opened his arms. Mohammad supported her until she reached her dad. Sarah fell into his arms and hugged him. "Oh, dad, I'm so glad to see you." Sarah cried. "I have a surprise."

"I think I can probably *guess* what it is," he said swallowing noticeably. "I'm going to be a granddaddy."

Mohammad kind of guided them both to the sofa. They seemed to only be aware of each other.

When they were seated, Mohammad said, "Ah, I'm going to go out and get some ice cream for dessert, maybe pick-up a few things at the grocery story, maybe get some *gas in the car.*"

Sarah looked at him with tears in her eyes and smiled, "We don't own a car, *habeebee!*"

"So, I'll get ice cream, pick-up a few things at the market, *buy* a car, and fill it with gas," Mohammad laughed, "You and your dad visit!"

Sarah held her dad's hand to her stomach. He felt the soft ripple of his grandchild as it swam beneath his daughter's heart.

"What are you doing here? Does Mom know?"

"I was headed down to the Feed Store and the old truck seemed to have a mind of its own. I wanted to see you so badly that I just kept driving." There were tears in his eyes. "I'm so *sorry*, Sarah. I shouldn't have let this go on as long as it has. When Martha told me about Sam, I wanted to kill him." He wiped a tear from his cheek. "I wanted to come and see you. I wanted to call, but..."

"I know," Sarah said, "You don't need to explain. You're here now, and that is all that matters."

Dave looked around the neat room. "Are you happy, Sarah? Is Mohammad good to you?"

"I'm happy, Dad. Mohammad is wonderful; his family is wonderful. You saw how he was just now; how he was making all kinds of excuses so we would have time to talk alone. I couldn't imagine myself with anyone else. The best thing that ever happened to me was marrying Mohammad."

Mohammad was gone for over two hours. When he got back, Sarah and her dad were sitting at the table. Her dad was just wiping his plate with a piece of pita bread. "That was delicious. What did you call it?"

"It's called *ma'lou'be* –upside down. My sister-in-law, Yasmeen, taught me how to make it when I stayed with her grandmother those three weeks I was visiting Mohammad's family.

"I have the ice cream and picked up some strawberries at the market," Mohammad said holding up two bags.

"Where's the *car?*" Sarah asked with a twinkle in her eyes.

"Parked out front with a tank full of gas," Mohammad laughed. "Don't you believe me?"

"Is it parked right next to where the *camel* is tethered?"

"Yep, right next to the camel," Mohammad grinned.

Dave listened to the banter and *knew* that Sarah and Mohammad were happy. He could almost feel his heart easing.

Dave asked if he could use the phone. He dialed Sarah's mom.

"Hello, Emily, this is Dave. I'm just calling to tell you not to wait up. I took a small detour."

Sarah couldn't hear what her mother was saying.

"I'm sorry I worried you. No, the truck didn't break down, and no, I didn't have a bad spell – in fact I am feeling good. I'll explain when I get home. See you later." Emily had said something and Dave replied, "Me too. Bye."

After ice cream with strawberries, and two more cups of coffee, Dave finally pushed his chair away from the table and said, "I really need to get going. It's a long drive back. I'm so glad that I came. Seeing you is better than any medicine."

He hugged Sarah at the door. Mohammad walked down to the pick-up with him.

They were awkward with each other. "Well," Dave said clearing his throat and looking out over the parking lot, "I can see you are treating Sarah well. And that is all that is important to me. She *chose you.* I just have to accept that and make the best of it."

"I love Sarah, sir. I will always take care of her."

"See that you do." Dave said getting in the pick-up. He didn't shake hands with Mohammad. He didn't look him in the face.

Mohammad stood in the empty street long after the tail lights of the pick-up could no longer be seen. He was glad that Sarah had been reconciled with her dad. He knew that Dave would never like him, oh, he would *tolerate* him for Sarah's sake, but he would always think that Sarah had married beneath her and wish that she had married *one of her own kind – a boy from home.* He sighed as he shoved his hands into his jeans' pockets.

Sarah had been watching from the window. She had been happy to see her dad; she was not happy with what she had seen.

When Mohammad came in the door, she dried her hands on a tea towel and went to him and put her arms around him, laying her head on his shoulder.

"You, my Arab *sheik,* are the most important person in my life. Don't you *ever* forget it!" Just then Mohammad's son raised a little fist and softly punched his Baba in the stomach. Mohammad felt the gentle punch and smiled.

Chapter 49

It wasn't easy explaining to Emily where he had been. When Dave got home, she was still up stewing. "Where have you been so long? I was worried sick."

Dave took off his jacket and hung it in the hall. "Is there any coffee?"

"I just made a fresh pot. I needed *something* to keep me up besides *worry*. *Where* have you been until this hour? It's been hours since you phoned. Why didn't you tell me where you were on the phone?"

Dave pulled out a kitchen chair as Emily poured him a cup of coffee."

"I went to see Sarah."

"WHAT!?"

"It just happened. I set out for the Feed Store and the old truck seemed to have a mind of its own. Before I knew it, I was parked outside her apartment."

"How did you know where her apartment was? You've been talking to Martha, haven't you?" It was obvious that Emily was angry. "What else have you been doing behind my back?" Emily looked accusingly at Dave, "You've had *contact* with Sarah?"

"I had a note from her."

"No mail came here from Sarah. How did you get a note from her?"

"I asked Martha to have Sarah write to me in care of her."

Emily was silent, biting the words that were boiling inside of her.

"Damn you, Dave Goldman. You *know* how I feel about this, and yet you deliberately go behind my back and ask Martha to tell Sarah to write to you in care of her. You are *all* against me!"

"*Damn it, calm down* Emily! Sarah is my daughter and I wanted to see her, especially after my stroke. I know how precious time is, and it seems stupid to waste it on things we cannot change."

"I suppose Sarah was *over the moon and half way to the stars* to see you?" Emily said sarcastically.

"Yes, Sarah was glad to see me. And, there is something else," Dave paused. "she's pregnant."

"I *knew* it! So, she is going to have a little *Moslem* baby, is she? I suppose Martha has known all along too?"

"Martha never said anything, but I am sure she must know. Sarah said that she speaks to Martha every week."

There was anger mixed with hurt in Emily's voice as she said, "Once again, *I'm* the *bad guy.* I am kept in the dark about my own daughter, about where my husband goes, and about what my sister knows. You are *all* against me. I have taken a very difficult stand, and none of you appreciate what it has cost me." Emily began to whimper and slip into her *martyr mode.*

"You have brought this on yourself, Emily. You're *in the dark,* as you so aptly put it, because folks don't want to rile you."

Emily got up and put her cup in the sink. "Well, I am as sure as Monday follows Sunday that *I* don't want to *rile you* nice people. I'll make up the bed in the spare room for you." She passed Dave without looking at him and climbed the stairs.

She didn't speak to Dave the next day or the next or the next. She would put his meals on the table and leave the room. Any attempt he made to engage her in conversation was met with silence.

She did, however, have *a lot* to say to Martha. She drove over to see her when she knew that Ken would be busy with the milking. She knocked on the kitchen door.

"Emily! This is a surprise. Come on in. I'll make a fresh pot of coffee."

"This isn't a social call, and what I have to say to you I would rather say to you outside."

"Okay," Martha said, "let's go out in the garden."

"No, let's walk down to the Spring House. I don't want Ken coming up from the barn and interrupting me."

When they reached the Spring House, Emily let loose.

"I understand you have been *conspiring* with Dave *and* with Sarah!"

"I don't know exactly what you mean? If you mean did Sarah write to Dave here? Yes, that is true. It was hardly a *conspiracy.* Dave thought you would be angry if he got a letter from Sarah at home and asked if it would be alright if Sarah wrote to him here. A scare like he had with his stroke makes a man think twice about what is important."

"You knew Sarah was pregnant, and you kept it from me! *I'm* her mother, not *you!*"

"Sarah asked me not to tell you. She has been longing to tell you but knew you would be unhappy. And, of course, you are Sarah's mother, *but you should start acting like it!*" Martha was getting angry, too. "What you have put that girl through is *just not right* – and it certainly *isn't very motherly!*"

Without thinking, Emily raised her hand and *slapped* Martha hard across the face. "How *dare* you say I am not motherly? At least *I am a mother* and more a *mother* than you will *ever be!*" The words were hardly out of her mouth before she regretted saying them.

Martha straightened her apron and looked out at the pond. She let the tears fall unheeded. "What you say is true." She paused and wiped the tears off her chin with the hem of her apron. I love Sarah *and Mohammad* as though they were my own. And *in my heart* they *are!*"

She walked back to the house leaving Emily standing there.

When Ken came up from the milking, Martha was on the front porch rocking. "What are you doing out here in the middle of the morning? This isn't like you at all."

"I just needed to rock a bit, love. Sometimes a body just needs to rock." Martha was still crying.

"What's happened?" he asked in alarm.

"Emily was over. She's really upset about the letter for Dave coming here and about the fact that we knew that Sarah was pregnant."

"She must have said more than that? What else did she say?"

"It isn't important, love. She said something that I am sure she regretted the moment the words were out of her mouth. You know Emily."

Ken pressed. *"What did she say?"*

Martha's lips trembled. "She said that...she said that *at least she was a mother and more mother than I would ever be."*

Ken knelt down beside Martha's rocker and put his arms around her. "Now, *you know* that Sarah *and* Mohammad *love you.* This past year, when Sarah has needed a mother – *you* have been there for her. *In our hearts* Sarah and Mohammad are like our own kids." He continued to hold Martha. "That time that Mohammad was helping me shovel snow off the roof, he was telling me that his grandmother used to say that *God writes the people we are to love into our hearts.* He was referring to Sarah, of course, but I have thought about that a lot; I think that *God has written Sarah and Mohammad into our hearts."* He paused and kissed Martha on the cheek. "You know, honey, we were childless for years, but *now* we have *two* children."

Ken chuckled and helped Martha up from the rocker. "Sometimes I feel like we are like that old Abraham and Sarah in the Bible. Sarah was ninety years old and barren; Abraham was a *hundred years old* – and yet God blessed them with a child. We have been blessed with *two!"*

"Didn't Abraham have a son from his wife's Egyptian servant girl –*Ishmael?"*

"I see your days at Sunday School have paid off," Ken laughed. "Abraham *did* have a son from her. Mohammad was telling me that Moslems trace their connection to Abraham through Ishmael. Abraham had Ishmael, so it seems *right and proper* to me – almost as though *it were written,* that *we* have Mohammad! He paused and ran his thumb along Martha's chin. "It's *surprising* what a man can learn shoveling snow off a porch roof."

Martha held Ken's hand. "You are nowhere *near* a hundred, and I am certainly *not* in my nineties; right now I *feel* about sixteen and I *remember* an eighteen-year old boy with whom I was madly in love." She turned and looked at Ken. "I am still crazy about him."

Emily knew she had been hurtful to Martha. She regretted having thrown in Martha's face her childlessness. She was sorry she had slapped her, *but Martha had really no right to have interfered as she had.* None of them realized how much *she, Emily,* had *suffered.* Emily knew she was right. She knew she had to *stand strong,* to *hold fast* to her convictions. If that boy, *Mohammad,* hadn't come into the picture things would be fine with Sarah and she wouldn't be carrying a Moslem Arab baby; things would be fine between her and Dave; he wouldn't be sleeping in the spare room and would *never* have had his stroke; she and Martha would be acting like sisters; she would *never* have said those horrid things to her if it hadn't been for him. Seen in a proper light, *Mohammad was to blame for everything.*

In her mind, if Mohammad were *out of the picture,* things would fall back into their normal place. *I have to think of a way to remove Mohammad,* she thought. *There must be a way of getting him and his baby out of Sarah's life.*

She didn't really think of Mohammad as *Sarah's husband;* she didn't really think of the baby Sarah carried *as hers.*

Chapter 50

Mohammad had marked the month of Ramadan on the calendar. It was scheduled to begin April 17th and end with *Eid al Fitr* on the 18th of May. He was glad it was in the spring. Sarah read what he had written and said, "I'm going to fast with you this year."

"No, you're *not, habeeptee.* The Quran recommends that pregnant women do not fast. You have to be sure that the baby gets the proper *regular* nourishment."

"You mean to tell me that your mother, during *ten* pregnancies, didn't fast? And that Hasna, when she was pregnant *seven* times, didn't fast?"

"That's right – they would make up the days later in the year. You can make up the days," he joked, "but you're *not fasting* while you're pregnant."

Sarah wrote something down on the calendar. "What are you writing down?" Mohammad asked.

"This is apparently one of those times when you are exerting your function as an Arab prince, and I wanted to be sure that it was *recorded,* oh Master*!"*

"You *better* obey me, *thou unworthy one,"* he said tickling her. "The Quran allows me to beat you – *with a feather* – for disobedience," he laughed.

Mohammad kissed her and hugged her. "You can't imagine how much I love you, Sarah."

She kissed him back and smiled, "I *do* seem to remember something about *more* than the stars in the sky, sand on the beach, and raindrops in the ocean!"

"That is about the *right tally,*" Mohammad smiled.

Sarah *did* listen to Mohammad and *did not fast,* but when he got up at three in the morning the first pre-dawn day of Ramadan, he was surprised to find the table spread and Sarah sitting there drinking orange juice. "I *won't* fast, but I *will* get up with you for the pre-dawn meal. I'll snack during the day, but we will have our big meal together when the sun goes down."

"Do you *always* get your way?"

"Generally, I am pretty *stubborn* you know." It was a statement, not a question.

"I am really touched that you are doing this."

Half way through *Ramadan* a huge box arrived from Mona and Manal. In it were tins of *kiek ou mamoul* cookies- Some filled with dates and some with walnuts. There were also large plastic bags of *sfeeha* (meat pies)*, 'ikraz* (spinach pies)*, kubbeh* (stuffed meat and cracked wheat patties), and several zip-lock bags of homemade pita bread. There was a note to Sarah. *Please put everything but the cookies in the freezer to use as you wish. For the kubbeh, heat some olive oil and deep fry until it is a light brown.*

Sarah opened a tin to look at the *kiek ou mamoul* cookies. Mohammad explained that the rings were stuffed with dates, and that the round *mamoul* were stuffed with a mixture of crushed walnuts, sugar and cinnamon. "These are always made at *Ramadan*."

"They look delicious. We'll have to try them *after if'tar* this evening. Mohammad was tickled when she used an Arabic word.

They had heard back from several of their applications and had been offered jobs upon graduation. They had even heard from one agency that hired Agricultural Engineers to work in the Emirates. They were interested in offering Mohammad a job. He had explained in the application that he was hoping to get a green card. They had written that that wouldn't be a problem.

They spoke with the manager of the apartments about remaining on campus until after Sarah had the baby. Again, there was no problem. The manager had said that they would need to vacate before the beginning of August when a new batch of married students would be seeking flats, but until then, they were welcome to rent the apartment for the months of June and July.

Almost six weeks from the day of their meeting with the Immigration officials, Mohammad received his green card in the mail! The very same day, Khalil and Mansur phoned and announced that they obtained visitors' visas and that they were coming to Mohammad's and Sarah's commencement! Khalil also added that Amr had been granted a visitor's visa and would be coming as well.

It seemed to be that all the *pieces of the puzzle* – to quote another cliché that Mohammad had picked up – *were falling into place. Subhan Allah,* Mohammad was pleased how well things were working out.

It was then that it happened.

Mohammad had gone to the library to study. Sarah had lain down for a nap. She found that she tired more easily now. The baby was quite active and Sarah sometimes examined her stomach looking for the *bruises!* She found that if she was up and moving, the baby tended to sleep. When she took a few moments to lie down, the baby seemed to wake up and want to do his *exercises* and show how *vigorously* he could *swim.*

She wasn't really sleeping, but dozing, when she heard someone knock on the door.

She got up, swinging her legs off the side of the bed, and levering her body off the mattress. She went to the door in her bare feet and opened it to find *Emily standing there!*

"*Mum?* Come in. Come in." Sarah moved aside so her mother could enter.

"I won't be coming in, thank you. Get your shoes on. I want to talk to you."

"We can talk here," Sarah said. She found herself bristling a bit.

"No, *if you would be so kind,*" Emily said unsmilingly, "I'd prefer to go someplace else to talk to you. I won't keep you very long."

"Alright, let me get my shoes and my purse."

Emily stood in the hall and waited.

They walked silently to the *Starbuck's* a block away from the apartment.

After they were seated and had cups of coffee in front of them, Emily started.

"You *do* realize, *don't* you, that your husband is responsible for your dad's stroke?"

Sarah was taken aback. "What does Dad's stroke have to do with Mohammad?"

"If it hadn't been for him, your dad would not have been under all that stress. I hope you *also* realize that it is because of your husband that I no longer speak to your Aunt Martha and Uncle Ken?"

"Whether you speak to Aunt Martha or don't speak to her has nothing to do with Mohammad!" Sarah found herself getting angry.

"I just want you to know that your marrying Mohammad has come between your father and me."

"So, what you are saying is – I just want to be sure I am clear about this – that *everything* that is wrong in your life is *directly Mohammad's fault?*"

"Yes, that's right." For a moment Emily looked completely pleased with herself. Sarah had understood what she had said perfectly.

Sarah left her coffee untouched.

"You've made no comment about me being pregnant. Surely, you have something to say about that?"

"Well, if you were *foolish* enough to have gotten yourself into this situation, I am not *foolish* enough to comment." Just at that moment, the baby decided to turn a somersault and Sarah's belly rippled noticeably.

Sarah put her hand on her belly and absentmindedly rubbed.

"Since you think Mohammad is responsible for all these things, I am *sure* you have a solution in mind." Emily had not picked up on Sarah's sarcasm.

"Of course, I have a solution in mind. You must divorce Mohammad and come home."

"What about *the baby?*" Sarah was really curious to see how far her mother's absurdity went. "I am going to have *his* baby; you do realize that?"

"Of course, I realize that. The solution is simple, though I realize it may be hard at first, you need to give him his child. He probably already has a wife back where he comes from anyway; he can give his Arab wife the baby to rear."

"This has been very *enlightening,*" Sarah said opening her purse and leaving a tip on the table. (Though one didn't tip at *Starbuck's)* "You *obviously* don't care that I happen to *love* Mohammad. You *obviously* don't care that this baby is not only his but *mine.*"

There were tears of anger in Sarah's eyes. "I was hoping that you had come so we could make up; so we could work on healing the breach between us. I was hoping that you would be pleased that you are going to be grandmother. I had *never* dreamed you were coming to ask me to *divorce* Mohammad and to *give up* my child!"

Sarah pushed her chair in. "I guess there isn't anything left to say except: I *will never divorce* Mohammad. I *will never give up* our child. If you are asking me to choose between you and Mohammad, Mohammad *wins hands down.* There isn't even a *shred of doubt* in my mind. If Mohammad were to get hit by a car and die today, *God forbid,* I would go and stay with Aunt Martha and Uncle Ken until the baby is born, and then I would take my child and go and live with *his* parents! I would *never* come to you. "

Emily sat there with her mouth opened in shock.

Sarah wiped the angry tears from her eyes. "I don't want you to think that I am crying because I am sad. I am crying because I am so *damn angry*." Then she smiled. "I am *glad* we had this talk. It has cleared up so many things for me. I was feeling sad because of the way things were between us. Now, I feel a real *peace*. It is as though a great weight has been lifted from my heart. I am *sorry* that I have disappointed you; that I am not the kind of daughter you wanted." Sarah looked around at the others who were drinking coffee, trying to seem like they *hadn't* been *listening*. "But right now, at this very moment, it feels as though you are someone I don't really know."

Sarah walked out of the coffee shop leaving Emily sitting there. Emily finished her coffee avoiding the eyes that surreptitiously looked at her.

Chapter 51

When Mohammad got home from the library Sarah wasn't home. He was a little concerned. He looked in the bedroom and the bed wasn't straightened as it usually was. It looked like she had been resting and then had just left. It was close to time for *iftar,* and the table hadn't been set nor was any of the food out ready to be heated. There was no note. If she went out, she always left a note saying where she had gone and when she expected to be back.

He was just going out the door to look for her when he saw her coming slowly up the steps. She was holding the railing and pulling herself up.

He went down the few steps to give her his arm. "You look tired, *habeeptee,* where have you been?"

Sarah smiled and took his arm. "I had a visitor today; I'll tell you about it over dinner. It's close to time for us to eat. Why don't you go wash and pray, and I'll heat up the soup."

"Are you sure? You look done in. Let me wash and pray and then I'll prepare things for *iftar.*"

"No, I'm fine, *really.*" Sarah said.

Mohammad walked over and wrote something down on the calendar. "It's another one of those days when I am going to be the Arab *sheik* and demand you lie down," he smiled. "I just want to make sure that *it is recorded.*"

He walked her into the bedroom, sat her on the bed, bent down and removed her shoes, and swung her legs up onto the bed. He covered her with Aunt Martha's crazy quilt. "You have a little rest, *ya albi* (my heart); I'll wake you when it's time to eat."

Sarah smiled, rolled to her side and was almost instantly asleep.

Mohammad washed and prayed. He put the soup on a low fire and stuck a tray of *ma'loubeh* in the oven along with a few of the *sfeeha* and *ikraz* that his sisters had sent. He made a salad of tomatoes and cucumbers and set the table. The sun had just gone down when he went in to call Sarah.

She was sleeping so soundly that he decided to let her sleep. He ladled out a bowl of soup for himself, and filled his plate from the oven. He turned the oven way down low, just hot enough so the food would still be warm when Sarah awoke.

She didn't awaken until almost eight. Mohammad was watching a basketball game on TV with the sound off.

"You shouldn't have let me sleep so long," Sarah yawned. "I wanted to have dinner with you."

"I kept things warm in the oven for you. Sit down and I'll serve you. Maybe we should write this day on the calendar today – *Arab Prince serves female slave,*" he grinned but his eyes were worried.

"*Female slave, huh?*" Sarah said, but she didn't protest and sat down and let Mohammad serve her.

Mohammad watched her eat. She seemed famished. He drank some orange juice and nibbled at a *sfeeha.* "So, who was your visitor today?"

"Guess? Maybe we should have a wager?"

"Come on, tell me who? I don't want to guess."

"My mother."

"*YOUR MOTHER?*"

"Yep, Mum. You, my friend, if you had guessed correctly would have: grabbed the brass ring, rung the bell, hit the bull's eye." There was bitterness in Sarah's tone.

"She came to *set me straight* on a few of the realities of her life. It seems that *I* am the cause of my father's stroke, her estrangement from her sister, and the fact that my father sleeps in the spare room."

"You mean *I'm* responsible, don't you?" Mohammad asked.

"Oh, she said *you,* but she meant *me.*"

"I gather she had a *solution."* Mohammad said. "This answer I *can* guess – *divorce me.*"

"Now, you have won the lottery. Except for one thing you forgot – the *baby."*

"The baby? I don't know what you mean."

"The baby would be a reminder that I had once made this *unforgivable* mistake of marrying you. Her solution was easy – though she did admit it might be difficult for me at first– I am to give the baby to your Arab wife to rear."

For a moment, Mohammad was speechless. "What Arab wife?"

"You know; the Arab wife you have stowed away in the Old Country." Now there *were* tears in Sarah's eyes. "You can't believe how truly hateful she was. How truly hateful she *is!*"

"What did you tell her?"

"I was really calm, though I did leave a *tip* at *Starbuck's* – nobody leaves a *tip* there. I told her that if anything ever happened to you, *God forbid,* that I would take our child and go and live with your parents."

"That must have gone over well," Mohammad said; his mouth was grim and his eyes were suspiciously bright.

"The funny thing is - I *meant it.* I couldn't stand to be with Aunt Martha and Uncle Ken, even though I love them dearly, because it would mean I might run into *her*. I think six thousand miles would be far enough away. I would never have to see her ever again, and she would never have to see me and our child."

Mohammad took her hand and raised it to his lips. "I'm *so sorry,* Sarah. If I had thought that things would turn out this way, I would never have asked you to marry me."

Sarah yanked her hand back. "Don't you ever say that! Don't you even think it! You are the best thing that ever happened to me! If you hadn't asked me, I would have asked you! I don't regret for one minute that I married you!"

Sarah's face was flushed; her eyes were bright with angry tears; then she began to laugh. "I think in another minute I would have shaken you, slapped you, and beaten you for even *thinking you shouldn't have married me.*" She paused. "Weren't you even a *little scared?*" she laughed.

"Maybe a *little;* I'm just so glad that I am taller than you and outweigh you," he laughed going over and pulling her out of her chair so he could wrap his arms around her. Her stomach rubbed against his, and their son must have awakened, for he stretched and with a tiny foot kicked his father right in the ribs.

"Let's leave the dishes until tomorrow and go to bed," Mohammad suggested.

"But I'm not sleepy," Sarah said.

"Neither am I," Mohammad smiled.

It seemed as though a great weight had been lifted. Sarah was content and happy. She went about the house humming *show tunes!* She had bought conversational Arabic language tapes and played them when Mohammad wasn't at home. She had picked up an English-Arabic Quran from the university bookstore; she started reading several *Suras* at night before she went to sleep.

Mohammad questioned her motivation. "You're not just doing this to get back at your mother, are you?"

He could tell that her response was genuine. "No, I can see where you might think that. But I have seen the way your parents and siblings were when they knew you wanted to marry me. They, at first, weren't happy about it, but then they *accepted* and genuinely *welcomed* me into the family. My mother, with all her Christian piety, cast me out. Your mother, with her simple devout faith, embraced me because she *feels that it is written by God that we should be together.* I am not saying that I am going to convert; what I am saying is that there is much I *want to know.*"

Sarah smiled and snuggled close to Mohammad laying her head on his chest. "It's kind of ironic, isn't it? Here I am, a farm girl from Iowa, wanting to be *not* like her mother but like her Middle Eastern *mother-in-law.*"

Mohammad's arms tightened around her. "You couldn't have complimented my mother more." His voice was husky as he kissed the curls on top of her head.

That week when Khalil called, it was Sarah who happened to pick up the phone.

"Khalil! How nice to hear your voice. *Inshallah* you and Mansur, Zaleena, the children and Amr are well. You can't imagine how excited we are that you, Mansur, and Amr are coming for our graduation. We are counting the days."

"You sound very well, Sarah, *illhumdillah.* How is my little nephew doing?"

Sarah laughed, "*He* may be a *She, but he* is getting bigger by the day. Every day he kicks me and punches me. It seems he has forgotten which of us is the mother and which the son."

Khalil laughed, "I recall Hasna saying the same thing when she was pregnant with Saleem."

"Let me give you, Mohammad. He is trying to pull the receiver out of my hand. Please, when you call your parents do give *Mart Ammie* my special greetings. Here's Mohammad."

"*Mart Ammie,* did Sarah just refer to *Yum'ma* as *Mart Ammie?*" Khalil asked.

"Yes, you heard right. She is listening to Arabic tapes, is peppering her conversation with Arabic words, and has taken to referring to *Yum'ma* as *Mart Ammie.*"

"Amazing."

Chapter 52

Sarah's pregnancy was going well, except she *was* worried she was putting on a lot of weight. She hadn't had any morning sickness; she hadn't had any particular *cravings;* her energy level, except for the day of her mother's visit, (which she attributed to *emotional exhaustion)* was good. She had joked with Mohammad that *if pregnancy made her feel so good, she should probably be pregnant all the time.* He had grinned and said *that could certainly be arranged and that he knew just the man!*

The Purdue Commencement was scheduled for Sunday, May 15th. Mansur, Khalil and Amr were scheduled to arrive on the 10th. She had phoned and booked two rooms in the *Holiday Inn* for the 10th through the 15th. On the 16th, the three of them were flying out to California to spend a week with Mona and Manal; they would be returning to Amman from LA.

A letter had come from the school with the instructions concerning graduation. Each graduate was given four free tickets (to be obtained from the Bursar's office); gowns and mortar boards were rented from the college bookstore; the appropriate color of the tassel and hood for each school was listed (for Agricultural Engineering it was a maize-colored hood and tassel). Graduates and their guests were advised to be prompt.

Sarah and Mohammad, together, had received eight tickets. They really only needed five: Mansur, Khalil, Amr, Aunt Martha and Uncle Ken. Sarah knew that her dad would probably not come, and she didn't want her mother there.

When Aunt Martha called that Thursday, she had a suggestion.

"Sarah, your Uncle Ken and I were thinking that we would drive down to Indianapolis and pick up Mohammad's brothers and bring them on to Purdue. We would like to meet them. It will be about dinner time when we arrive at your place, and we would like to invite you all out to the *Chinese Dragon*. We had wanted to invite them out to the farm for a day or two, *of course with you and Mohammad,* but realize that their schedule is probably pretty tight, and you and Mohammad will be busy getting ready for commencement and such. How does that sound to you?"

"Are *you sure?* It would be wonderful. I really want them to meet you and Uncle Ken, and *you* to meet them. I know you will see each other the day of commencement, but there probably won't be much time to visit."

"Let's plan on that then, love. How will we recognize them?"

Sarah laughed, "That is easy – they look a lot like Mohammad – in fact, they look *just like brothers!*"

"When Mohammad talks to them next, have him tell them that we are going to be picking them up. They need to look for the *biggest* woman in the crowd who is holding the hand of a gray-haired man with a beard," she laughed.

"If Uncle Ken runs into Dad, he can tell Dad that we have a ticket for him if he wants to come. I know he can't, but have him tell him anyway."

"I will, love. Now, you take care of yourself. I put a little something in the mail yesterday for the baby; you should be getting it tomorrow or the next day. Give Mohammad our love."

Two days later Mohammad picked up a parcel from Aunt
Martha in the lobby. Mohammad broke the tape of the box with
a kitchen knife, opened the flaps, and Sarah pulled a blanket
out of the box. It was folded in on itself and wrapped in a
plastic bag from the cleaners.

When she unfolded it she and Mohammad were stunned. *It
was a baby quilt of the farm!* Aunt Martha had appliquéd the
barn in red, the house in white with green shutters. There was
a light blue scrap of fabric that represented the pond; there
were even little yellow ducks waddling beside it. At the bottom
there was a hay wagon drawn by a brown horse. To the left of
the house there was a green pasture with two cows in it. On
the sidewalk leading to the rambling porch were two figures;
one was a man with a beard holding a milk pail; the other was
a rather *large* woman in an apron; the couple were holding
hands. Above the two figures had been embroidered in red
embroidery floss: *Grandma Martha, Grandpa Ken.*

Sarah went right to the phone and called Aunt Martha.

"We just opened the box, and Mohammad and I are stunned!
We are speechless! It is such an amazing gift. It is priceless –
you have sewn *so much love* into it."

"I wanted this little one to know that *he* or *she* has a Grandma
Martha and Grandpa Ken."

Sarah was close to tears. *She found she was close to tears a lot
lately.* Her hormones were certainly being affected by her
pregnancy.

"We don't know how to thank you for *everything* that you and
Uncle Ken have done."

"Well, you are certainly *more* than welcome. As far as we are concerned, *you* and *Mohammad* are like our own kids. We love you just as though you really are."

Sarah and Mohammad had taken to going for long walks after *iftar*. They would leave the campus and walk on some of the quiet residential streets, look at the lighted windows and imagine what the families inside were like. They especially liked strolling on *trash days*; it was amazing what folks discarded. One evening, they discovered *it. It* was a *baby bassinet.* It needed a new coat of paint, but otherwise it was perfect. It rested on detachable legs and had two large handles so it could be carried. They were examining it when an older lady came down the drive carrying a plastic bag of garbage.

She smiled at Sarah and Mohammad. "I can *see* that you folks are looking for a bassinet. When is your baby due?"

"I just passed my second trimester," Sarah returned the smile.

"We were looking for something *just* like this," Mohammad said.

"Well, someone *upstairs* must be watching out for you. I just *now* put this on the pavement. I thing you are probably the first ones to see it."

"Why are you putting it out with the trash, if you don't mind me asking?" Mohammad questioned.

"Oh, I *knew* it wouldn't be here in the morning when the trash is picked up. I knew someone, just like you two, would be by and take it. It was just sitting here waiting for its next home."

The woman looked almost lovingly at the bassinet. "This basket has been used for over a dozen babies."

A *dozen?*" Sarah remarked.

"My husband was Irish Catholic and crazy about kids. We had seven of our own – two girls and five boys. My married daughters used it for their babies. The youngest grandchild just turned one. My daughters have been helping me clean out the attic today and my Sarah said, 'Mom, it's time that *this* had a new home. I'm sure there is a young couple out there looking for this very basket.'"

Mohammad smiled, "My wife's name is *Sarah* too."

The old woman also smiled. "Well then this is definitely *meant* for you two."

"I'll show you how these legs fold up." She lifted the handles and handed the basket to Mohammad. "Just like this. The basket is just the right size to squeeze into the backseat of a car."

As Mohammad and Sarah walked down the street, each carrying a part of the bassinet, the woman hollered after them, "Good luck!"

Sarah's six-month check up was scheduled the following day.

She liked the nurse who worked in the doctor's office and they were on a first-name basis.

"How you doing, Sarah?" Nancy asked. "Come on back and let me weigh you, measure you, and take your blood pressure."

Nancy glanced at the chart she carried in her hand. "You've just completed your 26th week, I see. You must be carrying a big baby."

"Here," she said handing Sarah a robe. "Slip this on and take off your shoes."

Sarah stepped on the scales and was weighed. "I see you have added a little weight." She wrote the number down.

"Now, lie back on the table." She lifted Sarah's gown and measured Sarah's belly from the bottom of her breasts to her pelvis. She wrote the number down, then she put the tape across Sarah's belly and wrote that number down.

She moved a stethoscope to different parts of Sarah's belly listening for the baby's heartbeat. "Your baby has a good strong heartbeat," Nancy smiled. She moved the stethoscope to the other side and listened. Then she moved the stethoscope back to where it had just been and listened. She went back and forth several times.

"You can put your gown down and rest there for just a minute. I want the doctor to examine you."

"Everything is *all right,* isn't it?"

"Of course, this is just part of the routine."

Doctor Grey came in. Sarah liked him; he kind of fit the stereotype of a *country doctor:* twinkling blue eyes behind frameless glasses, bushy gray eyebrows, snowy white hair and rosy cheeks, though of course he wasn't a country doctor but was on staff at one of the prominent hospitals in the area.

"How are you feeling today, Sarah? Any morning sickness? Sarah shook her head. "Are you feeling especially tired?" Again Sarah shook her head.

The doctor took the stethoscope from around his neck. "Raise you gown if you wouldn't mind."

Sarah did. The doctor moved the stethoscope around different parts of Sarah' stomach just as Nancy had done. He listened, hummed to himself, and nodded.

"You can get dressed now, Sarah. Come into my office when you are dressed."

Sarah sat in the chair opposite him. He read through her chart, made a few notes, and then looked at her.

"Sarah, everything is fine. You're beginning to gain more weight, but that is to be expected. Your blood pressure is good. You say you have lots of energy. Your pregnancy is moving along well." He paused. Sarah's heart began to beat faster and her palms to sweat.

"Usually, we are able to tell before 26 weeks the presence of twins. Sometimes- rarely- this is not so. As in your case," he smiled.

"*Twins?*"

"Nancy heard *two* strong heartbeats on opposite sides of your stomach. When I listened to you just now, I could also hear *two* very strong heartbeats. Considering this, the weight you have put on and the growth of your stomach is all perfectly normal. With twins the due date is sometimes moved up." He looked at her chart again. "I would say that you will probably deliver the last week of June, perhaps a bit earlier.

"Why wasn't it possible to determine this before?"

"Sometimes the babies play *hide-and-seek*. When you came for your other appointments, the one twin, *apparently*, was *hiding* behind the other. That's why we only picked up one very strong heartbeat. Today, they must have been *playing together side-by-side.*"

"Twins; we are going to have *twins?!'* Sarah was stunned. "We *can't* have twins!"

The doctor smiled, "Oh *yes*, you *can* my dear."

When she got back to the apartment and put her purse down on the counter, Mohammad asked her how the check-up had gone.

"Everything is fine, except..."

"Except what?" Mohammad anxiously asked.

"Except we need *another* bassinet."

"Another bassinet?"

"We, my fine Arab prince, are going to have *twins.*"

At first, Mohammad just stared at Sarah, and then his chest seemed to *expand* as his smile got broader. "Twins! How great! Issa thought he had beaten me by being *first* – but he's having only *one*, and I, *Mohammad Omar Mansur,* am having *two!*"

Sarah went over and poked his puffed-up chest. "A little lesson in biology, my learned friend, **I** *am the one having twins*. And, before you get too puffed up, thou exalted Arab *sheik*, you just *may* be father of twin *girls,*" Sarah teased.

Mohammad put his hands on Sarah's belly and bent down and whispered, "*Baba bihibkum ou' lad'dee.*"

"What did you tell them?" Sarah asked twisting her fingers through Mohammad's curls.

Mohammad smiled and kissed her. "I told my *sons* that their father loves them."

That night as they lay in bed, Mohammad bent down and kissed *both* sides of Sarah's stomach.

"I'm just kissing my *boys* good-night," he said, eyes twinkling mischievously.

Chapter 53

Martha and Ken stood among the crowd studying the faces of the passengers coming through the door. They had checked the Arrivals Monitor and the flight from New York was deplaning at Gate 4.

As soon as Khalil, Mansur and Amr, had come through the gate, Martha excitedly nudged Ken. "There they are. Over there," she pointed. "It is incredible how much they look like Mohammad!"

The brothers had also been scanning the crowd. "That must be Sarah's aunt and uncle over there." Amr moved his head in the direction of an older couple. "They look just like Mohammad described them," he smiled.

Martha moved in front of the railing and said to them, "You *must* be Mohammad's brothers, if you're *not,* you are their *twins!*" she laughed. "We are Sarah's uncle and aunt," she said nodding her head toward Ken.

"Yes, *we* are Mohammad's brothers; and this is our good friend, Amr. It was very kind of you to come and meet us."

"Baggage Claim is this way," Ken said pointing. "We're parked in the lot just outside Baggage Claim."

Luckily all their bags had made the change from the international flight to the domestic flight.

Once they were settled in the back seat of the station wagon, Martha began to tell how *fond* she and Ken were of

Mohammad. She laughed and said, "He even calls, Ken here, *Pop.* Ken used to joke if Mohammad had a hard time getting a green card, that he would be willing to *adopt him!*"

"Mohammad speaks highly of you both. Almost every time we talk to him, he tells us about *Aunt Martha* and *Uncle Ken.* He sent us pictures of the ten days he and Sarah spent with you during their winter break," Mansur said.

"He is *so pleased* that you all have come to attend the commencement," Martha said."We had wanted to have you all out to the farm, with Mohammad and Sarah of course, but realized that your schedule is probably pretty packed, so we wanted to invite you to Sarah and Mohammad's favorite restaurant as our guests."

"You must be *our* guests," Khalil said. "We insist."

"It's already been settled; you're *our* guests," Ken said. "Mohammad said to take you to the *Holiday Inn* so you could leave your bags in your room and freshen up if you want. Then I'll come back and pick you up and take you to the restaurant."

Ken drove up to the front of the *Holiday Inn* and dropped them off. He opened the trunk so they could get their luggage out.

"I'll be back about 5:30 to pick you up," he said glancing at his watch.

"Thank you so much," they said shaking hands.

They were standing at the reception desk getting the keys to their rooms, when Khalil felt a tap on his back.

He turned around and was grabbed by Mohammad. "*Illhumdillah alas'salameh,* (thank God for your safe arrival)" he said hugging first Khalil, then Mansur, and then Amr. "We couldn't wait to see you!"

Sarah peeked from behind Mohammad's back and was soon hugged and kissed on both cheeks by her brothers-in-law and Amr.

"We didn't see you standing there," Mansur laughed.

"How could you *possibly miss me;* I'm as big as a house," Sarah laughed.

"You look lovely," Amr said. "Expectant mothers have a *certain glow.*"

"Why don't you wait here in the lobby, Sarah, and I'll go up with them and help them carry their bags?"

"I'll see you later," Sarah said kissing them once again on both cheeks.

On the way up in the elevator, the brothers kept talking all at once not really hearing what the other was saying.

Their two rooms were side-by-side with a connecting door. "I tried to get a room with *three* beds, but the best they could have done would have been to wheel a cot into a double room. I thought that would be a bit uncomfortable for the person getting the cot, so opted for two rooms with a connecting door. I hope that is alright?"

"It's perfect. Amr and I used to sleep in a room with twelve other men when we were in prison; and when we were boys, Mansur and I slept in a room with *thirteen.* I think we will be able to *manage* with two rooms and three queen-size beds," Khalil grinned.

"I'll let you get settled, freshen up, nap if you want, and then Uncle Ken and I will be back about 5:30 to take you to the restaurant. Oh, by the way, I have rented a car for while you are here. Sarah insists that I come and get you every morning at *three* so you can have *suhoor* with us."

"Sarah is *not* fasting, is she?" Mansur asked.

"No, I told her it wasn't *allowed* for women to fast when they were pregnant. She does, however, get up with me, snacks during the day, but waits to have *iftar* with me."

He hugged his brothers and Amr again. "I'll be back about 5:30. I am *so glad* you have come.

Aunt Martha and Uncle Ken had gone back to Sarah's, and no one was there. They sat outside on a bench and waited. At their feet was a large, old-fashioned laundry basket.

They saw Mohammad and Sarah drive up and swing into a parking spot just at the side of the apartment complex.

"Sorry, we weren't here when you arrived. Mohammad couldn't wait to see his brothers; we must have just missed you at the hotel; we had hoped to catch you before you left," Sarah said kissing her uncle and aunt.

"What's this?" Mohammad asked pointing at the laundry basket.

"This was Sarah's great-grandmother's laundry basket. When Sarah called and told us that you were having *twins*, I went right up to the attic and brought this down. Grandmother Wellman used it for all her babies when they were small. When they got so they could sit up some, she'd prop a little pillow in back of them, and put another little pillow in front of them, and it became a kind of playpen. She could move it wherever she was and talk to the babies as she worked."

"You have lined this, even added a ruffle and made a mattress for it!" Sarah said. "It's beautiful."

"Grandmother Wellman gave it to me when your Uncle Ken and I were first married. She thought it would be perfect for our babies. I can still hear her saying, '*Why Martha, this will be just grand for all the babies you are going to have. It is certainly better than keeping them in the bottom drawer of a dresser!*' and she would laugh and laugh. She was a good-sized woman like me," Martha smiled.

"When your little ones are big enough, you can put one in *each end* of the basket and let them play. You'll have a *basketful of babies!* Now, that *is* grand*!*"

Ken had reserved a table for seven at the *Chinese Dragon*. Martha was the life of the party. Khalil, Mansur and Amr were soon captivated by her genuine warmth and loved her humor. It seemed she had them laughing all the time with stories of *when-she-was-a-girl.*

"When I was a girl, we were poorer than dirt. My folks just barely were able to pay the taxes on the farm. It was the Great Depression and nobody had any money. Anyway, we didn't have running water in the house and Mother wanted to conserve the water in the well. She didn't want to waste it on washing clothes." Martha took a sip of water.

'So, every Monday my mother and we girls would carry bundles of dirty clothes down to the creek to wash. Well, to get to the creek we had to climb an old rail fence, walk across a pasture and climb another rail fence. This one day, we had just started across the pasture, when we heard *snorting* and *pawing*. We looked around and there was *the bull*. Granddad had failed to tell mother that he was letting the bull into the pasture that morning." Martha began to laugh.

"You never saw three people *fly*. Mother dropped the laundry basket, grabbed our hands and raced toward an old apple tree that stood in the middle of the pasture with that old bull snorting and trotting after us. She just managed to get us up into the tree and climb up herself before the bull reached us."

"What happened then?" Mansur asked.

"Why we sat in the tree and hollered for Granddad or Pa. We must have sat in that tree for close to an hour. Finally, Granddad came sauntering into the field. He patted the bull on its butt and put a rope around its neck. He looked up at the three of us sitting in the tree and spat – Granddad used to chew tobacco," Martha explained. "He said, '*Why, Mary, I thought today was laundry day. What are you doing sitting in a tree on laundry day?*' My mother always had a quick tongue; she replied, '*Why, Father Wellman, the girls and I thought it was such a pretty day that we'd just sit here for a spell and converse with your bull before doing the laundry.*'"

Khalil turned to Mansur and Mohammad, "Who does Martha remind you of?" In a chorus they said, "Sitteh Hasna!"

"We used to have a grandmother, God rest her soul, called Sitteh Hasna. She was short, round, had blue eyes, red hair and freckles. She was a wonderful storyteller. She always prefaced her stories with: *when-I-was-a-girl-and-not-very-pretty*. They then related some of Sitteh Hasna's wonderful stories.

By the time that waiter had brought dessert – fried bananas in a syrup with a scoop of ice cream beside it, they were all fast friends.

Khalil and Amr rode with Ken and Martha back to the hotel. Mansur rode with Mohammad and Sarah.

"You folks must be tired," Martha said. "And we have a long ride ahead of us. We should probably be on our way. We'll see you all again on Sunday. I hope you don't mind," Martha smiled, "but I'm a *hugger*." She hugged Khalil and Mansur and Amr.

Ken shook their hands and patted them on the back. "I'm real pleased to meet you. You have a fine young brother here," he said smiling at Mohammad.

"Thank you for picking us up at the airport and for the wonderful dinner," Mansur said.

"We are so glad that Mohammad has married into such a wonderful family," Khalil added.

"It was a pleasure meeting you both," Amr said.

That night as Sara and Mohammad finally turned in, Sarah snuggled close to Mohammad, as close as her growing belly would allow. "I'm so glad your brothers and Amr have come. I think they really liked Aunt Martha and Uncle Ken."

"Like them?" Mohammad chuckled as he kissed the top of her head. "All three of them were asking if I thought Aunt Martha and Uncle Ken would *adopt them!*"

Chapter 54

Yasmeen went into labor the morning of the 15th of May. She was awakened by a severe backache and the lower part of the bed felt damp. She swung her legs out of bed and saw that the skirt of her nightgown was *wet*. Her water had broken.

"Issa, Issa, wake up!"

Issa opened his eyes and tried to focus. "What is it? It's not time for *suhoor*, is it?"

"My water has broken; go wake your mother."

Issa snapped fully awake and dashed to awaken Nijmeh.

"*Yum'ma, Yum'ma,* you need to come. Yasmeen is having the baby!"

Nijmeh came to the door with a shawl hastily thrown over her nightdress.

She took in Yasmeen's wet night gown and saw the panic in her eyes. "Don't worry, *binti,* this is all very natural. Lay back down and let me see how far along you are. Your water has broken, and that's a good sign."

Nijmeh called to Issa. "*Yum'ma,* go get Im Najib, and then you and your father go downstairs and boil some water.

By the time Im Najib had climbed the stairs and entered the bedroom, Nijmeh could feel the baby's head at the entrance to the birth canal.

"I have to get to the hospital, *Mart Ammie!*" There was panic in Yasmeen's voice.

"You're doing fine, *binti*. I can see the baby's head. It won't be much longer. You're going to have this baby here. Don't worry," Nijmeh said reassuringly, "I had all my babies at home; in fact, I delivered Issa all by himself while I was doing the wash," she laughed at an attempt to reassure Yasmeen. Yasmeen *tried* to smile, but the pain was intolerable.

Im Najib got behind her granddaughter and supported her back as Yasmeen pushed. Yasmeen would pant, push, and then lean exhaustedly against her grandmother. Sweat was pouring off her brow; her nightgown was above her protruding belly and drenched.

"It won't be much longer, Sitteh, not much longer," Im Najib said. "You are doing very well."

Yasmeen moaned; she bit her lips so wouldn't scream. She pushed and paused; she strained and paused; she thought it would never end. She hadn't thought it would be like this.

"First babies are always hard," Nijmeh said, "but by the time you have had your tenth, you will be up, baking bread and preparing the meal for your family." Yasmeen thought to herself: *Ten! Issa is never touching me again!*

Nijmeh looked again between Yasmeen's legs. The baby had crowned.

"One more push should do it, *binti*. Yasmeen puffed out her cheeks, gave one mighty push and out slipped a very angry, very wet, very red infant.

Nijmeh held him by the heels and gave him a smart swat on his little red buttocks. He looked with black solemn eyes at his grandmother as though to ask: *What did I do to deserve being hit?* Nijmeh cut the cord and tied it off. She laid the infant against Yasmeen's chest.

He stared at his mother. Yasmeen ran a finger through his damp curls. "He certainly has a lot of hair, and look," she said smiling at her grandmother and mother-in-law, *"it's red!"*

What are you going to call him, habeeptee?"

We are going to call him *Jameel* – because he is so beautiful!" Yasmeen said.

Issa called Zaleena in Amman. She, then called Mohammad in Indiana.

Khalil, Mansur, Amr, Mohammad and Sarah had just sat down for the pre-dawn breakfast when the phone rang.

Mohammad answered. "Zaleena, *Marhaba* (hello), is everything okay?"

"Yes, I just wanted to tell you that Issa and Yasmeen have a son! He was born early this morning, our time.

"Yes, they are all well. Yasmeen had a very easy labor. The baby came so fast that your mother delivered him. He is a nice size baby, and he has *red* hair!"

"What did they name him?"

"They are calling him *Jameel*. Isn't that a lovely name?"

"Mansur is here; I'll let you talk to him."

Mansur took the phone from Mohammad.

"How wonderful," Mohammad beamed. "We have a new nephew, and he is born the day of our graduation! What a perfect gift."

Sarah called to Mansur, interrupting him, "Be sure to have Zaleena give them our congratulations and love."

Commencement Day was lovely. It was sunny and warm, but not hot. Ken and Martha got to Purdue early and had time to chat with Mohammad's brothers and Amr as they walked over to the auditorium and found seats together.

The orchestra started the procession and everyone stood as the professors and graduates marched into the hall. Once all the graduates were in, the Masters of Ceremonies motioned for everyone to be seated.

Khalil read down through the program. He spotted the names of Mohammad and Sarah. He was pleased to note that they had *both* graduated with distinction! There were speeches and presentations and *finally* the conferring of degrees. There were a lot of graduates.

The Master of Ceremonies called for the graduates from the School of Agricultural Engineering to please rise.

Tears pooled in Khalil's eyes as he saw Sarah and Mohammad in the line. He remembered a grief-stricken sixteen-year-old boy being handed a little two-year-old brother; he remembered his mother telling him of finding that same little two-year-old hiding among the pallets in the alcove with one of Khalil's shirts around his neck, sucking his thumb; he remembered a child who slept in one of his shirts every night for the seven years he was in prison. *Mohammad Omar Mansur, passed with distinction..*

Khalil looked over at Mansur, and there were tears running down his cheeks as well.

Sarah Goldman Omar Mansur, passed with distinction.

Aunt Martha wiped the corner of each eye with a lace handkerchief.

Standing at the back of the auditorium, tears flowing, lips trembling, stood Sarah's father.

When all the graduates had received their diplomas the Master of Ceremonies said to them, *Graduates change your tassels.* He raised his hands to the audience, "Family, friends, guests, I present to you the graduates of the class of 1990."

There was thunderous applause.

Amr had asked the receptionist at the desk that morning to recommend a fancy restaurant for a graduation dinner that night. She did. She was kind enough to call and book a table for seven for six-thirty that evening.

"I have taken the liberty of booking a table this evening at *Adelino's Old World Kitchen.* The receptionist at the desk highly recommended it. I had asked her for a place that served Mediterranean cuisine. I would like you all to be my guests in honor of Sarah and Mohammad," Amr said.

Dave headed back home as the sun was setting. The sky was a palette of red, orange and yellow. It was in vibrant contrast to his dark mood. This should have been one of the happiest moments of his life – *Sarah graduating with distinction* –and he stood in the back of the auditorium and didn't even feel he could go up and congratulate her. He saw her from a distance surrounded by Martha and Ken, Mohammad, and three men who must have been Mohammad's brothers; they certainly looked like him – at least two of them did.

He cursed Emily for being so *self-righteous,* so *unyielding,* so *uncompromising,* and so *unforgiving.* He knew there would be a row when he got back. She would put on her damn *mantle of martyrdom.* He hated how she had become; he wished she could have been more like Martha. *No one* in town *cared* that Sarah had married an Arab, a Moslem.

Night had fallen and the stars had come out; as he got closer and closer to home he found himself slowing down. *He didn't want to go home; he didn't want to see her.*

He drove up the dirt driveway at about two miles an hour – if that. He parked the truck in front of the garage. Emily had heard him pull in and park. She came out the door of the breezeway. Her hands were folded across her chest; there was a scowl on her face.

"Well, I suppose you went down to Purdue to see your daughter graduate," she said accusingly. "You obviously don't care a whit about what *I* might feel."

Dave didn't say a word as he turned the key in the ignition, put the truck in reverse and backed out of the drive. He didn't even turn around as he drove down the dirt lane. He ignored the shocked cry of: *"Dave, Dave, where do you think you're going!"*

Mohammad and Sarah drove his brothers and Amr to the Indianapolis Airport early the next morning, so they could catch their flight to California.

"You can't imagine how much it meant to us that you came!" Mohammad said. "It was just *perfect* having you here."

"We wouldn't have missed it. We are so proud of you both."

They checked in, got their boarding cards for both flights (they had to change planes), and waited for their plane to be called.

"I always hate these last moments when we are waiting to leave," Sarah said. "I hate *good-byes!*"

Their flight was called. They each hugged Sarah and kissed her on both cheeks. Mohammad hugged and kissed Amr and Mansur. When he got to Khalil, his voice trembled and there were tears in his eyes. The two brothers clung to each other for a moment.

"None of this would have been possible without you," Mohammad whispered. "I owe you so much."

Khalil was too choked up to speak. He just held Mohammad close to his heart and kissed him, his tears falling into Mohammad's curls.

He smiled through his tears and patted his heart as he looked at Mohammad's tear-stained face. He smiled at Sarah and Mansur and Amr. They were all trying *not* to cry but weren't succeeding.

Sarah slipped her hand into Mohammad's. They stood and watched until Khalil, Mansur and Amr had passed through security, waved a final time and disappeared.

"Let's go home," Sarah said kissing Mohammad gently on the shoulder. He just nodded his head; he still couldn't trust himself to speak.

Chapter 55

Mid-June another package arrived from Aunt Martha. Mohammad was excited when he brought it up to the apartment. Sarah was resting on the couch with her bare feet up on the coffee table. It was hot; she was uncomfortable; she had gained about 42 pounds. "I can barely see my feet!" she joked as Mohammad carried the box over to her.

"You *are* looking just a *tad* like Aunt Martha," Mohammad grinned. Look, she sent us another *surprise*."

"It *has* to be another quilt. When she was out here for our commencement, she told me she was working on a second quilt, but not to tell you."

He slit the tape on the box with a paring knife and lifted a baby quilt out of the box and handed it to Sarah. She removed the plastic bag and unfolded the quilt.

If it were possible, this quilt was even more creative, more beautiful than the first. This quilt was the farm in winter. The same gray house with green shutters had been appliquéd on it, except *this* time there was the figure of a man shoveling snow off the porch roof; beside the red barn was a *sleigh* drawn by a horse; she had even embroidered little *bells* around the horse's neck. Around the pond there were mounds of white fabric pieced to represent snow; there was the figure of a wobbly man trying to skate on the blue satin pond. The most amazing part was that Aunt Martha had added two figures sitting on a toboggan. The toboggan was sliding down a snowy slope.

Above each figure Aunt Martha had embroidered the names in red silk thread. Above the figure shoveling snow off the roof was embroidered: *Grandpa Ken; Baba* was embroidered above the wobbly figure on the satin pond; above the figures riding the toboggan were embroidered: *Grandma Martha* and *Mama.*

"I can't believe how *beautiful* this is. It captures those ten days we spent at the farm. It is *amazing,*" Sarah said. "Help me up, *habeebee,*" she said reaching her arms out to Mohammad. "I want to put this in the basket."

"It's a good thing I come from *good peasant stock* and am such a *robust Prince,*" he smiled lifting her off the couch, "or I would need to call in the neighbors."

The bassinet had been set up in their bedroom. Mohammad had given it a fresh coat of paint. A sheet with little ducks waddling across it covered the pillow mattress. Artfully draped over the foot of the bassinet was the quilt Aunt Martha had made of the farm in summer.

On the floor beside the bassinet was the old-fashioned laundry basket. A matching sheet, with those little ducks waddling across it, covered the pillow mattress. Over the end of the basket, Sarah draped the new quilt – the farm in winter.

She put her arm around Mohammad's waist; his arm was around her shoulders. "All we need now," Mohammad grinned at her, "are our *sons!*"

Sarah lovingly poked him in the ribs, "Or our *daughters!*"

"Or," Mohammad grinned squeezing her shoulders, "one of each!"

Aunt Martha arrived the Monday morning of the last week of June. All that day, Sarah had been particularly energetic. She had cleaned the apartment; cleaned out the kitchen cupboards; organized the dresser drawers; done a huge laundry, even ironed Mohammad's permanent press shirts!

Aunt Martha said: *You're nesting. I suspect you will go into labor tonight.* Sarah had said: *I still have another week to go.*

They had finished supper; the table had been cleared; the leftovers put away. Aunt Martha looking out the apartment window said, "There's a full moon tonight. Grandmother Wellman used to always say babies usually came during a full moon. An old wives' tale, I suspect."

When she turned around, Sarah was clutching Mohammad's arm and standing in a puddle of water. "My water broke," Sarah said as though surprised.

"Are you having any contractions, love?"

"I feel a little discomfort in my back and feel as though I have *gas,* but..." Just then a strong contraction hit. She bore down on Mohammad's arm. "Ooooooh, now *that* was a contraction!"

She started to pace the apartment. Around and around she and Mohammad walked. Around the sitting room, into the bedroom, back into the sitting room, down the tiny hall; around and around they paced.

Mohammad timed her contractions. At first, they were about ten minutes apart. She called her doctor. He said to call him again when they were five minutes apart. They could go to the hospital then.

"Don't worry, Sarah, first babies usually take their time in coming. It will probably be some hours before you deliver."

It *was* some hours. The sun had gone to bed and risen again before Sarah's contractions were finally five minutes apart. She was already exhausted. She hadn't slept, none of them had. The *anticipation* had kept them all awake more than anything else.

Finally, at about eight in the morning, Sarah called the doctor. He said that he would meet her at the hospital.

Aunt Martha was a *take-charge* person. She fished the car keys out of her purse, handed them to Mohammad and told him to get Sarah's packed overnight bag from the bedroom closet. With Mohammad on one side and Aunt Martha on the other, they guided Sarah out the door, down the stairs, and into the backseat of Aunt Martha's station wagon. She got in with Sarah; Mohammad drove.

As soon as they walked in the hospital doors, a nurse met them with a wheelchair. Sarah got in; Mohammad pushed; Aunt Martha followed carrying the overnight bag.

Sarah was wheeled into a hospital room. The nurse and Mohammad helped her up into the bed. The nurse laid a hospital gown on the bed. "Get undressed and put this on. Your husband and mother can help you."

"This is my aunt," Sarah said looking lovingly at Aunt Martha. She was a bit startled by the realization that she was *glad* that her mother wasn't there. She had half-expected that she would *want* Emily there in spite of all that had happened, but she *didn't*.

Mohammad and Aunt Martha helped her out of her maternity smock and into the hospital gown. She lay down on the bed. The contractions were fairly regular. She would pant when she had one, then when it was over she would relax. She held tightly to Mohammad's hand.

The nurse came back in with a paper cup of crushed ice and handed it to Mohammad. "How regular are your contractions, hon?"

"They are still about five minutes apart."

"You still have a little ways to go. First babies sometimes take their time," she smiled. "I'm going to shave you and get you prepped. Your husband is welcome to stay, or if you would rather, he can step out for five minutes."

Sarah had a death-like grip on Mohammad's hand. "He's not going anywhere," she gritted her teeth as another contraction jarred her body; "it's because of *him* that I am here!" When the contraction was over, Sarah looked up at Mohammad and smiled. "You *know* that was an *attempt* at humor?"

Three hours later, Sarah had still not dilated enough. The nurse put in a drip to increase the contractions. The contractions *did* come more frequently and were quite painful. It had been almost sixteen hours since her water broke.

A half-hour later the doctor came in to examine Sarah. He asked the nurse how far Sarah had dilated, how far apart her contractions were.

He smiled at Sarah and said, "Well, young lady, I think your twins are finally ready to be born."

The nurse handed Mohammad a green surgical gown, cap and mask. He slipped the gown over his clothes; Aunt Martha tied it in the back.

Sarah was wheeled into the delivery room still clutching tightly to Mohammad's hand. She was put on the delivery table and her legs were put into the stirrups. Mohammad stood at her side holding her hand, speaking encouragingly to her.

Sarah had been given a saddle block. The nurse rubbed Sarah's belly. The doctor looked up over the top of his rimless glasses. "Now when I say push, give one good strong push – but *only* when I say." He paused and placed his hands as though ready to catch something. *"Now push!"*

Sarah gave one strong push. Mohammad held both of her hands, the nurse rubbed her belly.

"Now, relax," the doctor said. "He looked down again. "I can see a head. *Now push!"*

Sarah pushed again and felt a tearing as the baby slid into the doctor's hands. Grasping the baby by the ankles, he gave it a quick slap on its buttocks. The baby blinked his eyes and started to squall. "It's a boy," he said as he snipped then clamped the cord and laid the baby on Sarah's chest.

Sarah looked at her red, crying son covered with a milky-white substance. He had gobs of black hair matted against his head. She touched her finger to his little quivering hand and he grasped it. *It was love at a touch!*

There were tears in Mohammad's eyes as he beheld his son for the first time.

"You can hold him for just a minute," the nurse said as she lifted the squirming infant from Sarah's breast and placed him in Mohammad's arms. Mohammad thought his heart would burst with love.

"I'll take this little fellow and clean him up," the nurse said taking the baby from Mohammad's arms.

The doctor looked again, and he saw the second black-haired baby presenting itself. "The second one is ready to come, Sarah. You're almost done. *Now push!*"

Again Sarah gritted her teeth and strained. Mohammad held her hands; the nurse rubbed her belly. The second child slid wetly into the doctor's hands. Once again the doctor grabbed the ankles and swatted the buttocks. Once again a baby opened its eyes and cried. The doctor smiled, "You have another son." He placed the second baby on Sarah's chest.

The little one looked solemnly at Sarah with big black eyes, as though wondering who she was.

Sarah spoke to him, "I'm your Mama. I'm your Mama." His little hand quivered and waved. Sarah touched the palm, and once again her finger was grasped in a strong grip. Once again *it was instant love.*

The nurse, again, placed a squirming infant in Mohammad's arms. Mohammad ran his finger across the little cheek, and as a reflex the infant moved his mouth in search of the finger.

Mohammad's grin could not be seen beneath the mask he wore. "We have two sons, *habeeptee, two sons!*" He bent down and kissed Sarah through the mask, still cradling his infant son in his arms.

"*Illhumdillah, Illhumdillah,*" Mohammad kept repeating. "God be praised. God be praised."

The nurses took the cleaned and swaddled babies and put them into plastic bassinets. "You can go and see them in the nursery," the nurse told Mohammad. "When your wife is all cleaned up, we will wheel her back to her room and bring the babies there."

Mohammad removed his mask and kissed Sarah. "I'll just go and look at our sons and meet you back in the room." There were tears of happiness in his eyes. "You can't imagine how much I love you."

"Sarah was in an exhausted euphoria. "Something about stars, sand, and raindrops, wasn't it?" she said.

Aunt Martha was standing at the nursery window when Mohammad came up to her. He was still wearing the green surgical gown. He removed the green cap and ran a hand through his black curls. He put his arm around Aunt Martha's shoulders and bent down and kissed her.

"We have *two sons,*" he said, "Sarah was wonderful."

When the nurse came to the window she asked which baby they wanted to see. Mohammad held up *two* fingers and said *Omar.* The nurse smiled and picked up a little baby from a blue, plastic bassinet. She motioned to another nurse to pick up another baby from his blue, plastic bassinet. The two nurses came to the window and held the babies for Mohammad and Aunt Martha to see.

They had receiving blankets wrapped tightly around them; around each wrist was a plastic bracelet that read: *baby Omar;* both infants were fast asleep. All that really could be seen, aside from their little hands, were their fat cheeks and their *thick black thatches* of hair.

"They are beautiful; just beautiful!" Aunt Martha cried. "I feel like *I'm a grandmother!*"

"You *are* their grandmother," Mohammad said giving her a hug.

Aunt Martha tapped on the window, "I'm your Grandma Martha," she said smiling through her tears.

"They are such nice size babies. How much do they weigh?"

The one weighs seven pounds, three ounces; the other weighs seven pounds, four ounces," Mohammad proudly said.

"What have you named your sons?"

"We had decided *if they were boys* to name them after my brothers *Khalil* and *Mansur.*

"We also wanted them to have American names. So we decided on *Khalil Kenneth* and *Mansur Matthew* – after you and Uncle Ken. In Arabic the masculine form of *Martha* is translated *Matthew.*

"Well, *isn't that something!"* Martha murmured through her tears.

When they walked back to Sarah's room, she was already sitting up in bed. The nurse had combed her hair and Sarah had on a new dressing gown. She looked exhausted, but *happy.*

Mohammad kissed her. "You got your *sons!"* she smiled. "Aren't they the most beautiful babies you have ever seen?" she sighed.

Aunt Martha kissed her as well. "Mohammad told me about the names, love. You don't know how touched I am."

Two nurses wheeled in the plastic bassinets. A bassinet was placed on each side of Sarah's bed. Both babies were sleeping on their sides, content in their cocoons.

"I see from the chart," the nurse said, "that you intend to breast feed your babies. When they awake, put the baby to your breast and guide your nipple into his mouth. He may not know what to do at first but keep your nipple in his mouth and he will soon latch on.

The nurse pinned a blue ribbon to the receiving blanket of one of the infants.

"What's the ribbon for?" Sarah asked.

"This is for you to know which baby you fed," the nurse smiled. "We have found with twins that sometimes a new mother feeds the same baby twice! Once you have fed one of your sons, pin this ribbon to his blanket and nurse the other one. You'll get the hang of it."

Mohammad went over and picked up one of his sons. He kissed him on the forehead and handed the sleeping newborn to Sarah. He then picked up the second newborn and kissed him on the forehead. He sat in the armchair next to Sarah cradling his son in his arms.

Aunt Martha took a camera out of her purse. "You two stay just like that. Now smile." She then took a picture of Mohammad holding both his sons and another of Sarah holding both babies. She snapped several pictures. "I'll get these developed tomorrow so you can send prints to your brothers and folks."

"There's one more photo that needs to be taken," Mohammad said. "Come sit here, Aunt Martha," he said getting out of the arm chair. Martha sat down and Mohammad put a sleeping newborn in each arm.

"Now smile." Aunt Martha *did* smile, though when the print was developed it showed tears in her eyes as she held her *grandsons* for the first time.

Chapter 56

The morning after she gave birth, an older nurse came in to talk to Sarah. "I'm sure," she said, "since these are your first babies you will have lots of questions. I'm here to help. I have been working in maternity wards for over twenty-five years, and I have had *two* sets of twins myself."

"I am *so glad* you've come," Sarah smiled. "I don't like to admit it, even to myself, but I am really floundering here; I don't think I know anything."

"Ask away, dear."

"I want to breastfeed my babies, but I'm worried that I won't have enough milk or that both babies will need fed at the same time or that I will be breastfeeding *all the time* and won't have time for anything else."

The woman chuckled. "There is a one-word answer to all three questions. *Yes!* Yes, you will have enough milk. It is kind of like *supply and demand;* the amount of milk you produce will be stimulated by their sucking – the more they *demand* to be fed, the more milk you body will *supply.*"

"Yes, there will be times when they will want to be fed at the same time."

Sarah interrupted her. "Is it possible to feed both my babies at the same time?"

"That's another *yes*. It takes a little practice and can be frustrating in the beginning, but it is certainly possible. I will show you how to do it. One advantage of feeding them together is that it *does* give you more time to do other things – like *sleep*," she laughed.

"Is it okay for me to have my newborns in the same bassinet?"

"That's another yes; you are making this very easy for me," she smiled. "I personally feel that newborn twins sleep better if they are in the same bassinet. They have been so used to being together in the womb that it makes the adjustment to the *world outside* easier for them. I kept my twins in the same basket. The only thing I did differently was that I placed one at the foot of the basket, and the other at the head of the basket. This way they weren't facing each other and each had, I thought, more breathing space. Once they gained weight, and I thought they needed more room to move about, I moved them to the same crib. They were in the same crib, head-to-foot still, until they were well over a year old."

"I personally feel that twins miss the *presence* of the other when they are separated," she said.

Almost on cue, both Khalil and Mansur started to cry and wanted fed.

"They must have heard us talking," the nurse laughed. "Here, I'll show you how to feed them both at once. She took pillows from the closet and placed them under Sarah's arms. On the one pillow she placed Khalil.

"Just kind of tuck his feet under your arm. Position his face so he can latch onto your nipple."

Sarah placed her nipple into Khalil's mouth. He moved it around and then spit it out. She placed it again in his mouth. Again he spit it out. Finally on the third try, she gently held the nipple in his mouth and wouldn't allow him to spit it out. He played with it a bit, and then *latched on* and began to suck. She put her right arm around him and cradled his head in her palm. He seemed to *watch* her as he sucked.

"There, he's doing fine," the nurse said.

She then took Mansur and placed him on the pillow under Sarah's left arm. It was a repetition of what Khalil had done. On the fourth try, Sarah held her nipple in his mouth and he finally *latched on* and began to suck.

"There, you're doing it!"

"I feel like a sow we once had on my father's farm," Sarah laughed. She cradled the black-thatched heads of her newborns in a palm of each hand. Each arm securely, lovingly, curled around a tiny form.

The nurse pinned the blue ribbon to the right side of Khalil's sleeper. She told Sarah, "I have put the ribbon on the right side, because he is nursing on the right side. Whenever you nurse him today, nurse him on the right side and his brother on the left. Tomorrow morning when you nurse, move the ribbon to the left side and nurse him only on the left side, and his brother on the right side. He'll be the *control baby*," she smiled.

"I don't understand. Why does it make any difference?"

"Even mothers of one baby will alternate breasts when they nurse. This keeps the milk flow even. Mothers of twins are already using both breasts at the same time, but some babies nurse more vigorously than others. This allows the one who is more aggressive in his nursing to stimulate the milk flow in both breasts."

"You will initially need help at home," she added.

"My aunt is staying with me for a week," Sarah said.

"You'll need to have someone around longer than that. Of course, your husband can help, but when he goes to work you will need someone to help."

Sarah looked down and both newborns were sleeping. The nurse put them back in their bassinets and removed the pillows. "Why don't you take a little nap as well," the nurse smiled.

They were all three sleeping when Mohammad softly came into the room with Aunt Martha. He felt this incredible warm feeling around his heart. "They're beautiful, aren't they?" he whispered to Aunt Martha.

"Yes, they are," she smiled touching his arm. "Let's go down to the cafeteria and have a cup of coffee," Aunt Martha said, "while they sleep."

Over coffee, Aunt Martha asked him if he and Sarah had decided about the job offer they had recently had for next year.

It had come *completely out of the blue* – another cliché that Mohammad had picked up. He had been approached with a job offer by their adviser. It seemed that an Associate Professorship position had opened in the Agricultural Engineering Department. The man who had been offered the position had turned it down. Mohammad's name had been raised by the Search Committee as a possible replacement. They all knew Mohammad; they knew the caliber of his work; he had graduated *with distinction;* they liked him, and *he was a known entity.* His adviser had all-but-said that he was a *shoe-in* – another of those clichés.

In addition to teaching a couple of undergraduate courses a semester, Mohammad would be involved in research concerning global soil and water conservation; an area in which he was particularly interested.

It would mean that they remained at Purdue. They would still need to move from Student Housing, but only from one apartment to another, not to a new city or State or country.

"We're going to take it if we are *officially* offered the position."

"I'm *selfishly* glad," Aunt Martha said. "I want to have those grandbabies handy enough that I can pop down to see them from time-to-time, and that you and Sarah can bring them to the farm."

"I'm glad you mentioned the farm." Mohammad hesitated for just a moment. "I was wondering," Mohammad smiled, "how you and Uncle Ken would feel if Sarah and the boys and I came to the farm for the month of July?"

"*Feel?* I would feel that the angel Gabriel himself had given me a gift from God!" Aunt Martha beamed. "But I thought that you and Sarah wanted to avoid the farm because of Emily?" she said seriously.

"There *is* that concern. But I think it is outweighed by the fact that we would like some *help* with the twins, at least initially. Your farm *feels* like home. We figured with the *four* of us, there would always be a set of arms to rock a little one. Sarah would be able to *rest* a bit that month and gear herself up for having *two* little ones on her own." Mohammad paused. "You always said her mother would come around once there were grandchildren; we are *hoping* that that is true. How could she see Khalil and Mansur and *not* fall instantly in love?"

Aunt Martha smiled, but thought to herself *you don't know Emily.*

It was decided as soon as Sarah and the newborns were released from the hospital, they would all drive up to the farm for a month.

When Martha was talking on the phone to Ken that night, she told him about Mohammad's proposal. Ken was ecstatic!

"I couldn't be more pleased! But what about Emily?" he asked rather soberly.

"Mohammad is *hoping* there might be some sort of reconciliation once Emily sees the twins, though I frankly doubt it. But, you never know, *miracles do happen.*"

"I did run into Dave at the Feed Store. He asked if Sarah had had her baby. I told him that she had had her *babies.* He said that he hadn't known she was expecting twins. He looked kind of sad about it. He asked me if I knew what her plans were for next year. Of course, I didn't know, but said that Mohammad had had several job offers. He asked me to tell him when I did know, as he would like to drive down to Purdue to see Sarah and his grandchildren before they moved."

"He didn't mention Mohammad, did he?"

"Nope, not a mention."

Mohammad was intrigued with the fact that Sarah was attempting to nurse both the babies at once and was initially *embarrassed* to see her sitting there with both breasts uncovered. All the women he knew in the camp breastfeed their babies, but they always had a shawl over their shoulders hiding the breast and the baby.

Sarah noticed his embarrassment. "I feel a bit *exposed, too*," she laughed. "It almost makes me feel *wanton*. Then I look at these two little guys and think that this is all *natural, beautiful,* and *maternal*." Her eyes twinkled, "Not to worry, I am never going to nurse them both in public unless I have a large shawl covering my *impressive assets*."

Mohammad had to grin, "They *are quite impressive!* Those are two pretty *lucky* little guys."

Chapter 57

Dave and Emily tolerated each other; divorce wouldn't have even entered their minds. There were days when Emily would have *liked* to have gone out the kitchen door, walked down the dirt lane, crossed onto the unpaved country road and disappeared. There were days when Dave thought of getting in his truck and heading west. He *had* done *just* that the night of Sarah's graduation. The furthest west he had gotten was the all-night adult arcade off the interstate. There weren't any cars in the parking lot, so he pulled over and slept in his truck until morning.

The following morning when Emily had gone down to the barn to check on the cows, Dave was there doing the milking. All Emily had said was, *I see you're back. Breakfast will be on the table when you're done.*

That afternoon, Dave moved his things permanently into the spare room. He and Emily *moved around* each other, saying not much more than *pass the peas,* and *it looks like rain.* Emily still went to choir practice on Wednesdays, attended church and Sunday school on Sundays, and went to Thursday-night Bible Study faithfully. The *mantle of martyrdom* she wore was *almost visible.*

Zaleena had been anxiously waiting for a phone call from Mohammad announcing the safe delivery of the twins. She had marked the predicted due date on the calendar. She knew that first babies sometimes went beyond their due date, but that twins sometimes arrived early. Every day she expected a call.

It was seven in the morning when the call finally came. The children were already dressed and having breakfast as they left the house at seven-thirty; Mansur and Zaleena both left at eight.

Zaleena picked up the receiver on the second ring.

"*Salam aleikum,*"

"*Aleikum, Salam* – Mohammad?" Zaleena asked.

"I wanted to catch you before you left for work. The babies have arrived, *illhumdillah!* We have twin *sons!*" Mohammad excitedly said.

"*Elf ma'bruk* (a thousand congratulations)! How is Sarah?"

"Sarah is fine, *illhumdillah*. She had a long labor, but she was amazing!"

"How big were the boys and what did you name them?" Zaleena asked. Mansur was at her elbow trying to listen to what Mohammad was saying. She motioned him away and mouthed: *Go call Khalil,* Mansur told young Omar, "Go call Ammo Khalil and tell him that Ammo Mohammad is on the line."

"The boys were a nice size, *ma'shallah,* the one weighed 7 lbs, 5 ounces; the other was 7 lbs, 4 ounces. They have lots of black hair."

"*What* did you name them?" Zaleena persisted.

"We have named them *Khalil* and *Mansur*. We also gave them American middle names: *Kenneth* and *Matthew* after Sarah's uncle and aunt."

There were tears in Zaleena's eyes. "How thoughtful that you named them after your brothers; here's Mansur; he wants to congratulate you," Zaleena said as she passed the receiver to Mansur.

"Elf mab'ruk habeebee. Inshallah everything is well. I am really touched that you have named your sons after Khalil and me. You can expect a *big present*," he laughed.

Khalil had just come in the door. "I'll give you Khalil, again *elf mab'ruk.*" Mansur grasped his brother on the shoulder and squeezed. "You have a grandson, Khalil!" he whispered.

"Mohammad, *habeebee, elf mab'ruk.*"

"Did Mansur tell you that we named one of the twins, *Khalil?*" Mohammad paused. "You have always been like a father to me, so I wanted to name my first son after you – like a good *son* would do." He laughed.

At first Khalil couldn't say anything, then finally he said, "You *are* as much my son as my brother. I am honored that you have named one of your sons for me."

"Please call *Yum'ma* and *Yaba* to tell them our news. I mailed out pictures today to you and to them. You'll get to see your *nephews/grandsons!* The boys *look* like us – they are *dark, and handsome,*" he laughed. "Sarah asked me to tell Zaleena that when she saw the boys, she thought of what Zaleena had told her about: *if the babies favor the father then that means that the mother loved the father better than the father loved the mother!* She is questioning *how much I love her.*" Khalil could hear the smile in Mohammad's voice.

Omar listened to Nijmeh's *trilling* on the phone. He turned to Issa and Yasmeen, "Mohammad and Sarah have had their babies! Apparently, all is well, *illhumdillah.*

Nijmeh came into the sitting room waving two handkerchiefs and doing the slow mincing steps that women did at weddings. "We have two new *grandsons, ma'shallah!* Sarah and the babies are fine, *illhumdillah!* Imagine *three* grandsons in one month!" She did a series of *Ah'ee's* and trills.

"What did they name the boys, *Mart Ammie?*" Yasmeen asked.

"They have named them after Khalil and Mansur."

"*Inshallah,* next year they will have a little *Issa,*" Issa smiled.

Sarah and Mohammad had been at the farm almost two weeks. Mohammad had gotten up early and gone to the barn, or worked in the fields, with Uncle Ken every day. Mohammad was a hard worker.

Uncle Ken had asked him what kind of work he had done at home. Mohammad had explained that it had been difficult for boys like him from the camp to work because there *was no work.*

"If we had not been refugees, and our families had remained in their villages, we would have been out working in the fields almost by the time we could walk. We would have herded sheep and goats, picked olives and figs, tilled the soil to plant wheat. My father and grandfathers were peasants, my brothers and I would have been peasants and tied to the land. When our fathers no longer had the land, they lost what defined them."

Mohammad continued. "In the camps, there was almost no work at all for the *men*. The only work *boys* could find was to sell religious cards with Suras from the Quran on them in the street, or they sold candy bars. If a boy was lucky enough to have a father who had a shop or a trade he went to work with his father when he was very young. My older sister's husband worked with his father, who was a carpenter, from the time he was ten. Her oldest son went to work with his father and grandfather when he was ten. Her six other sons all dropped out of school to go to work as day laborers. Her youngest child dropped out of school at eleven to work with my father building stone walls, digging gardens, that kind of thing."

Mohammad continued to fork hay down from the loft to the cow stalls beneath. "My sisters in California married two brothers who worked in their father's grocery store since before they were sixteen. They would work after school and weekends until ten at night. Sometimes Arab grocers in the States keep their stores open all night and their sons are *expected* to work."

He leaned against the hay fork and wiped the sweat from his brow. It was hot in July in Iowa, boiling in the hayloft.

"I suppose if the only Palestinian you met were me, you'd think we were all *lazy, privileged,* and *pampered.* That is far from the truth. A few boys like me, born in the camp, raised in its poverty, aware of how we had no chance to be more than uneducated day laborers, saw that *education* was the only way out. My father hammered this into my head. He kept saying to me, '*Don't be like me. Learn to read and write. Make something of yourself.'* My older brothers listened to him. They studied hard; they won scholarships; they excelled at college or university, so they could do as my father asked, *make something of themselves.*

"It is a part of our culture that the oldest is responsible to help his younger brother go on to school, and once that next youngest is finished with school, he is responsible to help the next, and so on. My oldest brother, Mansur, put my brother, Khalil, through school; Khalil put me through school, and Mansur put my youngest brother, Issa, through school. I have been blessed in being the *ninth* – the only one younger than me has already been put through school by Mansur.

"The siblings look out for each other. My married sisters' husbands sent me *pocket money* every month. They knew I couldn't work because of my student visa, so this was their way of *helping.* I didn't ask for their help; I didn't *expect* them to help, but they did.

"I think, in my case, my older brothers spoil me. They grew up in the poverty of the camp, and now that they are professionals and have money, thank God, they wanted to make sure that Issa and I had every opportunity, but they also expect that once we are making money, we will also help others. It is part of Islam to give *zakat* – a fixed amount of our income to others." Mohammad took a rest from pitching hay and wiped his brow again.

"We have no social security system at home. My older brothers also support my parents; they do it out of love, not just out of duty. They insisted that my mother no longer go out and clean houses. They *suggested* to my father that he no longer needed to go and repair stone fences and dig gardens – but he loves working the land, so he didn't listen to their *suggestion.*"

Mohammad laughed. "I know you all thought I was probably going a *little overboard* – another cliché I picked up – when I kept kidding about wanting the twins to be *boys*. This is also a philosophy with which I have been raised. A man *had* to have sons to support him in his old age. A daughter, when she got married, became part of another family. If a man had no sons, his old age would have been very bleak. He would have been dependent on the charity of his nephews or his neighbors."

Uncle Ken smiled as he distributed the hay that Mohammad was tossing down into the different stalls. "I think this is the most I have ever heard you talk! And you have sure explained a lot about Arab culture that I didn't know – a lot about *you* that I didn't know!"

Mohammad looked down at him and laughed. "You probably thought that I was just a spoiled, rich Arab boy whose daddy had a lot of money. You never saw me working, and yet I obviously had money – and I *do* – *my brother's money*. I think my brothers see it, not as a handout, but as an *investment*. They expected me to work hard in school and to *excel*. If I hadn't *excelled* they would have withdrawn their support and insisted I go back home.

"I *may* appear to be *pampered and privileged* – and I admit that I have been. But I have also *worked really hard* because I *knew* that my brothers were investing in my future, and I couldn't possibly disappoint them."

Sarah had a long talk with Aunt Martha. "Mohammad and I feel a bit guilty about coming up here to spend the month with you. We know that we could have managed with the twins on our own, especially since school is over and Mohammad hasn't started his new job yet, but we had no *family* at school, and we really wanted to share this time with you and Uncle Ken. It is so much easier having you two around."

"We are *so happy* that you are here. As I told Mohammad, *it is like the angel Gabriel himself brought us a gift from God.* It means a lot to your uncle and me that you feel at home with us," Aunt Martha said. "And just look at how well the babies are doing, bless their hearts!"

The babies were doing well; they seemed to be thriving in the country air. Sarah still nursed them whenever they were hungry. She sometimes nursed them both together, sometimes separately if one awakened before the other. She enjoyed those times when she could cuddle each one alone.

These first two weeks, it seemed that all the babies had done was eat, sleep, and need their diapers changed. The adults used *diaper-changing* time as a time to rock the babies and talk to them. It was one of the few times they were awake and *not* being nursed.

It was interesting that both newborns seemed to *recognize* Sarah's and Mohammad's voice. Whenever one of them spoke within hearing of the infants, the little one's eyes would look around as though *searching* for the face that went with the voice. Sarah had remarked to Mohammad that she had read where babies in the womb *hear* their mother and father's voices and *recognize* their voices after they are born.

The babies slept together in the old-fashioned laundry basket – head-to-toe – as the nurse had suggested. Sarah *did* notice that if either of the babies was fussy, and she put the other baby in the basket, the one that was fussy seemed to calm right down. They *did* seem to be more content when they were together.

One afternoon, at almost dusk, Sarah was sitting on the porch rocking Khalil; Mohammad, who had just come in from helping Uncle Ken in the barn, was rocking Mansur. Aunt Martha had gone in to make coffee, as Uncle Ken was just coming up from the barn. An old pick-up truck came up the lane.

"I think that's my dad's truck," Sarah said as her heart seemed to catch. Mohammad looked around the trellis with the climbing white roses.

"It *is* your dad. Would you like me to go inside?"

"No, stay right here. I'll go out and talk to him," she said placing a wide-awake Khalil in the basket.

Sarah walked out to the drive just as Dave was getting out of the truck.

"Sarah, I heard you were back," Dave said. "I wanted to stop and see you and see my grandsons."

Sarah hugged her dad. "Come on up. The babies are with Mohammad on the porch."

Dave walked reluctantly behind Sarah. This was his brother's house; this was his daughter; yet, he felt awkward – uncomfortable. Aunt Martha was just coming out the door with a tray of coffee cups and cookies.

"You're just in time for coffee, Dave. Pull up a rocker and sit a spell." She put the tray down on the wicker table and bent down and picked-up a wide-awake Khalil from the basket. "Now, there's a love," she said to the baby putting him against her shoulder.

"Sir," Mohammad said.

Dave just nodded his head.

Mohammad went over and said to Dave, "Perhaps you'd like to hold your grandson, Mansur?" He placed the baby in Dave's arms. Mansur's dark brown eyes stared at him as he waved a little fist.

Dave looked down at the little mite. He didn't look *anything* like Sarah.

Aunt Martha went over and placed the wide-awake Khalil in Dave's lap. "And this is your other grandson, Khalil," she said.

Dave looked at both of his grandsons and again thought: *they're nothing like Sarah.*

The babies started to squirm a bit. "Here, you better take them," he said to Sarah.

Sarah picked up Khalil; Mohammad took Mansur.

They placed the babies, side-by-side, on their backs in the basket and Sarah covered them with a knitted blanket that Mona had sent. "I'll leave them on their backs until they fall asleep, and then I'll rearrange them," she said to Aunt Martha.

Ken came up onto the porch. "Glad to see you, Dave. What do you think of our grandsons? Pretty handsome boys, aren't they? Look just like Mohammad."

Dave didn't quite know what to say, so he said nothing.

He shuffled his feet and got out of the rocker. "I probably should be going; Emily will probably have supper ready."

"You didn't drink your coffee," Martha said.

"Another time."

He hit his ball cap against his leg, and put it back on his head. "I'll be seeing you."

"I'll walk out to the truck with you, Dad," Sarah said slipping her arm through his.

"What did you think of your grandsons, Dad?"

"They'll do." He put his foot on the running board of the old pick-up. "Your mother hasn't said anything, but I think she would like to see you and the babies. She's a pretty hard nut to crack, but she *is* your mother, and those boys *are* her grandsons. If you have a mind to, you could bring them over to the house tomorrow."

"I don't think Mum wants to see me, and I don't think she'd be happy to see the twins," Sarah said. "The last time I saw her, she wanted me to *divorce* Mohammad and *give* the baby to him – we didn't know we were having twins at the time."

"I thought she had said something like that to you. She can be very *harsh*, but *she is still your mother.*"

"Let me think about it. I'm not making any promises."

"Do as you see fit," Dave replied." But I hope you decide to come."

Sarah talked it over with Mohammad, Aunt Martha and Uncle Ken. They were all a bit uneasy about Sarah taking the boys over to see Emily, though they all agreed that she had a *right* to see her daughter and grandsons and *hoped* that seeing the babies would soften her heart and bring about some form of reconciliation.

Mohammad suggested that Aunt Martha drive her over late tomorrow morning after Sarah had nursed the boys. Sarah reluctantly agreed.

Neither Sarah nor Mohammad slept well that night. They kept thinking about seeing Emily the next day. Martha and Ken also lay awake most of the night. They knew Emily and were *apprehensive* about how she would react when seeing Sarah and the boys.

Both Khalil and Mansur chose to wake up together and demanded to be fed. Mohammad arranged the pillows under Sarah's arms and placed each of his sons on a pillow.

When the first one finished nursing, Mohammad picked him up and put him on his shoulder to burp. And then when the second had finished did the same. He loved this contact with his sons. They would nestle their little heads into the crook of his neck and stare wide-eyed as Mohammad walked the floor and gently rubbed their backs.

After they had successfully burped, he laid them at the foot of the bed and changed their diapers. He joked with Sarah: *When we go to the Old Country, don't you dare mention in front of my grown nephews, or Issa, that I change diapers!*

With full bellies and clean diapers, they were soon asleep and content to be returned to their basket.

Late morning, after the babies had been nursed and changed, Sarah and Mohammad put them in their car seats.

Mohammad hugged her as she got in the front seat. "I'm glad you are doing this. I know it is hard, but it is good that you are making one more attempt. Remember how much I love you."

"Take care of them, Aunt Martha," he said.

"Don't worry. They'll be fine."

The nearer they got to her parents' farm, the busier the butterflies in her stomach became. "I'm really scared to see her," Sarah said to Martha.

"I know, love. But it *will* be alright. Your dad will be there, and I will be there."

Martha drove up the lane and parked the station wagon outside the closed garage doors. The windows had been rolled down, and Martha opened the driver's side door. "I'll sit here in the car and watch over the babies. You go in and see your mother."

Emily had heard the car drive up and came out of the breezeway. Her arms were folded across her chest.

"Well, Sarah, Martha," she nodded toward them. "To what do we owe this *pleasure*?" There was more than a hint of sarcasm in her voice.

"Hi, Mum. Dad was over last night, and he said that he thought you wanted to see me and see your grandsons."

"*Grandsons?* You don't mean to tell me you had *twins*?!"

"Didn't Dad tell you?" Sarah asked incredulously.

"Your dad and I don't talk much anymore other than to comment on the weather or to ask to *pass the peas.*" Emily looked meaningfully at Sarah. "And you know whose fault that is?"

Sarah chose to ignore the last comment. "Do you want to see the boys? They're sleeping in their car seats in the backseat."

Emily walked over and opened the backseat door. She glanced in at the sleeping infants.

"They look like little Arab babies, don't they? They are quite dark, and look at all that black hair. They don't look a bit like you or like *our* side of the family."

Martha felt the hairs on the back of her neck stirring. "You remember Great Uncle Abner, don't you? Why, he was so dark that Grandmother Wellman used to laugh and say, "Well, there's must have been some color in the family somewhere."

"She said *no such thing;* you're just making that up, Martha! Why we are as *white-as-white,* there was no hint of color in our family *until* now!"

Sarah could not believe what she was hearing. She turned to Dave who had just come up from the barn. "Sarah, Martha," he nodded, "I see you've come. Did you bring the boys?"

"Hi, Dad, yes, they're in the backseat," Sarah said absently.

"Did you see the boys, Emily?" Dave asked as he glanced in at his sleeping grandsons.

"I saw them." That was all she said.

"Aren't you going to come up on the porch and sit down?"

"No, I think we need to be going. The babies will want to nurse soon."

"*Nurse?* Don't tell me you are *nursing* and not giving them a bottle? It's so old-fashioned, so *common.* Everyone bottle-feeds their babies these days; I don't know of *one* mother who nurses."

"Lots of women are breastfeeding their babies these days. It's becoming quite popular. You are probably still thinking how it was when you were a young mother. It is now the 90's – and the *modern* trend is to breastfeed! *Now, you know one personally!*" Sarah said, "Me!" In spite of herself she was angry.

"I don't like your *tone* young lady! I am still your mother, and I won't have you talking to me that way!"

"Emily, *hush up!*" Dave said. "You have said quite enough.

"I apologize, Sarah. I thought things would be different. You go on and go," her dad said.

"That's right, *take her side.* If it hadn't been for her marrying that *damn* Arab, things would be fine for us – *for her!*"

"Come on, love, get in the car," Aunt Martha said.

Sarah got in, and she and Martha drove back to the house in silence. As Martha pulled in front of the house, the twins began to stir.

"It's time for their feeding," Sarah said. "Call Mohammad to help me get the boys out of their car seats, would you?"

The words were barely whispered in the breeze when Mohammad was there at the side of the car smiling.

He unbuckled the car seats and gazed down at his two sons. They were just blinking their eyes open, and their mouths moved as though in anticipation of the nipple.

"I think my little guys are hungry," he smiled. "Are you hungry, Baba?" he asked them. They wiggled at the memory of his voice.

Mohammad took Khalil out of his car seat and handed him to Sarah. He then picked up Mansur and put him on his shoulder. He glanced at Sarah, and his smile faded.

"I guess it didn't go as we hoped, huh?"

"Not quite. But it is okay; I'm fine, really."

Mohammad put his free arm around Sarah's shoulders. "I'm *so glad* that you and the boys have been written into my life. I love you so much."

"I know," Sarah smiled, "like the stars in the sky, the sand on the beach and the raindrops in the ocean."

That night the twins were sleeping peacefully at either end of the old-fashioned basket; the house was quiet except for an occasional *creaking* as it settled (even though it was over a hundred years old); there was the wonderful perfume of lilac coming through the open window; Sarah was in her familiar place, her head resting on Mohammad's chest, her breath gently moving the curly hairs beneath her nose.

Mohammad kissed the top of her head and chuckled, "You know what I am remembering?" he said smiling into Sarah's hair. "I'm remembering Khalil *warning* me *not* to get involved with an American coed. And I faithfully listened to him, *until I met you!*" he said kissing her curls again.

"Once I saw you, I *knew* that Allah had written you into my heart."

Sarah kissed his chest. "That is exactly what your mother said. She said that she was convinced that Allah had written our lives together."

"Look at us today," Mohammad said. "We are here, together, in each other's arms, and our two precious sons sleep over there in their basket. We have been truly blessed."

Coming soon:

American Sneakers in Palestine

A Palestinian Saga

Book 4

Coming soon:

American Sneakers in Palestine

A Palestinian Saga

Book 4

American Sneakers in Palestine

"We need to talk to the kids about the move," Sarah said as she set a cup of coffee down in front of Mohammad, but far enough away that two-year-old Amr (who was called *Andy* at daycare) could not reach the cup. "They won't be excited about the prospect of living in the West Bank for four years."

"It's a great job offer working for the UN," Mohammad said taking a sip from the mug. "We both get to use our degrees; get to do some real service in the West Bank, and the kids get a chance to really pick up Arabic, to get to know some more about Islam; get acquainted with their extended family; get to travel and *see the world*. Those sound like *positives* to me," he smiled.

"I'm afraid the kids won't see it that way," Sarah said sitting down at the table with him.

"The boys will be coming back to the States for college in two years, and Yasmeen will finish high school there, be removed from some of the temptations that seduce teenage girls here, and then be better prepared to return to the States for college. And this little guy," he said kissing Amr on top of the head, "will have picked up the accent and fundamentals of Arabic. He'll be speaking like a native!"

"The boys and Yasmeen aren't going to be happy about leaving their friends. They will argue that they want to finish their last two years of high school here. And, frankly, I can't blame them," Sarah said stirring a little sugar into her coffee. "They won't want to give up all their activities and opportunities to begin again in a new school six thousand miles away. As for

Yasmeen, she will really resent moving to a conservative society where her activities will be curtailed."

"It will be hard at first, I grant you, but look at the *opportunities* they will be having! It will be a once-in-a-lifetime experience for them!" Mohammad said excitedly. "They'll love the idea!"

"I *hope* you're right," Sarah said unconvinced.

He wasn't.

www.ingramcontent.com/pod-product-compliance
Lightning Source LLC
Chambersburg PA
CBHW051533250626
47157CB00001B/26